Rising from the Ashes

A Regency Romance about second chances and changing fate, inspired by P&P

Sydney Salier

To Michael

As always, thanks

Chapter 1

In March of the year 1808, Mr Collins, the heir presumptive of Longbourn, proposed to Miss Elizabeth Bennet who had just turned seventeen.

Given the chance, he probably would have chosen her older sister Jane, but Mrs Bennet had sent her most beautiful daughter to her brother in London when she discovered that Collins was coming to visit, with the intention of choosing a wife from her daughters.

Since Mrs Bennet disliked Elizabeth, her second daughter, for any number of reasons but particularly because Elizabeth had chosen not to be born a boy who would inherit their estate, the lady decided that Lizzy should make up for her shortcomings by marrying the heir presumptive. Mrs Bennet reasoned that if her daughter was married to the heir, when Mr Bennet passed on to his final reward, she herself would not only be able to remain in her home but retain her position as mistress of Longbourn.

When Elizabeth rejected his proposal, Collins applied to Mrs Bennet, who was also unable to get her daughter to agree to save her mother and her sisters from the hedgerows if Mr Bennet should pass away prematurely.

While Mrs Bennet worked to convince her husband of the need for Elizabeth to marry Mr Collins, she bemoaned Elizabeth's impertinence and stubbornness to Mr Collins, citing Mr Bennet's indolence which kept him from teaching his daughter the proper submissive behaviour, and claiming that Elizabeth needed a firm hand to guide her.

Mrs Bennet ever more frenziedly hounded Mr Bennet to assert his authority over his daughter until she eventually wore him down. Despite Elizabeth being Mr Bennet's favourite daughter, he capitulated.

Notwithstanding her protests that Mr Collins was a ridiculous and stupid man, Elizabeth Bennet was forced to become Mrs William Collins.

~A~

The day of her wedding, she and her husband travelled to Hunsford arriving late in the evening. Despite the lateness of the hour and the exhaustion of a day spent in a carriage, Mr Collins had insisted on joining his wife to complete the final stage of their wedding.

The following morning, they walked to Rosings so that Collins could present his wife to Lady Catherine de Bourgh, proving to his patroness that he had followed her orders and married one of his cousins.

Elizabeth was still tired and sore from the previous day and as a consequence was quieter than was her wont. The quiet demeanour seemed to please Lady Catherine and even though the interview was brief, the lady did them the honour of inviting the newlyweds to dinner.

When Elizabeth and Collins arrived at Rosings ten minutes before the appointed time, she was introduced to Lady Catherine's nephews, who had come for their annual visit.

Colonel Richard Fitzwilliam and Mr Fitzwilliam Darcy were quite irritated with Collins since he interrupted his wife almost every time she opened her lips to respond to a question.

Darcy in particular, since he had a better view of the lady due to their relative positions at the dining table, noticed the tension in the jaw and the shoulders of Mrs Collins. He wondered how such a lovely young lady could have married such a bumbling fool as the parson.

During the dinner, the gentleman tried to subtly deflect his aunt's inquisition of the charming young matron. As Darcy was only partly successful Lady Catherine still managed to discomfit her guest.

Mrs Collins answered quietly but honestly, causing Lady Catherine to exclaim, 'Upon my word, you give your opinion very decidedly for so young a person.'

It seemed that Mrs Collins' tolerance had its limits when she answered, 'I do beg your pardon, Lady Catherine. Since I was informed that you pride yourself on your frankness of character, I thought that you might appreciate that quality in others.'

'While I am all in favour of honesty, you should attempt to learn tact,' huffed the lady.

'I can assure you, your ladyship that I will ensure that my wife will be most attentive to her lessons,' Collins promised his patroness.

~A~

Being significantly more intelligent than her husband, Elizabeth could not resist correcting Mr Collins during their limited conversations. This circumstance as well as having made a bad start with Lady Catherine, caused Collins to take exception to his wife's behaviour.

He had been raised to believe that men were superior to women and must therefore ensure that their wives behaved in a properly submissive manner and never contradicted their husbands. It was therefore a part of his marital duties to teach his wife to display the proper deference towards himself.

While Collins was not a cruel man, he had learnt the correct behaviour of the head of the household from the example set by his father who taught his son that physical chastisement was the proper way to deal with the transgressions of the family members in his care.

Being quite inflexible, he could not accept that such behaviour was not universally practiced or even condoned. Therefore, as much as it pained him, he would follow in his father's footsteps.

Since Collins valued routine as he was not intellectually suited to deal with surprises, he set aside Sunday evening for the performance of all his marital duties.

The first order of business after dinner was to tally up his wife's transgressions for the week and administer all the week's chastisements, as permitted by law, in one fell swoop. Mr Collins, being a most law-abiding citizen ensured that he followed the rule of thumb precisely. The cane he used on his wife's back was never thicker than his thumb. Unfortunately for his wife, he had rather pudgy hands to go with his rather large and pudgy body.

Mrs Collins came to dread Sundays. While the physical punishment was bad enough, her husband also lectured her concerning the reason for the administration of every single stroke of the cane. She could not even protest, once she learnt that Collins considered her objections as grounds for punishment since a wife was never allowed to question her husband's opinions or actions.

Collins would then finish the evening with the performance of his other marital duties, which he disliked in equal measure as the first, to ensure that his wife would produce the heir required by their future estate. Naturally, the only proper way for his wife to receive his attention was for her to be lying on her back.

Every Sunday night Elizabeth cursed her mother while tears streamed into her pillow.

~A~

Three months into their marriage, Mrs Collins was pleased to inform her husband that she was with child.

He was overjoyed and proud of his manliness. Collins was also pleased that he could now suspend the second part of his marital duties until his heir was born and weaned, although he still continued his efforts to teach his wife the proper way to behave.

Several months later, when Elizabeth became too large to accept his chastisements, he suspended her lessons, saving them up for when she would be physically capable to receive them.

In due course, Elizabeth was delivered of a boy. As the birth had been a difficult one, she was allowed to hire a wetnurse to take some of the burden of looking after their heir off her shoulders.

Collins was ecstatic and proudly wrote to the Bennets to inform them of his prowess as a husband.

~A~

Elizabeth could not sleep. So, when her son woke in the middle of the night, she went to feed him.

As she was holding Henry Collins to her breast, she said quietly to the fractious infant, 'You poor mite, being saddled with a father like Mr Collins who will likely make your life hell no matter what you or I do.'

The boy squirmed. She looked at him with pity and crooned softly, 'And to add to your troubles you have a mother who would like to love you but cannot. It is not your fault that you were conceived in hatred. But I am not a saint. I am sorry, but I simply cannot love you.'

It seemed almost as if Henry Collins understood his mother's words as he suddenly clamped his gums shut, causing Elizabeth to cry out in pain. When she managed to detach her son from her breast, it was bleeding.

Fortunately, Elizabeth's cry woke Mrs Brown. When the wetnurse saw the damage which her charge had done to his mother, she suggested, 'I think I had better feed him from now on.'

Elizabeth gratefully agreed.

~A~

A month later Elizabeth was churched and allowed to leave the house again, to attend the christening of her son.

She was grateful that Mr Collins most graciously decided to allow her a few more days to regain her strength before resuming their former routines.

Before that could happen, a black edged letter was delivered to the Hunsford parsonage informing the residents that Mr Bennet had fallen victim to an accident and had passed away.

Naturally, Collins immediately insisted that Elizabeth should pack to journey hurriedly to Longbourn to pay their final respects. Due to the inclement weather, Collins decided it would be safer for his son to remain at the parsonage with his wetnurse.

~A~

The couple arrived in time for Collins to attend the funeral of Mr Bennet, while Elizabeth stayed at Longbourn with the other ladies.

As it was Saturday, Mr Phillips suggested that they should read the will immediately following the funeral and finalise all the papers since it would not do to do so on Sunday.

As expected, Mr Phillips confirmed that Mr Collins was now the master of Longbourn and that the entail was at an end. Collins was elated to sign the papers transferring full ownership to him.

Collins was not pleased when he discovered that Mr Bennet had appointed guardians for his daughters as he thought himself better qualified than the men Bennet had chosen. Mr Harold Phillips was the primary guardian and Mr Edward Gardiner the alternate guardian, if anything should happen to Mr Phillips.

Bennet had also bequeathed all his personal belongings and wealth to Mr Gardiner, who was to hold any monies realised from the sale of his possessions in trust for the support of his daughters. Gardiner assumed that Bennet wanted to ensure his wife could not squander her daughters' inheritance.

Despite those conditions, Mr Collins, having achieved his dream of being master of the estate, allowed Mrs Bennet and her daughters to remain in the house, although he insisted that the master and mistress's suite should be made available to him and his wife immediately, an order which Mrs Bennet grudgingly obeyed.

Once her belongings had been moved to another room, which ironically used to be Elizabeth's before her marriage, Mrs Bennet took herself off to that refuge and sulked.

~A~

Sunday morning saw the combined Bennet and Collins families attending services.

Despite her father's passing, Elizabeth felt better than she had in almost a year. She was regaining her physical strength, and, on this Sunday, she did not even have to listen to her husband's sermon as written by Lady Catherine de Bourgh.

That feeling of euphoria lasted until after dinner, when her husband came to her room carrying his cane. 'We have several months' worth of corrections to perform,' he informed his wife.

'Please, no. I am not yet strong enough,' pleaded Elizabeth but it was no use.

Collins had kept meticulous records and administered all the arrears, after which he went to his own rooms feeling a little lightheaded, which he put down to the exertions of having performed his duty to the best of his ability.

Elizabeth was left behind, lying battered on the floor where she had collapsed. Eventually she managed to crawl into what used to be her mother's bed dressed only in her shift. She immediately went to sleep, although it would be more accurate to say that she passed out and did not wake until late the next morning.

~A~

Chapter 2

Elizabeth was woken by a hysterical maid shaking her shoulder. 'Mistress, please wake up. It's your husband...' Sally cried.

'What about my husband?' Elizabeth asked as she blearily tried to open her eyes.

'I think he's dead,' sobbed the girl.

That statement had a galvanising effect on Elizabeth. She got out of bed as quickly as her battered body allowed and put on the robe which the maid held out to her, ignoring Sally's gasp as she saw her back since Elizabeth's shift did little to hide her injuries.

As soon as she was decently covered and moving stiffly, she followed the maid into her husband's chambers where she was met by Mrs and Mr Hill, who had been alerted by the maid's cries.

'I am sorry, Mrs Collins, but it seems your husband passed away in his sleep. I have sent for Mr Jones to come and confirm it,' said Mrs Hill, unsurprised by the slight and quickly suppressed smile spreading over Elizabeth's countenance.

Mrs Hill remembered the previous year when Elizabeth had begged her parents not to force her to marry the disagreeable man. Her experienced eyes also did not miss how carefully Elizabeth moved.

~A~

While they waited for Mr Jones, Mrs Hill accompanied Elizabeth back to her room to help her dress.

Elizabeth chose a simple dress which buttoned at the front to wear over her softest chemise.

Mrs Hill tutted when she saw Elizabeth's injuries. 'You should get Mr Jones to provide you with an ointment to soothe your hurts and speed up the healing process,' she suggested in a quiet voice.

'Thank you for your concern, but I always heal eventually,' Elizabeth tried to shrug off the concern to prevent herself from dissolving into tears at the quiet sympathy. 'But I would appreciate help in putting on my stockings since I am not very mobile today.'

'Of course, Miss Lizzy,' Mrs Hill agreed.

Elizabeth smiled at the affectionate appellation. She much preferred Miss Lizzy to Mrs Collins.

~A~

The apothecary arrived and confirmed that Mr Collins had died of an apoplexy. 'It is no surprise,' Mr Jones claimed. 'Being such a large man and with all the strain and excitement he experienced recently.'

As the widow, Elizabeth had attended the examination giving Mr Jones the opportunity to notice her difficulties in moving. He gave her a searching look, 'Perhaps I should examine you while I am here since you appear to be injured.' He reached out to Elizabeth who flinched back involuntarily.

'Miss Lizzy,' he said softly. 'You have known me since you were a child. I promise you that I will not hurt you.'

Elizabeth realised that she was trembling. She clenched her hands into fists to still the tremors. 'It is nought but bruises.'

'Still… if you would like to call Mrs Hill then I could attend to you in your chambers…' he said carefully as he suspected the cause of the bruises.

Considering in how much pain she was, Elizabeth reluctantly agreed.

~A~

After the examination, Mr Jones handed a jar of salve to Mrs Hill with instructions to apply it to her mistress twice a day, and he promised to send more.

When Elizabeth was fully dressed again, she faced him and was astonished at the furious expression on the face of this normally gentle man. 'You are very fortunate that you can still walk. That man could easily have crippled you. He is fortunate that he is dead because at the moment I would like to teach him what it feels like what he did to you,' Jones said with barely suppressed anger.

'I think he knew since I believe that is what his father used to do to him,' Elizabeth said quietly.

Jones shook his head. 'When people speak of the sins of the father being passed onto his son, I wonder if that was the true meaning of that expression.'

'I shall see to it that my son will never have to endure this kind of education,' Elizabeth vowed.

~A~

Since Collins had no family other than the Bennets, there was no need to delay the funeral by more than the time it took to make the casket.

He was buried on Wednesday, attended by Mr Phillips and Elizabeth, who would not be denied despite women being considered too weak and emotional for such occasions. She did her family proud and remained stoic throughout the service and the internment despite wanting to dance on Collins' grave.

When Elizabeth returned with Mr Phillips to his office to consult about the will, he informed her that Collins had left the estate to his son as expected. What did surprise Elizabeth was that in the marriage settlement, Collins had named Elizabeth as the guardian for his children and the estate.

Mr Phillips explained, 'Mr Bennet insisted on that clause.'

Elizabeth felt a slight quickening of excitement. 'What does that mean?' she asked her uncle.

'According to your husband's will, until your son reaches the age of one and twenty, you are in charge of him and the estate... irrespective of your age.'

'What about Mrs Bennet and my sisters? Who is in charge of them? What provisions did Mr Bennet make for them?'

Phillips looked uncomfortable. 'Bennet named me the guardian of all his daughters, with Gardiner as an alternate in case I cannot perform those duties, although in the case of Jane that will not be for much longer as she will reach her majority soon. Your mother is her own person.'

He sighed and would not meet her eyes. 'Your mother has her jointure of five thousand pounds, which was invested in the four percents since her marriage, but your father did not make any financial provisions for your sisters other than what was in his will.'

Since Elizabeth had not been allowed to attend the reading of the will, he briefly explained those provisions. 'Gardiner was planning to visit as soon as Madeline is feeling better, to take charge of Bennet's personal possessions which are to provide for your sisters. It may not be much since I suppose he expected to live long enough to see you all married...'

Elizabeth's sigh echoed her uncle's. 'I suppose most of Mr Bennet's possessions are his books. Uncle Gardiner can value those books, but I am prepared to accept those books in lieu of money to support my sisters, even though I suspect that they will not cover all the expenses for the period they will be living at Longbourn.'

She gave him a hard stare. 'Uncle, I want it clearly understood that while they live under my roof, they will obey my rules and I will not brook interference by any guardian. At least for those sisters who live at Longbourn.'

'What about your mother?'

'That will depend on Mrs Bennet's behaviour. After what she did to me, I am in no mood to be particularly tolerant.'

Phillips nodded. 'I quite understand. I believe it would be best for me to draw up a document ceding authority over your sisters to you while they remain at Longbourn.'

'Thank you, uncle,' replied Elizabeth. While she waited for Mr Phillips to finish the document, another thought occurred to her. 'What happens if my son should die?' she asked with concern. 'Not all infants reach adulthood.'

'Then, since the entail ended with your husband, as the widow of Mr Collins and the mother of the current owner, you inherit the estate.'

'Oh.' Elizabeth inhaled sharply. 'Thank you, uncle, I believe that I had better send for my son.'

~A~

When Elizabeth returned to Longbourn she was met with a mortified looking Mrs Hill.

'What is going on?' Elizabeth asked suspiciously.

'I am sorry, mistress. I am afraid that Mrs Bennet is insisting that we move her things back into the mistress's suite,' Mrs Hill explained.

'I see. You had better go and pack Mrs Bennet's things... into trunks and ready the carriage,' Elizabeth replied and went to beard the dragon. She found Mrs Bennet in the mistress's chambers ordering the maid to remove Elizabeth's belongings.

Elizabeth dismissed the maid and closed the door behind her.

'What do you think you are doing, Mrs Bennet?' Elizabeth asked in a cold fury.

'Now that that odious man is gone, I can return to my rightful place,' crowed Mrs Bennet. 'I had not thought that such good fortune could come from Mr Bennet's passing. Not only is he gone, but so is Mr Collins. I not only do not have to fear being thrown into the hedgerows any longer, but I do not have to give up my position as mistress of the estate... especially to you.' Mrs Bennet sneered and was just about dancing when she proclaimed her joy.

'Do you truly think that you deserve to be mistress of Longbourn?'

'Naturally. It is my rightful place which I have held for two and twenty years.'

'No, Mrs Bennet, I disagree.'

'What do you mean you disagree? It is not your place to disagree. And why do you call me Mrs Bennet? I am your mother.'

'No, you are not my mother. No real mother would sell her daughter into abject slavery to ensure her own comfort.'

'What are you talking about? I did not sell anyone into slavery.'

'Yes, you did when you forced me to marry Mr Collins.'

'What are you complaining about? You only had to bear him one child while I had to bear five, and since you refused to be born a boy, it was only right that you should marry Mr Collins.' Mrs Bennet dismissed her daughter's words with a flick of her handkerchief.

Elizabeth exploded into fury at the casual dismissal of her suffering. She ripped open the buttons at the front of her dress which, apart from a chemise, was still all she could tolerate on her back, and dropped it to the ground. She turned to ensure her mother could get a good look at the bruises which covered her from her shoulders all the way down to her thighs.

'Did Mr Bennet ever do that to you?' she asked as she whirled back to see a look of abject horror and fear on her mother's face. She picked up the dress and pulled it on again, holding it shut because of the lack of buttons.

Before her mother could respond other than to shake her head, she continued, 'did your husband do that to you every Sunday before expecting you to perform your marital duties... lying on a back which was constantly black and blue? And as you know full well, Mr Collins was significantly heavier than your husband.'

Mrs Bennet's mouth opened and shut without a sound coming out.

'That was the fate to which you condemned me. You quite cheerfully sold me into a lifetime of misery and agony just so that you could live in comfort. And not only that... Mr Collins informed me that you had advised him that I would need a firm hand to control me,' Elizabeth now screamed at her mother. 'And now you have the nerve to demand my position for which I paid dearly because of you.'

She took a deep breath to try to calm herself enough to speak. 'Well, no more. It makes me sick to look at you. I want you out of my house before nightfall. Do not ever set foot in Longbourn again because you will not be welcome.'

'You cannot do that. This is my home,' cried Mrs Bennet, panicking.

'This *was* your home. It now belongs to my son, and I am his guardian and make all the decisions in this house until he comes of age,' spat Elizabeth.

'But where will I go?'

'I do not care. You can go rot in the hedgerows as you have been promising for years, as long as you get out of my sight.'

Some of Mrs Bennet's maternal instinct came to the fore, or perhaps she was concerned about supporting her other daughters on the interest of her jointure. 'What about Jane and Lydia?'

Elizabeth gave her a disgusted look. 'Like Mary and Kitty, they have done nothing to me. They can stay.' She gave Mrs Bennet a hard look. 'Perhaps without you driving all the men away with your uncouth and grasping behaviour, they might even find decent husbands.'

Elizabeth walked over to the door and opened it. 'Goodbye, Mrs Bennet.'

~A~

In a daze, Mrs Bennet returned to the room she had occupied for the last few days. She did not even acknowledge her other daughters who had been drawn to the hallway outside the mistress's suite by the shouting.

When she entered, she discovered that several trunks were in the process of being filled with her possessions. 'It appears that my daughter is not wasting any time,' she murmured.

'Quickness seems to run in the family, Mrs Bennet,' replied Mrs Hill, who was supervising the packing, with an angry look. 'You were pretty quick to sell Miss Lizzy to Mr Collins.'

'How dare you,' snapped Mrs Bennet.

Mrs Hill huffed. 'I saw what that man did to the poor girl. He would have been condemned if he had treated a horse that way and I would not be surprised if you had told him to treat Miss Lizzy like that.'

'How was I to know he would go that far?'

'The signs were all there, but you refused to see them,' accused Mrs Hill, when a thought occurred to her. 'Or perhaps you did see the signs, but you did not care because you always hated your brightest daughter,' she said and saw a flash of fear cross Mrs Bennet's features.

They were interrupted when Lydia came into the room. 'What are they doing, Mama? Surely, Sally can carry your things back into your rooms without putting everything into trunks.'

'They are packing because that vexing Lizzy has decided to throw me into the hedgerows.'

'How can she do that? Are you not going to be mistress of Longbourn now that that horrible Mr Collins is gone?' Lydia asked in sudden concern. The girl had been mostly unaffected by the death of her father as he had not played a significant role in her life.

On the odd occasion when he had thought to interfere in her pleasure, Mrs Bennet had interceded for Lydia. Therefore, Lydia only saw the benefit of his death since she would not have to waste effort in getting her mother's help to countermand his orders.

When Collins and Lizzy had arrived, that man had not been around long enough to have any impact in her life. Once he passed away, Lydia had assumed that her mother would now have charge of everything, and she had looked forward to a life of unalloyed ease and fun.

'No, I am not, your hateful sister is seeing to that.'

'How can she do that?'

'When your father died, Mr Collins inherited Longbourn. He was a good man who was going to let all of us remain in our home. But now that he is gone, Lizzy's brat has inherited, and she is his guardian until he reaches his majority, and she can dictate who is to live here or who is to leave.'

Lydia's eyes widened. She whispered, 'Is she going to throw all of us out of the house?'

'You had better pray that she does not, because I am in no position to provide for you or any of your sisters,' Mrs Bennet declared just as the last trunk was closed.

Mrs Hill spoke up, 'the carriage should be ready,' and escorted Mrs Bennet as she left Longbourn for the last time.

Elizabeth watched the departure from the window of the mistress's suite.

~A~

Chapter 3

Mr Phillips sighed as he saw the Bennet carriage, loaded with trunks, stop outside his house and Mrs Bennet disembarked.

Once the lady was in the parlour and her trunks had been placed in the house, Phillips joined the ladies. He was just in time to hear Mrs Bennet complain to her sister how she had been mistreated.

'Fanny, for years I have told you not to be so greedy, but you can never restrain yourself,' he said when the lady tried to harangue him with her tale of woe. 'I would guess that Elizabeth has asserted her authority and shown you the door.'

'That ungrateful little hoyden. From the day she was born she never did what she is supposed to do.'

'Spare me your rant about her not being a boy. She had even less control over her sex than you did. Would you rather that Bennet had blamed you for only giving him daughters?' When Mrs Bennet's eyes were shooting daggers at him, he said, 'Never mind, I have no interest in hearing your complaints. You may stay in my house for a fortnight to find a cottage to live in. After that you are on your own.'

~A~

The sisters gathered for dinner, with Elizabeth sitting at the head of the table.

'Why did you throw mama out of the house?' demanded Lydia as soon as she was seated.

'I might have let her stay at Longbourn, but she tried to usurp my position. After all she has done, that was the last straw.'

'But she is still your mother. How can you do that to her?' accused Mary.

'She did not act like a mother to me. All my life she abused me and then she forced me to marry Mr Collins who abused me even more... at her instigation. Today she insisted that I should step aside and let her be the mistress of Longbourn.'

Jane, ever the peacemaker, questioned Elizabeth. 'You must understand that it would be difficult for her to give way to you since she has been mistress of the estate for over two decades. Could you not have given her time to become accustomed to the changes?'

'No, Jane, I could not. I understand your mother perfectly. She cares more about her position and comfort than about her daughters. But there was a more practical reason for insisting that she leave. There cannot be two mistresses in a house and Mrs Bennet would have attempted to undermine my authority constantly. And she would have wanted to continue to squander the income of my son's estate.'

Jane stopped to think about Elizabeth's words and reluctantly agreed.

'But how do you expect mama to live?' asked Lydia, refusing to accept the departure of her ally.

'Mrs Bennet will receive the interest on her jointure which is two hundred pounds per annum. For somewhere between fifty and eighty pounds a year she can rent a decent cottage and hire two maids of all works. That will leave her with at least ten pounds per month to live on. If you think that is a pittance for one woman, the Hunsford living was worth just over four hundred pounds. That amount was to support Mr Collins and myself and however many children we had, as well as to provide for their future.'

'If she has that much money, why did she always claim that we would starve in the hedgerows?' asked Kitty quietly.

'Because Mrs Bennet does not understand the concept of a budget or economy. Two hundred pounds per year is a very comfortable amount for one woman to live on, after all many families live on significantly less. For someone like Mrs Bennet who has never learnt how to economise it seems like a paltry sum since she will be unable to throw elaborate dinner parties. In the current circumstance she does not even have to support several unmarried daughters,' Elizabeth explained.

'So, you are not going to throw us out of the house too?' Kitty asked with a tentative smile.

'I am not planning on doing so, but I need you all to understand that there will be some changes in this house. Like... I will continue to provide your pin money each month but if you squander it, you will not get any more till the next month. And you are not allowed to steal from your sisters,' Elizabeth answered, giving Lydia a pointed look.

'But how am I going to survive on such a pittance?' cried her youngest sister.

'Fifty pounds per annum is hardly a pittance especially for a girl who is not out. Also, since we will be in deep mourning for the next three months and half mourning for another three, you will not need to spend any money on fripperies but can save it.'

'You mean that you expect us to stay at home for half a year?' Lydia protested.

'I shall expect you to stay home for three months. After that you may visit your friends, but you may not attend any parties for a further three months.'

'What makes you think you have the right to dictate to us what we can or cannot do?'

'Uncle Phillips, who is your guardian appointed by Mr Bennet, has ceded his authority to me for any of my sisters who live under my roof.' Elizabeth gave Lydia a hard look. 'While you are under my roof you are subject to my rules. If you do not like my rules, you may apply to Mrs Bennet or Uncle Phillips for alternate accommodation.'

Lydia brightened until Elizabeth added, 'Of course, I will not provide pin money to anyone not of my household.'

The young girl understood numbers and her mother well enough to realise that Mrs Bennet would never provide her with the kind of pin money Elizabeth offered as it represented a quarter of her annual income.

~A~

In the morning, Elizabeth sent the Bennet carriage to Hunsford to collect her son and his nurse.

Since neither Elizabeth nor Collins had left behind anything of particular value, she gave instructions that the rest of their possessions could be given away. As far as Elizabeth was concerned, those items were not worth the distress she would experience if she were to return to the house where she had spent such a traumatic year.

As soon as she sat down to breakfast she was joined by Jane.

'Lizzy, how are we going to manage without either of our parents or your husband?' she asked full of quiet concern.

Elizabeth gave her a rueful smile. 'I think we will manage well enough if you are prepared to help me.'

'What can I do?' Jane asked doubtfully.

'You know how to manage a house, do you not?'

'Y-e-s...'

'If you take charge of the running of the house, I can concentrate on learning how to run the estate.'

'But women do not manage estates.'

'Lady Catherine de Bourgh does, although I believe she does not do so very well. But there are books available on estate management and I am certain our neighbours will provide advice if I ask them. And surely you remember that Mr Bennet was a most indolent master. I suspect that it should not take too long for me to be at least at his standard.'

A pained expression flickered across Jane's countenance while Elizabeth grimaced and sighed. 'The others you mentioned would do even worse. Mrs Bennet might have set a good table, but she did not even know enough about the duties of a mistress to visit the tenants and Mr Collins knew nothing at all and was too stupid to learn.'

Jane slowly nodded as she considered her sister's words. 'I have to agree, and you were always the brightest of us. What about our sisters? How will you deal with them?'

'I have considered hiring a governess or companion for Kitty and Lydia to teach them manners and some basic accomplishments. This companion will also need to be a good musician to help Mary improve on the pianoforte.'

'And perhaps broaden her interests…' sighed Jane.

'Indeed. It might also help her if you asked her to work with you in managing the house. So that she will not feel quite so left out.'

Jane smiled a little ruefully. 'That is not quite such an issue anymore.' When Elizabeth raised a quizzical brow, Jane explained, 'Mary and I have become much closer over the past year and to my chagrin I discovered that you and she have much in common. Having been the invisible sister for so long, she has become extremely observant and in the right mood, she has a wicked sense of humour.'

'Oh no. Why did I never find out about this?' Elizabeth cried, feeling guilty for having ignored their middle sister.

'Because I saw how Mrs Bennet treated you and I preferred to be ignored rather than abused,' said Mary as she came into the room, having heard the last comments.

'I am sorry, Mary –' Elizabeth started to say only to be interrupted.

'There is no need for you to apologise, otherwise I have to apologise for hiding and letting Mrs Bennet vent her spleen on you,' Mary said. 'I suggest that we both adhere to your philosophy. *Remember the past only as it gives you pleasure.*'

The sisters agreed and they spent the rest of the meal discussing what they each planned to accomplish that day.

Since they were agreed on their tasks, immediately after they finished their meal, Elizabeth wrote to her Uncle Gardiner asking for his assistance to employ a suitably qualified lady to educate her sisters. She did not mention the other changes as she was still too angry with Mrs Bennet to present an unbiased account of happenings.

~A~

Late the following afternoon, when the Bennet coach returned to Longbourn, Elizabeth went outside to greet the new arrivals.

Instead of the nurse with her son exiting the coach, the driver climbed off the box and with a bow handed her a black edged letter with a grave demeanour. Suspecting the content, she immediately broke the seal and read the missive.

Rosings Park, near Westerham, Kent, 23rd March 1809

Dear Madam,

I regret to inform you that after your departure from Hunsford, a fever swept through the neighbourhood claiming the lives of several people, mostly the already sick, the old and the very young, including your son and his nurse.

As your son's death coincided with the arrival of your coach, I have taken the liberty of sending his body to you in the belief that you would wish to have him buried with your family. I pray that I have judged correctly.

Please forgive me for not attending to this matter in person, but my presence is required at Rosings Park as my aunt, Lady Catherine de Bourgh is also gravely ill.

I will see to it that, as per your instructions, your possessions are distributed to the poor in the area.

My sincere condolences for all your losses.

Your faithful servant

Fitzwilliam Darcy

While Elizabeth read the note from Mr Darcy, who must have recently arrived for his annual visit, the driver had removed a small coffer from the back of the coach.

When Elizabeth looked up, he said, 'Mr Darcy suggested that since your son died of a contagious fever, it would be best not to open the box. I am sorry, ma'am.'

Elizabeth was startled when she felt a gentle hand on her arm. 'Shall I call the undertaker and arrange for the funeral?' asked Mrs Hill.

'Yes, thank you. Perhaps Henry could be buried with his father,' Elizabeth replied in a daze as she wondered at the capriciousness of fate. Two weeks ago, she was chained in an abusive marriage and had a son who seemed destined to follow in his father's footsteps.

Now she had lost her father, her husband, and her son.

In the process she had gained an estate as well as her freedom.

For the first time in her life, she was free to be her own person.

The irony was that in just over one week it would be her eighteenth birthday, the age at which most young women came out into society.

~A~

Elizabeth kept the sealed coffer at Longbourn overnight. It seemed fitting to her that the young master of the estate should spend at least one night in the place he had inherited even though he would never see it.

She sat several hours next to the sealed coffin in the small parlour after informing her sisters of the news and requesting time to herself. While she sat watching over the tiny coffin, she felt an unexpected rush of anger, 'I struggled for all those months to give you life and now you die?' she railed.

As soon as the words passed her lips Elizabeth felt guilt wash over her and the anger was replaced by pity. 'I am sorry, Henry. I know it was not your fault. We were both the victims of circumstances.'

As she kept her vigil late into the night remembering the past year, she removed the note she had received from her pocket and clutching it, she recalled the one time, less than a year ago, when she had met the incredibly handsome gentleman who had so kindly sent it.

Elizabeth had been mortified by the pity in Mr Darcy's eyes when Mr Collins displayed the full extent of his ignorance and obsequiousness. But all through that interminable dinner, Mr Darcy had shown her nothing but respect and courtesy.

Eventually she took herself off to bed for a few hours of troubled sleep.

~A~

Chapter 4

Another day, another funeral, and another visit to Mr Phillips' office.

In the morning Mr Jones and the undertaker took the coffer to the cemetery where they had carefully opened the chest to confirm that the body within was indeed the remains of Henry Collins. Once Elizabeth, supported by Mr Phillips, had verified the identity of her son, the coffin was sealed again, and the funeral progressed in the normal fashion.

Afterwards Elizabeth again accompanied her uncle to his office. On this occasion they spent time dealing with the paperwork to transfer Longbourn into Elizabeth's name.

Having learnt how fragile life could be, Elizabeth requested her uncle to draw up a will for her to ensure the safety of her sisters and of Longbourn.

As Elizabeth was sitting in the deep, comfortable chair by the fire while she waited for Mr Phillips to prepare the document, the door burst open, and Mrs Bennet barged into the office. Without looking to see who else might be in the room she exclaimed to Mr Phillips, 'Brother, I have just come from the cemetery, and someone has been digging up the grave of Mr Collins. Are there graverobbers in town?'

'No, Fanny. Mr Collins' grave was opened to place his son next to him,' Phillips explained quietly.

Even though Mrs Bennet was a woman of mean understanding, she was quick to recognise something which in her mind would be of benefit to herself. 'You mean that Elizabeth's brat is dead too? How wonderful. Now she has no excuse to lord it over Longbourn. I can take back my rightful place,' crowed the matron.

Mr Phillips closed his eyes for a moment at this painful and embarrassing exhibition by his sister-in-law. 'No, Fanny. With the death of Henry Collins, his mother inherits the estate.'

'His mother? You mean Lizzy is to be the mistress of *my* estate? Permanently? This cannot be. Fate cannot be so cruel to me,' gasped Mrs Bennet. 'After all the trouble I went through to ensure that I would remain mistress of Longbourn. No brother, you must assist me in reclaiming what is rightfully mine so that I can show that little upstart the door,' Mrs Bennet continued her vindictive rant.

Elizabeth shrank back into her chair hoping that her mother would not notice her. After all the upheavals of recent weeks this tirade was simply too much. Had this woman not the slightest shred of compassion for a widow who had just lost her son, even if she had not even a modicum of motherly love for her second daughter?

In her despair she missed some of the conversation although she could guess the gist of it when she heard her uncle say, 'No, Mrs Bennet, you have no right to Longbourn. If you continue to carry on in this fashion, I doubt that you will be welcome in any home in this neighbourhood.'

~A~

Mrs Bennet eventually stormed out of the office, slamming the door behind her in frustration.

Mr Phillips rose and came to sit in the chair beside Elizabeth, handing her his much larger handkerchief to dry the tears quietly streaming down her face. 'I know it is difficult but try not to let her words upset you. She has always been a shallow, grasping woman with no understanding of the hurt she causes.'

Elizabeth forced a smile for her uncle. 'I know exactly what Mrs Bennet is like. After all I had seventeen years to experience her brand of... affection.' She wiped her eyes and blew her nose. 'Does that woman not realise that it was her grandson whom we laid to rest this morning?' she exclaimed in exasperation.

While anger might not be the healthiest emotion, it at least helped her to overcome her grief and deal with necessities.

Phillips ignored what he considered to be a rhetorical question and instead said, 'I have that will ready for you to read and sign.'

Elizabeth was grateful for the change of topic, and they finalised their business.

~A~

It was Sunday again and for the first time in nearly a year, Elizabeth looked forward to the day.

It seemed somehow appropriate that it was Palm Sunday, as she had her own triumph to celebrate, unlike the Palm Sunday of the previous year when her suffering had begun.

She attended services accompanied by her sisters and was greeted respectfully by her neighbours. Foremost amongst them was Charlotte Lucas, who invited Elizabeth and her sisters to sit with her family.

Once they entered the church, the reason for the invitation became obvious. Mrs Bennet was sitting in isolated splendour in the middle of the pew at the front of the church where the Bennet family usually sat.

Since the pew occupied by the Lucas family became rather cosy, the two oldest boys moved to the pew behind the rest of the family. When Mr and Mrs Phillips arrived, they took their usual seats, not in the Bennet pew, nodding at their nieces on their way past.

The vicar spoke well about Christ's suffering but also about enduring and overcoming adversity, a point which Elizabeth felt was directed at her. Despite the engaging sermon, Elizabeth was peripherally aware that Mrs Bennet was constantly fidgeting throughout the service. Possibly she wanted to search for her daughters amongst the congregation, but she managed to stop herself from turning around.

When Mrs Bennet finally rose at the end of the service and turned to leave the church, her eyes widened when she saw all her daughters sitting with the Lucas family in the pew four rows behind where she had sat. After one withering glare, she stalked out of the church with a pinched expression, not bothering to speak to the vicar or anyone else.

~A~

After leaving the church themselves, Elizabeth pulled Charlotte Lucas aside for a private word. 'What is going on?' she demanded.

'What could be going on?' Charlotte countered with pretended innocence.

'Our neighbours have never before shown such deference to me while they almost seemed to shun Mrs Bennet.'

Charlotte looked pained but answered, 'Your maid Sally was horrified by the state of your back and when Mr Jones kept sending jar after jar of ointment to Longbourn...' Charlotte shrugged. 'It is now common knowledge that you were forced to marry that brute of a husband and he had been encouraged in his actions by Mrs Bennet.'

Ignoring Elizabeth's blush on learning that her secret shame was known, Charlotte continued, 'Our neighbours, including the men, are gentle people and do not take kindly to deliberate and calculated abuse. And if you are worried... this knowledge has done you no harm. Your neighbours respect you for not trying to garner sympathy due to your experiences and they fully support you for evicting Mrs Bennet.'

Even though still blushing furiously, Elizabeth was relieved that her neighbours were not viewing her as a heartless monster who would condemn her mother to the hedgerows... especially as that woman had the means to live comfortably, if not lavishly.

~A~

As far as Elizabeth was concerned, the rest of the day was perfect.

She and her sisters spent it in relatively quiet pursuits, except for Mary who practiced a new piece of music on the pianoforte while Jane, Kitty and Lydia occupied themselves with sewing and embroidery.

Elizabeth had browsed through her father's library and discovered a couple of recent books on estate management which she thought might help her to get started.

While she reasoned that Mr William Marshall's book *On the Landed Property of England, an elementary and practical treatise* from 1804 would help her understand her duties as master of Longbourn, she also considered hiring a steward and was interested in what Mr John Lawrence thought important in 1801 when he wrote *The Modern Land Steward*.

When she went to bed that night, Elizabeth felt relaxed and confident of what the future might bring.

~A~

In the morning Elizabeth discussed with Jane and Mrs Hill the changes she wished to make to the master's suite to make it fit for her own use.

She loved the dark wood and simple lines Mr Bennet had favoured but thought the colours of the walls and soft furnishings to be too dark for her own taste. At least making those changes would be quicker than modifying Mrs Bennet's chambers. It could also be done while she occupied the mistress's suite.

Once she was installed in the master suite, Elizabeth planned to have everything in the mistress's suite sent to Mrs Bennet's new accommodation. Therefore, those rooms would need to be completely redecorated and furnished.

Elizabeth offered those rooms to Jane, once she herself vacated them, to give her sister a proper space where she could work on the business of running the house. Of course, she gave permission for Jane to decorate those rooms according to her own taste.

It seemed fitting to Elizabeth that they each occupied the rooms appropriate to their places in the household.

~A~

At last, after the upheavals of the previous week, Elizabeth was able to attend to the matter of Longbourn.

She thought that the first order of business must be to reassure the tenants that things would continue as they had done at least in the near future. Elizabeth hoped to make improvements to the estate once she knew what was happening now and what could be improved.

Elizabeth went to the stables since she would need transport because she would not be able to see every tenant today if she had to rely on walking.

As she looked around the available horses, she sighed. There was old Nellie, their one horse which was trained to side-saddle. Apart from the fact that Elizabeth hated riding side-saddle since it felt very insecure to her, Nellie was slow and probably would not be able to keep up all day.

The farm horses which doubled up for pulling the carriage were employed for ploughing, which was a much more important occupation for them at this time of year than pulling the carriage.

That left only Mr Bennet's gelding. But while riding on him astride was tempting, Elizabeth could not do so in her dresses. She was still pondering the problem when Mr Jamieson, the stablemaster, approached her.

'You'll be wanting some transport, Miss Lizzy? Pardon me, I meant to say Mrs Collins.'

Elizabeth smiled at the old Longbourn retainer. 'I prefer Miss Lizzy to Mrs Collins, Mr Jamieson, although perhaps we could compromise and settle for Mrs Elizabeth. And yes, I need to visit all the tenants and was just trying to work out how to ride my father's horse since I do not believe that Nellie is up to the task.'

Jamieson grinned. 'You are in luck, Miss Lizzy, in two ways. I was thinking that you might need transport and remembered that your grandmother used to use a gig. It's been gathering dust at the back of the shed, but I had it brought out, cleaned up and checked over. It's perfectly fine now and you can use it to get around.'

'That is excellent as far as it goes, but which horse can be spared to pull the gig and who can teach me to drive it?'

'That is the second piece of luck I mentioned. Horace,' Jamieson indicated Mr Bennet's horse, 'is trained to pull a cart as well as carry a rider and Bob the groom can teach you to drive and would be good for you to take along since it will be safer for you not to go alone.'

'If you can spare Bob...'

'I can spare him a lot more easily than we could spare you if anything should happen,' Jamieson declared firmly.

~A~

By evening, Elizabeth had visited all Longbourn tenants and was well satisfied.

Except for Mr Chambers who had *no time to waste on a little girl who had no right to meddle in the affairs of men*, the interviews had gone well.

The visit to the Potters was representative of her discussions with four out of the five tenants.

'Miss Lizzy, we were all very sorry to hear about your father passing away,' Mr Potter said nervously. 'And we were wondering what is going to happen now, especially as Mr Collins passed on too.'

'Mr Potter, please do not worry. Since my son fell victim to a fever last week as well, it seems that I have inherited Longbourn. I plan to keep all the leases going while I learn how to look after everything. I hope you will be willing to continue on and deal fairly with me while I will do the same.'

Potter heaved a sigh of relief. 'I'll be pleased to do so, Miss Lizzy. Mr Bennet might not have been the most involved master at Longbourn, but at least he was fair.'

'Be sure to let me know if there are problems. I am hoping that we can make some improvements which will make the estate more profitable for all of us.' Elizabeth was very relieved at the cooperative attitude of Mr Potter.

'Do you now? I heard some talk about some four-course rotation system which is showing real good results in Norfolk. I'd be interested to find out more about it...' Potter suggested with a sly smile.

'I suppose I had better make some enquiries,' Elizabeth agreed, pleased with her first foray into estate administration.

~A~

Chapter 5

The following day a letter arrived from Mr Gardiner informing Elizabeth that he had found a good candidate for a governess or companion for her sisters. He also requested permission to deliver the lady to Longbourn and bring his family to spend Easter with the sisters.

Elizabeth responded immediately with an invitation and then went in search of her youngest sisters. She found Kitty and Lydia in the dining room, listlessly breaking their fast.

Lydia gave her older sister a rebellious look. 'Why do we have to stay at home for months just because papa died? He never cared to spend time with us, so why should we care that he is dead?'

'He may not have been the best father but very few men spend time with their children. But he kept you in significant comfort and for that at least he deserves your respect.'

'But it is so boring to sit around the house with nothing to do,' Lydia complained.

'Since you are bored you will be pleased to know that Uncle Gardiner is coming for Easter, and not only is he bringing his family but also your new governess.'

'A governess?! Why would we need a governess? Mama said that no man wants an overeducated woman, but since I am pretty and lively, I am sure to quickly find a husband. Perhaps even an officer... they look so dashing in their red coats. Mama was always telling us about Colonel Miller.'

'Indeed. And she also said how he broke her heart when he left without a backward glance,' Elizabeth reminded her sisters. 'But to attract a good husband, you will need more than a pretty face and a lively demeanour. You will need accomplishments. At a minimum you will need to know what is involved in looking after a household. And you never know, the lady may be able to teach you things you might enjoy.'

Lydia looked mulish at that pronouncement, but Kitty tilted her head as she thought of the possibilities. Eventually she said to her sister, 'At least it will give us something to do while we are forced to stay at home.'

Although Lydia kept grumbling, she allowed herself to be mollified with the idea of some entertainment to break the monotony.

~A~

The Gardiners arrived late on Thursday afternoon with their three children, their nurse and Mrs Taylor.

All the sisters were glad to welcome their relations, as even Lydia was fond of her young cousins.

Once the governess had been introduced and everyone had refreshed themselves, they had an early dinner. Afterwards Mrs Taylor and Lydia helped the nurse to settle the children into the nursery, while Elizabeth invited Mr and Mrs Gardiner to the library for a conversation which also included Jane.

'I am sorry that we could not come to see you when your father died,' said Mrs Gardiner when they had settled with the beverage of their choice. 'I am expecting again, and I could not bear the movement of the carriage at the time. But I have been concerned about you. We had a rather brief note from Phillips telling us that you are living here alone.'

'Did Uncle Phillips tell you why or did he suggest there was a problem?' Elizabeth asked carefully.

Her uncle answered. 'He did not do either. He said everything was working out better than he had anticipated, but I felt that we had to come and see for ourselves. It would also give me the opportunity to carry out the last wishes of your father.' He hesitated a moment before he added, 'And after all, I am the guardian for all you girls.'

'Uncle, please forgive me for correcting you, but you are the alternate guardian if Uncle Phillips becomes unavailable... and really only for my sisters. Once I married, I was considered to be an adult. As a widow, I became a woman of my own commandment,' Elizabeth gently reminded Mr Gardiner.

'But you are only about to turn eighteen,' he protested.

'True but according to the will of my husband I am in charge of Longbourn. Also, Uncle Phillips trusts me to manage my inheritance and my sisters living in my home.' Elizabeth smiled to take the sting out of her words. 'Uncle Phillips even presented me with a document giving me authority over all my sisters who live at Longbourn.'

'Phillips appointed you as Jane's guardian?' Gardiner was all astonishment although after a few moments he started to chuckle. 'No wonder he did not give me any details.'

'But why is your mother not here to look after your sisters?' Mrs Gardiner asked.

Jane and Elizabeth exchanged glances before Lizzy said, 'You are aware that when Mr Collins inherited Longbourn the entail was broken, therefore when he died the estate went to our son, leaving me as guardian of Henry and in charge of Longbourn.' The Gardiners nodded as Elizabeth continued her explanation. 'Since Mrs Bennet refused to accept her new position in my house, I asked her to leave. She is currently residing with Uncle Phillips.'

Elizabeth grimaced when she added, 'You should also know that Mrs Bennet's only thought upon hearing that my son, her grandson, had died was to insist that she was entitled to take possession of Longbourn and throw me into the hedgerows.'

The initial shock of the Gardiners upon hearing the story was soon replaced by resigned acceptance. 'I was afraid that my sister would act in an uncharitable manner, but I did not expect her to behave quite so abominably.'

To lighten the mood, Jane smiled sweetly as she said, 'I find that Elizabeth is very well qualified to look after our sisters. Much as it pains me to say so, she is a better parent then either of our parents ever were.'

'Uncle Gardiner, instead of dealing with this in dribs and drabs, let me tell you what has happened,' Elizabeth proposed. When their relations agreed she proceeded to lay out for them what had occurred since Mr Bennet's funeral, leaving out only the severe beating she had endured. 'Now you can judge for yourself if we need assistance.'

Both Gardiners were amazed at the happenings. 'Little Lizzy as the master of Longbourn,' Gardiner said with a smile and nodded. 'Yes, I can see how that would be an improvement.'

'You were wise to request us to find a governess for your younger sisters,' mused Mrs Gardiner. 'As a widow a decade older than you, Mrs Taylor will lend greater respectability to you… if you choose to hire her.'

'Please, tell us about her,' requested Elizabeth.

Mrs Gardiner obliged. 'Margaret Taylor is the daughter of Baron Standish but when she married a young officer against the wishes of her family, they cut her off. He was killed in action about six years ago and being without sufficient funds, she had to take employment as a companion to a young lady. Her first position went quite well and six months ago Miss Thompson married to great advantage thanks to the accomplishments she had learnt from Mrs Taylor.'

'We know the Thompsons quite well, as I do quite a lot of business with Mr Thompson,' interjected Mr Gardiner. 'They are a most respectable family.'

'That was how we met Mrs Taylor and I thought her to be most congenial company as she is only a few years younger than myself. After Miss Thompson married, Margaret took another position with a certain Earl who has two daughters and a roving eye.'

Mrs Gardiner sighed. 'All was well as he was busy at his estate, while his wife and daughters were in town for better access to masters in the art of painting which is the younger girl's particular talent. While Mrs Taylor is an adequate artist, this young lady outstrips her talent. But that is neither here nor there. The point is that until three weeks ago, the Earl was out of town.' She hesitated.

'Let me guess,' said Elizabeth when her aunt was reluctant to continue. 'The Earl took one look at Mrs Taylor and thought her easy prey.'

'He did indeed but Margaret would have none of it and walked out… after delivering a ringing slap. Naturally, this makes it difficult for her to find another position in town.'

Jane sighed. 'Society is horribly unfair. Men are the predators, but women are blamed for being the victims.'

'Precisely. But there may be a most advantageous outcome for all. I can personally vouch for her being an excellent teacher and having impeccable morals. I believe your sisters would greatly benefit from her tuition.'

'There is only one question. How will she deal with having to take orders from a woman a decade younger than her,' speculated Elizabeth.

~A~

Once the Gardiner children had settled down for the night, Lydia invited Mrs Taylor to join her in the parlour where Mary and Kitty were waiting.

Mary, as the oldest sister present performed the duties of the hostess and served the tea which Mrs Hill had just delivered.

Lydia was curious as always and without waiting for anyone else to make polite conversation she asked bluntly, 'Why did you become a governess?'

Mrs Taylor decided since she had not yet been officially offered the position, she would not take the young lady to task about her lack of manners. Instead, she answered, 'I am a widow and since I do not have the funds to live without working, I am using my education to earn my living.'

'Did you not have a jointure?'

This time Lydia had gone too far with that question, and Mrs Taylor informed her, 'Miss Lydia, it is considered very bad manners to enquire into a person's finances.'

'Please forgive me for asking, but you seem quite young to be a widow,' Mary said, trying to deflect Lydia's question.

'My husband was an officer in the regulars, and he was killed in battle.' As Mrs Taylor answered, she noticed Lydia's eyes light up when she mentioned her husband's profession and decided to nip this interest in the bud. 'I should have listened to my parents and married a gentleman.'

'Your parents did not wish for you to marry a man in uniform?' Kitty asked in confusion as she remembered Mrs Bennet extolling the charms of a red coat.

'No, Miss Catherine, my parents thought I had made a poor choice, but I thought myself in love and since I was of age, they could not stop the wedding.'

'How romantic...' sighed Lydia with a dreamy look in her eyes.

She was shocked when Mrs Taylor said, 'How stupid.'

'What? How can you say that? You were marrying your love despite your parents' attempts at ruining your life,' exclaimed Lydia.

'My parents were trying to save me from a life of misery and poverty, but I was too stupid and headstrong to see this. I suspect I had been reading the same kind of novels you have, and my head was filled with romantic nonsense.'

'But surely it was wonderful to be loved,' Kitty asked quietly.

'Oh yes, it was wonderful until all we could afford to eat was barley bread and not much of that.'

'But surely an officer has enough money...'

'No, Miss Lydia. A Lieutenant earns barely enough to feed himself. He should never have proposed since he could not afford a wife.' Seeing the dubious look Lydia was giving her, she added, 'I will make an exception about discussing finances. A lieutenant earns about eighty pounds a year. Out of which he has to pay for his equipment and his food. So, you can see that there is precious little to spare for a wife.'

'Oh.' Lydia was shocked. She had considered herself hard done by because she received only fifty pounds a year in pin money. Until recently, her mother had supplemented that amount to what was probably more than a lieutenant's salary. And all she had spent that money on was ribbons, bonnets, and other treats.

Mrs Taylor sipped her tea and watched the youngest girls process the information. She felt satisfied that even if she did not get the position, she had at least made the girls think.

She also did not mention that her husband had expected her to receive a significant dowry and was only too pleased when her parents did not insist on a marriage contract, which would leave him free to squander the money. He had been most put out to discover his wife to be penniless.

~A~

The girls were still thinking about the information imparted by Mrs Taylor when the Gardiners and Jane joined them.

'Mrs Taylor, I realise that you must be tired, but my sister would like to have a word with you if you feel up to it,' Jane addressed the lady.

'I am not that tired and even if I were, I would prefer to ascertain the situation sooner rather than later,' replied Mrs Taylor and followed Jane to the library where Elizabeth was sitting behind the desk.

Jane withdrew while Mrs Taylor seated herself at Elizabeth's invitation.

After a few preliminary civilities, during which Elizabeth explained her preferred form of address, she asked, 'How do you feel about taking orders from a much younger woman? Myself to be exact.'

'Are you to be my employer?' Mrs Taylor asked in some confusion. 'Neither Mr nor Mrs Gardiner mentioned this.'

'I am the owner of the estate; therefore, I will be your employer if you are sanguine about taking orders from me. You were not informed before as my aunt and uncle were unaware of the full situation because I had no wish to submit the events which occurred to paper.'

Elizabeth spoke quietly but firmly, impressing Mrs Taylor with her attitude and poise.

'What do you require?'

'You have met my younger sisters. I am certain you have recognised that neither Kitty nor Lydia were taught proper manners. They also were not required by their parents to learn any accomplishments. My next younger sister, Mary, is devoted to practicing the pianoforte but could use instruction on how to improve her playing. Also, while her manners are quite proper, I believe that she is overfond of scriptures and would benefit from broadening her mind.'

'I can do all that, but would you mind answering a question for me?' When Elizabeth agreed, Mrs Taylor asked, 'How do you feel about corporal punishment?'

'You will not lay a hand on my sisters,' Elizabeth snarled as she surged out of her chair, leaning over the desk.

Mrs Taylor smiled and raised her hands placatingly. 'I simply wanted to know if you expected me to deal out that kind of chastisement, because I will not do it. I am pleased that we understand each other.'

Elizabeth relaxed back into her chair. 'I too am pleased by your attitude.' She grimaced and with a rueful smile added, 'Although I must confess, I would understand if once in a long while and in the heat of the moment, you delivered a single slap since I am fully aware that Lydia can be particularly trying. I simply object to deliberate and calculated cruelty.'

'I believe that I have better control of my emotions than that. However, I am relieved to know that you would not hold a single lapse in judgement against me.'

'I can acknowledge that everyone is human and therefore imperfect. As I said, I also know how irritating Lydia can be. But you have not answered my question. How do you feel about taking orders from me?'

Mrs Taylor smiled as she said, 'I have no qualms about taking orders from a sensible employer. You appear to be such a one.'

'In that case, Mrs Taylor. The position is yours.'

~A~

Chapter 6

The next morning, Good Friday, Mr Gardiner requested a private interview with Elizabeth.

Once they were comfortably settled in the library, Gardiner explained, 'I was going to discuss this with Phillips, but since you are the owner of Longbourn and have taken over the care of your sisters, I believe you are the person to whom I need to provide the information.'

'This sounds most intriguing. Please go on.'

'I believe that you are aware that your mother has a jointure of five thousand pounds which is invested in the four percents.'

Elizabeth nodded and Gardiner continued, 'It is customary that the interest of a jointure is part of the family's income... and is often used as the wife's pin money. In the early years of their marriage, Bennet took the interest but deposited it into a separate account... again in the four percents. Once I started my business, he invested the annual interest from your mother's jointure with me and reinvested any profits he made on those investments.'

Gardiner chuckled at the stunned look on Elizabeth's countenance. 'Before you ask, he kept the interest from the first four years in the four percents to ensure there was at least some money if my business ran into trouble.'

Elizabeth managed to get her voice to cooperate enough to ask, 'How much...'

'At present there is a combined total in excess of ten thousand pounds.'

'There was no mention in the will as far as I know, and Uncle Phillips did not say anything about funds invested with you. To whom does that money belong?' Elizabeth asked, worried that it might go to Mrs Bennet who would surely squander it.

'Since Bennet did not leave any specific instructions, one could argue it belongs to Longbourn and therefore to you. On the other hand, since it is not in the estate account, I was going to keep it safe for you and your sisters if Collins had not had the decency to shuffle off this mortal coil as expeditiously as he did.'

She did a quick calculation. 'So, between Mrs Bennet's jointure and Mr Bennet's investments with you, there would be at least six hundred pounds per annum in interest for all of us to live on, even if it were all invested in the four percents and even if we did not have Longbourn.' She shook her head. 'Why were we led to believe that we are poor? Or at least relatively so.'

'So that my sister could not spend it all on fripperies,' sighed Gardiner.

After giving Elizabeth a moment to absorb the information, he said, 'Of course, that does not include the money I can realise from the sale of the books, which Bennet wanted to be used for you and your sisters to live on until each of you married.'

'I gather that he made those arrangements before he forced me to marry Mr Collins?'

'He made those arrangements shortly after Lydia was born. But what do you mean he forced you to marry?'

'I had no wish to marry but Mrs Bennet would not be gainsaid since she seemed to think that I would allow her to remain at Longbourn as its mistress after father died.'

Gardiner noticed the expression which was a mixture of anger and hurt. He asked, 'I gather that yours was not a good marriage?'

'My husband had a heavy hand and had been encouraged by Mrs Bennet in his endeavours to break my spirit if not my body.'

It was Gardiner's turn to look pained. 'I had not realised things were that bad. No one mentioned that you had not married of your own free will.' Gardiner paused and sighed. 'I promised Bennet never to mention this, but I believe you need to know... Last Christmas he confided in me that he did not expect to see out another year.'

'But he died in an accident. He fell off his horse and broke his neck,' exclaimed Elizabeth.

'True. But I have wondered whether he was already dead when he hit the ground. It was his heart which was giving out.'

They both sat quietly while Elizabeth considered the implications. Eventually it was her turn to sigh. 'That explains much. I was angry at father for not providing for his daughters.'

Gardiner nodded in understanding. 'The question is, what do you want to do with this money now?'

'It is my decision?'

'As you are the head of the family remaining at Longbourn, you get to decide what to do with it,' Gardiner replied with a challenging smile.

Elizabeth responded to the unvoiced challenge. 'I would like to keep the investments in place for the moment, although the interest from Mrs Bennet's jointure will now go to her, any interest from the second account may continue to compound and I would like to reinvest any profits the investments make from your business. These funds will give my sisters quite adequate dowries.'

'That is an excellent... and generous decision.' Gardiner gave his niece a proud smile. 'But what about yourself? Do you not want a share?'

A mischievous grin spread over Elizabeth's features. 'If you allow me to keep the books, I will provide for my sisters while they live here. As for the rest, I do not need it. Without our parents at Longbourn squandering the income, I expect to make significant savings with which to improve the estate, giving me an even bigger income.'

'Well said, my dear. Although if you have excess funds, I should be happy to invest them for you,' Gardiner said with an answering laugh.

'Just one thing... I do not wish for word of this to get out, since I prefer not having to deal with fortune hunters.' She did not say that she also did not wish to deal with demands from Mrs Bennet or certain sisters for additional funds with which to buy fripperies. As that thought passed through her mind, she felt a sudden pang of understanding for some of her father's motives.

~A~

Saturday, the first day of April 1809, the anniversary of Elizabeth's birth dawned bright and clear, tempting Lizzy out of the house at the crack of dawn.

In the past two weeks her bruises had almost completely faded, and she felt full of energy. Putting on a sturdy pair of half-boots, a coat and a bonnet, she quietly slipped out of the house. The dark colours of mourning made her well-nigh invisible as she made her way to her favourite destination.

The last time she had watched the sun rise from Oakham Mount had been on her last birthday. It seemed like a good omen that on this birthday she could again enjoy the freedom of walking as she pleased.

Her conversation with her uncle the previous day had also mitigated some of the sense of betrayal she had felt about her father, leaving her to feel lighter than she had for the past year.

Breathing deeply from her brisk walk, she sat on her customary perch and waited for the sun to crest the horizon. As the light spread across the countryside Elizabeth felt her spirits lift as if the sun was not only lighting up the world but her soul which had been stranded in darkness for the past year.

She opened her arms and revelled in the feeling of being reborn.

~A~

Much as Elizabeth would have liked to, she did not linger past the sunrise and hurried back to Longbourn.

She was pleased when she discovered that Sally had a bath ready for her. 'Happy birthday, Mrs Elizabeth. I thought that you might allow yourself to be pampered for once,' her maid greeted her. Ever since her conversation with the stablemaster, word had spread throughout not only Longbourn but the whole neighbourhood about her preferred form of address.

Elizabeth happily acquiesced as she felt that a bath would be the final cleansing which she needed to start a new year and her new life.

~A~

Elizabeth entered the dining room to be greeted by all her family with their best wishes for her birthday.

Six-year-old Bethany Gardiner presented Elizabeth with a (somewhat misshapen) wreath of flowers. 'I picked them myself,' she proudly declared and insisted on placing it on Lizzy's head.

'This is wonderful. Thank you,' Elizabeth managed to say with a smile despite the happy tears threatening.

'You look very pretty now,' Bethany stated firmly with a big smile before allowing her mother to persuade her to attend to her breakfast.

~A~

When they had all finished their meal, Elizabeth's sisters presented her with small gifts, after which Mrs Gardiner asked Elizabeth to come to their room for a few minutes.

Lizzy was astonished when her aunt presented her with several lengths of fabric for new dresses. 'Aunt, while I appreciate the gift, you are aware that we are in mourning.'

'Certainly. But you will be in mourning for only a few months, after which you will need to dress appropriate to your new station. At least you have time to make up the dresses to have them ready when you need them.'

Elizabeth ran her hands over the materials, and this time she could not stop her tears. 'They are so beautiful,' she sobbed as her aunt pulled her into an embrace. It had been a long time since Elizabeth had felt cherished and for the first time in what seemed forever, she allowed herself to abandon her stoicism and cried on her aunt's shoulder like the young girl she still was. She felt like all the hurt and pain was being washed away by her tears.

At last, the storm of weeping passed, and Elizabeth pulled away from her aunt who handed her a handkerchief, which she used to good effect. 'Thank you, Aunt Madeline. I am sorry I made such a spectacle of myself.'

'There is no need to apologise. It is fully understandable that you would at times feel overwhelmed. A great deal of responsibility has been placed on your young shoulders. Just remember that you are not alone, and your uncles and I are always willing to help.'

Elizabeth tilted her head as a thought occurred to her. 'There is a matter upon which I would appreciate your advice. As you can imagine,

I do not wish to be addressed as Mrs Collins and Miss, or worse, Mrs Bennet would be equally as bad. At present many people call me Mrs Elizabeth, which is perfectly adequate amongst my neighbours, but I will need to use a surname for business. Since I love you and Uncle Gardiner, I considered using that name…'

Mrs Gardiner observed the pensive look on Elizabeth's face and asked, 'Are you concerned about how your uncle and I will feel about you using the name, or your mother?'

'Mostly the latter…'

Mrs Gardiner thought for a moment when an idea came to her. 'Do you remember my family name before I married your uncle?'

Elizabeth's brow wrinkled as she searched her memory. 'I believe it was Brooks, was it not?'

'Correct. While your initials will revert back to EB, it is different enough not to cause you problems. Since I have no further use for it, may I gift you with my name?'

Elizabeth said carefully, 'Mrs Elizabeth Brooks.' Her eyes lit up and she threw her arms around her aunt. 'I like it excessively. Thank you for my best birthday present.'

Soon afterwards she shared the news of her new name with the rest of the family and the staff, who approved thoroughly of the change.

~A~

The rest of the day proceeded quietly with the sisters taking turns to play with the Gardiner children while the others spent time with their aunt and uncle.

Mrs Taylor had settled into what used to be Elizabeth's room and was getting to know her charges. She discovered that her friend Madeline had been correct in her estimate that Mrs Bennet had a very limited understanding and had attempted to shape her daughters in her own image.

She considered it fortunate that the potentially most difficult sister was only thirteen years of age, and while she was badly spoilt, Lydia was not stupid. Mrs Taylor hoped that the brief conversation about finances on their first evening would have a salutary effect.

In Mrs Taylors's estimation, Kitty only followed Lydia because she had been neglected by both parents and despite being nearly two years older than Lydia, she was more likely to quickly improve her ways if gently encouraged.

She finally turned her attention to Mary. 'I understand from your sister that you have a great love of music but have lacked proper instruction to help you improve your performance.'

'I am mostly self-taught as Mrs Bennet could not spare funds to hire a music master for me,' replied Mary with a bland expression. 'I am given to understand that you are an expert on the pianoforte?'

'That is correct. Mrs Gardiner said that was one of the major criteria your sister insisted upon when she specified the qualifications for this position. I believe Mrs Brooks wanted you to have the opportunity to be the best you could be.'

'Perhaps you would like me to play for you so that you may judge how much you have to teach me?'

'Please, that would be best,' Mrs Taylor agreed.

Mary led the way into the next room, leaving the doors open to the parlour where the rest of the family were talking, and opened the pianoforte.

A small smile played about her lips as she sat down and started to play her favourite piece without bothering to select a score. She was halfway through the first section of the Moonlight Sonata when all conversation stopped in the next room.

Mary's smile became wider when she saw the raised brows of Mrs Taylor, after which she focused on the music, becoming absorbed in its strains. While her playing was still in need of improvement, it was not as dull and stilted as it had been in the past.

She stilled as the last note faded away. After a moment of complete silence, Mary was drawn back to the present by thunderous applause.

'I never knew you could play like this,' exclaimed Jane.

Elizabeth grinned and remembered an earlier conversation with her sister about hiding herself. 'I suppose all that practice did pay off after all,' she said to Mary with twinkling eyes.

~A~

Later in the day, the servants of Longbourn had a final surprise for Elizabeth.

Mrs Hill requested that Elizabeth should step up to the master suite to give her opinion on a matter which the housekeeper refused to divulge.

When Elizabeth entered the rooms with Mrs Hill, she discovered that they had been transformed. Gone were the dark walls and dark fabrics which had been replaced by pale green walls and cream curtains. The furniture was still dark wood, but now it complemented the lighter colours.

The theme was carried from the sitting room to the bedchamber and onto the dressing room, where all of Elizabeth's garments had been placed. A few cushions in a sunny yellow added warmth and brightness.

With a pleased smile at Elizabeth, who took in all those changes with an expression of wonder and delight, Mrs Hill indicated several paintings. 'I wondered which of these pictures you would like to have in your rooms?'

'You must have worked day and night to make all these changes so quickly,' Elizabeth exclaimed and startled the housekeeper into a blush by giving her a quick hug.

'It was not so bad since I had lots of help. Everyone wanted to do what they could to get it ready,' Mrs Hill shrugged off the praise but was secretly delighted at her mistress's response. That open appreciation was a major reason why all the staff had worked hard to finish the rooms.

'Please convey my thanks to everyone for their hard work.'

'I will, but you have not said which pictures you would like.'

Elizabeth selected three landscapes, one for her bedroom and two for her sitting room. When Mr Hill with the aid of the footman John hung the picture with a view from Oakham Mount in her bedroom, she heard the older man say, 'I told you she would pick that one.'

The last surprise as she slipped into bed was that the mattress and all the bedding were new as well. She had never before slept in such a comfortable bed.

~A~

Chapter 7

On Easter Sunday, the sisters, accompanied by the Gardiners and Mrs Taylor arrived a little early for services.

The vicar greeted them on arrival, seemingly having waited for them. He escorted them to the empty pew at the front of the church, where the small plaque saying Bennet, had been replaced by one professing Longbourn.

'It is only right, Mrs Elizabeth,' said the vicar only to be stopped by Elizabeth.

'Thank you, vicar. You are most kind. But I would beg you for one more kindness. Thanks to my Aunt Gardiner, nee Brooks, I have decided that I would like to be known as Mrs Elizabeth Brooks.'

The old gentleman gave her an understanding look and said, 'I shall be happy to address you as such,' and returned outside where soon afterwards could be heard the less than dulcet tones of Mrs Bennet, complaining when she heard that she had been barred from the Longbourn pew by the vicar and was required to sit elsewhere. Mrs Bennet ended up joining her sister and her husband.

~A~

Tuesday morning, after the Gardiners left Longbourn, Mrs Taylor sought an interview with her employer.

'Mrs Brooks, as you suggested, I have spent the last few days observing your sisters.'

'And despite that you did not leave with the Gardiners?'

Mrs Taylor smiled at the quip. 'Indeed, not. I am made of sterner stuff, but I wished to discuss with you methods of rewards and punishments which I hope will be successful... and do not involve physical violence.'

'You intrigue me. Please explain.'

'I understand that your sisters' pin money is fifty pounds per year, which you plan to give them at the rate of four pounds per month, plus an extra two pounds at Christmas.'

'That is correct.'

'I would like to suggest that you raise that amount by a potential two pounds per year, but instead of giving it to them each month, you give your younger sisters one pound each week.'

'I presume you have a reason for this.'

'I do not wish to offend you, but I believe that your youngest sister is somewhat mercenary,' Mrs Taylor said and when Elizabeth reluctantly nodded, she continued, 'I therefore propose to fine her one shilling for each infraction of the rules which we will set.'

Elizabeth thought about the suggestion while the governess waited patiently. 'I believe I can see the point of the weekly payment. Lydia, and to a lesser degree Kitty, will learn more quickly the consequences of bad behaviour.'

'Precisely. And it will be easier for them to remember the instances which caused them to be penalised since they will all be within a sennight. If we were to work on a monthly schedule, there would be more arguments because they would likely forget their infractions.'

'This arrangement has the potential to save me quite a bit of money, especially in the first few months.' Elizabeth grinned as she considered this solution to the dilemma of forcing Lydia to cooperate without resorting to physical inducements.

'The short-term savings will pay for the additional pin money in the long-term,' Mrs Taylor agreed. 'Now that we are agreed on this issue, I have prepared a schedule of lessons which I would like to discuss with you.'

The ladies spent the next half hour discussing Mrs Taylor's ideas. At the end of their conversation, Elizabeth was well satisfied with the schedule, and she was amused by the list of infractions which would cost her sister one shilling each.

Elizabeth even provided two small ledgers in which Mrs Taylor could record Lydia's and Kitty's misdemeanours. Although she was reminded of the records Mr Collins had kept, she was pleased that her sisters would be spared those kinds of consequences.

~A~

Mrs Taylor found her charges at breakfast since the youngest Bennet girls liked to sleep late.

They were not well pleased when Mrs Taylor informed them that in future, she expected them to break their fast no later than by eight in the morning as their lessons would begin at nine and were to occur every day except Sunday.

The complaints by Lydia were vociferous but stopped when she was told that she was to receive her pin money in weekly instalments. Mrs Taylor gave the reason for this change as an opportunity for the girls to learn budgeting, as they would have to save up money if they wanted to have a new dress.

Lydia's good humour vanished again when Mrs Taylor handed them the list of infractions and explained that they would lose a shilling for each one.

- *Rudeness / throwing a tantrum*
- *Deliberate disobedience*
- *Refusal to attend to lessons / chores*
- *Lying*
- *Tardiness*
- *Leaving Longbourn without permission / chaperone*
- *Flirting with members of the opposite sex*
- *Dressing inappropriately for a girl not yet out*
- *Stealing – also known as borrowing without permission*

'But if you deduct a shilling for each time we do anything wrong, how shall we ever be able to afford new dresses?' cried Lydia.

'If you learn to mind your manners and comply with the rules of the house you will not lose any money. And even if you lose part of your pin money, you may still be able to buy some fabrics. In that case, although you will not be able to commission having the dress made by a seamstress, you can still sew it yourself,' Mrs Taylor explained patiently.

'Lizzy will never allow you to treat us so badly,' Lydia expostulated, refusing to accept that her days as a favourite and indulged child were over.

'I discussed this with Mrs Brooks, and she is in complete agreement with me. And I must warn you, this is the last time that your obstinate attitude will be tolerated. You have until tomorrow to become reconciled to the new rules.'

~A~

Midmorning, Elizabeth received a note from Mr Phillips informing her that Mrs Bennet had found a cottage to rent and requested her mother's belongings which were still stored at Longbourn to be sent to the new address.

Mr Hill accompanied the carts carrying Mrs Bennet's chattels and returned with an inventory signed by the lady and notarised by Mr Phillips, confirming that all her belongings had arrived in good order.

Mr Hill handed the document to Elizabeth and said, 'This was Mr Phillips' idea. He also sends his compliments and says that you owe him a shilling.' Hill chuckled at Elizabeth's puzzled expression. 'It's at the end of the list.'

The last item on the inventory was indeed – 1 shilling in lieu of a missing doily. Elizabeth looked up at her faithful retainer raising a quizzical brow.

'Mr Phillips paid that to shut her up and to stop her from coming here to claim her supposedly missing property. But I seem to remember that particular item as one Mrs Bennet ruined one night when she was in her cups by dropping a candle on it. Between the wax and the charring, it was not fit to be used any more. She was only lucky that the candle went out and it did not catch fire and burn down the house.'

Elizabeth shook her head in disgust. Would that woman never be satisfied? The answer was simple – no.

Instead of complaining, she smiled at Hill as she said, 'I shall gladly reimburse Uncle Phillips. The peace of this house is worth much more than one shilling.'

~A~

That afternoon Elizabeth visited her uncle and handed over one shilling.

After that business had been completed, she asked his advice how to go about changing her name to Brooks to ensure the change was legal.

Elizabeth was pleased to discover that she could call herself anything she wished, as long as it was not with the purpose to defraud anyone.

If she wanted the change to be permanent and official, all she had to do was to put an advertisement into a newspaper to make the notification official.

Relieved with the simplicity of the process, Elizabeth asked her uncle to send the notification to the paper and update all her documents with her new name.

It felt good to now be officially Mrs Brooks.

~A~

She was not so sanguine at five minutes to nine the following morning when Lydia sauntered into the dining room where Elizabeth and her other three sisters as well as Mrs Taylor were finishing their breakfast.

Mrs Taylor was prepared and had already recorded the incident in the ledger which she presented to Lydia to sign as acknowledgement of her actions.

'La, what a joke. You cannot make me sign this silly ledger.'

'If you do not sign, I will get these witnesses to sign on your behalf and fine you another shilling for refusing to obey an order.' As Lydia opened her mouth to start screaming and throwing a tantrum, Mrs Taylor reminded her, 'If you throw a tantrum, that will be yet another shilling.'

Lydia's mouth snapped shut as she stared at the implacable expressions of Mrs Taylor and her oldest sisters while Kitty kept her eyes on her plate, refusing to be drawn into the conflict.

In the past, Lydia's tantrums had been her most potent weapon since her father valued his peace and her mother was amenable to crocodile tears. If that ploy was denied to her, how was she to gain the upper hand?

Her memory of crocodile tears sparked an inspiration.

Lydia managed to squeeze out a few tears as she took on a mournful expression. 'I am sorry. I was only late because I barely slept a wink. Ever since out dear papa passed away, I have had trouble sleeping at night.'

Mrs Taylor's expression took on a doubting cast before she shot a questioning look at her employer.

'That is the exact method Lydia used to employ to get Mrs Bennet to countermand Mr Bennet's edicts,' Elizabeth said blandly and after a moment's thought, added, 'You should also know that my sisters hardly knew their father. I only knew him because I was interested in learning.'

'I see. Thank you, Mrs Brooks.' Mrs Taylor acknowledged the information as she took up her pen and dipped it into the ink. She wrote *Refusal to sign the register* and on a separate line she added *Lying about grief for her father keeping her awake*.

She looked up from the ledger and advised, 'Lydia, you had better consider your actions and attitudes. At this rate, not only will you forfeit your pin money for the week, but you will be in debt... a debt which will be carried forward to the next week.'

Since Lydia could not argue against the judgement made by the lady and her older sister without being penalised again, Lydia focused on something she could refute. 'I did not give you permission to address me by my given name,' she said haughtily.

'I do not need a child's permission to address her in a familiar fashion. Until you can behave like a lady, you do not deserve the be addressed with a courtesy title.'

When Lydia opened her mouth to start yet another argument, Kitty lightly touched her hand and said, 'Lydia, no more. Come, eat your breakfast. We are already late for our lessons.'

Lydia grudgingly acquiesced.

~A~

The following Monday morning Lydia was most put out again when she received her pin money for the previous week.

She held up a coin in each of her hands. 'I am supposed to have a pound of pin money per week. How am I supposed to survive on only two shillings?' she stormed.

'You should have considered that before flaunting the new rules in this house. But considering that you have no need to spend money at present, you have nothing to complain about. You have a stout roof over your head, a comfortable bed to sleep in unmolested and you do not need to go hungry,' replied Elizabeth who was passing out the pin money to her sisters.

'I did not get any breakfast twice last week.'

'You were informed on several occasions that breakfast is served between the hours of eight and nine in the morning. If you choose not to attend breakfast at that time, you have only yourself to blame if you go hungry. Instead of whining, you should be grateful that we did not fine you for being late on those days, otherwise you would not have received any money at all.' Elizabeth shrugged. 'I felt that you missing breakfast was punishment enough. If you disagree with that judgement, I will be happy to apply the rules exactly.'

Elizabeth reached out as if to take Lydia's coins from her, only to have her sister snatch her hands back. 'You are horrible,' the girl spat and rushed out of the room.

Kitty was pleased enough to receive fifteen shillings, having learnt quickly that following Lydia was an expensive exercise. Instead, she discovered that her efforts to apply herself to her lessons garnered praise and attention which she had never before received.

Each evening over dinner Elizabeth had enquired about her sisters' activities for the day. Any praise Mrs Taylor expressed for her students' achievements, Elizabeth and Jane warmly seconded.

Since Mrs Taylor dealt with any reprimands immediately, they were never raised during dinner, ensuring that this time was pleasant for all the sisters... apart from Lydia's whining, of course.

~A~

While during the second week of the new regime Lydia still lost the majority of her allowance, she was surprised when she received praise for her mathematical ability.

'Why did we never hear that we have a mathematical genius in our midst?' asked Elizabeth when informed of this development at dinner that evening.

'Mama never wanted us to learn manly accomplishments,' replied Lydia with a shrug.

'Manly accomplishments? How can looking after the household accounts be a manly accomplishment? After all, every lady needs to know how to budget for food, clothing, and other household necessities,' exclaimed Jane.

The sisters exchanged startled glances.

'No, this could not be possible...' breathed Mary.

'Jane, do you remember that it was Aunt Gardiner who taught us about household accounts,' Elizabeth reminded her sister.

'And we taught Mary...'

'Mama knows how to count,' interjected Lydia. 'But she always said no lady should ever need more than that. I always knew that numbers were easy, but having mama fuss over me was much nicer than have her screaming at me the way she did at Lizzy.'

Jane mused, 'I never thought about it before, but speaking about this brings to mind that Mrs Hill was always doing the household accounts. Mama said that was part of her duties.'

Mrs Taylor added her own advice. 'While it is indeed part of the housekeeper's duties, it is incumbent on the mistress to check those figures to ensure that the housekeeper does not cheat the family.'

'I believe we now have an explanation why Mrs Bennet is such a spendthrift and could never stick to her budget,' expostulated Elizabeth with a shake of her head and an unladylike huff. 'I believe I had better send a note to Uncle Phillips, suggesting that he might want to keep an eye on her spending, otherwise she might squander a year's income in the first month.'

Jane was the first to think of an application of Lydia's new-found talent. 'I believe that since numbers come easy to you, Lydia, you might enjoy helping me with the household accounts.'

Now it was Elizabeth's turn to grin. 'And once you have mastered those, perhaps you would enjoy expanding your education into the realm of estate accounts.'

Lydia was uncertain whether to be chagrined at having more lessons added to her schedule or pleased with the praise by her sisters. In the end, pleasure won out since even someone as self-centred as she was, craved acceptance from her family.

~A~

Chapter 8

A few weeks later, Mrs Taylor approached Elizabeth in the library regarding one of her pupils. 'Elizabeth, I would like a word with you if you have the time,' Margaret Taylor asked, forgoing formality since she and Elizabeth had developed a friendship and they had decided to use their given names when in private.

Elizabeth allowed that she was at her leisure and offered a seat to her friend.

'Did you know that Catherine has an excellent eye for colour and design?' Margaret refused to call the girl Kitty.

'I do remember that she used to love drawing until Lydia made fun of her for what she called Kitty's scribbling.'

'I set the girls an exercise asking them to draw one of the rooms in this house but redecorated to their taste. While Lydia was adequate at the task, I would happily live in the room Catherine designed,' explained Mrs Taylor and handed over a sketch. 'See for yourself.'

Elizabeth took the sketch and exclaimed, 'That is the back parlour which we never use because it is too dark. Even in summer when it would be pleasantly cool, no one wants to spend any time in it.'

'Would you be willing to let Catherine oversee the redecoration of that room?'

Elizabeth broke into a wide smile. 'I would be delighted to do so. Summer is almost upon us, and it would give us a pleasant room to take tea in the afternoon to escape the heat.'

~A~

Kitty was thrilled to be put in charge of the redecoration even though she had to work with Lydia who was in charge of the finances to give her a practical application for her own lessons.

Five days before midsummer's day, Kitty, Lydia, and Mrs Taylor invited the other sisters to examine the completed project.

The parlour was now decorated in light blues and whites with dashes of yellow, giving it a light and airy look, perfect for a cool retreat on a hot summer's day.

'This is truly wonderful,' exclaimed Elizabeth, a sentiment which was echoed by her sisters. 'Although I hope that you have not bankrupted us to create this delightful haven,' she teased.

Lydia grinned and took Elizabeth's hand turning it palm upwards to place six shillings in her hand. 'This is left over from the budget Mrs Taylor set us,' she said proudly.

'Lydia was most exacting that I should not overspend, so we had to be creative,' Kitty explained with a deprecating smile which did nothing to hide the excitement she felt at the wholehearted praise by all her family. 'Fortunately, since we wish to use this room in summer, we were able to save on the curtain material. Rather than a good, heavy brocade we used a light and cheap cotton but by adding embroidery at the edges it still looks elegant.'

'The budget was quite modest,' added Mrs Taylor who seemed very proud of her students, justifiably so.

Elizabeth looked at the money in her hand and made a quick decision. 'Since you must have worked very hard to achieve this, you deserve a treat,' she said and handed three shillings to each of the girls, who beamed at her.

Lizzy had the feeling that the exuberant smiles were caused more by the praise than the financial reward.

~A~

To celebrate the occasion the sisters and Mrs Taylor took their tea in the newly refurbished room.

Once the girls had calmed down from explaining the details of their project, Elizabeth reminded them, 'You girls must have been excessively focused on your task since you appear to have lost track of time.' Receiving puzzled looks, she added, 'It has been three months since father died. You may change your dresses to half mourning if you wish.'

'Does that also mean that we may leave the house again to go visiting?' Lydia wanted to know.

'If you are finished with your lessons for the day, and you have permission as well as being accompanied by a chaperone, then you may indeed go and visit your friends. Or perhaps you would like to invite Maria Lucas for tea tomorrow and show off your achievement.' Elizabeth smiled and gestured at the room.

She was stunned and proud when Lydia looked to Mrs Taylor and politely asked, 'Might we invite Maria to come at three? We should be finished with our lessons by then.'

Margaret Taylor smiled. 'If you both focus during lessons, we can finish half an hour earlier to give you time to get ready.' When the girls excitedly chattered to one another, she turned to Elizabeth and winked.

~A~

The following day appeared much brighter at Longbourn as four of the sisters wore gowns in various shades of lavender or mauve instead of black.

Margaret Taylor continued to wear her light grey dresses, but she now added subtle blue ribbons to brighten the look.

Elizabeth also opted for grey. It was not that she was feeling particularly mournful, she simply abhorred lavender as a colour. Since she also disliked violet and mauve, grey was the only acceptable colour left to her.

At breakfast, Mary questioned her sister, 'Is it not customary to mourn a husband for a year?'

'I am sorry if my choice of apparel shocks you, but I am not enough of a hypocrite to pretend mourning that man. I have been wearing mourning colours out of respect for our father, not my husband. And before you ask, if I had followed custom in mourning my son, I should have worn white for six weeks.'

Mary sighed and nodded in acknowledgement. 'I beg your pardon; I had not considered the circumstances.'

'There is another factor for changing my garb. At least, in this heat, grey is much cooler than black,' Elizabeth commented with great relief.

~A~

By Michaelmas, the difference in the Longbourn household was immeasurable. By the time the sisters finished their period of half-mourning they were almost unrecognisable.

Jane had blossomed being given responsibility for the household. Gone was the languid young woman who had not been allowed to do anything since she was too beautiful to bother herself with such mundane things as housework.

She had spent much time in the kitchen, a room from which she had been banned by Mrs Bennet, to learn the intricacies of preparing a meal. While she had no intention ever to cook, except as a last resort, now she knew what was required in that domain.

As a consequence, menus at Longbourn became a delight for the diners. While the meals became less elaborate, they were exceedingly tasty as Jane always chose dishes for which the produce was in season. This had a further benefit of reducing the money spent on food at Longbourn significantly. A fact which delighted Elizabeth who was trying to save as much as possible to provide funds to improve the estate.

Mary, who unbeknownst to her family had always had an interest in botany, introduced Jane to the stillroom, where they created perfumes to delight their sisters, as well as salves and other preparations which they distributed to the tenants who could not afford to purchase these basic treatments.

In return, Mary had come out of hiding and allowed her sisters to teach her how to present herself to best advantage. When she discarded her tight bun in favour of a softer hairstyle, she was no longer the plain daughter which Mrs Bennet had derided. Admittedly, few women could hold a candle to Jane when it came to physical beauty, but that still allowed for plenty of scope to be exceedingly attractive rather than merely tolerable.

Mary still practiced the pianoforte and admitted that while she had hidden her talent in the past, there were still many things which Mrs Taylor could teach her since that lady had an exceptional talent when it came to music.

With some encouragement, she even considered opinions other than Reverend Fordyce. But that was an ongoing project.

The younger girls were flourishing under the care of Mrs Taylor. Once the lady took on their education and Kitty felt appreciated, she had not been much of a problem. While in the early days of the lady's tenure Elizabeth had been grateful that it was predominantly the governess who had to deal with Lydia's whining, the youngest girl had started to accept the new rules. To top it off, in recent times there had even been a week when Lydia had received all of her allowance.

~A~

Over the summer, Elizabeth started to grow into her role as master of Longbourn.

She read every book and pamphlet on estate management on which she could get her hands. She spent hours each day on studying tomes on farming techniques and animal husbandry.

She spoke to her neighbours and to their stewards. While some of the men advised that she should engage a steward and not worry her pretty little head about such things as managing Longbourn herself, many of them were helpful giving advice on any topic related to her concerns.

Slowly but surely, she garnered the respect of her neighbours and her tenants as a competent master. That is not to say that everything went perfectly. She made some mistakes when she thought that she had understood and applied what she had found in books, only to discover that the information she had gathered, applied to a different county with different soils or climatic conditions. But as she was prepared to acknowledge her blunders and then go ahead to fix them, no one held those things against her.

She pushed herself hard, even when her sisters advised that she should take time for herself occasionally. But she had a reason for working as hard as she could so that she fell into bed exhausted most nights.

That exhaustion allowed her to go to sleep.

While she presented a calm and competent front to her family, servants and all her friends and acquaintances, she was troubled by nightmares. In her dreams she relived the worst parts of her life when she was trapped in her marriage, or she found herself running until she dropped with exhaustion but never escaping and coming to a safe haven.

Focusing on estate matters to the exclusion of all else before going to sleep, sometimes allowed her to escape the dreams.

Yet gradually, as the months passed the nightmares became less frequent.

~A~

During those months, Mr Phillips called at Longbourn once a month to see if he could be of assistance to his nieces. When he saw the improvements of not only the sisters but also the house and the estate, he was most impressed and said so during a conversation with Elizabeth just after they had finished the harvest.

'Please, uncle, do not be too fulsome in your praise. We had had our share of... ah... issues, but somehow, we muddled through.'

Phillips laughed at Elizabeth's chagrined expression. 'My dear niece, do you not know that the purpose of mistakes is to learn from them?'

Elizabeth joined in his laughter. 'Well, what can I say, we had many opportunities to learn.'

Becoming serious once more, Elizabeth said, 'I am glad that you have come today. There is something I wish to do, but I would like your advice before I go ahead.'

Seeing his niece fidget, Phillips became concerned and curious. 'I will help all that I can.'

'You know the Russells who have the lease on the farm which adjoins Longbourn?'

'Yes, that farm is part of Netherfield. What of it?'

'Well, Mr Russell wants to move, and I want to buy the farm. I thought that Mr Morris might not want to bother trying to find another tenant...'

'You are doing well enough to buy more land?' Phillips was all astonishment causing Elizabeth to blush.

'The harvest was good, and our expenses are significantly reduced these days. And Mrs Potter's brother would like to move closer to his sister, since she is the only family which he has left, apart from his own of course. He is in Gloucestershire, where he stayed to help his parents. But they passed away a few months ago...'

Phillips grinned. 'So, you have a potential tenant which Morris does not know about. Since you are likely correct when you think he probably does not want the bother of finding a new tenant, he should be amenable to making his profit from selling the farm at a good price.'

'Will you make the enquiries and negotiate for me?'

'I will do so without letting on who the potential buyer is. He might think you to be silly enough to pay an inflated price.'

'I am prepared to consider a fair price only.'

Phillips smiled, pleased that he could be of service to his niece.

Six months later, Elizabeth was ecstatic to add a sixth tenant to her roster.

~A~

As Elizabeth's competence grew, there was only one notable hold-out in her acceptance as master of Longbourn.

Word was passed on to her that one evening at the Red Bull tavern, several of the tenant farmers were spending an evening enjoying a pint or three.

The men were discussing the relative merits of the various landowners when Elizabeth's name was mentioned in a most favourable light by several of her tenants, as well as the tenants of Netherfield.

Chambers exclaimed, 'You call yourself men? Taking orders from a slip of a girl who knows nothing about farming. All those newfangled ideas she has. Mark my words, come harvest time you'll see that I was right to stick to what my father and grandfather did.'

The other farmers figured that Chambers was worried about his farm as it was not producing what it once did, but since he was not prepared to listen and change his ways, there was no point in arguing with him... Especially since Chambers was known to be an obstreperous drunk.

~A~

Chapter 9

Since her eviction from Longbourn Mrs Bennet had often considered moving to another area but she could not bring herself to go to a place where she did not know a single soul. Even though her friends amongst the four and twenty families refused to call on her while she was in deep mourning other than to gloat about her reduced circumstances since word had spread about her treatment of Elizabeth, at least here her sister was prepared to maintain contact.

For the first several months Mrs Bennet railed against her second daughter for cruelly tossing her out of her home and refused to listen when her sister and Mr Phillips told her she only had herself to blame for what had happened.

During their annual sojourn to Longbourn, the first Christmas after Mr Bennet's death, Mr Gardiner visited his sister in her cottage at the edge of Meryton at the behest of Mr and Mrs Phillips to attempt to get Mrs Bennet to see reason.

'Brother, it is wonderful to see you,' Mrs Bennet greeted Mr Gardiner excitedly when he stepped into the small parlour and grasped his hands. 'Perhaps you will be able to make Elizabeth see sense and get her to step aside to allow me to resume my rightful place at Longbourn. Martha's husband is useless and refuses to listen to me.'

Stunned by his sister's immediate demand, Gardiner did not bother with a greeting, instead answering, 'Fanny, you do not have a rightful place at Longbourn after the abominable way you behaved towards Elizabeth.'

'What do you mean... abominable? I ensured that Lizzy had a husband and a home which no one could take away from her. All I expected in return was to remain in my home when Mr Bennet passed away.'

'How could you possibly think that Elizabeth would feel charitably towards you after you forced her into such a brutal marriage? And to think you even encouraged that man.'

'How was I to know that he would be so very bad? I just thought she simply needed a firm hand to bring her to heel. Mr Bennet always let her run wild and she never listened to me.'

'You are saying that you knew she never listened to you and yet you expected her to step aside and let you continue as mistress of the estate?' Gardiner shook his head at Mrs Bennet's steadfast refusal to acknowledge her own culpability.

'She is too young to act as a proper mistress.'

'She is the same age as you were when you married Bennet and she had the advantage of growing up on an estate. Something you cannot claim.'

'But...'

'No, Fanny. You were wrong to force Lizzy to marry that man. You were wrong to expect her to defer to you. You are wrong now to complain. And furthermore, she is now doing a better job than you ever did or ever could.'

'You cannot possibly mean that. I heard tell that the table she sets is positively parsimonious.'

'As it happens, Jane is acting as the mistress of Longbourn and is responsible for the menus, for which Lizzy has set a perfectly adequate budget and unlike you they are sticking to it. Lizzy is also more involved in the running of the estate than your husband ever was. I expect it will not be long and she will be an excellent master of Longbourn.'

Mr Gardiner hesitated since he knew his next words would hurt his sister more than anything else he had said so far, but in fairness to Elizabeth, it needed to be said. 'Lizzy is also better at raising your daughters than you or your husband ever were.'

'How can she raise her sisters; she is only a child herself.'

'Lizzy is a bright young woman who has learnt manners and accomplishments despite your constant attempts to make her and Jane act like you did at their ages.'

'Do you not understand that was why Lizzy had to leave. How is Jane supposed to catch a husband if Lizzy is always interfering and stopping Jane from putting herself forward.'

'You mean to say that you forced Lizzy onto that man so that you could then have the opportunity to force Jane to behave like a harlot?

'How dare you use such a horrible word,' screeched Mrs Bennet.

Gardiner was unmoved and unapologetic. 'Quite easily because I remember that I used to be mortified by your behaviour when you were pursuing Bennet. Unfortunately, I was too young at the time, and nobody would listen to me when I advised against that match.'

Mrs Bennet ignored most of his statement and only focused on the portion she felt that she could refute. 'I was right to behave as I did since he married me.'

'Bennet was a fool to marry you. But he paid for his mistake since you nagged him into an early grave.'

For the first time her brother's words made an impact. 'Are you saying that I am to blame for my husband's death?' whispered Mrs Bennet.

Gardiner sighed and felt ashamed that he let his sister goad him into putting his feelings into such blunt words. 'I think you picked the wrong man to marry. Once he realised your lack of intelligence and character, he despised himself for falling for you. This in turn caused him to despise you. He repaid your shrill and nagging ways by making sport of you at every opportunity.'

Mr Gardiner saw the information penetrate his sister's limited understanding. Since he had gone this far, he decided he might as well continue. He shrugged as he said, 'The discontent and tension in your marriage took its toll on his health. You pretended to nervous prostration to get your own way. Bennet truly did suffer from nerves, and I believe that was what killed him.'

Mrs Bennet shook her head. 'Since you believe that, you have to admit that I was right when I feared for his early death which would leave my girls and myself homeless,' she claimed and crossed her arms as she returned to the main topic of their conversation. 'I kept hoping that Jane would make an advantageous match as she could not be so beautiful for nothing. How is she supposed to get a rich husband if she refuses to use that beauty? After all, wealthy men are only interested in beautiful women.'

'I am a wealthy man and while I appreciate Madeline's beauty, I would never have married her if she did not possess intelligence, accomplishments and a sterling character.'

Mrs Bennet tried a different strategy. 'But how can I assure that the girls will find husbands if I am banished to this miserable cottage.'

'You could always invite your daughters to come live with you,' suggested Gardiner who was getting more irritated with his sister by the minute.

'Live with me? How can you suggest such a thing. My jointure is barely enough to keep me housed, fed, and clothed. As you probably know, I have only ten pounds per month to live on. How could I possibly have any of my girls live with me. Especially when in a few months I can at last get rid of all these ghastly widow's weeds and need to buy a new wardrobe.'

'Fanny, your daughters are not in any rush to marry. Elizabeth has hired a governess to teach all the girls the proper manners of ladies and ensure that they will have all the necessary accomplishments. I believe that they will have a better chance at making good matches without you making a spectacle of yourself by pushing the girls at men.'

'But...'

'Most men do not want a woman to push her daughters at him. It makes them wonder what is wrong with the daughters if the mother is so desperate to marry them off.'

'But...'

'I am sorry, Fanny. But your daughters are in better hands now than they have ever been.'

Seeing the calm determination in her brother as he refuted all her arguments made an impression on Mrs Bennet at last.

'You think me a bad mother?' she suddenly asked as she collapsed into a chair.'

'I think you are a mother who was given a very bad example to follow.' Gardiner relented as Mrs Bennet appeared to grasp that her way of dealing with her daughters had been counterproductive.

He only stayed a little longer to ensure Mrs Bennet was well enough before he returned to Longbourn where his wife, their children and nieces waited for him with a great deal more cheer.

~A~

Painful and vexing as Mrs Bennet's conversation with her brother had been, it had been profitable as she at last had an inkling how misguided she had been, and she stopped making demands.

After that conversation, whenever the lady encountered any of her daughters, they greeted her politely, but none of them stopped to converse with her, not even Lydia.

Since her own hurt pride stopped her from extending an olive branch to her daughters, Mrs Bennet was forced to rely on Mrs Phillips to provide her with news of her girls. To that end she asked Mrs Phillips to resume her close connection to the girls.

She was chagrined when she learnt that Elizabeth and the governess were succeeding in slowly educating even her youngest to be accomplished ladies.

~A~

Mrs Phillips was pleased when her sister stopped railing against her fate and her daughters as Mrs Phillips had always been fond of her nieces as she was unable to have children of her own. In recent months the lady had been torn between love of her nieces and love of her sister.

Even though Mrs Phillips, like their neighbours, disapproved of Mrs Bennet's actions towards Elizabeth, she could not abandon her sister, whom she loved regardless, to being shunned by everyone. She had felt obliged to be the one support her sister had left.

Now that her nieces were out of mourning, and Mrs Bennet appeared somewhat reconciled to her situation, Mrs Phillips looked forward to resuming her habit of inviting the girls to tea, dinners, and card parties.

~A~

During one visit for tea, which was attended not only by the sisters but also Lady Lucas, Mrs Long and Mrs Goulding, the topic of remarriage for Elizabeth was raised by the ladies.

Lady Lucas was particularly keen to canvas that topic as she hoped one of her sons could become the next master of Longbourn. 'So, tell me, Mrs Brooks, now that you are out of mourning, how soon are you planning to remarry to ensure that there is a man in charge of your estate again?'

'Remarry? I have no such plans. I shall be much too busy managing my own estate,' Elizabeth exclaimed, feeling vexed that the lady would suggest that she should give up her new freedom.

'But surely, you cannot mean to continue in this way,' exclaimed Lady Lucas. 'While I think it admirable of you to have stepped in to take up the reins when your father and husband passed, ladies are not suited for such an occupation.'

Jane could see her sister was starting to bristle at the implied insult to her abilities and interjected, 'Lady Lucas, as much as it pains me to speak ill of the dead and of our father, no less, but as everyone knows, he was a rather indolent master. In the short time since she has been in charge, Elizabeth has already become a better manager than Mr Bennet ever was.'

'But it appears to me to be quite unseemly for a young woman to perform a man's job. And you must also consider the future of the estate. Who shall inherit Longbourn?'

Elizabeth gave her a tight smile. 'Since the entail has ended, it is my decision to whom I will leave the estate. I am certain that since I am blessed with four sisters, at least one of them will produce a child who will be able to carry on our family at Longbourn. There is no need for me to risk another marriage.'

Mrs Phillips shot an angry look at Lady Lucas for having brought back bad memories for Elizabeth of her late husband and supported her niece. 'While it may be unusual for ladies to manage estates, it is certainly not unheard of. And Lizzy is doing a wonderful job. Mark my words, I predict it will not be long before she is one of the most respected landowners hereabouts.'

~A~

Chapter 10

More than two years had passed since Elizabeth inherited Longbourn, and she was watching the last of the harvest being loaded onto carts while sitting astride Horace's back.

Even though she generally used the gig when she had to cover more ground than she could by walking, on some occasions it was more convenient to ride. Since she still considered the side-saddle to be an impractical and dangerous contraption, she was now wearing a split skirt which appeared modest while allowing freedom of movement.

Against the expectation of many people, her experiment with crop rotation which she had implemented the previous year was a success. Seeing the improved harvest, Elizabeth wished she could have started a year earlier, but the planting had been finished by the time Longbourn became hers.

Instead, she had spent the first year speaking to her tenants, discussing what she had learnt from books and securing agreement to try her ideas.

The previous year there had been an improvement in yield on the fields where the appropriate crops could be planted, but they had to wait until this year to see the full benefit.

Elizabeth was pleased with and for the tenants. The tenants were very pleased with their new master in return.

As she was completing her tour of inspection, Elizabeth noticed an unfamiliar carriage heading away from Netherfield, making her wonder if a potential new tenant had come to view the estate.

~A~

Her question was answered in the affirmative when her friend Charlotte Lucas came to call the following day.

Charlotte was the daughter of Sir William Lucas who several years earlier while he was mayor of Meryton, had made a speech to the King and Queen when they were forced to briefly stop in the town. The King had been so impressed by his erudition that Mr William Lucas was granted a knighthood. As a consequence of his elevation, Sir William had sold his business and bought a small estate which he renamed, Lucas Lodge.

While Charlotte was seven years older than Elizabeth, the two had been friends for many years, each of them enjoying the intelligent company the other provided.

The two had remained friends even after the horrible faux pas by Lady Lucas. Elizabeth still remembered the mortification in Charlotte's expression when she came to Longbourn to apologise for her mother's thoughtless and insensitive enquiries.

'Charlotte, you are not to blame for your mother's actions,' Elizabeth had reassured her friend. 'Considering the behaviour of my own mother, I would be the worst kind of hypocrite if I held you responsible for Lady Lucas' insensitivity. And before you say anything else, I know that like many mothers, she was motivated by concern for her children.'

'I was afraid that you would think us fortune hunters… which technically she is but she is also aware that my brothers are nothing like he who shall not be named,' Charlotte said with a crooked grin. 'But I am still trying to think of a way to make amends.'

Elizabeth ignored the sally and simply asked, 'You truly wish to help?'

'If there is anything that I can do, just name it.'

'Let it be known that I will never again be forced into marriage. Even if a man thinks that a compromise would sway me, it would have the opposite effect. Someone who thinks to force me into marriage is *the last man on earth I could be prevailed on to marry*.'

'I assure you that I will make certain that everyone in our community will know your feelings on this matter,' Charlotte had been only too happy to promise.

Charlotte made good her promise and it was now an accepted fact in Meryton and its environs that if in the unlikely event that Mrs Brooks should eventually decide to marry, it would only be by her choice.

~A~

Elizabeth had just finished updating her books with the details of the harvest when her friend was announced. 'Your timing is exquisite as I have just this minute finished my chores for the day,' said Elizabeth in greeting.

'I thought that I would pass on the latest intelligence mother provided to me,' Charlotte explained with a mischievous smile since Lady Lucas was one of the most energetic gossips in the neighbourhood. 'Mrs Phillips has it on the very best authority that Netherfield Park has been let to a Mr Bingley, a young man of large fortune.'

'The gentleman must be excessively decisive as he viewed the estate only yesterday.' When Charlotte looked surprised at Elizabeth's response, she added, 'I saw a strange carriage leaving the estate yesterday and wondered about the reason.'

'Perhaps this new tenant will be more to Jane's liking, as Mrs Phillips claimed that he was a very handsome young man and her husband confirmed that he is single.'

'There is no reason to assume that he would be interested in Jane rather than one of the other ladies in the area. Perhaps you would be more to his liking.'

Charlotte tilted her head and gave her friend a disbelieving look. 'When has a gentleman ever been interested in anyone other than the most beautiful lady hereabouts,' she scoffed.

'Just because all the other gentlemen have proved to be shallow, it does not follow that Mr Bingley will be so. Perhaps he will prove to be more interested in inward beauty...'

'While you are gracious to say so, we all know that Jane is also blessed with inward beauty as you call it,' Charlotte replied ruefully.

'Ah, well. We can speculate all we like but until the gentleman settles into Netherfield, we cannot know what will happen.'

Having delivered her news, Charlotte remained in relaxed conversation for another hour before returning to Lucas Lodge.

~A~

Two weeks later, the ladies at Longbourn were informed that Mr Bingley and his party had taken up residence at Netherfield Park.

Elizabeth considered whether to pay a visit welcoming them to the neighbourhood in her capacity as master of the estate like the gentlemen of the area were doing. She was still dithering the next day while working in her study putting off making a decision when Mr Hill announced a caller, 'Mr Darcy would like to pay his respects to Mrs Collins.'

Elizabeth's eyes widened in shock accompanied by a sharp indrawn breath. Recovering quickly, she said, 'Please show the gentleman in and bring coffee.'

She rose and greeted the gentleman as he entered. 'Welcome to Longbourn, Mr Darcy.'

Darcy was stunned seeing the vibrant young woman whom he remembered as the very young wife of the ridiculous parson of Lady Catherine. When he met her, he had felt pity for Mrs Collins who had seemed both angry and afraid, trapped in what he suspected was a marriage of convenience.

The difference between then and now was remarkable. Now she seemed alive and confident.

'Mrs Collins, thank you for receiving me. Since I have come into the area to visit with my friend Mr Bingley, I wanted to take the opportunity to express my condolences on your losses in person, belated as they are.'

'Thank you, Mr Darcy. I hope that you will accept my belated thanks for your efforts on my behalf when my son died,' Elizabeth replied as she stepped away from her desk and gestured to one of the chairs by a small table next to the second window. 'Will you sit and take refreshments?'

'It would be my pleasure,' Darcy answered and realised that he meant it, as the pleasant smile and relaxed attitude of the lady invited an equal relaxation in him.

As they sat down, a maid carried in a tray and deposited it on the table. 'I believe that you used to prefer coffee. Is that still the case?'

When Darcy confirmed that coffee was still his preference, Elizabeth fixed his cup the way he liked it before pouring her own.

'Thank you, Mrs Collins,' said Darcy and noticed a slight moue of distaste flicker across his hostess's expression.

'Mr Darcy, please forgive me for correcting you but these days I prefer to be known as Mrs Brooks as neither of my previous surnames engender pleasant memories,' she said gently.

She was rewarded by a nod as he said, 'I quite understand, Mrs Brooks. There is nothing to forgive.'

'Pardon me for not having kept up with events in Kent. How are Lady Catherine and Miss de Bourgh?'

'I am afraid that Lady Catherine did not fully recover from her illness, and she was left in a much-weakened state. My cousin, on the other hand I am pleased to say has blossomed in the past two years. Having been confined to her rooms at the time, she did not become ill. Now it is she who administers Rosings while my aunt is the invalid.'

'I am pleased for Miss de Bourgh. I remember her fondly. Please pass on my regards to her when you next see her.'

'It will be my pleasure although I expect it will be many months before I can do so in person. But what of yourself? How is your family?'

'My sisters are all very well. I would introduce you, but they are all out on various errands or simply visiting friends as we had not expected visitors today. The only reason you find me at home is because I had to finalise the accounts from the harvest.'

'I had not meant to call at an inconvenient time...'

'Be easy, Mr Darcy. I had just finished and was considering calling on Mr Bingley to welcome him and his party to the area.' Elizabeth noticed a somewhat shocked expression on her visitor's face at her words and with raised brows gave him an impish smile. 'I was going to do so not as a single woman but as the master of Longbourn.'

'The master of Longbourn?' echoed Darcy in confusion.

'Indeed. As you may have gathered, when I returned here it was because my father had died, and my husband inherited the estate. Yet within a few days my husband also became deceased, and as you know, my son passed away as well less than a week later. Those circumstances left me in possession of the estate. Being the owner of Longbourn makes me its master despite my sex. Although I suppose one could argue that I am both the master and the mistress of the estate.'

Darcy's expression cleared as he considered her words. 'I beg your pardon. I had not meant to imply any impropriety. I simply had not considered your unusual position.'

As he thought upon the situation further, he was hard pressed not to smirk as he considered the reaction of Miss Bingley if Mrs Brooks did come to call. It would be delightful to see the lady's misconceptions challenged and soundly refuted.

'I suppose it is very similar to your cousin, Miss de Bourgh, except of course that I am a widow,' Elizabeth replied with a slight shrug. 'When I considered calling on Mr Bingley, I had thought to offer him my insights on becoming the master of an estate without previous experience since I understand that his family was in trade.'

'You are quite correct, Mrs Brooks and while I am here to help my friend learn how to administer an estate, I have no experience in coming into such a situation without prior education. After all, Pemberley has been in my family for many generations and my father taught me my duties from an early age.'

'While you were educated in estate administration from childhood, it must still have been difficult to take on the responsibilities for such a large estate as Pemberley at such a young age as you did.'

They continued discussing their respective estates and their ideas and approaches to the administration of their responsibilities for another hour. Neither realised how much time was passing until Darcy took the last sip of coffee in his cup and noticed it was cold.

He glanced at the clock above the mantle and exclaimed, 'Forgive me, I had not meant to take up so much of your time.'

Elizabeth followed his gaze and replied with a rueful smile, 'I am equally at fault. I confess it is rare that I can discuss my ideas and concerns with a gentleman and feel like I am being treated as an intelligent and competent adult. I thank you for a most pleasurable conversation.'

~A~

Darcy soon made his farewells and left Longbourn feeling rather bemused.

He had expected to make a brief courtesy call on Mrs Collins when he realised that Bingley's estate was next door to the home of the lady, now a widow, whom he had briefly met when she was the wife of his aunt's parson.

His initial surprise at being received in a well-stocked library rather than a delicate lady's parlour was nothing to the amazement he experienced during their conversation.

Gone was the frightened child he remembered from Rosings. Instead, he had spent a most enjoyable hour conversing with an experienced and confident master of her estate.

Mrs Brooks had said that she appreciated being treated like an intelligent adult, yet it was nothing to the pleasure Darcy had experienced from being treated as a person rather than prey. Not once did the lady flirt, simper or agree with him when it was obvious that she did not. Yes, they had discussed his estate, but it was in relation to farming methods or issues he had overcome, never once was it about the monetary value of his home or the number of balls he had given.

Were it not for fear of contravening propriety, he would quite cheerfully have spent the rest of the day in company with this delightful lady, rather than returning to Netherfield and dealing with his hostess.

Miss Bingley was his friend's younger sister who had her cap set on Darcy. While she was beautiful, elegant, intelligent and had been educated in one of the best lady's seminaries, her character was such that Darcy would never consider tying himself to such a vicious and mercenary virago.

Darcy sighed and caught himself thinking, it was a pity that Mrs Brooks was not better connected.

~A~

As it was getting late, Elizabeth decided to wait until after the harvest assembly, which was scheduled for the next day, to call on Mr Bingley.

Instead, she reviewed her conversation with Mr Darcy. As she had said to him, it had been an unalloyed pleasure to converse with a gentleman who treated her as an equal in competence. That he was exceedingly handsome had only added to her enjoyment.

She planned to mention the visit to her sisters, but when they returned home and excitedly reported on their own outings, it slipped her mind.

~A~

Chapter 11

At Longbourn three ladies were getting ready to go to the harvest assembly. Even though her older sisters and Mrs Taylor would have allowed seventeen-year-old Kitty to come out, she opted to wait a little longer, for which Lydia was grateful.

Mrs Hill, whose cousin was Mrs Nicholls, the housekeeper at Netherfield Park, advised the sisters to wear their second-best dresses which they usually only wore when going to the theatre or the opera on their infrequent visits to London. Their best ballgowns, which had not yet had any outings, had been a present from Mrs Gardiner on her last visit.

Since the servants' grapevine had informed Mrs Hill that Miss Bingley and Mrs Hurst were rather high in the instep, she wanted her ladies to be elegant and fashionable while still adhering to proper etiquette for a country assembly.

As a result, instead of muslin, Jane, Elizabeth and Mary wore their silk gowns in shades of pale blue, sage green and soft primrose respectively. The gowns were subtly embellished with embroidery and ribbons in slightly darker shades. All the sisters had refused to add lace, as excessive use of it had been Mrs Bennet's passion.

With their hair pinned up becomingly to ensure their necks would remain cool during the dancing and leaving only a few tendrils to soften their looks they all looked rather exquisite, at least in Mrs Hill's supposedly unbiased opinion.

~A~

The ladies of Longbourn arrived at the assembly and were greeted enthusiastically by their friends.

'My, are we fancy tonight,' teased Charlotte Lucas, noticing her friends' finery.

Elizabeth sighed although she smiled as she replied, 'Mrs Hill simply refused to let us attend in our usual gowns. I believe she wants us to make a good impression on our new neighbours.'

'Or she does not want to give the cats an excuse to bare their claws,' Charlotte posited.

'I gather you have heard some rumours as well?' Mary asked.

'What can I say… this is a small community and servants will talk. And while I cannot afford to be turned out in such style,' she indicated the sisters' gowns, 'I am pleased that at least some of us can display proper elegance… without going over the top.'

Their conversation was interrupted by the approach of several of the younger gentlemen requesting various sets from the ladies.

Ever since she had come out of mourning, Elizabeth had been excessively popular with the younger sons of their neighbours since she had an estate of her own. Even after she made it known that she had not the slightest interest in marrying again, the young men kept trying to convince her of their suitability and their undying devotion.

At least the gentlemen had enough sense to realise that thanks to Charlotte, her attitude was well known, and since Elizabeth was greatly liked by her neighbours, any attempt to compromise her into marriage would end badly for themselves.

~A~

The first set finished, and the sisters and Charlotte gathered by the refreshment table at the end of the room to secure glasses of lemonade, when there was a stir by the entrance.

The doors opened and the party from Netherfield, which consisted of two ladies and three gentlemen made their entrance.

The two ladies were fine women, with an air of decided fashion. One gentleman was good-looking with a pleasant countenance, and easy, unaffected manners. The second merely looked the gentleman, but the third, whom Elizabeth immediately recognised as Mr Darcy, drew the attention of the room by his fine, tall person, handsome features, and noble mien. The tableau was only marred by the decided way in which the younger of the ladies clung to the arm of Mr Darcy.

Sir William Lucas, in his role as master of ceremonies, bustled up to the group to welcome them and to affect introductions to the leading families of the community.

They had not got far before Darcy said, 'Sir William, please pardon me, but I have seen an acquaintance whom I wish to greet,' and led the way towards Elizabeth.

Darcy bowed to the lady. 'Good evening, Mrs Brooks. It is good to see you again. I hope that you are well?'

'Good evening to you, Mr Darcy. I am in excellent health, thank you for asking. I hope you are the same?'

When Darcy smiled and answered, 'Indeed. Would you allow me to introduce my companions to you?' Miss Bingley who had clung to his arm all the way across the room shot him an angry look.

How dare her Mr Darcy request permission of some country nobody to introduce herself to this lowborn nonentity. It was bad enough that Caroline had to endure introductions to these mushrooms, but they should be honoured to be granted an introduction to herself.

Ignoring the look of displeasure on Miss Bingley's countenance, Elizabeth smiled politely. 'I would be pleased to meet your companions, Mr Darcy.'

Darcy introduced Bingley, Bingley's sister Mrs Hurst and her husband Mr Hurst, and finally Miss Bingley, mentioning that his acquaintance with Mrs Brooks stemmed from an introduction by his aunt, Lady Catherine de Bourgh. All but the last greeted Elizabeth politely, while Miss Bingley was barely civil in her hauteur.

Elizabeth graciously acknowledged them, and in return she introduced her sisters and Charlotte Lucas.

It was immediately obvious that Bingley was completely smitten by Jane's beauty, and he requested her next set, which she granted happily.

Darcy was not in the least surprised at the request and suspected that his friend had just found his latest angel. Instead of concerning himself with his friend, he asked, 'Do you dance, Mrs Brooks?'

'I do indeed.'

'In that case would you honour me with your next available set?'

'My fifth set is still unclaimed... which will be the fourth set since your arrival,' she replied sweetly. Although she sounded as if she was simply being helpful, she was reprimanding whoever had caused the party to arrive late.

Darcy smiled and bowed as he replied, 'Thank you for clarifying. I would not wish to risk missing my dances with you.' He had noticed the reprimand and was amused by the subtlety. Only Mr Hurst caught on as well and managed to stifle a laugh. The Bingley siblings seemed to be oblivious, either too focused on their company, or in the case of Miss Bingley fuming that her Mr Darcy had asked another lady to dance before he had requested any dances from her.

~A~

Darcy did his duty to his hostess and her sister by dancing once with each of them.

Instead of dancing the fourth set, he was stalking around the edges of the room, avoiding potential friend and known foe alike, displaying his customary fearsome scowl without even being aware of its presence. A number of people noticed that he always appeared to be on the opposite side of the room from the ladies in his party.

He was relieved when he could approach Mrs Brooks for their promised set. Darcy bowed to the lady with a smile. 'I believe this is our dance,' he said and offered his arm.

'Indeed, it is, sir,' Elizabeth answered with a smile as she accepted his arm and let him lead her to the dance floor.

When the music started, they danced in amicable silence for a few minutes during which Elizabeth noticed the relaxed and pleasant expression on her partner's face.

When they had a chance to speak, Elizabeth teased, 'Pardon me for asking, but do you have a twin brother? One who stalks around the edges of ballrooms with a fearsome expression?'

Darcy gave her a chagrined smile as he said, 'I am afraid I must own to the fearsome expression. I find it rare to have amiable company at a ball and experience has shown me that that expression will keep all but the most persistent hunters at arm's length.'

'Since your scowl is ineffective on the most odious of company, perhaps you should adopt a different tactic? After all, you have created a self-fulfilling prophecy.'

The dance separated them briefly. When they came together again Darcy asked, 'Please explain.'

'Your scowl is intended to keep away unpleasant company. But since those kinds of people will not be deterred, whatever you do, you only succeed in keeping away people whose company you might enjoy.'

'And since I never meet anyone pleasant at a ball, I keep scowling...' Darcy answered her grin with one of his own. 'Do you have a suggestion how I might overcome this impasse?'

'Am I correct in assuming you adopt your attitude since society abounds with too many matchmaking matrons and their enthusiastic offspring?'

'That is a part of my reason.' Elizabeth raised her brows encouraging him to continue his explanation, which he did once the dance brought them together again. 'I also find it difficult conversing with people whom I do not know well.'

A thought occurred to Elizabeth which caused her to laugh. As Darcy started to look affronted to have the lady laugh at him after he confessed a weakness, Elizabeth hurried to say, 'I beg your pardon, Mr Darcy. When you gave your explanation, I had a thought about which incongruous topics we might converse during our dance. Perhaps which kind of manure would be best for various crops.'

That quip startled Darcy into laughter, restoring his good humour. 'Perhaps that is a topic which we might discuss at another time. Your neighbours might consider us rather eccentric if they overheard that particular discussion.'

'As you wish. In that case let us return to our previous topic. How to enjoy a ball without raising expectations.'

'I am most anxious to learn.'

'Go to a ball and dance only with wallflowers and only ever dance once with any lady. The ladies will be grateful and since you only dance once, that will not raise their expectations. And perhaps the fact that you danced with them will encourage other gentlemen to request dances. And you never know, those dances might lead to a happy outcome for both.'

Darcy smiled as a thought occurred to him. 'But if that happens, there will be fewer wallflowers for me from which to choose.'

'At least you have the advantage over ladies as you have a choice about whether to request a dance, while ladies have to wait to be asked and then have very few excuses to refuse.'

'Have you found a way to refuse an unwanted request?'

'I have very few reasons to do so. In our community it is well known that I attend assemblies because I enjoy dancing but have not the slightest interest in finding a husband. Therefore, I will never dance a second set with any gentleman.'

Darcy was astonished to hear that Mrs Brooks had no wish to remarry, but the casual way she spoke about it, made him feel that she truly meant it.

Before he could comment on that fact, she smiled and added, 'Also, since there are more ladies than gentlemen in our community, I can always claim, truthfully mind you, that I wish to sit out a set to give other ladies an opportunity to dance.'

'Do you use that excuse often?'

'Twice at every assembly.'

'I am grateful that you had a dance available since you appear to be an exceedingly popular lady.'

'I believe Longbourn is the reason for my popularity,' Elizabeth said, her smile only partly hiding her cynicism. 'I believe that you may be familiar with that concept.'

'Indeed. Hence my reluctance to dance.'

They finished their dance in thoughtful silence on the part of Darcy and contented silence for Elizabeth. Since the gentleman had been considerate and helpful in every one of their few interactions, she was pleased that she might have been of small assistance to him in overcoming his discomfort at balls.

~A~

The music stopped and Darcy offered his arm to Elizabeth. 'Where would you like to go?' he asked.

'I would dearly love to get a lemonade and then I would like to see if one of my sisters or friends is sitting out the next set so that I may have their company.'

'Shall we find you sisters first and I would be happy to fetch a lemonade for you. Perhaps you would even allow me to sit with you and we could continue our conversation?'

'Mr Darcy, if you sit out a set with me after dancing another, you might give rise to the expectations of my neighbours.'

'Surely, no one can think it amiss if the master of Longbourn converses with the master of Pemberley,' claimed Darcy with an innocent expression which caused Elizabeth to chuckle.

'You certainly have a way with words, Mr Darcy. Especially for a man who claims to find it difficult to converse with relative strangers.'

'Ah, but you are a stranger no longer. Our acquaintance is of more than three years duration.'

'Very well, sir. If we find one of my sisters or friends, you will be welcome to join our party.'

They did indeed find Charlotte Lucas to be unoccupied for the next set, whereupon Darcy fetched refreshments for them all and they spent the next half hour in pleasant conversation.

Darcy learnt a great deal about the neighbourhood and about his temporary neighbours. In a brief lull in their conversation, he tried to remember when he had last been able to have a pleasant and intelligent conversation with two ladies who were not members of his family. The unsurprising answer was... never.

The only surprising thing that occurred was, that not once in the whole time he spent with the ladies did Darcy's fearsome scowl make an appearance... until Miss Bingley and Mrs Hurst joined them.

~A~

Chapter 12

Fortunately for Darcy, the seventh set was about to begin and having already learnt that Miss Lucas was not engaged for that set, he made the request, and she was happy to grant him those dances.

A moment later, John Lucas came to claim Elizabeth.

Before Miss Bingley and her sister knew what was happening, they were left standing on their own... again.

As they lined up for their dance John Lucas looked suspiciously at Elizabeth, whose eyes were dancing with mirth. 'What is so amusing? Do I have a spot on my face or something similar?' he asked.

Elizabeth swallowed her laughter and straightened her expression as she answered. 'I should not be so unkind to laugh at a lady whom I only just met, but I must confess that I have found Miss Bingley's attitude somewhat... ah...'

'Supercilious? Haughty? Disdainful? Arrogant? Exasperating? Vexing?' her partner supplied, causing Elizabeth to laugh.

'I must commend you on your vocabulary. I gather that I am not the only one who has observed the lady's superior attitude.'

'Quite. The lady has made it perfectly obvious to all that she considers us unsophisticated bumpkins who should feel honoured by her presence.'

Elizabeth smiled and nodded. 'I am afraid that I found amusement in her sour expression when Mr Darcy asked Charlotte to dance the moment she joined us, and I suspect he mostly did so to escape that lady's company.'

'At least some good has come of it. Charlotte looks like she is enjoying her dance,' said John and nodded towards his sister who was in animated conversation with Mr Darcy.

Elizabeth followed his gaze and surprised herself by feeling an inexplicable stab of something she could not name.

~A~

Unsurprising, Charlotte Lucas had also noticed the expressions of Mr Darcy and Miss Bingley.

As they commenced their dance, Darcy noticed the barely suppressed laughter on his partner's countenance. Having just spent a most pleasant half hour in the lady's company he felt comfortable enough to ask, 'Miss Lucas, would you care to share the cause of your amusement? I too would appreciate an opportunity to enjoy some levity.'

Charlotte could not help but blushing at being found out. 'I beg your pardon, Mr Darcy but I could not help but notice your reaction to a certain lady, which seems peculiar considering the hints scattered by this lady. Although her reaction is quite comprehensible in the circumstances, I suspect that her hints are based on wishful thinking rather than reality,' she answered as obliquely as she could.

Darcy sighed theatrically. 'It seems this community is blessed with a multitude of intelligent and observant ladies,' he replied without confirming or denying her assumptions.

'Do not be troubled, sir, our neighbours abhor foxhunting and are sympathetic to the vexations of foxes. I confess, they might put out lures to *snare* a tasty prey, but they do not actively hunt. Foxes are quite safe in these parts. We have even been known to give sanctuary to prey.'

'Indeed? Perhaps you would be so good as to point out such safe havens?'

'I believe you will find every estate other than Netherfield to be welcoming if approached in a friendly manner.'

'I thank you, Miss Lucas. I shall keep your advice in mind.'

~A~

The lady under discussion could hardly contain her own vexation.

'I wonder what those ghastly women did to force Mr Darcy to converse with them, and to request a dance from that plain one,' snarled Miss Bingley while maintaining her supercilious smile which she considered the height of fashion when amongst such peasants as the ones at this assembly.

While Miss Bingley was intelligent, after all, she prided herself on having mastered (rather than learnt the basics as her teachers claimed) three modern languages at that expensive and exclusive seminary which she had attended, she did have one significant blind spot. To her any member of the gentry who owned a farm was a farmer and a farmer was, by her definition, a peasant. Peasants were obviously beneath someone as wealthy and educated as she was.

It never occurred to her to examine the incongruity that she did not apply those standards to Mr Darcy. She seemed unable to grasp that by her definition he would be a farmer as well. But not only was he related to the nobility since his uncle was the Earl of Matlock, but he also owned a large estate, and such estates were the location of stately homes and could therefore not possibly be farms.

While she dreamed of being mistress of places such as Chatsworth House, or even better, Blenheim Palace, she was just realistic enough to know that those positions were out of her reach. Instead, she focused on Pemberley as its master was a friend of her brother.

Since Miss Bingley only knew that Pemberley was considered one of the largest and most beautiful estates in the country, she was resolved to become Mrs Darcy, the mistress of Pemberley. Although once they were married, Miss Bingley would insist that she and Mr Darcy would predominantly live in his house in town. In the summer when the air in London was noxious, she would be willing to remove to Pemberley as long as they could host a houseparty.

Her detractors, of which there were many, foremost among them Mr Darcy and his cousin Colonel Richard Fitzwilliam, claimed that she wanted to be Mrs Pemberley since she did not care a pin about Darcy.

As she considered herself practically engaged to the gentleman, she was now fuming that he had walked away from her with barely an acknowledgment.

Mrs Hurst did not want her sister to throw one of her famous tantrums in this venue, she therefore said placatingly, 'Mr Darcy is being a perfect gentleman. Miss Lucas is the daughter of our host, Sir William

Lucas. He is obliged to dance with the female relations of his host.' Mrs Hurst forbore to add, *just as he danced with you for the same reason*.

The lady did not have any illusions as to Mr Darcy's attitude towards her sister. She knew that the gentleman barely tolerated Caroline since she was the sister of his friend. But as the youngest of the Bingley siblings, Caroline had always been indulged and had never been told *no*. As a consequence, she had become accustomed to always get what she wanted.

Louisa Hurst hoped that her brother would soon grow up enough to assume his role as the head of the family and pull Caroline into line. Until then, her sister would rule the roost and cause vexation to all with whom she came into contact.

~A~

Meanwhile Miss Bingley found another cause for vexation as she noticed her brother dancing for the second time with Miss Bennet.

She remained in place, expecting Mr Darcy to return his dance partner to their previous location. She was frustrated again when she saw the gentleman escort that plain woman to a spot at the other side of the room where he met up with the other woman to whom Mr Darcy had introduced her earlier. Caroline wracked her brain. What was the name of that woman again? Oh yes, it was Mrs Brooks.

She had just decided to make her way to the group when the musicians struck up the penultimate tune for the evening and Darcy led Miss Bennet to the floor while Bingley partnered Mrs Brooks.

Foiled yet again, Miss Bingley remained in place and fumed.

~A~

Bingley was pleased for several reasons that he had a chance to dance with Mrs Brooks.

Even though she was not his type, she was a very pretty young lady and an excellent dancer. He also wanted a chance to speak to her since Darcy had briefly mentioned she might be helpful to him in his current position. He wondered to which position his friend referred.

'What did Darcy mean when he said that you have information which would be useful to me?' he asked once they commenced their dance.

'He meant that you have no background in managing an estate. Two and a half years ago I was in the same position when I inherited Longbourn, which is my family's estate.'

'Is it not unusual for a lady to inherit a property?'

'It is, but there were exceptional circumstances with which I will not trouble you during a ball. Suffice it to say, that I am the master of Longbourn, and I had to learn how to deal with the myriad issues that come with the position.'

'Surely Darcy can teach me all I need to know,' exclaimed Bingley.

'Mr Darcy learnt his duties from an early age and potentially takes some knowledge for granted... but which you do not have. Since I also was not trained to take the reins of an estate, I made some mistakes in the early days. I thought that you might benefit from my hard-won expertise so that you avoid those mistakes.' Elizabeth smiled impishly at the bemused expression of her dance partner.

Bingley was grateful that the dance separated them long enough that he could accustom himself to the information Elizabeth had imparted.

'Forgive me for being pedantic, but since you are a lady, does that not make you the mistress of Longbourn, rather than the master?'

'When you look at it from the point of view of semantics, you are correct. BUT the roles for the master and the mistress of the estate are quite clearly delineated. As I do not have the time for both, my oldest sister is currently performing all the duties of the mistress of the estate, just like your sister will be doing for you, as I was given to understand. Since I own the estate and perform all the duties incumbent on the master... by that definition I am the master of Longbourn.'

'I see...' mumbled Bingley and looked up to see his friend watching him with a slight smirk twitching his lips.

That amusement pulled Bingley out of his fugue, and he smiled at Elizabeth. 'Since Darcy thinks that your knowledge would be helpful to me, I shall be grateful to learn from you.'

Another thought occurred to him. 'Perhaps *your* sister would be willing to guide *my* sister in her new duties. After all, Caroline is in the same position as I am when it comes to estate matters. We are complete novices.'

'I will speak to my sisters and see what can be arranged,' Elizabeth promised and surmised that based on his brilliant smile, Bingley had hopes of spending more time with Jane, while she was teaching Caroline.

'Thank you, Mrs Brooks. Would it be convenient for you and your sister to call on my sister?'

'I believe we have free time the day after tomorrow.'

'Excellent. I shall ask Caroline to sent you an invitation.'

~A~

On their return to Netherfield Miss Bingley was in a fractious mood. Seeing how irate his sister was, Bingley decided not to mention the arrangement he had agreed with Mrs Brooks.

Instead, he resigned himself to listen to Caroline's displeasure with the evening.

Eventually he tired of her vitriolic description of everything and everyone. 'If you had not been so conceited, you could have danced or conversed with our neighbours and enjoyed yourself.'

'You think that I would dance with one of those peasants? I was afraid that those clumsy louts would step on my dress and tear it,' huffed Caroline. 'I just spent a month's allowance on this dress, and I will not have one of those... ah... people ruin it.'

'If you are afraid for your dress, you should have worn something less elaborate, like the other ladies,' muttered Bingley.

His sister ignored the comment and ranted on, 'And as for conversation, what would any of those bumpkins know about elegant discourse.'

'I suspect that they know a lot more than you do,' said a sleepy-eyed Hurst laconically and delighted in watching from half lidded eyes as his sister-in-law turned an interesting shade of puce, which clashed horribly with her gown.

Caroline shot a furious look at Hurst before turning to their guest. 'Surely you agree with me Mr Darcy, since you were forced to endure half an hour complete of what passes for conversation in these parts.'

Darcy sighed. He hated being rude, but he did not have a choice, and perhaps Miss Bingley would at last get the message that he was not interested in her. 'I hate to disagree with you, Miss Bingley, but I had a most enjoyable conversation with Mrs Brooks and Miss Lucas.'

'What topics could these mushrooms have in common with a refined gentleman like yourself?'

'The ladies were kind enough to provide me with information about the neighbourhood in general and Netherfield Park in particular.'

'Why would you want to concern yourself with anything in this benighted neighbourhood?' Caroline asked dismissively.

'Because your brother is leasing Netherfield Park and wishes to learn the administration of said estate. To that end he needs to know about conditions hereabouts.'

'Surely tomorrow would have been soon enough to delve into such matters, rather than at a ball,' Bingley exclaimed in astonishment.

'Perhaps, but it afforded me the opportunity for a pleasant and intelligent conversation, which is a rarity for me at a ball at any time and has never before occurred when speaking to a lady, let alone two.'

That casual comment combined with an equally as casual seeming look at Miss Bingley was enough to shock her almost speechless. 'Never?' she breathed.

'Never.' Darcy confirmed, causing Miss Bingley to press her lips together until they formed a barely visible line as she glared at the sniggering Mr Hurst. If looks could kill, he would have expired on the spot.

~A~

Chapter 13

As the sisters were tired, they did not speak much on their return to Longbourn but sat in contented silence.

In contrast, breakfast the next morning was much more boisterous as Kitty and Lydia were eager to hear all about their evening.

'Jane was quite the belle of the ball,' Elizabeth teased. 'She was the only lady whom Mr Bingley asked for a second set.'

Jane's cheeks turned pink but refused to be outdone. 'Perhaps so, but I was not the lady whom his friend asked for a dance first, even before requesting dances from his hostess and her sister. Is that not so, Lizzy.'

'You are quite correct, Jane, but you forgot to mention that he danced the last set with you,' Elizabeth responded with a grin, refusing to be embarrassed.

'Who is this friend that you act like he is something special,' queried Lydia.

'He is Mr Darcy of Pemberley in Derbyshire, and he is reputed to be exceedingly wealthy,' Mary informed her younger sisters. 'He is also one of the most handsome gentlemen I have ever beheld, and he appeared to be interested in Lizzy.'

'I had not realised that we had such an eligible gentleman in our midst,' commented Mrs Taylor who also broke her fast with her charges. Being prompted for more information by Kitty and Lydia, she added, 'His mother was Lady Anne Fitzwilliam, the sister to the current Earl of Matlock. Mr Darcy inherited his estate five or six years ago. Ever since then, because of his wealth and connections he has been much sought after by the ladies of the ton.'

'Have you met him?' Kitty asked.

'No, I have not. I believe he was but eighteen years of age when I married and since then we have not moved in the same circles.'

As Mrs Taylor could or would not provide any more information, Lydia turned to Elizabeth and gushed, 'He must have been quite smitten with you to ask you to dance as soon as you were introduced.'

'I do not believe he was. I simply happened to be the only lady in this area with whom he was already acquainted.' Elizabeth smiled at the surprised looks from her youngest sisters. 'Do you not remember that I mentioned him before? He is a nephew of Lady Catherine de Bourgh, whom I met when I first arrived in Hunsford, and he is the gentleman who so kindly arranged for Henry's remains to be returned to us.'

She hesitated a moment considering whether to inform her sisters of the courtesy shown her by the gentleman before adding, 'He also called on me the day before yesterday to tender his condolences in person, when he discovered that we are neighbours.'

'Why did you not mention he called on you?' asked Jane.

'It slipped my mind in the excitement of preparing for the assembly, and I did not think it of any great moment,' replied Elizabeth.

Jane rolled her eyes. 'Only you, Lizzy, would forget to mention a visit by a handsome gentleman.' Jane shook her head, thinking that her sister's aversion to men must run deep if even such a handsome man could not stir her interest. 'I confess I did wonder how he knew to address you as Mrs Brooks and if you have been keeping secrets,' she teased to see how her sister would respond.

But Elizabeth refused to be drawn on the subject. 'Well, now you know, but you have diverted our attention from you and Mr Bingley long enough. Did you enjoy getting to know the gentleman?'

Jane capitulated and told her sisters, '*He is just what a young man ought to be, sensible, good-humoured, lively; and he has such happy manners.*'

'*He is also handsome,*' teased Elizabeth, '*which a young man ought to be if he possibly can. His character is thereby complete.*'

'I was very much flattered by his attention.'

'His attention is even more pronounced than you might think. He asked if you would be willing to teach his sister the duties of the mistress of an estate.'

'Is that not something she would have learnt at that exclusive seminary for ladies of which she is so proud?' asked Mary.

'As far as I can tell, those seminaries focus on accomplishments to catch a husband. They do not appear to teach what to do with him once you have caught him,' Elizabeth quipped cheekily.

'Lizzy, be careful in what you say. Mrs Taylor might scold you for setting a bad example for us,' teased Kitty with a laugh.

'I thank you for the reminder, Catherine. It is good to know that you have become such a proper young lady.' Elizabeth said to her sister who preened just a little as Elizabeth only called her Catherine when she acted with propriety.

Still smiling, Elizabeth turned back to Jane. 'You have not yet said if you would be willing to instruct Miss Bingley.'

'I am willing to teach, but is the lady willing to learn?'

'I suppose we will find out soon enough. Mr Bingley indicated that he would suggest to his sisters to invite us to tea tomorrow.'

Having dealt with that subject, the sisters discussed their plans for the day.

~A~

Foremost amongst the tasks for the day was one which Elizabeth did not relish. She had to deal with Mr Chambers.

Since the man had refused to consider the improvements which she had instigated with the other tenant farms, his harvest had yielded considerably less than the others, making it impossible for him to pay the rent.

As much as she hated having to do so, Elizabeth knew that she could not continue allowing him to remain as her tenant. Owning an estate was a business, not a charity. At least all the Chambers' children were grown up and able to make their own way in the world.

Therefore, she visited Mr Phillips to arrange terminating the lease unless he could pay the rent.

~A~

The situation at Netherfield was less amicable when the family rose several hours later.

Darcy had enjoyed the quiet morning and gone for a ride before he had to deal with his hosts. He returned just in time to hear raised voices in the dining room.

Miss Bingley addressed her sister. 'I already know all I need to know. Charles is simply trying to spend more time with his latest angel,' she scoffed.

'Caroline, you may not have any interest in learning the duties associated with the role of the mistress of an estate, but I am,' Mrs Hurst contradicted.

Darcy stopped in the hallway, thinking his friend had hit on a clever ruse to spend more time with Miss Bennet. He was unsurprised that Miss Bingley was not in favour of such an occupation but was pleased to hear that her sister was prepared to take advantage of an opportunity to learn.

'I have already learnt everything I need to know to be Mrs Darcy.'

The gentleman under discussion repressed a derisive laugh which was audibly echoed by Mr Hurst. 'I hate to disappoint you, but you have not learnt anything useful at that overpriced seminary. How many painted tables or covered screens do you think a house needs? And no man cares how well you net a purse.'

'I also learnt to be an excellent hostess, to preside over the exquisite dinner parties and balls which Mr Darcy and I will host during the season.'

'You know perfectly well that Darcy does not like those kinds of entertainments,' Charles Bingley's voice cut in. 'Apart from that, you need to accept that he will never offer for you.'

'Charles, what would you know about this. Mark my words, before we return to London, Mr Darcy will recognise that I am perfect for him. I have all the accomplishments required by a lady of the first circles.'

'But he despises the ladies of the first circles. You heard him last night. He said he had never before had an intelligent conversation with a lady. Considering that you have prattled at him for years, that should tell you that he is immune to your charms.'

'He was simply in a bad mood. You know what he is like at parties. He was always thus. You will see that he will be most congenial when he is just amongst friends.'

That comment caused Darcy to consider his options. Because Bingley was his friend, he had always been civil to his sisters. It seemed that despite acting with only cool politeness Miss Bingley had determined that he was interested in her. It occurred to him that since he had never shown an interest in any lady, their long association had given her the mistaken impression that she had a chance.

His distraction caused him to miss some of the conversation until he heard Caroline say, '… I play the pianoforte exceedingly well.'

'No, Caroline, that talent is only useful so you can entertain your husband on long winter-nights when you are snowed in at your country estate,' Bingley refuted his sister yet again.

Before the siblings had a chance to continue their bickering, Louisa Hurst cut in. 'No matter what we learnt at that seminary, I for one shall be glad to discuss the duties of an estate mistress with someone who has practical experience in such matters. Charles, did Mrs Brooks indicate which day would be convenient for the ladies?'

'The lady said that they will be free tomorrow.'

'Excellent. I shall send them an invitation to tea.'

'No, Louisa, you shall not do so. As the mistress of the house, it is my decision who comes to visit, and I have no intention of lowering myself to deal with peasants,' interjected Caroline coldly. She particularly did not want her brother to spend more time with his latest angel and she most definitely did not wish for Mr Darcy to continue his acquaintance with the lady whom he found so intelligent and charming.

Darcy, upon hearing those words took exception to Caroline's attitude and was about to storm into the dining room but was arrested in his movement when he heard his friend exclaim, 'That is quite enough, Caroline.'

Rising from the Ashes

The words were accompanied by a crashing sound as Bingley had stood up and hit the table with his fists. He was leaning threateningly towards Caroline. 'How often do I have to tell you that those people whom you choose to denigrate are landowners who have owned their estates for generations and are therefore gentry. Unlike us, who are the children of a tradesman. On the social scale those people are well above us in rank.'

'You cannot be serious, Charles. They are farmers who get their hands dirty,' Caroline attempted to refute her brother's word by shouting louder than he did.

'Any good estate owner will on occasions get his hands dirty when it is necessary to get the harvest in and a storm is looming,' Hurst angrily interjected.

'I have had enough of your attitude, Caroline,' roared Bingley at the same time. After a moment of shocked silence, he moderated his voice. 'This is my house and I decide who will be invited. Not only that, but I also decide who acts as my hostess.'

Bingley turned towards his older sister and asked politely, 'Louisa, would you be so good as to take on the duties of mistress of this house and estate?'

Louisa Hurst smiled with pleasure mixed with relief. It appeared that her wish from last night was being granted and her little brother was growing up. It seemed that overnight the little puppy had matured and developed an impressive set of teeth.

'I would be honoured to take on the position as mistress,' Louisa replied graciously and was surprised when her husband took her hand and gave it a gentle squeeze.

Caroline ignored her sister and shouted, 'You cannot do this to me! You are going to make a laughingstock of me by putting Louisa into my position.'

'Yes, I can do this! Because if I do not, you will make a laughingstock of us all and no one in the county will respect us.'

'But how can I prove to Mr Darcy that I will be perfect as the mistress of Pemberley if you replace me as hostess of Netherfield,' Caroline voiced her real concern.

'How often do I have to tell you that Darcy has no interest in you. No matter what you do, he will never offer for you,' Bingley refuted Caroline's concerns yet again.

'If Mr Darcy is not going to offer for me, we are wasting our time in this savage backwater. I insist that you take us back to London.'

'I have no intention of leaving but will be only too happy to send you to town with your maid.'

'You are insufferable,' shouted Caroline and rising from her seat, stormed out of the room to head upstairs.

She was so focused on her anger and disappointment that she did not see Darcy, who had stepped away from the door and was headed towards the library to wait out the end of the argument.

~A~

When she gained the safety of her chambers, Caroline slammed the door and threw herself into the chair by her vanity.

She stared wretchedly at her reflection and saw a beautiful young woman of one and twenty with strawberry blond hair and a luscious figure, dressed in the latest fashion.

How could her brother claim that Mr Darcy was not interested in her? Ever since she had met her brother's friend four years ago, she had worked hard to gain his approval.

Caroline had displayed her many accomplishments. As she had mentioned to her brother, she excelled at the pianoforte and singing, she also could dance with exquisite grace.

She engaged Mr Darcy in conversation by speaking about the people he knew and shared her intimate knowledge of all their peccadillos. She was always accommodating and agreed with all his opinions, regardless of her own ideas.

Coming to Netherfield, Caroline had thought it would give her weeks of opportunities to fix Mr Darcy's attention on her, but now Charles was threatening to send her back to London by herself. She could not allow that.

She simply had to stay near Mr Darcy. Surely, with all she had to offer, he would not rebuff her. No, despite her brother's dismissal of her as his hostess, she would remain and prove to Mr Darcy that she was perfect for him... one way or another.

~A~

Chapter 14

Louisa Hurst had made good on her promise and invited the ladies of Longbourn, who arrived punctually in Elizabeth's gig.

The whole party had gathered in the drawing room and Caroline, who observed the arrival of their guest from the window, sneered, 'Good heavens, they are travelling in a gig. Do they not even have a carriage?'

'I am certain they do own a carriage, but their horses are probably needed in the fields,' commented Hurst, who was lounging by the fire with a glass of wine.

'What would horses be doing in a field?' asked Caroline with a frown.

'Pulling ploughs, or perhaps carts if they are still bringing in the harvest, or they might be busy delivering supplies. Any number of things,' Darcy pointed out in a reasonable tone of voice, although like Hurst he was suppressing a desire to roll his eyes at the ignorance of country matters displayed by the lady.

Bingley listened avidly, glad that Caroline was asking these questions, saving him from displaying his own lack of knowledge.

'Why do they not have horses devoted to that purpose?'

'On most smaller estates, horses are used for multiple purposes and in general the needs of the farm have priority over carriage duty to go visiting. Having a gig as well as a carriage makes good sense and shows they have the money to spare for the extra horse.'

'But what if it should rain, they will get drenched in that gig.'

'If it is raining, chances are that the horses will not be needed in the fields and are available to pull the carriage.' This time it was Hurst to explained, although his tone made it clear even to Caroline what he thought of her inexperience, causing her to colour as well as her temper to heighten.

Before she could expose further naïveté, or comment on the pecuniary disadvantages of their neighbours, Elizabeth and Jane were announced.

~A~

Most of the residents of Netherfield greeted the sisters genially, while Caroline could only muster haughty civility.

'Thank you for accepting my invitation,' said Louisa warmly. 'I am grateful for the opportunity to improve my knowledge about estate matters.'

'We are very happy to be in a position to offer our assistance as we know how difficult it can be taking on responsibilities unexpectedly,' Elizabeth responded to Louisa's enthusiasm with a friendly smile.

'Perhaps before we delve into more serious matters, you would care for refreshments?' suggested Louisa, which everyone was pleased to accept.

While Louisa served the tea, Caroline addressed Elizabeth. 'I am given to understand that you are managing the estate?'

'I do indeed,' Elizabeth replied with a smile, wondering where this line of enquiry might lead. She found out very quickly.

'Is that not a very masculine thing to do? Surely your father or husband would be better suited to the task.'

'I am afraid that both are incapable of managing Longbourn –' Elizabeth started to explain, only to be interrupted.

'You show a considerable degree of arrogance and conceited independence to claim to be superior to the men in your family,' Caroline attacked.

In the background Hurst muttered, 'It takes one to know one.'

Elizabeth smiled sweetly. 'I am sorry that you feel that way, but as I was trying to explain, my father and my husband are unable to manage Longbourn... as both are dead.'

Bingley and Louisa cringed and even Caroline realised her faux pas but refused to acknowledge it. 'So, you are acting as mistress of the estate until your son inherits?'

'No, Miss Bingley. There is no son. I inherited the estate and own it outright. Therefore, I am the master of Longbourn, not its mistress.'

'If you are not the mistress of the estate, how can you teach anything to us. We certainly have no wish to usurp the role of gentlemen.'

'Miss Bingley, you may rest easy. I have no intention of teaching you anything. My sister, Miss Bennet is acting as the mistress of Longbourn and has agreed to pass on her knowledge to the acting mistress of Netherfield. I am only here to advise your brother on local conditions.'

Caroline, who had been in the process of taking a sip of tea, spluttered as the beverage went down the wrong way.

To ease the tension caused by her sister, Mrs Hurst asked Jane, 'How long have you been acting as the mistress of your estate?'

'Since Easter, two years ago,' Jane answered and returned the smile. 'I confess I was a little worried at the beginning, but as Elizabeth claimed to have complete confidence in me, I could not let her down. I was also fortunate to have many people to help.'

'I am curious though. What is different about being the mistress of a house in the country rather than in town?' Louisa was honestly curious.

'In town, few people have gardens which produce the food needed by the household, therefore most supplies come from shops, whereas in the country you will rely heavily on what is grown on your estate. This is particularly important to remember as the shops are not as easy to reach. And if the gentlemen indulge in sport, the game they shoot will find their way to your table.'

'I had never considered those aspects of gentlemen's sport,' commented Louisa in chagrin.

'And then of course, the mistress of the estate is expected to visit the tenants to speak with the women, who are generally reluctant to speak to the master. It will be your responsibility to discover issues with tenants and to help mitigate those problems.'

Not wanting to make any assumptions, Louisa asked simply, 'Whose help did you have?'

'The biggest help was and still is, is Mrs Hill, our housekeeper. She has worked for our family for nearly two decades and knows everything and everyone at the estate. Mrs Nicholls is her cousin, and you can be sure she can be of great assistance to you.'

Caroline huffed at Jane, 'You cannot possibly suggest that we should take orders from a servant. Servants take orders from their betters.'

Jane disregarded the stubborn attitude as she addressed Louisa, 'A good housekeeper is worth her weight in gold, and you are fortunate to have one of the best in the county. Whenever there was no mistress resident at Netherfield Mrs Nicholls has been acting in that role.'

'Just like Mrs Reynolds does at Pemberley,' interjected Darcy and was rewarded by a grateful smile from Jane, as Caroline shot the gentleman a horrified look and refused to comment further.

'So, you are saying that we already have an expert resident at Netherfield,' Louisa asked with a pleased smile.

'Indeed, but I thought it might be wise for you to have a second opinion pertaining to the duties of a mistress.'

'Or perhaps you thought that I would be more likely to listen to you than a servant.'

Jane's eyes twinkled as she said, 'I said no such thing.'

~A~

Bingley listened with growing pleasure as Louisa and Miss Bennet discussed the various duties the lady performed at Longbourn.

While he had been annoyed with Caroline's attitude, Miss Bennet and Mrs Brooks had handled his sister with aplomb. He was pulled from his absorption when Elizabeth asked, 'Mr Bingley, would you like to discuss Netherfield and my experiences?'

Bingley reluctantly dragged his eyes away from Jane to pay attention to Elizabeth. 'Indeed, I would,' he said with an amiable smile. 'But I am concerned that our discussion will interfere with our sisters'.'

'Perhaps we could adjourn to your study?'

'That would be ideal, as all the records and maps are there. Would you have any issues with Darcy and Hurst joining us? As a lady...'

'Mr Bingley, I thank you for your concern, but I assure you that as a widow and the master of Longbourn I am not as constrained in my actions and company as my sisters. I trust you gentlemen to act like gentlemen... especially as my neighbours are very protective of my wellbeing.'

The gentlemen and Elizabeth excused themselves from the ladies in the drawing room and relocated to the study, where they all took seats around a table by the window, which was covered in maps. Although, as a nod to propriety, they left the door ajar.

Once they were seated, Elizabeth addressed Bingley. 'I hope you do not think it presumptuous of me to give advice on this subject, but two and a half years ago I had to take on the administration of my estate without any real preparation. Although I had an advantage over you, as I had grown up at Longbourn and for several years had visited the tenants.'

'Pardon me for asking, but did you lose your mother at an early age as well?'

'No. Mrs Bennet is still alive,' Elizabeth said repressively, but after seeing the confused expressions of the gentlemen she softened slightly. 'Being the daughter of a solicitor, she never learnt about the duties of her new position.'

'But did not –' Darcy started to say.

'Please accept that mine was a dysfunctional family and leave it at that,' Elizabeth cut short his query. 'Suffice it to say that when I inherited Longbourn, only my four sisters and I continued living at Longbourn. And before you ask, Jane is two years older than I am. Our other three sisters are younger. The youngest, Catherine and Lydia are being educated by a governess. Our middle sister Mary is helping Jane with her duties.'

'Do you have a steward?'

'I have considered hiring one, but I have not found one whom I would trust. They all seem to think that because I am female, I would be easy to defraud... by them rather than the merchants with whom I need to deal.'

'At least I do not have that problem to deal with,' muttered Bingley.

'No, but the merchants will take one look at you and think you an easy mark because of your youth and inexperience, although perhaps since your family was in trade, you have contacts who will deal fairly with you.'

'You do not have problems with merchants trying to take advantage of you?' Darcy asked.

Elizabeth grinned at him. 'Not anymore. I found they come in three categories. One group is honest and will deal fairly with all. The second group tried to cheat me and were most annoyed when I called on my two uncles, one who is a very successful respectable tradesman, the other an equally intelligent and competent solicitor.'

'What about the third group,' asked Bingley when Elizabeth paused.

'Ah. The third group.' She chuckled. 'They are the ones who were overconfident, thinking that in dealing with a young female they would always get the better of a bargain. I do not know how they feel or what they did when they discovered they were wrong in their assumptions.'

The three men laughed along with Elizabeth and felt their respect for the young woman grow. Hurst commented laconically, 'They act the same way when they think a man is a drunk,' before he grinned and winked at Elizabeth.

'I hope that you will provide me with a list of merchants as well as your evaluation of them,' requested Bingley.

'Indeed, and I came prepared.' Elizabeth pulled a sheet of paper from her reticule. 'I have also included the goods in which they trade.'

Darcy looked over Bingley's shoulder to peruse the list. 'That is a most valuable intelligence, Mrs Brooks. I was wondering how to unearth this information.'

'You could do the same as I did. Talk to people, ask questions. That should be easy for you, Mr Bingley, as you have such an amiable manner.'

Darcy was reminded of the conversation he had had with Miss Lucas about approaching people in a friendly manner. He could see how his friend had the advantage over him in that respect. Perhaps this would be a good neighbourhood in which to hone his own skill in that area.

Meanwhile Bingley asked, 'And who are the people to whom I should speak?'

'Since Mr Darcy mentioned how involved his housekeeper is at Pemberley, I am sure he too would recommend Mrs Nicholls, as she has to deal with many of the merchants in her own role. She also knows the tenants since, as Jane explained to your sister, she has been visiting them when there was no mistress resident at Netherfield.'

'Is there anything Mrs Nicholls does not know?' Bingley asked, only half joking.

'If you discover such a lack, please let me know.' Elizabeth was pleased that Bingley did not seem to mind dealing with servants or women as equals. If he was truly interested in Jane and she came to reciprocate that interest, Bingley's attitude boded well for her sister's potential happiness.

She dismissed that thought and returned to the subject at hand. 'I recommend that after you have spoken to Mrs Nicholls, you visit all the tenants and speak to the men. Your sister can speak to the women. They can all tell you about local conditions and what problems there are.'

They continued discussing the conditions and people of the area in greater detail for another hour, after which Bingley begged, 'please, no more for today. As interesting as this discussion has been, I fear that my head will explode with all the information crammed into it. Perhaps we can continue this another day?'

Elizabeth was happy to agree, and they re-joined the ladies in the drawing room.

~A~

No one was particularly surprised when they only found Mrs Hurst and Jane Bennet speaking with Mrs Nicholls.

The housekeeper had been coaxed into sitting with the ladies while she imparted relevant information about Netherfield to Mrs Hurst. Once the others entered the room, Mrs Nicholls immediately excused herself.

Jane turned to her sister. 'Lizzy, I hope you do not mind but I have invited Louisa to come and spend the day at Longbourn tomorrow, to see how we deal with things.'

Elizabeth raised a brow at Jane's familiar use of Mrs Hurst name but made no comment. She only said, 'Of course, I do not mind. You know perfectly well that you are welcome to invite anyone you like.'

Bingley immediately jumped on the chance. 'Perhaps we might all be permitted to call on you?'

Elizabeth happily agreed to the scheme and soon after called for her gig to return to Longbourn.

~A~

Chapter 15

Elizabeth and Jane had just left Netherfield when a coach approached the manor at a very sedate pace.

Darcy, from his habitual place by the window recognised the crest on the coach. He turned to his friend and enquired, 'Did you by chance extend an invitation to anyone in the Fitzwilliam family?'

Bingley scratched his head and frowned. 'No, not recently.' Suddenly his expression cleared, and he smiled. 'Although I do remember telling the Colonel that he would always be welcome at my house if I ever had my own estate.'

Darcy nodded towards the coach which was just coming to a halt and said, 'I believe he may have taken you at your word. The Matlock coach has just arrived.'

Bingley and Darcy hurried outside and were just in time to see Colonel Richard Fitzwilliam being helped out of the carriage by his batman.

Fitzwilliam gave Bingley a weak grin. 'I hope your invitation still stands, as I am trying to find sanctuary from my mother's fussing.'

'Of course, you are always welcome and by the look of you I believe I can understand why the countess would be fussing. You look like hell.'

The Colonel smiled although it looked more like a grimace. 'I must have improved. Yesterday Bennings,' he nodded towards his batman, 'you remember Corporal Bennings?' Bingley and Darcy nodded at the Corporal in greeting. 'Anyhow, as I started to say, yesterday Bennings claimed I looked like death.'

Darcy held out his hand towards his cousin. 'I suppose on that scale, if hell is an improvement over death, I would hate to see you before. I am glad to see you more or less in one piece.'

'It was a close thing that he is in one piece and not several pieces. But if you pardon my saying so, the Colonel needs to get off his feet again and somewhere that does not move... right quick,' grumbled Bennings.

'Of course. Come inside and I will have Mrs Nicholls make up some rooms for you.'

'I have already arranged for that,' said Louisa who had come to greet their newest guests. 'Welcome, Colonel Fitzwilliam. I have asked the housekeeper to put you in the suite next to your cousin.'

'Thank you, Mrs Hurst.,' the Colonel said with a grateful smile.

'I will take the Colonel straight up if you do not mind,' said Bennings who was still supporting Fitzwilliam.

'Not at all, Corporal. Please make yourself at home, Colonel.'

Darcy took Richard's other arm and very slowly led his cousin to his rooms, which the ever-efficient Mrs Nicholls had kept ready for occupation at a moment's notice. Along the way, Darcy was thinking that it would be interesting to discover what harrowing fate had brought Richard to this juncture.

~A~

Once Richard was contentedly ensconced in a comfortable chair with a footstool, he breathed a sigh of relief.

'How bad are you?' Darcy demanded.

He was rewarded by a crooked grin. 'Not as bad as it looks. It was just that being jostled about in a carriage caused quite a bit of pain.'

'Then why did you travel, could you not have stayed in London?'

'I suppose I could have, but being cosseted and fussed over by mother would have driven me insane. This was the closest place to town I could think of to get away from her.'

'Are you not afraid that she might follow you here?'

'No, since I told her I would go to Pemberley. In about a fortnight I will send Johnston back with the carriage.' The Colonel still managed his usual grin at the subterfuge.

'Are you trying to get Johnston into trouble? Even without changing horses, it does not take a fortnight to make the return journey to Pemberley.'

Richard sighed as he admitted, 'We left town at dawn and travelled mostly at a walking pace.' He held up a hand as Darcy was about to burst into speech. 'I am in no danger anymore; I am simply in pain and need time as well as rest to heal properly.'

While Richard was relaxing, Bennings explored the suite. On his return to the sitting room, he said with a cheerful grin, 'Seems like I will be enjoying my stay. The bed looks right comfortable.'

'While I might be prepared to share a tent with you in Spain, I draw the line at sharing a bed with a reprobate like yourself,' growled the Colonel in mock disdain.

'There is no need to worry that you will keep me awake with your snoring. The lady has put us in a suite with two bedrooms.'

'What do you mean, my snoring? It is you who keeps me awake with your wheezing all night.'

Darcy watched the banter between the two men with relief. While Richard did indeed look like he had been to hell and back, the irreverent teasing of his batman seemed the best indicator that the Colonel was indeed on the mend.

~A~

The following morning Richard declared himself perfectly content to spend the day in his rooms with only Bennings for company while most of the others went to Longbourn.

Miss Bingley declined to accompany the party as she claimed to suffer from a headache, a situation for which the others were grateful.

Hurst accompanied his wife in the carriage, while Darcy and Bingley followed on their horses. As the intention of the visit was for Louisa Hurst to see firsthand the duties of the mistress of an estate, the party reached Longbourn just after breakfast.

Once they arrived, Bingley claimed that he too wanted to know more about this aspect of life in the country, joining his sister as well as Jane and Mary as they went about their duties. As he had nothing better to do, Mr Hurst tagged along and observed with pleasure how well his wife was dealing with this new situation.

~A~

As the group went to follow Jane on her visit to the Potters, Darcy was left standing forgotten by the window of the parlour, sporting an amused smile.

The only other occupant of the room noticed his expression and started to chuckle. 'I confess that I did wonder if Mr Bingley had come to discuss which crops do well in this climate as opposed to Derbyshire, or whether he was more interested in less... ah... manly pursuits.'

'I would have thought most people would consider it very manly to pursue a lady.'

'I just hope he does not raise expectations which he is disinclined to honour.'

'I confess I have seen my friend fall in and out of love on many occasions. This time he seems more serious.' Elizabeth raised a quizzical brow and Darcy clarified. 'He only mentioned your sister's beauty once since he met her.'

'Thank you, Mr Darcy. That is reassuring,' replied Elizabeth.

After a moment's hesitation she completely changed the subject. 'I need to inspect the fences on the home farm, which I was going to do tomorrow, but since Mr Bingley does not require our presence, would you care to accompany me on my walk?'

'Thank you, Mrs Brooks. I would enjoy stretching my legs for a change.'

~A~

They set out, going past the stables to collect Bob, who always accompanied Elizabeth on her outings.

In answer to Darcy's query about her unusual chaperone, she said with a grin, 'I believe Mr Jamieson, the stablemaster, only keeps Bob on because he can keep up with me when I am walking.'

Since she was setting a brisk pace, Darcy could well understand the need for Bob.

As they walked, Elizabeth pointed out features of her estate, and improvements she had made and others she considered making. Darcy responded with suggestions of what had worked for him at Pemberley.

When they did not speak, they each thought about their companion.

Darcy was impressed by the ability Elizabeth possessed in not only continuing the administration of the estate as her father had done but making improvements. She was so very different from the society ladies he had met in the past.

Those ladies would stroll languidly while Elizabeth strode with purpose. Instead of sporting a bored demeanour, Elizabeth's eyes were sparkling and there was a vibrancy about her which drew him like a magnet.

It was such a pity that she was not better connected because in every other aspect she seemed to be absolutely perfect.

For a moment he considered that as the owner of her own estate, she would make the perfect wife for a second son, such as his cousin Richard, who needed a wealthy wife as he had no expectations.

But the instant the thought crossed his mind, he felt such alarm at the image of Elizabeth in the arms of his cousin that he could barely breathe.

Refusing to consider the matter, especially his reaction to the idea, he wrenched his mind back to the present and focused on his surroundings.

'What is the matter with those fields?' he indicated the area on the other side of the fence. 'They appear untended.'

'Those fields belong to the farm being leased by Mr Chambers,' Elizabeth answered with a grimace. 'I am afraid that he is very traditional and refused to listen to my suggestions about improving his yield with crop rotation.'

Darcy nodded in sympathy. 'I too had a couple of tenants who were reluctant to embrace new ideas. It took me several years to convince them to use the new farming methods.'

'At least you are a man, and your tenants knew you and expected you to manage your estate. Mr Chambers objects to take suggestions, as he was heard to put it, *from a slip of a girl who should not get above her station to think she can meddle in men's business*.' Elizabeth paused and sighed. 'I was told he then proceeded to tell people that I should get myself a husband and added in graphic detail to which activities I should confine myself,' she added with a slight blush.

'I gather he is something of a misogynist.'

'He is simply a man of our times. It is a rare man who can accept that women have the ability to learn things other than household matters.'

'You should know that I have read Mary Wollstonecraft's book and I quite agree with her that women should be allowed to be educated.'

'You think then that women should improve their minds by extensive reading?'

'Indeed. I have never understood why any man would want a wife who has not the ability to hold an intelligent conversation.'

'Perhaps because these men are incapable of holding an intelligent conversation themselves?' suggested Elizabeth with an impish grin.

Darcy could not help but chuckle at the impertinent comment.

'Perhaps you are correct. But if you live on an estate there are long evenings which will be spent predominantly in company with one's spouse, with no other people about. I have always felt that such time will be more pleasurable if one can spend it in elegant discourse. After all, one cannot spend all of one's time reading.' Darcy delicately forbore to mention that while there were other pleasurable activities in which a couple might engage, even those could not take up all evening. One had to have some conversation at some time.

'My father would have disagreed with you. He spent every minute he could in his library. But I suppose he was an exception.'

'Was he the one who collected all those books I saw in your library?'

'Indeed, and I was fortunate that he allowed me to read anything I liked.'

'If he allowed you to delve into matters generally considered unsuitable for ladies, did your father teach you to manage your estate, since you have only sisters?'

'I wish that were true, but I must confess that he was a rather indolent man, who did not encourage his tenants to move with the times and that is now causing me some issues.'

Elizabeth nodded in the direction of the neighbouring fields. 'Since Mr Chambers has refused to use the new farming methods, his harvests have been getting progressively worse. He is at the point where he cannot pay his rent and I had no option but to send him a notice to cancel his lease.'

She shrugged. 'Not only do I miss out on the rent this year, but I need to allow the fields to lie fallow for a year to let them recover. For that reason, I cannot in good conscience get a new tenant until then.'

'Have you considered getting a tenant who will work to improve the fields by planting turnips while you waive the rent and possibly pay him a small amount to live on?'

Elizabeth stopped and stared at Darcy. She closed her eyes and shook her head. When she opened them again, a chagrined smiled played about her lips. 'No, Mr Darcy. I had not considered that option. It had simply not occurred to me.' Her smile broadened. 'That is a brilliant notion. Now I only have to find someone who would be willing to take on such a project.'

'I am pleased to have been of assistance.' Darcy smiled and bowed.

He did not realise how his smile coupled with his respectful attitude affected his companion.

Elizabeth thought that if she had not sworn off men for all times, this gentleman could be a serious danger to her equilibrium. Fortunately, it appeared that while he seemed to enjoy her company, it was only as a fellow landowner and perhaps a fledgeling friend.

~A~

Colonel Fitzwilliam had been able to rest for a day and was now in a state to take an interest in his cousin's affairs.

They had the chance for a private conversation after dinner in his suite. 'So, pray tell, who are those neighbours you visited today? They must be very interesting if even Hurst bestirred himself.'

Darcy grinned as he answered, 'I believe the major incentive for Hurst was the fact that Miss Bingley refused to join the party.' He then went on to describe the inhabitants of Longbourn and their offers of assistance to Bingley and to Louisa Hurst.

Richard had listened carefully and became interested in what Darcy did not say. 'What about this Mrs Brooks? What is she like?'

'As it happens, you have met her,' Darcy said with a smile as he dragged out the suspense.

'I greatly doubt it. I would remember a beautiful widow who owns her own estate. But Mrs Brooks is completely unknown to me.'

'When she became a widow, she changed her name as her married name has too many unpleasant associations...' Darcy paused again but eventually took pity on his cousin's curiosity. 'She used to be Mrs Collins of the parish of Hunsford.'

Richard was taken aback. 'She was the meek young wife of that idiot parson of Aunt Cat?'

'Indeed. Although you would hardly recognise her now.' Darcy went on to wax lyrical about all the accomplishments and abilities of the lady, unaware how much his cousin read into his effusions.

'It seems that you have developed quite an interest in the young lady,' Richard commented with a delighted smile when Darcy eventually stopped speaking.

That comment startled Darcy, but all he would say was, 'It is a pity that she has no worthwhile connections.'

Richard just raised his brows and shook his head at his cousin's comment, knowing that if he pushed, Darcy would dig in his heels and refuse to consider what would be good for him. But he was curious to meet the lady again.

~A~

Chapter 16

At Longbourn, the ladies spent time readying the estate for winter, but since they were up to date on their various tasks, it left them time for their own interests.

Elizabeth and Mary were practicing a duet on the new pianoforte which Elizabeth had bought recently. While it was not the best and most expensive instrument, it was much better than the one on which they had learnt.

Since in recent years, Longbourn had become a much more peaceful home, Elizabeth had not felt the need to escape its confines by taking long walks. As her duties required her to spend time outside and she felt more at ease at home, she had taken the time to practice on the pianoforte more regularly.

It also helped having Mrs Taylor in the house, who assisted and encouraged the sisters. Even Jane discovered to have a modest talent for the harp.

~A~

After the visit to Longbourn, Mrs Hurst spent some time putting her newfound knowledge into practice, while Bingley and Darcy dealt with preparing the estate for winter. Since Hurst had no duties, he and Richard spent a considerable amount of time playing chess or simply relaxing by the fire in the library while the Colonel slowly recuperated.

During that period, hardly anyone noticed that Miss Bingley spent most of her time in her rooms. When someone realised, they assumed that she was sulking, and left her to her own devices.

When the residents of Netherfield were not busy with their tasks, they visited the various neighbours and established friendly relations with all. As a result, they received many invitations to sundry events, many of which were also attended by Jane, Elizabeth and Mary.

One time, when Darcy visited Longbourn, he discovered that Elizabeth knew how to play chess. Not only that, but they were also evenly matched. After that they enjoyed many a game when the opportunity presented itself.

~A~

Sir William Lucas was a most gregarious neighbour and had invited some friends to a small social gathering.

Because his own younger daughter Maria was allowed to attend, the youngest Bennets and their governess were invited as well as the three older sisters.

As soon as the sisters arrived, Kitty and Lydia sought out Maria. Mrs Taylor and Mary took up a position nearby to keep an eye on the girls, although these days it was more a precaution than a necessity.

After greeting their hosts, Jane and Elizabeth found Charlotte waiting for them to lead them to the side of the room, hoping to catch up on the latest news.

'I hear that you have been getting to know our new neighbours,' Charlotte said with a lifted brow, inviting the sisters to share their experiences.

Jane smiled sweetly as she answered, 'Indeed. I find the company of Mrs Hurst most congenial. She is quite eager to experience life as the mistress of an estate,' and had the mischievous pleasure of seeing their friend's expression cloud.

Charlotte huffed, 'You know perfectly well that was not the neighbour of whom I was speaking.'

'Her husband is also quite charming when not in company of their sister,' Elizabeth added for good measure.

Rolling her eyes, Charlotte demanded, 'I would like to know all you have to tell me about Mr Bingley and Mr Darcy.' She looked at Jane and Elizabeth in turn when she mentioned the names.

Jane put a placating hand on Charlotte's arm. 'I find Mr Bingley to be a most amiable gentleman, but you must remember I have only met him a few times so far.'

'Then I hope you will be pleased that we expect to see him tonight,' Charlotte informed her friends. 'I confess that when I have seen him in your company, he appeared quite smitten,' she allowed.

A movement by the entrance caught her attention. 'And speaking of the gentleman... it seems that he has arrived.'

The party from Netherfield without Miss Bingley had arrived and were being greeted by Sir William, to whom they introduced Colonel Fitzwilliam who was making his first foray into Meryton society and was leaning on a cane.

The sisters and Charlotte could hear Sir William exclaim, 'Capital. Capital,' before three of the gentlemen excused themselves and came towards them.

Darcy introduced his cousin, but as soon as greetings were complete, Bingley managed to manoeuvre Jane away from the group, a move which raised equally knowing smiles on all four faces.

The Colonel broke the impasse by commenting, 'I cannot fault Bingley's taste,' but realising that he had slighted the other ladies, he added, 'since Miss Bennet is the exact type of beauty he favours.'

Charlotte smirked as she said, 'Colonel, when you are in a hole, you should stop digging. Did they not teach you that in the army?'

'In the past I would have expected to hear that sort of comment directed at me by you,' Darcy laughed at the Colonel's discomfiture.

Richard recovered his aplomb as he lied, 'Indeed. I was not taught any such thing, since my superior officer used to be in the navy. No digging allowed at all on a ship.'

Following the laughter at his quip, the group chatted pleasantly for a few minutes until they were joined by Mrs Taylor and Mary, who said to Elizabeth, 'Lady Lucas has requested us to perform, and I was hoping you would join me in a duet.'

While Mary's playing had improved over the last two years, her voice, although better trained now, was still weak. Whenever a piece of music required singing, Elizabeth was the preferred performer.

Elizabeth shook her head in mock exasperation. 'So, we are to sing for our supper. Very well, we shall oblige Lady Lucas but please do not complain if our performance is not up to the standard to which you are used,' she added for the benefit of Darcy and Fitzwilliam. Quickly making the introduction between the Colonel and Mrs Taylor, she and Mary went in search of their hostess.

Darcy and Charlotte noticed the Colonel looking carefully at Mrs Taylor. 'I believe that the introduction was superfluous. Unless I am mistaken, you used to be married to Lieutenant Taylor, were you not?'

'I was indeed. And I believe I remember my husband speaking about a dashing Lieutenant Fitzwilliam in the Horse Guards.'

'By dashing I hope you mean that I was always dashing into the thick of the fighting,' Fitzwilliam retorted with what seemed to be an almost embarrassed smile. 'I confess I was young and stupid at the time and thought myself to be immortal. I have learnt better since.'

Mrs Taylor looked at the cane and nodded in understanding.

Before they could speak further, they were interrupted by the strains of a song. Instead of the expected instrumental duet, Mary had convinced Elizabeth to sing *Voi Che Sapete* as Mary played the instrument.

Darcy and his cousin listened spellbound while Charlotte and Mrs Taylor exchanged knowing looks.

~A~

Later in the evening, Darcy told Elizabeth, 'I received a letter from my cousin Anne. She was pleased to hear that you are doing well and thanks you for your greetings.'

'I too am pleased to hear that she is feeling better these days. I wish I had had a chance to get to know her while I was at Hunsford.'

'Did you not have a chance to speak to Anne in all the time you were there?' Darcy asked in surprise.

'While Lady Catherine and Mr Collins pontificated, it was unwise for anyone else to venture a comment.' Elizabeth grimaced as she attempted a weak joke, 'Neither Miss de Bourgh nor I had the option to go against the wishes of our warders.'

'Ah, yes. Now that you mention it, Anne did say that she too hoped for a friendship between the two of you, but as you say, you both were being constrained by dragons.'

He tilted his head as an idea occurred to him. 'Perhaps it is not too late. Now that Anne is in charge of Rosings she can send and receive mail. You have much in common since you both had the responsibility of an estate thrust upon you quite unexpectedly at about the same time. Would you be agreeable if I were to suggest to my cousin that you could compare experiences via correspondence?'

Although startled by the suggestion, Elizabeth replied sincerely, 'I would be delighted to correspond with Miss de Bourgh.'

~A~

'What are you doing?' asked Richard in the library at Netherfield where he and Darcy had retreated for a nightcap.

Darcy glanced up from the desk by the window and with a haughty expression said, 'It should be obvious even to an illiterate soldier that I am writing a letter.'

'Just because I have no interest in obscure literature, that hardly makes me illiterate. But what is so urgent that you are writing this letter now. Would not the morning be early enough to do so?'

'I am sending a note to our cousin.'

'You are writing to Anne?'

'Indeed.'

'That brings me back to my question. Why do you have to write to her now?'

'Because I want the letter to be sent first thing in the morning. And before you interrupt me further, I am suggesting to Anne that she might like to correspond with Mrs Brooks,' Darcy replied and gave his cousin a brief explanation.

Richard suppressed a smile and said, 'Then get on with it so that we can have a nightcap and a conversation.'

Since Darcy was only writing a short note, he was soon finished and joined his cousin by the fire.

'Remind me to thank Bingley for finding an estate in such excellent surroundings.'

'You have yet to see any of the surroundings,' protested Darcy.

Richard grinned. 'I am speaking of the remarkably lovely ladies with which this area abounds.'

That comment caused Darcy to chuckle, albeit somewhat exasperatedly. 'Of course, you would notice the members of the fair sex. You always had an eye for the ladies, but do you not think it is about time that you settled down? Is not your current condition proof that you are not immortal?'

'Ah... but you know perfectly well that I am not in the same lucky position as you. I have to marry with an eye for financial security, but I have no wish to consider fortune as the only criteria if I am to spend the rest of my life in the company of a lady.'

With a pained expression, Darcy said, 'I have considered that as a wealthy landowner, Mrs Brooks would be a good match for you to allow you to retire from the army.'

'She would be a good match... for you too,' retorted Richard who had noticed the ease with which Darcy conversed with the lady and the pains he took to assist her.

'Richard, you know that I too have certain constraints. I am expected to marry a lady from the first circles to ensure that Georgiana has the opportunity for an advantageous match.'

'Do you truly think that the daughter of a gentleman with an estate of her own is not an ideal match for you? After all, need I remind you that you are but an untitled gentleman.' Richard shook his head at his cousin's stubborn refusal to see what was best for him.

Seeing that Darcy was unmoved he continued, 'As her second guardian I am just as concerned that your sister should have a good marriage, but we may have very different ideas what constitutes a good match. I would prefer her to marry a man with whom she can be happy rather than excessively rich.' He grinned before he added, 'Naturally, I would not object if she could have both.'

'Yes, my foremost concern is that Georgiana should be happy. I simply do not want to risk her missing out on her perfect partner due to the unsuitability of my wife.'

'Can you imagine Georgiana wanting to marry a man who would object to your choice in wife?'

'N-o-o-o, but the fact remains that Mrs Brooks has no connections other than two uncles, one of whom is a country solicitor and the other is in trade.'

'Of course, we do not have any embarrassing relations at all...' Richard commented sarcastically and had the pleasure of seen Darcy's ears turn pink. But the Colonel was enough of a strategist to change the subject now that the seed had been planted.

~A~

When the sisters and Margaret Taylor returned to Longbourn, they were having tea in the parlour and discussing the evening.

Lydia and Kitty waxed lyrical about the wonderful time they had with their friend.

After they had run down, Elizabeth mentioned to her sisters Darcy's offer to facilitate communication between herself and Miss de Bourgh and the reasoning behind his suggestion.

'Mr Darcy is certainly going out of his way to be helpful to you,' said Jane with a speculative look.

'Indeed, he is very generous with his assistance, but I suppose that the main reason is that his cousin has been isolated much of her life. It must be difficult for her to make new acquaintances.'

'Indeed,' Mary echoed with a bland smile. 'Mr Darcy is quite unstinting in his concern for his family.'

Mrs Taylor suppressed a smile at the sisters' teasing of Elizabeth who remained oblivious. To ensure it would not get out of hand, she urged the youngest girls to retire for the night. 'After all, just because you were permitted to attend a party tonight, does not mean you will be allowed to neglect your lessons tomorrow.'

While Kitty and Lydia put up a token resistance, they did obey with alacrity.

Once they were gone, Margaret Taylor poured herself a cup of tea and added her own comment. 'Colonel Fitzwilliam mentioned to me that he had never before seen his cousin being so relaxed and helpful to anyone outside of his immediate circle.'

'I am pleased that Mr Darcy feels this way. I feel honoured that he should consider me a friend.'

'Lizzy, can you not see that Mr Darcy seems much more interested in you than could be explained merely by friendship,' Mary was getting exasperated with her sister's wilful blindness.

Elizabeth's countenance took on a pained expression. 'I truly hope that you are wrong. Can you not understand that the idea of another marriage terrifies me utterly. I am in the lucky position to have an independent fortune and therefore no need to marry. Why should I give that up and risk a lifetime of misery.'

'Would you truly prefer a lifetime of loneliness?' whispered Jane with tears in her eyes.

'An aching heart is less painful than never being allowed to speak my mind.' Elizabeth still could not bring herself to speak more clearly about her marriage.

'I promise you that most men are not like that!' cried Jane.

'Perhaps not. But I still see no reason to risk it.'

Since the mulish look on Elizabeth's countenance only became more pronounced the more her sisters pushed her, Mrs Taylor changed the subject, allowing everyone to relax again.

~A~

Chapter 17

The following morning Elizabeth headed for Oakham Mount, the destination of choice whenever she felt in need of solace.

The discussion about the gentlemen with her sisters on the previous evening was still running through her mind and had triggered another one of her nightmares. Elizabeth loved her sisters dearly, but sometimes she wanted to shake them and to beat some sense into them.

Could they not understand that it was not her fear of a repetition of the physical abuse she had suffered which made her wary of another marriage.

For once in her life, she was in charge of her own destiny. She did not have to defer to any man. She was allowed to have and utter opinions of her own without fear of reprisals. How could her sisters expect her to give up her freedom and independence to become less than nothing in the eyes of the law?

During her marriage she had silently railed against the injustice that she had not the slightest recourse in law to end her suffering. Now that she had her freedom, Elizabeth could not envision giving it up.

Sitting on Oakham Mount and watching the sun rise, she slowly felt the anger and the tension draining away. As she relaxed, she thought about the object of her conflict with her sisters. He was so very different than her husband had been.

Mr Darcy was intelligent, kind, and exceedingly handsome. Yet he was still a man and according to the law he had total power, and his future wife would have no rights.

No. Elizabeth was determined. Even if by some miracle he was indeed interested in her, for her peace of mind it would be better to only be friends with the gentleman.

~A~

As usual, Darcy was up at the crack of dawn and went for his customary ride before breakfast.

His cousin's words, casual though they were, had haunted him during the night, but Darcy was determined to do all he could to ensure his sister's happiness.

He was not paying particular attention to his route until he crested the top of Oakham Mount and found it already occupied.

~A~

The last thing Elizabeth wanted was to see the gentleman who had occupied her thoughts so much.

Fortunately for her peace of mind, he was distantly friendly when he greeted her and asked her permission to join her in admiring the vista.

They chatted of inconsequentials until Darcy remembered something he had been meaning to follow up. 'I have been wondering why you suggested to Bingley that he should get his information from Mrs Nicholls, rather than the steward, Mr Thompson.'

Elizabeth fidgeted and refused to meet his gaze for several moments. Eventually she sighed. 'Mr Darcy, you must understand that I have no wish to cast aspersions on anyone's character, but I simply cannot bring myself to trust Mr Thompson.'

'Do you have a reason for this lack of trust?'

'No, which is why I am reluctant to speak of it. I am afraid that Mr Thompson and I do not see eye to eye. It could be as simple as the fact that he is very traditional and has an exceedingly low opinion of the capabilities of women.'

She grimaced and sighed. 'While Mr Thompson has never insulted me outright, he has often insinuated that I am incompetent and should not be in charge of Longbourn. And yet...'

'Do you think he may be dishonest?'

'I simply do not know. All I can tell you is that I am always most uncomfortable in his company. He always displays the courtesy due to my station, but I always feel that he is untruthful. He appears to be paying lip-service to the conventions. As I said, it could simply be that he believes that women should always be subordinate and subservient to men.'

As soon as Elizabeth put her feelings into words, she recognised at last that Thompson's attitude mirrored that of her late husband. As realisation hit her, she started to tremble uncontrollably as memories flooded her mind.

'Elizabeth, what is wrong? Can I help?' Darcy cried in alarm and reached out to support her.

Visions were clouding Elizabeth's mind and eyes. She saw a tall man who seemed to be holding a cane rather than a riding crop. Darcy, who in a moment of stress, used her given name became one with the memory. That hand reaching for her was the last straw. Elizabeth panicked and gasped, 'No,' but not in answer to the question.

At least today she was outdoors and had room to move. In her confused state, Elizabeth whirled away from Darcy, picking up her skirts and ran as fast as her feet would carry her... away from what she perceived to be danger.

She blindly rushed down the hill at full tilt, automatically heading for Longbourn and safety, leaving behind a totally confused and worried man.

Darcy considered following Elizabeth but judged that chasing a distraught woman was possibly the worst thing he could do. Instead, he untied and mounted Hermes, riding very slowly towards Longbourn.

He needed to ascertain that the lady arrived safely at her home. Perhaps, after she calmed down, he could find out what had disturbed her so greatly.

~A~

Elizabeth was almost back to her home and on Longbourn lands when the panic started to recede.

Her wide-eyed stare focused as reason returned to her mind. She was breathing heavily, partly due to running and partly due to the overwhelming panic she had experienced. As she slowed down, she felt her legs burning and would have stumbled if Mary had not suddenly appeared next to her and reached out to support her.

'What is wrong? Has someone hurt you?' cried Mary in concern, taking in the dishevelled appearance of her sister as she led Elizabeth to a nearby bench in her garden.

Elizabeth gratefully collapsed onto the support of the bench and took some shuddering breaths while shaking her head.

'No one hurt me. At least not recently.'

'Then what happened to bring you into such a state?'

Too exhausted and wrung out to watch her tongue, Elizabeth answered completely truthfully for the first time. 'I suddenly remembered my life with Mr Collins in vivid detail. How he used to beat me and lecture me simply for speaking honestly.'

A sob escaped her lips, and a dam broke inside her. 'I was not allowed to have any thoughts or opinions of my own. Even a look could be misconstrued by him, and he would punish me... every Sunday night. And now you urge me to subject myself to that kind of torture again?'

Never having had the opportunity to fight back against her husband, who was dead and beyond her reach, she now lashed out at the only person available. 'Why would you do such a thing? What have I ever done to you that you would want to see me beaten till I am black and blue and can barely move. I thought you loved me, but you want me to suffer unspeakable cruelty.'

Mary sat next to her weeping sister in stunned horror as the words poured from Elizabeth's lips. Never had she imagined the kind of life to which her sister had been subjected.

'Lizzy, I am sorry. I had no idea about the kind of suffering you endured. I never imagined that anyone could be so cruel. Especially to you who are the kindest and most wonderful sister anyone could hope for.' Mary reached out to clasp her sister's hands, tears streaming unnoticed down her own cheeks. 'Please believe me when I say that I only want to see you safe and happy. If that means that you stay single for the rest of your life, I will pray that you find the happiness and contentment which you deserve.'

Mary babbled on for what seemed an eternity until her words of apology and comfort truly registered with her sister.

Realising what was going on, Elizabeth shook herself and gasped, 'Mary, please stop. I am sorry I lashed out at you. It is not your fault what happened in the past. I should not have said what I did.'

She pulled Mary into an embrace. 'I do not know what happened that made me say those things.'

'I think I know what happened,' Mary retorted and pulled back a little to look her sister in the eye. 'Ever since you came back, you pretended that everything was well. You did not wish to burden us with your pain and kept it bottled up. It festered like a boil. Like a boil, once it is lanced, all the sickness pours out. Perhaps you will now be able to heal.'

'How did you become so wise?'

'I had years to observe while being ignored. I suppose it gave me a different perspective.'

Elizabeth took a deep breath and slowly released it. 'Thank you, Mary. I do feel better now.'

'In that case, shall we go inside and break our fast?'

~A~

The sisters made good use of the handkerchiefs they always carried and were on their way to join their family in the dining room, when a rider slowly approached Longbourn.

Remembering what had happened at Oakham Mount, Elizabeth urged Mary to go inside while she spoke to Mr Darcy.

As soon as Darcy dismounted, Elizabeth approached him. 'Mr Darcy, I must apologise for my behaviour earlier.' She hesitated, wondering if she should reveal the cause for her distress.

'There is no need to apologise, I was only concerned for your wellbeing and that you reached your home safely.'

'I thank you for your concern. I am afraid I made quite a fool of myself, but I was suddenly overcome with memories of the past and needed to get away.'

Darcy did not really understand what the problem had been but as he did not want to pry into her private affairs, he accepted her explanation. He smiled reassuringly. 'As long as you are safe and sound, I am content.'

'I am perfectly well now,' Elizabeth replied with an untroubled smile. 'I was about to break my fast with my family, would you care to join us?'

Darcy felt relieved that he had not been the cause of her distress and seeing her relaxed smile reassured him. 'As much as I would enjoy your company, but since I promised Bingley that we would investigate a potential drainage problem immediately after breakfast I had better return to Netherfield now.'

He took his leave and Elizabeth joined her sisters, feeling better than she had in a long time. Perhaps Mary had been correct, and she was starting to heal at last.

~A~

While most residents of Netherfield Park were busy with estate business and socialising, Miss Bingley entertained herself with gathering information about their neighbours, two ladies in particular.

She was getting exceedingly vexed when the worst she could discover about Jane Bennet was that she had two uncles in, what Caroline considered, trade and her dowry was less than the twenty thousand of Caroline's fortune, but she hoped it would be enough to convince her brother that Miss Bennet was only interested in him for his wealth.

Attacking Mrs Brooks was even more difficult. At dinner that night, Miss Bingley tried to make much of the fact that Elizabeth had changed her name to Brooks after she became widowed.

'I wonder what scandal she is trying to hide by using a false name,' she suggested with pretended concern.

'She is probably trying to hide that she is a much better person than you will ever be,' murmured Hurst, causing Caroline to want to murder him... yet again.

'She did not like her married name,' Darcy commented casually. 'I knew her late husband and cannot say that I blame her.'

'Was her husband some sort of criminal?' Caroline asked avidly.

'No, much worse than that. He was a fool. He did not realise what a treasure he had in his wife,' was the unwelcome answer which Darcy delivered with a bland smile.

Miss Bingley fought a valiant rearguard action. 'Still, she and her sisters will find it difficult to attract husbands as I have heard that they are poor as church mice. Their father never put any money aside for dowries.'

'I congratulate Mr Bennet for keeping his daughters safe, even after his death,' said Richard and lifted his glass as if in toast. 'No fortune hunter will give them a second look if they think the ladies are poor.'

Hurst could not resist the opportunity to snipe. 'Even twenty thousand pounds cannot attract a fortune hunter thanks to Caroline's personality.'

Ignoring Hurst, Caroline huffed, 'What kind of dowries could any of them have?' Why did Colonel Fitzwilliam have to be so irritating as well?

'I would estimate that Mrs Brooks' fortune is at least seventy-five thousand pounds,' said the irritating Colonel.

Miss Bingley stared in consternation at Fitzwilliam. 'How could she have such a large fortune? How did you find out about it?'

'She is the owner of Longbourn, an estate which has been in her family for many generations. In my experience, an estate that size would probably clear at least two and a half thousand pounds a year. To calculate the value of the estate, you multiply the annual income by thirty... at least an estate this close to London.'

Darcy smiled wolfishly and added to his cousin's comments. 'Mind you. I would not be in the least surprised if the income was significantly higher than that.'

'I bow to your greater expertise,' Richard replied and literally bowed as much as he could while sitting at the table.

Being stymied on all fronts, Caroline Bingley decided that she had to step up her campaign, if she wanted to succeed. It was getting urgent for her to succeed.

~A~

Chapter 18

Over the next several days, Elizabeth thought about her outburst with Mary.

Ever since her husband's death she had tried to forget about her marriage and get on with her life as if that year had not happened and therefore had never spoken about her experiences except in the most general terms.

Part of the reason was that she simply wanted to forget, but also because she had wanted to protect her sisters from being disturbed by the extent of her suffering.

While her sisters were all aware of the last beating, she had received from her husband, because Sally had spoken of her bruises to all and sundry, the girls had thought it a one-time happening. Elizabeth had never mentioned the weekly beatings she had received.

Elizabeth had not wished to frighten her sisters into thinking that such calculated cruelty was the norm in a marriage. After all, she had never seen her father raise his hand against Mrs Bennet, despite the woman's outrageous and irritating manner.

Uncle Phillips might shake his head over his wife's antics, but Aunt Phillips never acted as if she was in pain. And considering the wonderful relationship her Aunt and Uncle Gardiner had, she was certain that at worst they might have a heated discussion.

She now realised that it had been a mistake not to speak of it, for several reasons.

Not only had those emotional wounds festered and prevented true healing to occur, but by keeping her sisters in ignorance of potential pitfalls, it made them vulnerable, expecting all men to be non-violent.

Jane in particular was still in the habit of trying to see the best in people. Such naïveté could be dangerous if she met the wrong man.

After much soul-searching, Elizabeth decided to speak to her sisters.

~A~

The following morning, during breakfast she asked Mrs Taylor to suspend lessons for the day as she wished to have a discussion with her sisters as well as the governess.

Elizabeth chose the library as the stout door would ensure that they would not be overheard.

Once they had all settled into the comfortable chairs, Elizabeth took some deep breaths to help calm her nerves.

'I have realised that I have been remiss in not telling you about what happened to me during my marriage. I thought to protect you from some unpleasant truths so as not to frighten you off the idea of marriage for yourselves.'

Elizabeth paused to gather her courage and after asking her audience to hear her out before asking questions, she went on to tell her sisters about her experiences.

As expected, Jane and Kitty were the most affected, with the younger girl turning green and gulping so as not to cast up her accounts. Jane had tears streaming down her cheeks as she struggled to comprehend how anyone could act in such a manner.

Lydia was the most vocal. 'What a monster. I am glad that he is dead, but I wish that he should have suffered for what he did to you.'

The other sisters added their own version of that sentiment, creating quite a hubbub.

Elizabeth waited until they had quieted somewhat before she shocked them even more, 'I do not believe that Mr Collins was a monster as he did not enjoy what he did to me. But in a way that was worse as he believed he was doing his duty.'

'How can beating your wife be considered a duty?' exploded Kitty.

'He was a fool and excessively rigid. He was raised to believe that men are superior to women in every way, but in particular in intellect. Like many men he considered me, or any woman other than Lady Catherine, to be on the same level as a child. Children have to be taught proper attitudes and behaviours, and even the bible says, spare the rod and spoil the child.'

Mary huffed, 'Book of Proverbs 13:24. Although I felt guilty about disagreeing with the holy book, I always thought that was a ridiculous statement. Now I have changed my mind. Now I know it is a dreadful sentiment.'

Elizabeth's lips quirked in a small smile. 'Careful, Mary. Soon you will be as secular as I am.'

'I do not care if they call me a heretic, but I will forevermore disagree with that proverb,' Mary retorted fiercely.

'I am very pleased to hear you say that. But to get back to the point I was trying to make. Even though it was horrific from my perspective, Mr Collins thought of himself as a good Christian.'

Several of the sisters displayed various grimaces of distaste and Jane added, 'Considering the kind of marriage you had, it is no wonder that you did not want us to recommend Mr Darcy as a potential husband.'

Elizabeth sighed. 'That is one reason. But are all of you aware that according to the law, once you marry you are no longer considered to be a person in your own right? You belong to your husband... literally. He owns you, just like everything you own becomes his property as well. Even the clothes you wear will belong to him. You have no rights.'

'None at all?' gasped Kitty, looking close to tears.

'The only thing your husband is not allowed to do is to kill you. In everything else he may do with you as he wishes.'

'But why would any woman want to marry? Why did mama push us to find husbands as quickly as possible?'

'Women do not have many options to earn a living. And even those few options are fraught with danger,' Mrs Taylor said. 'In my previous position, the master of the house wanted to take liberties with me.'

'But that is so wrong,' gasped Jane.

'It is wrong, but it is also quite common. And ofttimes the woman being importuned has no way to resist or escape. And if she is unfortunate, she becomes with child; at which point she is fired without a character.'

'That is even worse.' Jane's shoulder slumped as she considered the plight of servants and even impoverished gentlewomen.

'Which is why most women are prepared to take the risk and marry. At least they cannot be fired for producing a child,' Elizabeth said.

She let that information sink in for a moment and then said, 'On the other hand, I still believe that a marriage with the right man can be delightful. Look at the Gardiners. I have never seen a couple so perfectly suited and exceedingly happy.' She gave her sisters an encouraging smile. 'I hope that if you choose to marry you will find as good a man as our uncle.'

'So, you are advising us to be careful in our choice of husband,' Mary said with a frown. 'But did I understand you correctly? Did you say we had a choice whether to marry or not?'

'You all have a choice.'

'But how can that be? Mama always said that unless we marry, we would starve in the hedgerows,' Kitty asked with a worried frown.

'She also claimed she would starve in the hedgerows when our father died. Yet she is living quite comfortably in her cottage, and I have not noticed her looking ill-fed,' Elizabeth reminded Kitty.

Elizabeth let her gaze wander over each of her sisters. 'I want you to know that each of you will have a respectable dowry when the time comes. This can be used to create a settlement for you if you choose to marry, or you can use the interest on that dowry to live on if you choose to remain single.'

'From where do those dowries come? Mama always complained that papa was not providing for us.' This time it was Lydia who was curious.

'Father did save for us from the day he married. He did not tell Mrs Bennet about that money because he was certain that she would have wanted to spend it on fripperies.'

All the sisters' faces lit up on hearing the news.

Lydia, always interested in numbers asked, 'How much did he save?'

'The interest from Mrs Bennet's jointure. Two hundred pounds per year.'

Kitty's face fell as she calculated. 'While that is over four thousand pounds, it is still less than what mama has, and she said that she cannot support all of us on that money.'

'Compound interest, you ninny,' exclaimed Lydia with a grin. 'Even at four percent that should be about seven thousand pounds by now.'

'And since most of it is invested with Uncle Gardiner, the return is ten percent on average,' Elizabeth informed her sisters.

Lydia pursed her lips as she calculated. 'At ten percent that would make it about fifteen thousand, but you said not all of it is with Uncle Gardiner, so it will be somewhat less,' Lydia said with a grin. 'Split between the five of us, that is at least two and a half thousand. At a ten percent return, we each have about two hundred and fifty pounds per year.'

Elizabeth's grin answered Lydia's enthusiasm. 'Although the interest from Mrs Bennet's jointure has been used to support her these last two years, reducing the amount to something in excess of thirteen thousand, that money will be split between the four of you. And as long as you do not all marry within the next few months, it will continue to grow.'

The relief in the room was palpable, which even Elizabeth's warning could not diminish. 'I must warn you though. If you marry without my approval, you will forfeit that dowry. That should discourage fortune hunters from inducing you to elope.'

~A~

As the sisters had much to absorb and consider, Mrs Taylor arranged for tea to be delivered.

After everyone had been served, Jane addressed Elizabeth, 'I do not think it is fair that you should not receive a portion of those dowries. Especially as you have housed and fed us since papa died and seem to be willing to do so until we leave home. And not to mention that you also provide us with pin money.'

Her statement caused the other sisters to nod in agreement.

Elizabeth felt very proud of her sisters as she said, 'Rest easy, Jane. Father had arranged for his books to be used to provide the funds for your support.'

'But the books are still here.' Mary gestured at the walls.

'I agreed to support you in return for keeping the books, which by my estimate cover the cost of your keep. And Longbourn can easily afford the expense since neither Mr nor Mrs Bennet is spending me out of house and home.'

'And you have made improvements to the estate,' Lydia commented. 'Even I can see that.'

'Indeed. We have an extra tenant, and due to some other improvements, I arranged, the home farm is much more productive than it has been in years, reducing our food bill. Especially with Jane and Mary's excellent management of the household.' The sisters beamed at the praise.

Elizabeth considered whether to share the information about her finances and decided against it.

She was proud of the fact that with the new tenant and the increased yields of the home farm, much of which was sold, Longbourn had made close to three thousand pounds this year. She expected that in the next year the income would be less since she would miss out on the rent for Mr Chambers' farm until the field were recovered enough to be farmed again. Although a crop of turnips, like Mr Darcy suggested would provide a small profit.

Even though she had used the excess profits from previous years plus the bulk of money in the estate accounts to buy the extra land, she would be able to invest the profit from the current year with Mr Gardiner. This would earn interest adding to her total annual income.

Instead of going into those details, she merely said, 'So, while it is technically not my responsibility to look after you, I can afford to do so. And in return, I get to keep all my old friends.' She gestured at the books.

Kitty gave Elizabeth a pensive look. 'I am sorry, but I never considered whose responsibility it was to take care of us after papa's passing. I am now sure that it was not supposed to be you.'

Elizabeth gave her a reassuring smile. 'Uncle Phillips was to be your primary guardian with Uncle Gardiner as an alternate if something should happen to Uncle Phillips. As I said before, Uncle Gardiner was supposed to sell the books which would have provided sufficient funds for Uncle Phillips to rent a cottage for all of you and Mrs Bennet and still provide you with pin money without touching the money set aside for your dowries.'

Mary pulled a face of distaste. 'I can just imagine living with Mrs Bennet in a cottage. There would never have been any peace and none of us would have accomplishments.'

'But we would all have too much lace on our dresses and mama would complain how poor we are,' added Jane.

'And then she would have importuned Lizzy for extra funds,' said Lydia with a shudder. 'Not only that, but I would also still be bored to distraction without anything to do.'

'It sounds like you all agree that things have worked out for the best,' said Elizabeth with a smile and received answering nods. 'And do not forget, Longbourn is now mine and will remain so.'

'You earned it,' Mary muttered as she remembered Lizzy's pain.

~A~

After the drain of the morning's conversation, Elizabeth declared a holiday for the rest of the day.

They were happily ensconced in the drawing room, reading or working on embroidery when Hill announced visitors.

Bingley, accompanied by Darcy and Colonel Fitzwilliam, entered and greeted the assembled ladies. Once they were enjoying refreshments, Bingley explained the purpose of their visit.

'Our neighbours have been most welcoming since our arrival, and I thought I would like to repay their kindness. I have therefore decided to give a ball and would like to invite all you ladies to attend.'

'Mr Bingley that is very kind of you, and I will be most pleased to attend as I am certain will my two oldest sisters. But as you know our youngest sisters are not yet out,' Elizabeth answered.

'And since I am required to attend my charges, I must regretfully decline,' Mrs Taylor apologetically informed Bingley.

'Mrs Brooks, would you consider making an exception? Would you allow your sisters to attend the ball at least until supper?' Fitzwilliam offered seeing the disappointed looks on Kitty's and Lydia's faces. He did not mention that he also wished the opportunity to spend time with their governess. 'Since I am unable to dance for the foreseeable future, I will spend the evening watching the entertainment and I will ensure that no harm will come to the young ladies,'

'But who will protect them from you, Colonel,' teased Elizabeth who had seen the same mournful looks, followed by mounting hope.

Seeing that Elizabeth was at least considering allowing the youngest girls to attend the ball, Mrs Taylor suggested, 'Perhaps we could reach a compromise? I will be happy to sit with the girls and we can all watch the entertainment. And after supper, I can bring my charges home.'

Seeing the pleading look of four pairs of eyes directed at her, Elizabeth capitulated. 'Very well, you may attend but you will not dance, and you will not consume any alcohol, is that clearly understood?'

Since the girls agreed, Bingley had the opportunity to request the first and the supper sets from Jane, as well as a set each from Elizabeth and Mary.

Darcy also requested a set each from Jane and Mary before turning to Elizabeth. 'I know that you have said that you do not usually dance more than once with any gentleman, but do you think you could make an exception for a friend and grant me the first and the supper set?'

Elizabeth blushed and fidgeted with her teacup, feeling a strange sensation in the pit of her stomach caused by the intense look Darcy directed at her.

Eventually she remembered her old motto, *my courage always rises at every attempt to intimidate me*. Taking a deep breath she said, 'Very well, Mr Darcy. I should be pleased to dance those sets with a friend.'

She thought that the brilliant smile which he directed at her should be classified as a deadly weapon.

Bingley and Fitzwilliam suppressed grins of their own at Darcy's reaction.

~A~

Chapter 19

The highly anticipated ball was only two days away and all the ladies in the area were busily preparing their gowns and accessories.

Miss Bingley was no exception. She ensured that her best ballgown was ready for the event. While she cared not whether the locals were going to be impressed by her ensemble, she wanted to be a credit to Mr Darcy when he opened the ball with her.

Although she was getting somewhat frustrated as he had not yet requested the first set from her, she kept reassuring herself that he was possibly taking it for granted that they would dance that set together.

Her hopes were dashed as she passed the open door of the library after dinner and heard the teasing voice of Colonel Fitzwilliam, 'Well Darcy, only two more days and you will be able to dance not only the first but also the supper set with the delightful Mrs Brooks. Should I speak to the musicians and bribe them into playing a waltz for the supper set?'

'That will not be necessary, and I suspect it would only be counterproductive since I do not believe the lady would be prepared to be manhandled. I prefer to have the opportunity to dance both dances with the lady,' Darcy replied casually.

Caroline could hear her brother sigh. 'Pity. I had considered arranging for a waltz myself, but I would not wish to be responsible for suspending your pleasure, particularly as you seem to have lost your customary reserve since arriving in Hertfordshire.'

'Well, what can I say, Bingley. For the first time in years, I do not feel like prey, and it is mostly thanks to Mrs Brooks.'

'Perhaps Caroline will get her wish and we will be brothers, although not in the way she hopes,' Bingley said dreamily as he considered the wonderful personality of Miss Bennet.

As Caroline could not hear Mr Darcy denying the suggestion, only Fitzwilliam's amused chuckle at his cousin's embarrassed expression, she panicked.

After all these years of her campaign to become Mrs Darcy, she would ensure that Charles and Mr Darcy would become brothers... but on *her* terms.

~A~

Darcy woke up with a pounding headache and feeling much too warm. He carefully opened his eyes and was relieved that the light in his bedroom was dim.

As he became more aware of his surroundings, he realized that most of the heat was at his back. On investigation he discovered that the heat source was in the shape of a female form... a nude female form; a fact which he established by reaching behind him and only encountering the feeling of soft skin.

He closed his eyes again with a groan, hoping that this was just a bad dream.

The groan had alerted his bedpartner to his wakeful state, and she whispered, 'Good morning, my love.'

As he had feared, the voice belonged to Miss Bingley.

'I need to speak to your brother.' Grateful to be wearing his nightshirt, he got out of bed and strode to his dressing room without a backward glance.

~A~

Two hours later, Darcy was ensconced in the study with a smug Miss Bingley and a bewildered and bleary-eyed Charles Bingley.

Darcy observed the siblings and came to a decision.

He addressed Bingley. 'I must tell you that when I woke up this morning, your sister was in my bed.' Darcy held up his hand before Bingley could do more than open his mouth.

'I need you to know that I do not remember the latter part of last evening or the night, which leads me to believe that I was drugged, since the last thing I do remember clearly was congratulating myself on

138

having had only two glasses of wine all evening despite everyone urging me to consume more.'

While Miss Bingley's countenance remained bland her brother looked terrified at that statement. 'What are you saying?'

'I believe your sister drugged me and then let herself into my room and climbed into bed with me. I would most certainly never invite her.'

'But do you not keep the door to your room locked…' Bingley was struggling to come to grips with the tale. Could his sister truly be that desperate to marry Darcy?

'Since she was the mistress of your house, she had all the keys until you replaced her with Mrs Hurst. I would not be at all surprised if she had held back the key to my room during the change, allowing her access to importune me at her leisure.'

'That is not a nice thing to say about your fiancée, Mr Darcy,' purred Caroline, unconcerned about the implied insult since she knew that she had the upper hand.

'I am simply stating facts,' Darcy replied coldly. 'But since I am a gentleman, even if you are no lady, I am prepared to marry you… but there are certain conditions.'

While Caroline beamed at the statement, Bingley gave his friend a worried but grateful look. 'Thank you, Darcy. You are a true friend.'

'Not at all,' Darcy said ambiguously. 'Now that we have established how this situation came about, I thought it a good idea if I explained to you what will happen going forward.' He indulged in a wolfish smile.

Caroline thought that grin was caused due to the anticipation Darcy felt for intimacies with her. 'I know just how it will be. In one month, we will have a grand wedding in St George's on Hanover Square, after which we will go on a wedding tour for a month before returning to London and enjoying the season. At the end of the season, we will retreat to Pemberley for the summer, and I shall greatly enjoy hosting a ball during the houseparty for all our dearest friends,' Caroline declared in raptures.

'You are incorrect on all counts.' Darcy replied as his grin widened even further. 'We will marry no earlier than a year from now in Scotland where you will spend the intervening period on one of my estates.'

'Why do you want to wait a whole year? What if Caroline is with child after last night?' exclaimed Bingley in confusion. Although he was grateful that Darcy was prepared to marry Caroline, the delay seemed counter to the reason for marrying in the circumstances. And even though Caroline was... difficult, she was still his sister and he wanted to protect her.

'I am insisting on this period because I am certain that I was incapable of rising to the occasion, not only because I was drugged but because I could not do so if completely sober... at least not with your sister.'

Miss Bingley coloured, although at the moment no one cared if it was in embarrassment of the topic raised, or in anger at the not so very subtle insult.

'But I still do not understand why that long a delay, especially if nothing happened?' Bingley asked ignoring the slight.

'To ensure that if she is expecting, I will not give my name to another man's child. Only a Darcy will inherit Pemberley. If a child arrives within eight months, there will not be a wedding, as I refuse to accept soiled goods.'

Both Bingley siblings blanched at his words.

'B-b-but...' stammered Bingley. Surely Caroline would not...

'I am not at all eager to be married to your sister, but if it needs to be done, I will ensure that there is no cuckoo in my nest. I also will not allow her to use the occasion to lord it over anyone. There will not be the slightest fuss. This wedding will occur in complete obscurity. She may only be attended by you and your sister but no one else will be present.'

Distracted from the length of the engagement period and other conditions, Caroline asked, 'But surely, you would not deny me a society wedding as the proper introduction to the ton.'

'There is no need to introduce you to society,' Darcy claimed, and Caroline was mollified by the statement as her fiancé seemed to imply that all of society already knew her. She was shocked when he continued, 'Since it would be a great embarrassment to acknowledge you as my wife, you will never again appear in society.'

'WHAT? You cannot mean to keep me cloistered at Pemberley!'

'Certainly not,' said Darcy and Caroline heaved a sigh of relief until he added, 'as I will not allow you to pollute the shades of Pemberley with your presence. Immediately after the wedding ceremony, you will return to my Scottish estate and only I will return to Pemberley.'

'You expect me to remain at your estate in Scotland?' Her voice was getting shriller with every word.

Yes.'

'By myself?'

'Yes.'

'But what shall I do there?'

'I care not.'

'How long do you expect me to languish in the wilderness?'

'For the rest of your life.'

'You cannot mean that. As your wife I have the right to be the mistress of your estates,' cried Caroline, now thoroughly worried.

'As my wife you are my property and must obey me. If I decide that you shall spend the rest of your life in isolation, then that is what you must do.'

'That is not fair!'

'It is the law,' Darcy sneered. 'Consider yourself fortunate that I am not a violent man. According to the law I could beat you within an inch of your life every single day and no one could object to it... least of all you.'

'Why would you be so cruel to me?'

'Because I have not the slightest intention of rewarding you for your abhorrent behaviour.'

'But I do not wish to spend my life in what is effectively a prison.'

'You should have thought of that before you drugged me and forced your way into my bed.'

'But I only did that so that you would marry me and let me take my rightful place in society.'

Bingley had sat and listened in growing horror as his friend explained to his sister the terrible fate which awaited her. He wondered if Darcy was trying to convince Caroline to withdraw her demand that he should marry her by painting the most appalling picture of her future. He was still wondering about Darcy's intentions when he was even more shocked at what his sister seemed to be confessing.

In that moment, he stopped wondering and his sympathies swung completely into Darcy's favour. 'Caroline, are you admitting that you engineered this compromise to force Darcy to marry you? He did not invite you to his rooms?'

Miss Bingley realised that she had inadvertently given herself away and tried to show her actions in a better light. 'You know how shy Mr Darcy is around ladies. I knew that he wanted me as his wife but was only too nervous to ask me. So, I thought to help him along.'

Bingley shook his head as he considered his sister. 'Based on his reaction, you misjudged his interest. Whether you did so deliberately after I told you he would never offer for you or because you fooled yourself into thinking he liked you is beside the point...'

He trailed off as another thought occurred to him. 'Caroline, is there any merit to Darcy's fear that you might be with child from another man? Is that why you took such a desperate action?'

Caroline turned scarlet and could not meet her brother's eyes.

~A~

'WHO WAS HE?' Bingley roared and startled his sister into raising her eyes to meet his glare.

'His name is George Wickham,' she whispered, cowed into revealing the truth by the ferocious look with which her brother held her spellbound.

'Wickham!' exclaimed Darcy.

His interruption caused the siblings to turn to him. 'I gather you know him?' asked Bingley.

'I most certainly do.'

'Indeed, since you are the cause for his misfortunes,' spat Caroline.

Darcy collapsed back into his chair roaring with laughter. 'Wickham is the architect of his own misfortunes. He is the worst gambler ever to frequent the gaming hells of London where he squandered the bequest from my father as well as the money, I paid him in lieu of the living which he did not want.'

'What money?'

'The three thousand pounds he requested since he did not wish to take orders and become a respected clergyman.'

'You paid him for the living?'

'I most certainly did and with the greatest of pleasure. A libertine such as he should not be inflicted on the congregation of Kympton.' Darcy smirked. 'I gather he forgot to mention that little detail. While he is an atrocious gambler, he is an expert liar.'

Caroline ignored the sarcastic comment. 'But he seemed like such a gentleman.'

'If you liked him that much, why did you not marry him?' asked Bingley who was getting tired of the distractions. 'Especially since...' he looked at her midsection.

'I wanted to marry him when I thought him a wealthy gentleman. But then I found out that he was only the son of Mr Darcy's steward. You cannot possibly expect me to marry a servant.'

'Did he ask you to marry him?' Darcy asked. 'I expect that Wickham would have been delighted to marry you for your dowry.'

'Well, not in so many words, but he did say that he would like to, but he could not keep me in the style to which I am accustomed because you had cheated him out of his inheritance.'

'Let me guess, when he discovered that despite giving up your virtue to him, he could not induce you to marry him and hand over your dowry, he then suggested that you should compromise me into marrying you. After the wedding he would be your devoted lover as long as you kept him well supplied with money.' Darcy chuckled mirthlessly. 'I suppose he was not quite so blunt, but I would bet that was the gist of Wickham's plan.'

Seeing Caroline's embarrassed reaction to Darcy's words, Bingley briefly covered his face with his hands while he shook his head. After a moment he dropped his hands. 'Darcy, please accept my apology for the embarrassment you have suffered. Would you mind giving us some privacy. Caroline and I have to discuss her future... which of course does not include you.'

'I accept your apology. I only hope that you can arrange things to avoid a scandal. I would not wish Miss Bennet to be embarrassed by your sister.'

'Oh, lord, I had not even considered that complication,' groaned Bingley as Darcy left the study.

~A~

Darcy requested a passing servant to deliver coffee to the library, where he went to wait for the uproar to die down.

He encountered his cousin lounging by the fire. 'Where have you been all morning?' Fitzwilliam enquired.

'There has been a misunderstanding which needed to be cleared up.'

'What misunderstanding?'

Darcy considered for a moment but as he was now certain that Miss Bingley would be evicted from Netherfield, he thought it advisable to inform his cousin of the circumstances to ensure he would not ask too many awkward questions. 'This needs to stay confidential...' he began.

~A~

As a result of the conversation between Bingley and his sister, Caroline was locked in her room until after the ball.

Bingley informed Darcy that once he had the leisure to do so, he planned to take his sister to London, find George Wickham and get him to marry Caroline.

Knowing how slippery Wickham was, Darcy offered the use of his estate in Scotland if Caroline's paramour could not be found.

~A~

Chapter 20

Jane and Mary each donated their second-best evening gowns to their youngest sisters, as these dresses needed the least modifications to fit the girls.

As they were trying on the dresses, Mrs Taylor suggested to the sisters, 'You know Catherine, your sister Elizabeth and I had thought to allow you to come out several months ago. Do you think now is the time to do so?'

Kitty was obviously torn as she looked between her governess and Lydia. 'Well...'

Mrs Taylor was exceedingly proud when Lydia said to her older sister, 'Kitty, I know you delayed so that I would not feel left out. But this ball is too good an event for you to miss out on.' She grinned impishly. 'And if you are dancing, I get more attention from the handsome Colonel.'

Kitty blushed with pleasure and threw her arms about Lydia. 'Thank you for understanding.'

'Do not worry. It will be my time soon enough. And given the conversation with Lizzy the other day, I am not in a hurry to lose my independence.'

'Considering Lizzy's experience, I am not at all sure I want to get married either, but I would like the opportunity to dance and have fun,' Kitty replied with a grateful smile.

Kitty and Lydia spent the intervening days each embroidering a fichu in complementary colours, which would be used to make the gowns suitably modest for younger girls.

Mrs Taylor refreshed a gown she had worn to the last ball to which she had escorted Miss Thompson as her companion. The rich dark blue complemented her eyes, causing Kitty and Lydia to view their governess in a new light.

As they were getting ready to leave for Netherfield, Lydia, in her usual forthright manner, tilted her head as she appraised Mrs Taylor and said, 'I had never noticed it before, but you are an exceptionally handsome lady.'

Mrs Taylor smiled and graciously accepted the compliment in the spirit it was given. The ladies carefully deposed themselves in the carriage to minimise wrinkling their gowns and the party set off to enjoy their evening.

~A~

The receiving line at Netherfield consisted only of Bingley and the Hursts, who greeted their guests warmly.

As they welcomed the party from Longbourn, Elizabeth informed them, 'Mr Bingley, we had a slight change in plans and Catherine has decided that she is ready to come out into society. She will therefore be permitted to dance.'

Bingley immediately understood the implied request and asked Kitty for the fourth set, for which he did not yet have a partner.

As other guests were arriving, they moved to the ballroom where they were greeted by Darcy, who was standing just inside the door, near his cousin.

At the instigation of Bingley, Mrs Hurst had arranged for a table and several chairs to be set up in a position to provide the best view of the activities. Being near the door, Lydia would be able to greet friends without leaving her companions.

While greetings were exchanged with friends who had arrived earlier, Elizabeth took the opportunity to take Darcy aside a few steps. 'Mr Darcy, might I ask you for a favour?'

'Certainly, dear lady, what can I do for you?'

'Catherine has decided to take advantage of this ball as her coming out. Unfortunately, since we are rather short of gentlemen in our family, she has no one with whom to dance the first set, and I wondered if...'

'You wish me to dance the first set with your sister?'

'Indeed, if you would be so kind?'

'And with whom shall you dance?'

'I shall be quite content to watch Catherine enjoy herself. And if you stand up with her for the first set, I believe she shall not lack for dance partners for the rest of the evening.'

Darcy felt torn. He had looked forward to dancing with Elizabeth but on consideration it was probably wiser to only dance once with the lady. 'Very well, I am honoured that you are asking me to stand in loco parentis to your sister, who is not so very much older than my own. But I hope that you do not expect me to abdicate the supper set to anyone else,' he added with a teasing smile.

'No, Mr Darcy. I am selfish enough to look forward to that set and intelligent conversation during supper.'

'I shall do my best to entertain you,' Darcy replied.

Kitty was astonished and rather flustered when Darcy requested to open the ball with her. 'But were you not planning to dance with Lizzy?'

'Catherine, at your first ball you should dance the first set. Since our father is not here to dance with you, Mr Darcy has agreed to do the honours.'

'It will be good practice for me for when my sister comes out and attends her first ball,' the gentleman explained with an encouraging smile.

'And do not forget, I will have plenty of opportunity to dance later,' Elizabeth reassured her sister.

'Thank you, Lizzy. I appreciate you giving up this set for me. I know how much you looked forward to it,' Kitty said innocently before turning to Darcy. 'Thank you, Mr Darcy, I would be honoured to dance the first set with you,' Kitty said and curtsied prettily.

Elizabeth was grateful that the attention was off her, as she blushed and hoped that Mr Darcy had missed the import of that comment.

Her hope was in vain, as Darcy did indeed hear that comment, but wisely chose not to embarrass Elizabeth further and pretended not to have heard.

~A~

Kitty did indeed cause quite a stir when Darcy led her to the dance floor for the first set and Elizabeth was proven correct since her sister danced virtually every set afterwards.

Charlotte, who also did not have a dance partner, came to speak to Elizabeth. 'It is very generous of you to forgo dancing with that delightful gentleman,' she teased her friend.

'What makes you think that I would have danced the first set with him?'

'Because he always dances with you first before any other lady has a chance.'

'Well, since tonight is a formal ball with supper, I have agreed to dance the supper set with the gentleman,' Elizabeth replied without mentioning her other plans.

Charlotte nodded knowingly. 'I should have realised. Given the choice of a single set, since you never dance twice with a gentleman, Mr Darcy wisely chose the one which would give him the most time with you.'

'I confess that I find it most agreeable to have the opportunity of intelligent conversation with a friend while having supper,' Elizabeth agreed casually. Too casually in her friend's opinion.

~A~

When Jane and Bingley started their first set together, Jane who had noted an absence asked, 'Is not your sister joining us tonight?'

'I am afraid that Caroline is busy packing for her departure on the morrow. It appears that the country air does not agree with her,' Bingley replied evasively.

'It is a shame that she should not find the country to her liking. But I suppose that not everyone is suited to the quiet life we lead.'

'Whereas I cannot think of any place I would rather be than right here,' Bingley said with a smile as he truly wished he could remain at Netherfield in the company of Miss Bennet forever.

He shook himself out of the reverie caused by gazing into the eyes of his most charming partner. 'Unfortunately, I shall have to leave your enchanting company for a few days, since tomorrow I shall have to escort my sister to London and make arrangements for her future wellbeing.'

'Will you be gone for long?'

'Hopefully I will see Caroline well settled within a week or so. After that I shall be most eager to return to... Netherfield,' Bingley replied with a pause as he decided which identity to use and opting for the more innocuous one. But then he could not resist to ask, 'Shall you miss me?'

'Of course, I shall miss... both you and your sister.'

Bingley heard the hesitation and smiled mischievously as he said, 'I am sure my sister will be pleased to be missed,' eliciting a merry laugh from Jane.

~A~

Lydia had a surprisingly pleasant evening. As she was sitting with Mrs Taylor, some of the youngest girls who were allowed to attend the ball came and sat with her. Their parents relieved of chaperonage for a brief period took to the dance floor themselves.

Since Mary was quieter than her other sisters, she did not attract quite as many dance partners, but was pleased when John Lucas asked for her supper set as well as the last set for the evening.

Any time the sisters were not dancing, they joined the group sitting with Lydia and Mrs Taylor. Colonel Fitzwilliam entertained them with sanitised versions of his heroics, told in his inimitably droll fashion.

He was heard to say that he felt like a thorn surrounded by roses, but he too appeared to be having a delightful evening.

~A~

At last, it was time for the supper set. Darcy had sat out the previous set, after having danced once with each of the other Bennet sisters and once with Charlotte Lucas.

Lady Lucas wondered if her daughter might have a chance with the gentleman as they seemed to be on friendly terms and tonight, he had danced with her daughter but not yet with Elizabeth. Her hopes flew out the window as Darcy led Elizabeth to the dance floor for the supper set.

'Are you enjoying your evening, Mr Darcy?' asked Elizabeth when their first dance allowed conversation.

'I am, indeed, Mrs Brooks. I find the company here in Hertfordshire exceedingly delightful.'

'I am pleased to hear you say so. I must also thank you for dancing with Catherine earlier. Your example has inspired quite a number of gentlemen to request dances from her.'

'I am pleased to have been of service. I hope that my sister will have an equally as pleasant a time when it is her turn, although I fear that London society is not as gentle.'

'Perhaps you should consider bringing her out locally in your neighbourhood before exposing her to the pitfalls of London.'

'I would gladly do so, but due to my reticence I know hardly anyone around Pemberley,' he confessed.

'You do not know your neighbours?' Elizabeth asked in shock.

Darcy gave her a chagrined smile as he said, 'Only a very few. I do not have the gift of making friends or even acquaintances on my own. I believe that the last few weeks I have come to know more people than in the ten years prior.'

'Oh, dear. That is a conundrum,' Elizabeth said as she shook her head. After a moment, her expression brightened. 'I know just what you should do. If you are so inclined, why not bring your sister to Netherfield. You said yourself that you know more people here than in Derbyshire...'

Darcy's smile answered hers as he said, 'I think it a wonderful idea. I believe that my sister would be delighted to meet you and your sisters if you would allow an introduction.'

'I would be most pleased to meet your sister and I am certain that my own sisters will feel the same way.'

Having settled that subject, they finished the rest of the dance in comfortable silence.

When the music for the second dance of the set started, they received a surprise.

Despite his preoccupation with Jane, Bingley had not missed that Darcy was dancing with Kitty during the first set. Thinking to help his friend despite his denial, he talked to the musicians and had arranged a small change. In response to his request, they started to play a waltz.

Darcy was startled to hear the music and asked Elizabeth, 'Do you know the steps to the waltz?'

She looked unhappy as she replied, 'Yes, I do know the steps, but I am not comfortable to dance the waltz.'

'In that case, would you prefer to sit down?' Darcy asked, hoping she would say no but fearing that she would say yes.

His fears were justified. 'I am sorry, Mr Darcy but yes, I would prefer to sit out this dance.'

'Of course,' he said and offered his arm with a bow. As they made their way to the table with the rest of their party, which at present consisted only of the Colonel, Mrs Taylor and Lydia, Darcy shot a withering look at Bingley, whose sly grin turned to chagrin when he realised that he had miscalculated.

'Does your sister not like to waltz?' Bingley asked Jane.

'No, she does not.'

'Whyever not? I think it is a most delightful dance,' protested Bingley.

Jane smiled sadly. 'You know nothing about my sister, otherwise you would not ask this question.'

'You are obviously correct, but you have not answered my question,' he persisted.

'Mr Bingley, Elizabeth believes that the waltz is a dance for couples. Since she is not interested in being part of a couple, she does not wish to dance the waltz.'

'Not interested in being part of a couple? Are you saying that Mrs Brooks has no interest in… ah… potential marriage?' Bingley just barely prevented himself from naming Darcy, but he thought it diplomatic not to do so.

'Precisely,' Jane answered.

'Oh…'

They spoke no more for the rest of the dance, but the enjoyment had gone out of the occasion for Bingley as he realised that his good intentions had probably hurt his friend.

~A~

Despite the problem about the waltz, everyone's mood lifted over supper.

Elizabeth and her sisters, along with their dance partners from the supper set, occupied one of the tables set up in the dining room.

Bingley apologised for the last-minute change to the program. 'I had not realised that not everyone loves the waltz.'

Darcy smiled in resigned fashion and explained to their companions, 'My friend is the most amiable person I know, and he finds it difficult to believe that not everyone is as good natured as he and does not love all that he does.' He shot a sideways glance at Bingley and teased, 'You should have heard him on occasion urging me to dance when I was not in a mood to be pleased by anything.'

'I find it difficult to believe,' said Elizabeth. 'Not the part where you said Mr Bingley is most amiable, but your claim that you do not like to dance. I have never noticed such a reluctance.'

The Colonel interjected, 'You have never seen Darcy at a ball in London.' He then proceeded to regale his audience with stories about Darcy's reluctance to participate in social activities.

After a while, the others managed to divert him, and conversation was lively and ranged over a variety of topics.

The rest of the evening was pleasant for everyone concerned, but eventually they had to say goodnight and return to their homes.

~A~

Chapter 21

Darcy woke at his usual time but instead of immediately getting up he stayed abed thinking about the previous evening.

He had surprised even himself at the anger he felt towards Bingley when he was denied his second dance with Elizabeth, although sitting out that dance had allowed him further conversation with the lady. But this reaction caused him some concern.

In the stillness of the morning, he had time to think about it and he came to the conclusion that he was in serious danger of falling hopelessly in love with Elizabeth. Despite the lady being everything delightful, and as a landowner whose estate had been in her family for generations making her quite eligible, he still had reservations about how a relationship with the lady would affect Georgiana.

After an hour of soul-searching, he decided that he needed to get some distance from Elizabeth to be able to think clearly, as her mere presence made him want to forget about the duty which he owed his family.

To that end he thought it best if he accompanied Bingley to London, albeit not sharing a carriage with him and Miss Bingley.

This course of action also had the advantage that, as he knew Wickham better than anyone else, he had a greater chance of tracking down the scoundrel.

~A~

Having made his decision, he rose and ordered his belongings to be packed before going in search of Bingley and his cousin.

While Bingley was still catching up on sleep after his late night, Richard was already having breakfast. Since Mrs Taylor had taken Lydia back to Longbourn after supper, the Colonel had no more reason to remain at the ball and had sought his bed at a reasonable hour.

Once Darcy had filled his plate and joined his cousin at the table, he said without preamble, 'I have decided to go to London to help Bingley find Wickham.'

'So, you are running away.'

Darcy sighed and shook his head. 'I need time to clear my head. I thought that once Bingley's problems are sorted out, I will take Georgiana to Pemberley for Christmas. I think we could both do with some peace and quiet. Apart from that, I have been away for too long, I really need to attend to several issues in person.'

'How long are you planning to stay at Pemberley?' Despite his often irreverent attitude, Richard sympathised with his cousin. He knew the amount of responsibility resting on Darcy's shoulders and how conscientious his cousin was about duty. Although on occasions Richard was known to prod Darcy to get him to consider his own happiness for a change, rather than always putting everyone else before himself, this time he held his peace.

Darcy gave him a grateful smile for being supportive. 'I will be back in time to visit Rosings at Easter. I promised Anne to continue my assistance with the estate.' He had another bite before he asked, 'What are your plans?'

'If Bingley is willing to put me up a while longer, I will stay here. Now that Caroline is no longer a problem, I find that Hurst is staying sober for much longer periods and is quite good company.'

'I suppose having congenial neighbours has nothing to do with your decision.'

'That is simply a delightful bonus.'

'In that case, since I thought to let Bingley use my carriage to return to London, I shall leave you here to recuperate and if you like, I will send my small carriage back with him for your use.'

'Thank you. I would appreciate having my own transport.'

~A~

Since Darcy did not wish to see Caroline Bingley, he set out on his favourite horse before she made an appearance.

He had timed his departure to allow him to call at Longbourn at a reasonable hour, to make his farewells to the ladies... one lady in particular.

Upon his arrival, Mr Hill took him immediately to the library, where Elizabeth sat, reading a letter. She looked up and greeted him with a smile. 'Good morning, Mr Darcy. I have just received a letter from your cousin, Miss de Bourgh. She writes that she would be most happy to exchange experiences with another lady landowner.'

'I am pleased that I was able to facilitate this exchange,' replied Darcy with an answering smile.

'But you did not come to discuss my correspondence.'

'No, I did not. I am afraid that since family business is calling me back to London, I have come to say farewell.'

'Oh. Will you remain in London for long?'

'Probably only for a few days and then I will take my sister to Pemberley for a few months.' Seeing that Elizabeth tried to hide her disappointment, he explained, 'I have been gone from my estate for too long. While I thought that Bingley would need my assistance, I was prepared to stay, but since many of his neighbours, you foremost amongst them, are willing and able to provide advice, I can return to my own duties.'

'Of course, Mr Darcy, I quite understand. But I hope you will not take it amiss if I say that you shall be missed... by everyone. You have made many friends in the short time you were amongst us.'

'I too shall miss the friends I have made, although I hope to visit sometime next year.'

'I shall look forward to your visit.'

As they were both getting somewhat tongue-tied, Darcy hurried to say goodbye, feeling curiously reluctant to leave.

~A~

During their return to London, Caroline Bingley sat listlessly in Darcy's carriage looking out the window without seeing the changing landscape.

Her mind was busy remembering how she had arrived in this situation.

During August she had received an invitation to attend a houseparty at the beginning of September given by Mr and Mrs Grantley, the parents of one of her friends from the seminary she had attended. Since Charles had been busy with some business with the solicitors, she was accompanied only by her maid.

During the visit she had met several pleasant young gentlemen. While none of them were truly of the first circles, one or two were younger sons and the rest had all appeared to be wealthy members of the gentry. The most outstanding amongst them was Mr George Wickham. He was charming, intelligent and oh so handsome. He had been quite the favourite amongst all the ladies, but he seemed to be most interested in herself.

It was such a welcome change after the excessively proper civility she had endured from Mr Darcy for all the years that she had known him. Mr Wickham had been most attentive, and Caroline had felt flattered. It did not take long until she was completely besotted with the gentleman.

She was still uncertain of exactly how it had happened, but one convivial evening, when she had perhaps consumed more wine than was good for her, Mr Wickham had ended up in her bed. He was still most considerate the next morning and she had hopes of an advantageous marriage, until she discovered George's background.

At that point she realised that he had singled her out for her connection to Mr Darcy. While she was angry to start with, the charming rogue soon convinced her that between them they had the makings for a perfect future.

Unfortunately, Mr Darcy had proven to be too intelligent and suspicious. Now she was in the unenviable position of being taken to London for a potentially forced marriage at best or being sent into exile at worst.

Neither future appealed to her. She was still in low spirits when they arrived in London in the late afternoon.

~A~

The Bingley siblings had risen early because Bingley was determined to make an immediate start in finding Wickham. After weeks of being drilled in responsibility, he was at last starting to grow up and he was determined that he would no longer allow Caroline to dictate his actions.

They had barely finished their morning meal and adjourned to the drawing room when an unexpected visitor was announced, 'Mr Wickham, Lord of Winsten Castle, to see Miss Bingley.'

Bingley turned to his sister who gasped at the announcement as the colour drained from her face.

'What do you know about this?' he demanded.

'Nothing. I had not expected to see him until I was settled at Pemberley,' whispered Caroline, startled into honesty.

'Well, since it saves me the trouble of finding him, I will see him now.' Bingley turned to the butler. 'Show Mr Wickham in.'

~A~

Wickham entered the room and immediately upon spying Miss Bingley, he burst into speech.

The first words which came from his lips astounded his audience. 'Please, Miss Bingley, tell me that you are not engaged to Darcy.'

'I am not engaged to Mr Darcy,' answered Caroline in confusion.

'Thank heavens. I feared that I was too late.' Once he had that answer, he appeared to relax and turned to Bingley. 'Please forgive my impulsive behaviour, but I had to know if there was still a chance I could offer for Miss Bingley.'

Bingley shook his head in confusion at this most unprecedented behaviour. Taking refuge in custom to gain some time, he requested his sister to make the introductions.

Once the formalities had been completed and they all took seats, Bingley asked his sister, 'Is this *the* Mr Wickham?'

'Yes, Charles.'

'The one with whom you conspired to trap Darcy?'

'You know about this? Oh, my lord, do not tell me that you went ahead with that harebrained scheme,' Wickham exclaimed as he paled.

Caroline's eyes flashed as she replied heatedly, 'I did not have a choice as I missed my courses last month.'

Wickham briefly closed his eyes as he grimaced. 'I hope he did not hurt you?'

'No, he did not as he was insensible all night and, in the morning, he would not even look at me.'

'That is the priggish Darcy we all know and love.' Wickham said in relief until the meaning of Caroline's earlier statement penetrated. 'Are you saying that you are with child?' he asked.

'I suspected that I might be. Mr Darcy suspected the same thing, which is why he refused to marry me.' Before Wickham could comment further on her condition, she added, 'Although as of last night, I am now certain that it was a false alarm.'

Wickham was smiling broadly as he said, 'I am pleased beyond measure that you are still available.' He glanced briefly at Bingley but considering what they had already discussed so freely, he decided to ignore the man and asked, 'Since that is the case, would you consent to marry me instead? I know that I do not have the position or the connections, but I would very much like you to be my wife.'

Before Caroline had a chance to answer, Bingley asked suspiciously, 'What brought about this change of character? I was given to understand that you are a scoundrel and a wastrel who leaves debts and spoiled women behind on a regular basis.'

'Ever since you and more particularly Miss Bingley moved to the country, my luck changed.' Wickham chuckled and shrugged. 'They say that you can be lucky at cards or lucky in love. All my life I was lucky with the ladies, but I was losing money hand over fist whenever I touched cards.'

Wickham was sporting a grimace of chagrin as he said to Caroline, 'Then I met you. After you left for Hertfordshire, for the first time in my life I surprised myself by missing someone. The more I missed you, the more I won at cards. I have had two months of the most unbelievable run of luck.' He paused to emphasise the next point. 'I won in excess of one hundred thousand pounds.'

'How much?' gasped both Bingleys.

'You heard correctly. But that was not all. Last week I was playing against Carruthers and on the last hand he bet an estate which had been in his family for the last eighty years.'

'You won an estate?'

'It is only a small one and the income from it is less than a thousand pounds, but it does come with an unusual clause... The owner is called the Lord of Winsten Castle.' Wickham smiled his most beatific smile as he turned back to Caroline. 'His wife is known as the Lady of Winsten Castle. Does that sound like a title you would enjoy?'

'Lady of Winsten Castle,' Caroline repeated dreamily. 'Yes, I would like that excessively.'

'In that case, would you do me the honour and marry me?'

'But why would you suddenly want to marry me?' Caroline asked in confusion.

'Because I understand you and I feel like you understand me. We are both mercenary. While most people would be horrified, I like that about you since with you I do not have to pretend to be... noble.'

Wickham did not mention that he had also enjoyed her enthusiasm in their amorous activities, although his heated gaze roaming over her figure reminded her of those occasions. Caroline had shown a great deal of native talent in that aspect, which had been so very different from the fumblings of the young girls Wickham used to seduce.

Caroline stared open mouthed at Wickham for several very long moments. Suddenly her expression softened, and a small laugh escaped her as she realised that for once in her life a man liked her for herself even though she was considerably less than perfect. It was a heady feeling, and, in that moment, all her ambitions flew out the window.

'In that case, I would love to marry you,' she said with a beaming smile which was answered in equal measure by Wickham.

Bingley sat off to one side, shaking his head in consternation. Having steeled himself to deal firmly with his sister and her lover, discovering that his new resolve was unnecessary was quite frustrating.

~A~

Bingley was still coming to terms with the new situation, when yet another visitor was announced, and a moment later Darcy strode into the room.

'Bingley, I had an idea how to find...' Darcy trailed off, seeing his quarry sitting comfortably near Miss Bingley and holding her hand.

As he stared in open-mouthed wonder at the apparition, Miss Bingley sat up straighter and announced with a smug smile, 'Mr Darcy, I believe that you know my fiancé, Mr George Wickham, Lord of Winsten Castle.'

'Lord what?' exclaimed Darcy.

'Lord of Winsten Castle,' said Wickham as he rose to his feet. His smile echoed that of Caroline, but with more amusement. 'It is good to see you, Darcy. I am glad that you stopped by. I have been meaning to give you this,' he said as he reached into his coat and retrieved an envelope which he handed to Darcy.

Darcy accepted it without thinking and kept staring at the tableau.

'Are you not going to open it?' prompted Wickham.

Coming to his senses again, Darcy looked at the envelope and reluctantly opened it. When he retrieved the enclosure, he gasped. 'This is a bank draft for three thousand pounds!' he exclaimed.

Wickham shrugged negligently. 'That was my best estimate of the debts you have bought up over the years. Let me know if I still owe you more. I do not want you to be out of pocket on my behalf.'

Smiling to himself Wickham thought that it was worth the money to see Darcy's expression which was composed of a mixture of disbelief, horror, and consternation.

Bingley took pity on his friend and after sending for coffee, proceeded to explain the happenings of the morning.

~A~

Chapter 22

Bingley was kept busy with his solicitor over the next few days arranging the marriage contract, after Darcy helped Wickham apply for a common licence on the first day.

Having had long conversations with Jane as well as Elizabeth, Bingley had learnt a great deal about entails. How they were generally created so that an owner could not sell the estate to cover debts and not even use the estate as collateral for a mortgage. To safeguard Caroline and her future children, Bingley insisted on Wickham creating an entail. But unlike the one at Longbourn, Winsten Castle could be inherited by the eldest daughter if there was no son.

Or, if a tragedy occurred and they had no surviving children, the estate could be inherited by a son of Caroline's siblings, who did not have an estate. The entail went on to detail alternatives if those conditions could not be met.

Caroline's marriage settlement was her own dowry of twenty thousand pounds plus another fifty thousand supplied by Wickham, which Bingley insisted upon, remembering that Wickham was an inveterate gambler. The interest on Caroline's dowry was to be her pin money, and the interest on the other amount was intended for the couple's living expenses.

Wickham was torn between amusement and anger at the conditions set in place for his marriage. But whenever his anger threatened to become dominant, he reminded himself that Bingley was aware of his previous financial problems caused by his gambling.

The amounts which Bingley stipulated were based on the fact that while Wickham had won more than one hundred thousand pounds, the story of his success had spread, and all his creditors had come to call and collect the debts he owed. Having suddenly more money than he ever dreamed of having, Wickham had paid up, wanting the chance to live long enough to enjoy his newfound wealth and wife.

Bingley's knowledge and experience with contracts were a great boon in these proceedings. During all those negotiations, on occasion Wickham was heard to mutter, 'Darcy, you have much to answer for, providing too much information to your friend.'

Exactly one week after Wickham's proposal, he and Caroline were married. Bingley stood up with his sister while Darcy did so for Wickham.

'I just wanted to make certain that you did not weasel out of this,' Darcy told the groom just before his bride walked up the aisle on Bingley's arm in their local church.

Again, it was not the society wedding for which Caroline had hoped but at least she had the satisfaction to read the announcement of her wedding in the paper.

Mr Charles Bingley of Netherfield Park in Hertfordshire is pleased to announce the wedding of his sister, Miss Caroline Bingley to Mr George Wickham, Lord of Winsten Castle. All their families and friends are pleased to wish every happiness to the Lord and Lady of Winsten Castle.

Immediately after the ceremony, said Lord and Lady of Winsten Castle, departed to take up residence in their new home.

~A~

'Thank heavens that went off without a hitch,' sighed Darcy as he collapsed into a chair in his study.

Bingley wholeheartedly agreed. 'Until they signed the register, I too was afraid that Wickham would change his mind.'

Darcy gave his friend a look full of chagrin. 'I, on the other hand, was afraid that your sister would remember that I had offered to marry her if she was not with child.'

'You worried for no reason, my friend. Not only was Caroline not going to miss the opportunity of being addressed as My Lady, but she also had no wish to languish in the wilds of Scotland for the rest of her natural life.' Bingley laughed as he added, 'I did not get a chance at the time to congratulate you on your clever ploy.'

'While I abhor that under the law women have no rights once they are married, on occasion there are advantages to those rules. They are usually enough to convince a lady that my greeting her politely does not constitute a compromise or a proposal of marriage.'

Bingley did not know how to respond to that comment, so he changed the subject. 'What are your plans now?'

'On Monday Georgiana and I will return to Pemberley until the spring. And what are your plans? When you return to Netherfield will you be courting or proposing to Miss Bennet?'

'I will indeed. I have never before met a lady whose kindness and compassion exceeded hers.'

'Not to mention her beauty,' teased Darcy.

Bingley smiled and shook his head. 'While her beauty is undeniable, it is her personality which has captured my interest. It is a pity that you will not be able to spend Christmas with us. I confess that I am curious to meet Miss Bennet's relations who will be joining the ladies for the festive season.'

Darcy squirmed a little in his seat at the reminder. 'Ah, yes. The ladies' relations from Cheapside.'

Bingley gave Darcy a hard stare. 'You sound just like Caroline. Please remember that my family is in trade. Why should it matter that Mr Gardiner makes his living from a respectable trade. According to what Miss Bennet and Mrs Brooks have related to me about their aunt and uncle, they are an elegant and sophisticated couple, who are responsible for the genteel and proper behaviour of the sisters.'

Darcy grimaced in embarrassment. 'My apologies. I am afraid that my ingrained prejudices are showing. While I have no issues with your background, I find it difficult to put my feelings aside for people whom I do not know.'

'In that case I suggest that you should get to know them before you judge them.'

'I am sure that you and Richard will send me detailed reports of what I am missing.'

'You can count on it.'

~A~

Bingley did not wait for Darcy and his sister to quit town, but returned to Netherfield in Darcy's smaller coach, since his own coach was at the estate, providing transport for the Hursts.

Immediately after Bingley had refreshed himself on arrival, he was beset by the Hursts as well as the Colonel clamouring for information. Louisa and her husband were shocked to discover Caroline's fate.

Fitzwilliam on the other hand was roaring with laughter. 'Do you mean to tell me that Wickham has made his fortune? Not only that but he came by it honestly?'

'It appears that way. He also redeemed all those debts which Darcy had bought over the years,' Bingley said and related the encounter in greater detail.

'Oh, I wish I could have seen Darcy's face when Wickham handed him that cheque,' Richard mourned but was pleased that his cousin was not out of pocket anymore. He still was unhappy about Wickham's attempt at eloping with Georgiana, but he thought that being married to Caroline would be Wickham's punishment. They must have met almost immediately after that scoundrel left Ramsgate.

Bingley sighed. 'I confess that I was pleased that Wickham was so willing to marry Caroline. Much as Caroline irritates me, I did not wish her to be truly unhappy. After all, she is my sister, and ridiculous as their attachment appears to everyone, I believe they deserve each other.'

Louisa agreed with him while Fitzwilliam thought it funny how Bingley's last statement echoed his own thoughts.

~A~

News of Bingley's return to Netherfield came to Longbourn via the servant's grapevine the same evening.

Elizabeth noticed Jane's pleased expression when Mrs Hill casually mentioned that Mr Bingley was back in residence. As soon as they had a private moment, she commented, 'You appear much happier tonight than you have been since the ball at Netherfield.'

'I am pleased that Mr Bingley has returned as quickly as he has. I was afraid that it might take longer to arrange his sister's future.'

'And were you afraid that other things might interfere with his return?'

Jane refused to meet Elizabeth's eyes as she said, 'Mr Bingley has many friends and acquaintances in town, who might wish for him to remain and partake of all the entertainments available. You know how amiable the gentleman is.'

'Indeed. I sometimes wonder if he is perhaps a little too amiable, letting himself be influenced by his friends and family.'

'I confess that the same concern had occurred to me,' Jane sighed and looked at Elizabeth to judge her sister's reaction who nodded but smiled.

'While that may have been true when he arrived here, it seems the young man is starting to grow up. He has been most diligent in learning about his estate and...' Elizabeth hesitated whether to share her other thought.

'He has taken care to restrain his sister's... ah... attitude,' Jane completed the sentence for Elizabeth.

'Indeed.'

'Do you think that he would make a good husband?'

Elizabeth raised both brows at the question. 'You are considering him in that light?'

'He is the most amiable man of my acquaintance and I enjoy talking to him. He cares about people, his family, his friends and even the tenants at Netherfield. He tries to do his best for the people about whom he cares, and when he misjudges and makes a mistake, he is not afraid to apologise and then try to fix things.'

'Since you want my opinion...' Elizabeth paused while Jane nodded vigorously, 'I would say you could do much worse. But there is no need to rush. Take your time to get to know him better.'

'You think that if he should propose I should request a long engagement?'

'I think that would be better.'

'But what if I decide that we will not suit? Will it not cause a problem to end the engagement?'

'As long as you are the one to end it, your reputation and that of your sisters will not suffer. But you might want to suggest a courtship instead... for both your sakes.' Elizabeth smiled and reached for Jane's hand. 'If he is serious about you and the right kind of man, he will give you the time to be certain. If not...'

'If he does not respect my need for certainty, especially if he should get angry, I will know that he is the wrong man for me.' Jane tilted her head as she asked, 'You think of this as some kind of test, do you not?'

'Yes, Jane. Since I wish for you to have only a happy marriage, I would like you to be as certain as it is possible to be before you commit yourself. You know what they say... Marry in haste and repent at leisure. So, take your time. If Mr Bingley loves you, he will be content to wait.'

Jane could feel the hidden sadness in her sister, who tried so hard to be supportive about something which still pained her so greatly. 'Oh, Lizzy. I just wish that you could forget the past. You are such a wonderful and caring person. You deserve all the happiness which you could have.' Jane smiled somewhat sadly. 'Is it not your maxim to only remember the past as it gives you pleasure?'

Elizabeth squeezed Jane's hands. 'Some things are harder to forget than others.'

'Very well. I shall not push you, but you cannot stop me from wishing that you will find peace and happiness sooner rather than later.'

'Dearest Jane. I have peace and contentment. That will do well enough for now.'

Jane had to be content with that answer, but she hoped that her sister would heal in time.

~A~

It was but one day later that Jane was able to put her sister's advice into practice.

Fitzwilliam accompanied Bingley to Longbourn to keep the ladies occupied while Bingley sought a private interview with Miss Bennet.

As soon as they were in the small parlour, with the door partly open and Mrs Hill stationed not far away, Bingley led Jane to the window seat at the far end of the room.

Jane noticed Bingley fidgeting as he gathered his thoughts.

'Miss Bennet, there is a question I wish to ask, but before I do so, I must inform you of the happenings of the last two weeks, as I would not wish for you to give me an answer without knowing all the facts,' he said in a rush.

'Mr Bingley, what can have happened to put you into such a state?' Jane asked in concern.

He responded with a weak smile. 'My sister acted with a callous disregard for the proprieties, as a consequence she was married the day before yesterday.'

Considering that Mr Darcy had accompanied the siblings to London, and the extreme nervousness of Mr Bingley, Jane feared the worst. While she could tell that Elizabeth was fighting her attraction to Mr Darcy, Jane now feared that the gentleman had become unavailable due to the machinations of Miss Bingley.

Not wanting to speak the name, Jane asked, 'Whom did your sister marry?'

'A Mr George Wickham, the son of Darcy's former steward.'

'Did Mr Darcy arrange the marriage?' Jane wondered if the gentleman had facilitated the marriage to escape Miss Bingley's clutches.

Bingley looked puzzled at her question until he understood what she had not asked. 'Not at all. Although I must confess that Caroline did try to compromise Darcy, it was after she had... ah... met Mr Wickham.'

'But now your sister is Mrs Wickham?'

'That is correct.'

'Mr Bingley, that information is not the sort of thing one should bandy about. Why are you telling me this?'

'Because I did not wish to approach you under false pretences. While a scandal was averted, there is still the possibility that rumours will surface. You should not be caught by surprise and regret your choice if you should give me a positive answer. You see Miss Bennet, I have come to love you most deeply and my dearest wish is for you to agree to become my wife.'

'Mr Bingley, the answer I wish to give you has nothing to do with what you just shared with me,' Jane said and saw Bingley's face fall as he expected her to reject his proposal. She hurried on before he could speak. 'Would you consider a courtship?'

He closed his mouth with a snap and considered Jane's words. 'A courtship, you say? You are not saying no?' he asked hopefully.

'Mr Bingley, we have only known each other for a short time. Since marriage is for a lifetime, I think it would be wise if we knew more about each other. I would not wish for us to marry and in six months we discover that we are unsuited. I think it would be prudent to spend those six months to become much better acquainted.'

'I suppose that would be wise.' Bingley said and thought for a moment. 'Pardon me for asking something so personal, but I have heard a rumour that your sister's marriage was… unhappy. Is that why you are reluctant to rush into marriage yourself?'

'Indeed, Mr Bingley. While Elizabeth has not warned us off marrying at all, she has recommended caution. I hope that is agreeable to you?'

'Miss Bennet, while I would love to marry you tomorrow if I could, I want you to take as much time as you need. I will be ready whenever you are.'

Bingley gently raised Jane's hands to his lips. 'You are worth the wait.'

~A~

Chapter 23

Life settled down at Longbourn and Netherfield as the residents prepared for Christmas.

Bingley called regularly on Jane, who was relieved that the gentleman was content to spend time getting to know each other.

The other frequent visitor to Longbourn was Colonel Fitzwilliam. Since he wanted to spend time with Mrs Taylor, whose duties had been upgraded from governess to companion to the younger girls, he often found himself occupied as a training aid.

During his visits, Mrs Taylor had one or the other of the girls acting as hostess, plying the Colonel with refreshments and conversation. He took his role in good humour, comparing the sisters to his ward. Fitzwilliam thought that it would do Georgiana a world of good to be included in these lessons and hoped that Darcy would make good on his promise to bring his sister to Meryton.

Meanwhile he enjoyed the rewards of his patience when he could sit and converse with Mrs Taylor while the girls were busy with other lessons which did not require her direct supervision.

~A~

The butler entered with the mail on a salver while the residents of Netherfield were at breakfast and presented the letters to Bingley.

Bingley who always delighted in receiving mail, sorted through the letters until he came to one not addressed to himself.

'Richard, there is a letter for you, he said and held out the missive.

'Darcy has not been gone long enough to write to me.'

'It is not from your cousin, as I do not recognise the hand,' Bingley said as Richard looked at the handwriting and groaned.

'How did my mother discover where to find me?'

'If she tracked you down to my home, I hope it is not bad news?'

Richard quickly broke the seal and scanned the lines in his mother's distinctive hand. 'It is bad news, but not the kind you are thinking about.' He shook his head and sighed. 'They want to spend Christmas with me.'

'Does that mean that you will go back to town? I had hoped for your company for at least another month or two.'

'If my mother gets her desire, you will get your wish as well.' At Bingley's puzzled look he added, 'Mother tells me that parliament goes back into session on the seventh of January, leaving too little time for my father to go to Derbyshire and back, especially as the roads are notoriously bad in winter. So, they are hoping to cadge an invitation to Netherfield.'

Blood drained from Louisa's face. 'Are you saying that the Earl and Countess of Matlock would like to spend Christmas with us?'

'And they would like to drag my brother along as well,' Richard confessed. While he loved his family, his mother's concern about his future, regardless if it was what he considered fussing about his health or her attempts at matchmaking, were too heavy handed for him to like spending too much time in her company.

Bingley recognised that his sister's reluctance was caused by her being flustered by the idea of hosting members of the nobility. 'While I would be honoured to have your family as my guests, I am not certain that we could provide the kind of environment to which they are accustomed.'

'It may shock you, but that is not an issue. They are surprisingly relaxed when in the country, away from the harpies of society. The problem is that the women in my family have a habit of giving advice. At least mother is much better informed than my aunt, Lady Catherine.'

Louisa looked uncertain but bravely said, 'I would be honoured to host your family for as long as they like.'

The sentiment was heartily seconded by Bingley.

As there was no escape, Richard bowed to the inevitable. At least the early start of the season enforced a limit on their stay.

~A~

While Louisa Hurst prepared Netherfield for their distinguished guests, at Longbourn, their long-awaited guests arrived.

Mrs Gardiner and her four children came for their annual visit on the Saturday before Christmas to allow them to spend as much time as possible in the country. As this was a busy time for his business, Mr Gardiner planned to leave London early in the morning the day before Christmas Eve to join the rest of the family for the celebrations.

Kitty and Lydia had spent the previous days preparing the nursery for their cousins, who ranged in age from ten down to two.

The sisters and Mrs Taylor eagerly greeted the new arrivals. As soon as everyone had refreshed themselves and warmed up with hot drinks, Kitty and Lydia took their cousins into the snowy garden so that could romp around after sitting in the carriage for several hours.

Meanwhile the older sisters and Margaret Taylor imparted all their news to Mrs Gardiner.

'So, you are being courted by Mr Bingley? I confess that I am pleased to hear that he did not immediately rush into an engagement,' Mrs Gardiner said with an approving smile.

'As it happens, he did propose and I asked for a courtship instead,' Jane informed her aunt.

Madeline's smile widened. 'Please forgive me if it offends you, but I must say, that removing the influence of your mother has been of great benefit to you. I knew your uncle for more than a year and we courted for six months before he asked me to marry him.'

'Have you ever regretted marrying our uncle?' Jane could not resist asking. Ever since Elizabeth had confided her experiences, she had become concerned about the potential dangers of marriage.

Mrs Gardiner pursed her lips as she gave the question serious consideration. 'I suppose that the best answer I can give you is… not usually. There have been days when your uncle and I had disagreements and sometimes it was difficult to discuss the issues. But we learnt that it is better to deal with the discomfort and embarrassment of honest discussions, as it helps us understand each other better, which reduces arguments in the long run.'

Elizabeth listened and caught herself envying her aunt for being allowed to express her own opinions. She well remembered Mr Collins' objections if she ever uttered an opinion which did not reflect his own. Elizabeth had never even been allowed to query his opinion. Having had time to think about it, she now suspected that he had been afraid that Elizabeth wanted him to explain the reasons for his thoughts, which she was certain he would not have been able to do, as all his learning had been by rote.

That night, Elizabeth found it difficult to go to sleep as she kept wondering whether her uncle was the exception or the rule when it came to men.

It was sheer coincidence that those musings led to Elizabeth wondering how Mr Darcy would deal with an inquisitive wife whose opinion differed from his.

~A~

The other topic, which was eagerly discussed with Mrs Gardiner, especially by the youngest sisters, was their other neighbour.

Mrs Gardiner was amused when Lydia told her, 'It is such a pity that Colonel Fitzwilliam is so old, although he still looks quite dashing in his regimentals.'

Margaret Taylor cut in, 'Lydia, remember what I told you about officers. It is very rare that one of them can afford to support you in the style to which you are accustomed. Would you really like to do your own cooking and cleaning, without the help of servants?'

'No, I would not. But that does not stop me from admiring a fine figure of a man. I am so pleased that he is visiting so often. Otherwise, we would always have to practice our manners and conversation with our sisters.'

'Is the Colonel visiting so very often?' Mrs Gardiner asked with a sideways glance at her friend. 'I wonder why?'

Kitty grinned. 'We all think that he is sweet on Mrs Taylor, even though she denies it.'

'How often do I have to tell you, just because the Colonel and I have become friends, it does not follow that anything will ever come of it.'

Mrs Taylor reminded her charges with a stern expression. 'Remember, we are both poor.'

~A~

Although that subject was dropped at the time, later in the evening, Mrs Gardiner had a private conversation with Mrs Taylor.

'Now, Margaret, tell me the truth, how much of what Kitty said about Colonel Fitzwilliam is based on fact?'

'It does not matter. He has made it quite clear that as a second son, he has no expectations and needs an heiress. And I have learnt my lesson with my disaster of a marriage. You cannot live on love alone and when you cannot afford even the most basic things, love does not survive.'

'Surely, his family would not let him suffer. I do remember the Fitzwilliams when they visited Pemberley. They seemed to be a caring family.'

'You met the Fitzwilliams?'

'Not the Earl and Countess, although at the time they had not yet inherited the title, but I do remember seeing their sons since they were good friends with their cousin, the young Mister Darcy, when they occasionally came to my uncle's shop.'

'The Earl may be caring, but he is still traditional, and you know perfectly well that the aristocracy does not like to split property, as that would mean that in a few generations, there would be nothing left to split, and they would lose power.'

Madeline shook her head sadly. She wanted to see her friend in a happy marriage like herself, as she thought Margaret much too young to remain a widow forever. And although her friend did not say it, Madeline felt that Margaret had come to care greatly about Colonel Fitzwilliam.

She was curious to see the two of them together but, as there was nothing she could do at present, she changed the subject. 'Since Jane is being courted and the younger girls all seem to be thriving under your care, what is happening with Lizzy? Is she still determined to remain single for the rest of her life?'

It was Margaret's turn to shake her head as she sighed. 'I am afraid that it will take some time for Elizabeth to learn to trust. For a while I thought that she and Mr Darcy might have a chance. They have become good friends and he always treated her with respect. But he left very suddenly, and we do not know when, or even if, he will return.'

They continued to discuss the family a little longer, and Mrs Gardiner came to the conclusion that her favourite niece would need more time to come out of her shell. She hoped that Elizabeth's courage would be great enough.

~A~

The next day being Sunday, the inhabitants of Longbourn attended services where they met the party from Netherfield.

Before Elizabeth had a chance to introduce her aunt, the Colonel exclaimed, 'Good heavens, can it be? Miss Madeline Brooks? Is it really you?'

'Colonel Fitzwilliam, I would hardly have recognised you. The last time I saw you, you were still at school and visiting the Darcys during your holidays,' Mrs Gardiner responded with a delighted smile. 'I am flattered that you remember me. But I must correct you, I am now Mrs Edward Gardiner.'

'I have an excellent memory where lovely ladies are concerned,' Fitzwilliam said gallantly.

Hurst murmured quietly, 'I suppose that stands you in good stead. It would never do to confuse one lady with another... especially in the morning.' The twinkle in his eyes was suggestive, but fortunately only Bingley and Corporal Bennings heard the comment. The latter had to strain his resolve to the limit not to burst out laughing.

As he had not heard Hurst, Fitzwilliam continued theatrically, 'I suppose you never realised that I was quite devastated when you left Lambton.'

'Surely not, Colonel. We barely knew each other,' Madeline Gardiner laughed at his antics.

'You may not have known me, but I was hopelessly in love with you,' averred Fitzwilliam.

Margaret Taylor became curious. 'Why was it hopeless?' she asked, thinking that perhaps in his youth the Colonel, as the son of an Earl had considered her friend unsuitable because of her lack of rank.

'Because a sophisticated lady like Miss Brooks, had not the slightest interest in a fifteen-year-old swain.'

'Very sophisticated indeed,' laughed Madeline, 'I was the grand old age of nineteen.'

Everyone joined in her laughter, including Margaret, who was relieved at hearing the explanation.

Once they calmed down, Elizabeth performed the introduction of her aunt to Bingley and his family. As the service was soon to start, they postponed further reminiscences until later.

~A~

Chapter 24

On Monday afternoon, Richard's relations arrived, and Louisa Hurst was grateful that they were indeed gracious and pleasant.

The Earl and Countess declared themselves eminently satisfied with the suite which consisted of a sitting room and two bedrooms with a dressing room each, which had been prepared for them.

Robert Fitzwilliam, Viscount Fanshaw was pleased to be allocated the rooms next to his brother, although he teasingly complained that Corporal Bennings occupied the second bedroom in Richard's suite, while his own valet had to make do with a bed in his dressing room as he did not have a second bedroom.

The brothers were quite close as there was only two years between them. They had attended school at the same time, during which period their initials had given rise to a number of nicknames. The most popular ones were never mentioned in polite society, particularly since the brothers could not agree on attributing the appellation of Rough and Ready, as both insisted that neither of them was Rough.

When they had a few moments of privacy, Richard told his brother, 'Thank you for keeping mother of my back for this long. I suppose it would have been too much to ask for to have peace for any longer.'

'I was hoping I could oblige you further, but she was about to start scouring the country for you. There was nothing for it but for me to tell her that I had met Preston at the club, and he had mentioned you were at Bingley's place in Hertfordshire.'

'Well, it could not last forever, and as I said, I am grateful for the reprieve.'

Robert grinned at Richard. 'Since you are in my debt, you can make up for it by telling me about the lovely ladies in this neighbourhood.'

'Very well, but... no poaching.'

~A~

Once the Fitzwilliams had refreshed themselves, they joined their hosts and the Colonel in the drawing room, where Louisa had tea ready for them.

After everyone had been served, Lady Matlock asked Richard, 'What have you been doing with yourself while you were hiding from me?'

'Recuperating in peace and quiet,' Richard answered with an unrepentant grin.

'I have been concerned about you, especially when I sent letters to Pemberley which you did not answer. I would have thought that at least Darcy would have the courtesy to send a note to let me know you were not there to respond to the letters.'

'Well, since Darcy was not at Pemberley, he would not have known that you were trying to correspond with me.'

'He was here too? I should have known. You two were always as thick as thieves.'

Lord Matlock, taking pity on his younger son, interjected, 'You are looking much improved. The country air has done you good.'

'What can I say. Thanks to Bingley I had clean air, good food and pleasant company. And thanks to Bennings I was never allowed to over-exert myself.'

Lady Matlock smiled even as she shook her head. 'Now that you had your rest and recreation, will you return to town with us in the new year? The season is starting quite early, and you might find yourself an heiress at last. I have not forgotten that you promised to retire from the army when you married.'

'Mother, while I feel better, I will not be able to dance and am not inclined to dance attendance on the latest crop of brainless beauties. I shall be better off to remain here... if Bingley is prepared to put up with me.'

'Richard, you know that you are welcome for as long as you like,' Bingley reassured his friend, but otherwise he and his sister kept quiet as it was obvious that the countess needed to have her say and he did not wish to have her ire directed at himself. He was unsurprised that Richard had chosen to recuperate away from the familial environs.

'Thank you, Bingley. I knew that I could count on you,' Richard replied with a grin.

The Earl looked closely at his son and noticed a look of pain which Richard was trying to hide. It seemed that while his son was on the mend, it would be some time before he was truly well. Lord Matlock wondered if Richard would recover enough to return to his duties or whether he would be prepared to retire... even without an heiress. The Earl was willing to set Richard up in civilian life if he would let go of his pride which had kept him in the army, citing that he had no wish to live on charity.

Lord Matlock saw that his wife wanted to argue further but knowing it would only make Richard more determined to thwart her, he asked instead, 'Tell me about your neighbours. Is there anyone hereabouts who is interesting? Perhaps someone who would be a worthy opponent at chess?'

Richard grinned and said, 'Now that you mention it, I believe there is someone whom you would like to meet, and as it happens, we are invited to dinner tomorrow.'

~A~

As they were getting ready to go to bed, Lady Matlock was excited to pass on to her husband the intelligence she had gathered via her maid.

'I believe I have discovered why Richard would rather stay here than return to London with us,' she said with considerable relief and explained, 'Lucy heard it mentioned that Richard is interested in Mrs Brooks of Longbourn.'

Since Lady Matlock had discovered that her son was interested in a widow who resided at Longbourn, she assumed that it must be the owner. After all, Richard had always declared that he needed an heiress and according to her information, the lady fitted the bill perfectly. She was therefore curious to meet Mrs Brooks of Longbourn.

Not knowing anything different, so was her husband, especially since Richard had lauded the lady as an excellent chess player.

~A~

Mr Gardiner arrived at Longbourn at noon, having been able to finish his chores in time to allow him to join his family.

Once he had greeted everyone and warmed up, Lydia and Kitty took the children outside to play to wear them out to ensure they would be happy to go to bed early, allowing the adults to spend an enjoyable evening with their guests.

Taking the opportunity of his children's preoccupation, Mr Gardiner had a brief meeting with Elizabeth to discuss her finances.

'It seems we both enjoyed a most profitable year,' he exclaimed when Elizabeth informed him of the excess profits she was hoping to invest. 'I just wish your father had seen fit to stir himself to the same kind of industry and economy. If he had, there would have been in the vicinity of five thousand for each of you at the time of his death and you would have been spared...'

Elizabeth grimaced at the reminder. 'Perhaps it would have been different, but I doubt that Mrs Bennet would have allowed me to escape. I am sorry, uncle, but that is a fruitless supposition. We cannot change the past. I am only grateful that it has worked out for the best in the long run.'

Gardiner sighed. 'I am sorry too. It was thoughtless of me to speculate on what might have been. What I was trying to say, very badly I admit, is that I am exceedingly proud of what you have achieved.' He smiled and patted her hand.

Elizabeth returned the smile as she said, 'I confess that I would not have been able to do so well if not for the assistance and advice provided by you and Uncle Phillips.'

'It was the least I could do,' protested Gardiner and was chagrined when Lizzy smiled impertinently at him, as if to say *I know*. He was grateful that his niece did not hold that against him.

~A~

Lydia had worn out the children and Mrs Gardiner, assisted by the nurse, gave the children their dinner early and put them to bed while the sisters, Mrs Taylor and Mr Gardiner welcomed the first of the guests.

Elizabeth had invited Sir William and Lady Lucas, as well as Charlotte and John to join them for this casual pre-Christmas party. Since John Lucas had danced twice with Mary at the Netherfield ball, Elizabeth thought to give them a chance to spend some time together in a casual setting. Elizabeth hoped that by inviting the other members of the family, it made her attempts at matchmaking less obvious.

Mrs Gardiner had just joined the party when two coaches from Netherfield arrived.

As Richard knew everyone, he made the introduction of his family, who were pleasantly surprised by the gentility displayed by all the sisters, even the youngest who were on their best behaviour.

Fortunately, being in the presence of an Earl prevented Sir William to reminisce about his investiture at St James' Palace, although Lady Lucas felt entitled to monopolise Lady Matlock's time.

Robert Fitzwilliam had been forewarned about the beauty of the local ladies and set out to charm the ones not obviously claimed, while his father spoke to Elizabeth.

'My son tells me that you play chess,' he said with a doubtful look.

Elizabeth felt torn between amusement and irritation as she said with an impertinent smile, 'He is quite correct, although I have not had the opportunity to play against him. I would expect that as a military man he would excel at strategy.'

'He does,' said the Earl with a proud smile. 'The only one in the family who has a chance against him is his cousin, Darcy.'

'Mr Darcy is indeed an excellent player,' Elizabeth confirmed. She wondered if she should tell the Earl that as of the last game she had played with the gentleman, they were even, but considering what he said about the Colonel, that would sound like boasting. Instead, she offered, 'Perhaps one day while you are here, you would do me the honour of a game?'

'I would be delighted. I always enjoy finding a new opponent whose strategy I do not know,' the Earl agreed and added paternally, 'But I promise I will take it easy on you.'

'As you wish,' Elizabeth said agreeably and promised herself to do her level best to trounce him.

Lady Matlock, even while being distracted by Lady Lucas, observed Elizabeth conversing with her husband and was pleased with the ease and grace she displayed. Yes, she decided, even though she was not classically beautiful like her older sister, Richard could do much worse than this charming young lady.

~A~

The party went into the dining room and suddenly Lady Matlock felt concern when Elizabeth took her seat at the head of the table, as the lady had not considered the implication of Elizabeth's ownership of Longbourn. Although Lady Catherine used to occupy the head of the table, that lady was nobility and significantly older than Mrs Brooks.

Therefore, while it had been said that they would not have a formal seating arrangement, she felt that Elizabeth should not have usurped her uncle's position at the table. If the young woman was to marry Richard, the countess feared that she would have to spend considerable time and effort teaching her proper manners and precedence.

At least, being seated next to Elizabeth, gave her the opportunity to get to know her potential daughter-in-law. 'I understand that you have been a widow for nearly three years.'

'That is correct,' Elizabeth replied, wondering about the direction of this conversation, although she had started to have a suspicion when she saw the countess looking around the rooms as if estimating the value of everything she saw.

'Since it has been so long, you must be anxious to find another husband to provide an heir to this estate,' the lady continued fishing for information.

'Good heavens, no. I have no intentions of marrying any time soon, if at all. I shall be perfectly content to will Longbourn to one of my sisters' children.'

'Are you not being rather selfish, placing such a burden on your uncle until then?' Lady Matlock exclaimed in surprise at the vehement denial.

Lord Matlock who had overheard the exchange said sympathetically to Gardiner, 'I imagine it must be difficult for you to divide your time between London and Longbourn to look after not only your business, but also the estate and your wards.'

'I am sorry to contradict you, but I am not the guardian for my nieces,' Gardiner replied with a bland smile and waited for the explosion from Elizabeth.

Before Elizabeth could object, Lady Matlock asked, 'If you are not the guardian of the sisters, who is?'

'I am,' Elizabeth said with a saccharine smile and was gratified to see two pairs of eyes turned to her in consternation. 'I am also the master of Longbourn. So, you see, I am being quite selfless as far as my relations are concerned, since I shoulder the responsibility not only of my sisters, but also of *my* estate,' she said, emphasising the possessive pronoun.

This time it was Lord Matlock who exclaimed, 'But surely you must need a man to administer the estate properly.'

'Not at all. Why would I want to hand over my property to some man to destroy everything I worked so hard to achieve? Especially since Longbourn is more profitable now than it ever was while it was in my father's care.'

'But women cannot manage an estate!'

'All evidence to the contrary,' Elizabeth growled.

Richard had overheard part of the conversation and suspected that his mother was trying her hand at matchmaking and failing miserably. While he thought it amusing to hear Elizabeth contradict his parents, he sensed that the lady was getting irate at having her competence questioned by guests in her house and judged it prudent to intervene before his parents were evicted from Longbourn.

'Anne is doing quite well, and she has been in charge of Rosing for a similar length of time as Mrs Brooks has had the running of Longbourn. By the bye, speaking of Anne, have you looked in on Aunt Catherine recently? How is the old dear?' he asked facetiously.

Fortunately, the comment diverted his parents, and the rest of the dinner was pleasant as everyone chose less controversial subjects for conversation.

~A~

Chapter 25

At the end of the meal, Elizabeth turned to her uncle, 'Will you be so kind and look after the gentlemen?' before she led the ladies to the drawing room, leaving the men to enjoy their port and cigars.

As soon as they had relative privacy, Lord Matlock asked Gardiner, 'Is your niece truly as competent at managing her estate as she seems to think?'

'I believe that she is not quite correct in her estimate,' replied Gardiner who was amused when he saw the Earl nodding as if to say *I just knew it*. After pausing for effect, he added, 'Elizabeth is much better than she gives herself credit.' The stunned look was worth more than a dozen apologies. Gardiner's lips quirked as he raised his glass in salute.

'But how can this slip of a girl from an unimportant family...'

'She is intelligent, well-educated and determined to ensure that her sisters will not be forced to marry for financial security.' Gardiner briefly considered mentioning that his niece had had a bad marriage but decided that her past was a private matter. 'In that determination she is completely different from her father. Although he was intelligent and very well educated, he was also indolent. And while some people might call Elizabeth many things, some not so flattering, indolent is one word which will never be used.'

Sir William chuckled at Gardiner's explanation and added his own opinion. 'Lady Lucas once had the idea of securing the lady for our oldest. She made the mistake of mentioning the idea to Eliza in public, and it took months for our neighbours to speak to my wife again.'

'It sounds like your neighbours are very protective of Mrs Brooks,' Lord Matlock commented cautiously.

'Indeed, my lord, and pardon me for saying so, but you had better make sure that your lady wife understands that.'

Rising from the Ashes

~A~

At the other end of the table, the younger men, who were all of similar age, had gathered. Like young men everywhere, the main topic of conversation was the ladies.

Since the Viscount was somewhat more observant than his parents, or possibly less convinced of his own superiority, he had noticed that of the adult ladies, only Miss Lucas seemed to be unattached. He was curious as to the cause because while Miss Lucas was not as overtly beautiful as Miss Bennet, she was most pleasing to the eye... at least to his eyes.

He enquired of her brother, 'Please forgive me if my enquiry offends you, but I had wondered why such a lovely lady as your sister is still single?'

'I am afraid part of the reason is the Bennet sisters. Compared to Jane Bennet, most women appear plain... even when they are not,' John hastened to add when the Viscount looked thunderous. 'I speak of the perception of the majority of men when they compare my sister with Miss Bennet. Of course, having only a small dowry is not helping either.'

'So, you are saying that a lovely and intelligent woman is being ignored because she is relatively poor and not fashionably beautiful.'

'Is it not always so?'

Robert looked thoughtful as he murmured, 'Not always, no.'

~A~

Lady Lucas had also overheard Lady Matlock's attempt at matchmaking for her son. Having learnt her lesson two years earlier, she felt it was incumbent on her to make up for her own blunder by distracting the countess from pestering Elizabeth any further.

To entertain the company, the ladies took turns at performing and Lady Matlock was impressed by the level of expertise being displayed. 'I had not thought to hear such excellent performances outside of London society,' she commented, while listening to Mary playing the pianoforte.

'Mrs Taylor has been a godsend to the Bennets,' Lady Lucas replied to the rhetorical comment, as it gave her an opening to praise her own daughter. 'Even my Charlotte benefitted as the lady was happy to share her expertise.'

'Indeed. Perhaps your daughter could be prevailed upon to display her art?'

Charlotte was just taking a seat at the pianoforte in response to her mother's urging, when the gentlemen entered the room. She was utterly shocked when the Viscount came up to her and offered to turn the pages for her. Since Charlotte was too dumbstruck to speak, she simply nodded, earning her a smile from the gentleman as he sat down next to her.

While Charlotte sorted through the music for a score suitable to her abilities, she asked quietly, 'Do you know anything about music?'

'My cousin, Georgiana, nods when she wishes for me to turn a page. I hope that is acceptable to you?'

'Quite acceptable, thank you.'

Charlotte's performance, although not outstanding, was creditable. When she finished, several of the others entertained the assembled party until Mary played a reel and Bingley could not resist but to ask Jane to dance.

As several others also wanted to dance, Mrs Taylor offered to play for them and since he still could not dance, Richard offered to turn the pages for her.

Only Mary paid enough attention to notice that the Colonel turned the pages at regular intervals, but it was always the same score, no matter what Margaret played... obviously from memory.

When the guests declared they had danced sufficiently for one evening, they soon afterwards said their goodbyes.

~A~

As soon as the Matlock carriage pulled out of the gates of Longbourn, Richard vented his spleen at his parents.

'How the devil could you be so incredibly rude to our hostess?' he growled as he attempted to keep his voice down and not air his grievance in public. 'You treated her like she was a side of beef which you were examining and found wanting.'

'Look, son, I understand that since you have feelings for Mrs Brooks, you want to protect her, but that is no reason to be so rude to your mother,' the Earl cautioned.

'You were no better than mother, telling the lady that she is incompetent to administer her own property.' Richard could feel himself getting ever hotter under the collar and took a few deep breaths to get his temper under control. 'She is a gentlewoman, a widow, the owner of Longbourn and the head of her family. And despite all that you insulted her, telling her that she should give precedence to her uncle who is a guest in her house.'

'I had no idea that she is the head of the family and when I saw her take the seat at the head of the table, I thought that she was an unmannered country hoyden,' Lady Matlock cut in, attempting to explain her behaviour. 'And as for examining her, I wanted to ascertain whether she would make an acceptable wife for you.'

'I have not the slightest interest in Mrs Brooks other than as a friend. While she is everything lovely and intelligent woman, and may I add a most accomplished and competent landowner, she is also not interested in me.'

Before the argument could deteriorate even further, the Viscount spoke up, 'I think it would be best if we waited with this discussion until we have some privacy.'

His family reluctantly agreed, and the rest of the journey was completed in tense silence.

~A~

At Longbourn the atmosphere was considerably lighter. One could almost say frivolous.

Once all the guests had taken their leave Elizabeth and Lydia dissolved into laughter.

'What is so funny?' asked Jane, who had sat at the other end of the table and had not heard any of the conversation which had caused such hilarity.

'Oh, Jane, please forgive me, for laughing at our guests, but if I did not laugh, I would be exceedingly angry,' Elizabeth crowed and did her utmost to regain her equilibrium so that she could relate her earlier conversation with the Earl and Countess of Matlock.

Elizabeth need not have worried, as Jane was furious on her behalf. 'How dare they? What were they thinking, behaving in such a manner?'

'I believe that I can shed some light on the subject,' said Margaret Taylor. 'As you know, I have spoken to Colonel Fitzwilliam on a number of occasions.' This statement caused several grins and nods from her employer and charges. 'He has mentioned that his parents are keen for him to retire from the army and his mother in particular keeps pushing him at various heiresses. Elizabeth, you being the wealthiest single woman in the neighbourhood, must be of considerable interest to them as a potential wife.'

'Did Lady Matlock truly think that such an intrusive interview would make me favourably disposed towards the Colonel?'

'Most young ladies in London would not consider that interview to be unreasonable. Lady Matlock is a mother trying to ensure that a young woman is suitable to join her family. Being a countess, it would not occur to her that any lady could possibly be disinclined to be so honoured.'

'Yes, well. While I cannot argue with your logic, the lady will have many surprises in store for her unless she changes her attitude.'

~A~

At Netherfield, the Fitzwilliams found privacy for a family discussion the following morning by sequestering themselves in the library.

As soon as the servant who had brought a tray of coffee to the room closed the thick door behind him on his exit, Lady Matlock addressed her younger son. 'About last night...'

Richard slouched back in the big wingchair which he occupied and crossed his arms over his chest. 'Yes?' he said noncommittally.

'I was given to understand that you had taken an interest in Mrs Brooks. Yet you claim to have no feelings for her. She also claims that she had no interest in marriage. How do you explain all those contradictions.'

'I have no need to explain anything. You on the other hand have a lot of explaining to do to justify your rude behaviour,' Richard refused to back down from his viewpoint.

'As I told you, I needed to find out if Mrs Brooks is an appropriate partner for you.'

'Mother, I am old enough to decide if a lady is suitable for me. I have been out of leading strings for decades. I am perfectly well equipped to decide who will suit me.'

'Very well, since you are being deliberately obtuse, I needed to establish if Mrs Brooks is acceptable for our family.'

'In the same way as you have established the suitability of all those heiresses which you threw at me. In case you have not noticed, I did not like any of them. You are therefore quite unsuited to evaluate potential brides for me.'

'Surely, eventually there must be one heiress who appeals to you.'

'So far, I have not met a single heiress with whom I would like to spend the rest of my life. But just to satisfy my curiosity, what gave you the cockeyed idea to choose Mrs Brooks as a potential bride?'

Lady Matlock squirmed in her seat before she answered, 'While it is undignified to listen to servants' gossip, they are often aware of things which people prefer to keep quiet. My maid informed me that according to the servants you were interested in the widow at Longbourn.'

Richard ignored his mother's justification but could not help but laugh at her misunderstanding. 'So, you heard that Longbourn is owned by a widow and since I reportedly am interested in a widow at Longbourn, you concluded that it must be Mrs Brooks. Is that correct?'

'Yes, but what is so laughable about that?'

'Had it not occurred to you that in many households there is more than one widow?'

'More than one...'

'The widow in whom I am interested is Mrs Taylor,' Richard stated and settled further into his chair, while waiting for Lady Matlock to come to the right conclusion... and for her to explode.

'A governess? Have you lost your mind? What arts and allurements did she use to gain your interest?' asked a furious Lady Matlock, but before Richard could answer, she continued, 'She must think that as the son of an Earl you are well-to-do and is attempting to secure her future.'

'She is a companion, not a governess and she knows perfectly well that I have no expectations,' Richard replied to the tirade, doing his best to control his temper.

'In that case, you will stop this nonsense immediately and focus on winning her employer. While Mrs Brooks is impertinent and no great beauty, at least she has an estate which can keep you in comfort.'

'No.' Richard's reply was quiet but also implacable in his anger.

~A~

Chapter 26

Hearing that implacable *No* from her younger son was too much for Lady Matlock.

She turned on her heel and stormed out of the room. Her control lasted long enough that she was several steps from the door before tears started streaming down her face.

Soon after her wedding, the then Viscountess had found out that her father-in-law had been a bad or at least unfortunate manager of his estates, having made several investments which lost money. Each new scheme, designed to recoup his fortune had only ended with more losses. After the old Earl's death, a dozen years ago, her husband had inherited an estate badly in debt, making it impossible to provide for their younger son. The current Earl had made significant inroads into restoring the earldom, but funds were still tight.

This state of affairs caused many sleepless nights for Lady Matlock, as she was terrified that Richard would be killed each time he was sent to the continent. Seeing him so badly wounded after his latest return made her frantic. She needed to protect him, and the only way was for him to leave the army. But without funds, he could not afford to do so.

For that reason, the countess had scoured the ton and even considered the daughters of various tradesmen to find a woman who would be able to provide the resources to keep the Colonel out of harm's way.

But he had rejected every candidate she presented to him. And now he had fallen for a penniless companion and refused to consider any other woman? It was too much.

She rushed into her dressing room and managed to reach her chamber-pot just in time before she cast up her accounts.

When she was reduced to dry retching, she collapsed onto the floor, and fumbled for her handkerchief to wipe her mouth and dry her tears.

As she drew a shuddering breath, a wave of heat engulfed her body causing her to curse under her breath. Why did she have to suffer through the change at this point in time when she needed all her wits about her? Instead, she slept badly, waking drenched in sweat and feeling exhausted, and during the day those flashes of heat which overcame her, made her waking hours a misery.

Between the wretchedness of her physical state and the relentless fear for her son, she was reaching the end of her resources. Yet she had to remain strong and maintain an unruffled façade not only to her family but also the outside world.

She slowly regained her feet and stumbled to the washstand to splash cool water on her face and rinse her mouth.

Lady Matlock dried her hands and face, carefully adjusted her clothing and tidied her hair. Looking into the mirror she sighed and squared her shoulders. She was ready to face the world again. She had to be.

~A~

In the library the Earl looked at his younger son and sighed. 'She worries for you.'

Richard echoed his father's sigh. 'I know, father. But those empty headed and insipid maidens she throws at me just make me feel old. They are so very young they make me feel like I am robbing a cradle.'

Across the room, Robert huffed, 'I know just how you feel.'

The Earl ignored the interruption and asked, 'Tell me about Mrs Taylor.'

Richard looked wistful. 'I enjoy her company; she makes me feel alive again. Her conversation on a great variety of subjects is delightful. She is warm and caring.'

He grimaced and shrugged. 'I confess that I have considered if we could somehow manage to make our funds stretch far enough to live at least in modest comfort, since Margaret has indicated that she does not require an extravagant lifestyle. All the years I have been in the army, I have saved as much of my honorarium and bonuses as I could and invested the money.'

The wistful look returned. 'I was going to propose to her tomorrow.'

Lord Matlock nodded thoughtfully, unsurprised by Richard's hopes. 'Tell me about her background.'

'When she was barely one and twenty, she married a young lieutenant against her family's wishes. As a consequence, they withheld her dowry making life difficult for the couple.' Richard did not mention that he suspected Taylor had married her for her dowry and was disappointed when it was not forthcoming. 'About a year later, he was killed in battle. Since then, she has made her own way as a governess and companion to respectable young ladies such as the Misses Bennet.'

'Why did she not return to her family when she became a widow?'

'She has too much pride to go begging to the people who rejected her,' Richard explained, causing the Earl to chuckle.

'I can see why you feel an affinity for the lady.'

Richard shrugged and grinned as he said, 'You know, I met her about ten years ago, before she married.'

'How could you meet her? Surely you did not move in the same circles.' The Earl was surprised and concerned about the company Richard might have kept.

'Ah, but we did. You obviously do not remember Miss Margaret, the daughter of Baron Standish.'

'She is Standish's daughter? Good grief,' Lord Matlock chuckled. 'That at least should appeal to your mother,' he said absentmindedly as he considered the situation. After a few moments he advised, 'I recommend that you propose to your lady, sooner rather than later.'

'You support my wish to marry Mrs Taylor?' Richard gasped.

'Son, I want you out of the army. If you think that between your savings and the sale of your commission you have enough to live adequately, I believe that I can find enough to help things along.'

'Father, you know I do not want charity. Especially as I know how straitened your own finances are,' Richard protested.

Lord Matlock grinned and suddenly looked very much like his younger son. 'Things have improved considerably and while there is still room for improvement, I am in a position to afford a modest wedding present.'

As Richard sat up straighter, his brother chimed in with a wide smile, 'I thought that you were a man of action. What are you waiting for?'

'Only for the carriage to be readied,' Richard replied and headed for the door.

~A~

When Richard arrived at Longbourn, he walked into cheerful chaos.

It seemed every single person in the household was busy decorating the house with greenery they had collected earlier that morning.

He had barely walked in the door when he was accosted by Lydia. 'Colonel, you are just the man we need. None of us are tall enough to hang the boughs over the fireplace. Do you think you could rescue a houseful of damsels in distress?'

Richard laughed as he bowed. 'It has been some time since I was called upon to be a knight errant, but it would be my honour to assist in such a dangerous task, even though I was most remiss and have not brought my white charger.'

'It is fortunate that you did not. Mrs Hill would be most put out with hoofprints in the parlour,' Mrs Taylor said as she came up to them with an armful of garlands.

While Richard busied himself, draping the garlands as directed over the fireplace, he asked, 'I am pleased that I can be of assistance, but is not Mr Gardiner able to help?'

'He promised he would hang the mistletoe when he returned, but at present he is visiting his sister,' Mrs Taylor informed him.

Soon after, Lydia rushed off to help one of her cousins, giving the Colonel the opportunity to ask quietly, 'Mrs Taylor, would it be possible to speak privately for a few minutes? There is something I wish to ask.'

The intense look which accompanied the question sent shivers down Margaret's spine. 'We can use the small parlour which we usually avoid in cold weather,' she said and led the way.

Since they left the door partially open, they walked over to the window to avoid being overheard. Mrs Taylor turned to Fitzwilliam. 'What did you wish to ask?'

Richard had imagined this moment many a time, but now that it was reality, he, who normally was never at a loss for words, found himself tongue-tied. 'Ah...' he started and stopped.

He nervously took Margaret's hands and drawing strength from them he plunged into speech. 'Margaret, you know that I have not much to offer you except a small cottage in the country and a loving heart, but that is yours forever. Despite that lack, I hope that you will grant me your hand in marriage.'

'You truly wish to marry a penniless widow?'

'You are a priceless treasure,' he declared sincerely.

'As long as that country cottage is occupied by you, I would love to join you and be your wife,' Margaret replied with a soft smile.

Richard returned the smile and pulled her towards him. A moment later their arms wrapped around each other, and they sealed their engagement with a kiss, which started out gentle but ended up leaving them breathless.

~A~

Elizabeth was having a wonderful day with her family and particularly her cousins who revelled in romping in the snow which had fallen overnight.

The expedition in the morning had been a resounding success and they had gathered enough greenery to decorate every room at Longbourn.

For Elizabeth there had only been one slightly discordant note. A couple of times she caught herself wanting to turn to Mr Darcy to help retrieve some mistletoe which was out of her reach or to point out some high-spirited antics of her young cousins, only to remember that he had quit the county.

Whenever that happened, she hoped that he was having a wonderful time with his sister at Pemberley. But there could be no doubt that she missed her friend.

Elizabeth was just thinking about Darcy again as she climbed off a chair, she had used to reach high enough to attach the final bit of mistletoe in the drawing room when Richard and Margaret joined the group.

Taking one look at the couple, Elizabeth and her relations could immediately tell that they were indeed looking at a couple.

Seeing the reaction of the people in the room, the Colonel gave them a smile and a bow as he announced, 'I have some news to share with you which is exceedingly happy for me, but I just realised it may be rather sad for you. Mrs Taylor has just agreed to become my wife.'

As he said the last words, he looked at Margaret with such joy that even Elizabeth could not but be convinced that her friend was likely to have a good marriage. She therefore rushed to them to offer her congratulations.

~A~

At Pemberley Darcy was having a quiet but pleasant time with his sister, although he too found it disconcerting that he kept wanting to share a thought, an interesting paragraph of whatever he was reading or even a beautiful sight, only to remember that Elizabeth was not with him.

Georgiana noticed his distraction and one evening gathered her courage to ask about the cause.

'I am sorry, my dear, I had not realised that I was not attentive to you.' He hesitated, as he had not considered confiding in his much younger sister, even though she would be affected by his decisions.

'You have been most attentive, but I have noticed you looking over your shoulder on a number of occasions as if you wanted to speak to someone and then you always look disappointed.'

'I had not realised I was so obvious, but I confess that I miss a friend whose company I enjoyed greatly while I was in Hertfordshire.'

Georgiana tilted her head as she asked, 'Is this friend Mrs Brooks?'

'How did you know about Mrs Brooks?'

'You mentioned her in your letters… every single one.' Georgiana grinned when she realised that she had managed to startle her brother. 'Please tell me about her.'

Seeing the entreaty in his sister's eyes and needing someone to talk to about the lady, Darcy related all about his interactions with Elizabeth.

In the end it came as no surprise when Georgiana asked, 'Are you in love with Mrs Brooks?'

'I believe that I am,' he said reluctantly.

'She sounds perfect. Why are you not happier about it?'

'While the lady is perfect, she is just a gentlewoman of no great consequence. I worry that if I were to marry her, your chances at a brilliant match could be greatly reduced.'

'Brother, do you truly believe that I would want to marry a man who is put off by you being married to a wonderful gentlewoman rather than a titled harridan?'

Georgiana's phrasing of the question elicited a startled laugh from Darcy. 'When you put it like that...'

'So, when will I have a chance to meet this lady?'

'I thought that we could visit with Bingley after my annual visit to Rosings. Mrs Brooks suggested that you might be able to come out into society on a limited basis in the country, to give you some experience before tackling a London season. She offered to introduce you to her neighbours, whom I found quite congenial.'

'In that case, spring cannot come soon enough,' declared Georgiana.

Now that he had cleared the air with his sister and gained her support, Darcy too could hardly wait for spring to arrive.

~A~

Chapter 27

Richard did not stay at Longbourn much longer, leaving the family to their preparations for Christmas day, an occasion to which the residents of Netherfield had been invited before the additional guests had arrived.

Given that no preparations had been made at Netherfield to provide a Christmas feast, Elizabeth had extended the invitation to include the Fitzwilliams. As Longbourn was already catering for sixteen people, the addition of three more was no hardship, but it could have been difficult to go from zero to seven at Netherfield.

When questioned by Jane about the invitation, she explained that she was prepared to be amused if there was a repeat of the performance at dinner. 'And I confess, I found the Viscount all that is charming. That he seemed to like Charlotte makes me think well of his taste.'

Elizabeth hesitated before she added, 'It occurs to me that his parents must have some good qualities to raise two such excellent sons.'

~A~

Upon his return to Netherfield, Richard was unsurprised to be summoned by his mother.

The moment he entered the sitting room in his parent's suite, he told her, 'Before you say anything, I must inform you that I have just proposed to Mrs Taylor, and she has accepted.' He waited for a denouncement of his actions and was astonished when it was not forthcoming.

Instead of delivering the expected tirade, Lady Matlock rose from her seat and embraced Richard. 'I am exceedingly happy for you.'

'You are not angry at me for going against your wishes?' Richard asked in astonishment.

His mother pulled back a little to look him in the eye. 'For years I have prayed that you would find someone for whom you would be prepared to quit the army. I admit that I wanted you to marry a woman who could bring sufficient funds into the marriage to allow you to live in comfort, but not at the expense of your happiness.'

The lady sighed. 'I am sorry if I seemed...' seeing a disbelieving look and a raised eyebrow she amended her words, '...*was* overly officious. My only excuse is that I love you very much and wish to see you happily settled and safe.'

Suddenly her face sported a gamin smile. 'I am also keen to hear the patter of little feet around Matlock.'

Richard could not help but laugh at the quip and tightened his embrace. 'I love you too, mother,' he said simply, but it was enough to cause Lady Matlock's eyes to mist.

Later in the evening, Lady Matlock was pleased to announce to the rest of the residents, 'Richard has just given me the best Christmas present I have ever received. He is engaged to be married and will resign his commission,' which caused everyone to offer their congratulations and instigated a small impromptu party.

Robert Fitzwilliam smiled as he sat back and wondered if his own arrangements for a Christmas present would be successful.

~A~

On Christmas morning, when the party from Longbourn arrived at the church for Christmas services, the residents from Netherfield were already waiting for them.

While Richard rushed to greet his fiancée, Lord and Lady Matlock approached Elizabeth.

After brief greetings, Lady Matlock said, 'Please accept my apology for my inappropriate behaviour the other night. I jumped to conclusions and made unwarranted assumptions.'

Elizabeth was rather astounded that the lady was apologising and with complete sincerity. She therefore said with a polite smile, 'I accept your apology, as I understand that you were worried about your son.'

Lord Matlock, not to be outdone in civility by his wife, addressed Elizabeth. 'I too owe you an apology, Mrs Brooks. I based my opinion of women managing estates on my sister who was adamant that she knew everything better... to the detriment of my niece's estate. I forgot that since Anne took over from her mother, Rosings is becoming profitable again.'

In response, he received Elizabeth's best impertinent smile as she said, 'I will be perfectly happy to forgive your misguided words, if you are prepared to make a small restitution... You still owe me a game of chess.'

Matlock laughed as he bowed. 'It shall be my pleasure.'

~A~

While Lord Matlock and Elizabeth spoke, his wife turned to her son and Margaret.

'Mother, I would like you to welcome my fiancée,' Richard said with a proud and happy smile.

'Mrs Taylor, you are indeed a most welcome addition to our family. I had despaired of Richard ever finding a woman who meant more to him than the army,' the lady said and opened her arms to embrace her new daughter, who was happy to respond to that invitation.

'I thank you for the welcome, but please, would you call me Margaret.'

'I would be delighted, and you must call me Eleanor in private. Lady Eleanor will do for public occasions.'

Lord Matlock added his own welcome just in time before they had to enter the church.

~A~

The service was quite pleasant as the vicar spoke about the peace and joy of the season. At the end, the congregations exited and briefly mingled to exchange Christmas greetings.

The gathering was just starting to break up when an unfamiliar carriage displaying a crest on its side pulled up in front of the church.

On recognising the conveyance, Robert Fitzwilliam smiled and approached the occupant who exited. 'Standish, it is good to see you again,' he called out, catching the attention of the gentleman.

Henry Standish, a good-looking young man of six and twenty, smiled and extended his hand in greeting. 'Fanshaw, it is good to see you too. But tell me, where is she?' he asked, looking around excitedly.

Robert nodded in Richard's direction and said with a grin, 'Your sister is to be my sister.'

Standish followed his gaze and recognised Richard, who had been pointed out to him once, years earlier. He strode over to the couple who were staring at him, having heard Robert call his name.

'Henry?' whispered Mrs Taylor, still staring wide eyed in complete disbelief.

'Is it really you, Margaret?' Standish asked as he searched her features nervously. As soon as she nodded, he threw propriety to the wind and engulfed her in a bearhug.

When Richard considered taking offence at a strange man embracing his fiancée, Robert lightly placed a restraining hand on his arm and said, 'Siblings who have not seen each other in a decade.'

After enjoying the embrace of her younger brother for a minute, Margaret recalled herself to her surroundings and slapped the young man on the shoulder. 'I see, you still have not the slightest notion how to act in public,' she said with a laugh that was half sob.

Standish released her, although keeping hold of her hands as he answered with an impertinent grin, 'What can I say. I have not had my big sister reminding me of propriety every five minutes for the past decade.'

Margaret was still slightly dazed as she asked, 'How did you find me?'

Her question was answered in a roundabout way when Robert said with a bow, 'Merry Christmas.'

~A~

After briefly being introduced to everyone it was obvious that Standish had to be invited to join the party at Longbourn.

While the Bennet sisters kept the Gardiner children busy enthusing over their presents, Margaret took the opportunity to briefly catch up with her brother.

They sat in a corner of the big drawing room, surrounded by the Fitzwilliams, while Henry gave her the news of their parents. The joy of seeing her brother again was somewhat dimmed when he informed her of her mother's passing four years earlier and her father's death only four months ago. Despite the circumstances of her separation from her family, Margaret was saddened to hear of her parents' passing.

'After we heard of your husband's death, father relented and was looking forward to seeing you again. But you never returned. Why not?'

'I had too much pride to go where I was not wanted. Father had made it quite clear that I was never to darken his doorstep again.'

When questioned Margaret explained how she had made her living, causing Henry to sit and shake his head. 'Four years ago, I was supposed to attend the season in London, but due to mother's death I stayed at the estate. Just think, if I had been in London, I could have encountered you while you chaperoned your charge to various functions.'

'We might indeed, although I am uncertain whether we would have recognised one another,' said Margaret. Another thought occurred to her, and she turned to Robert. 'But why did you send for Henry?'

'I saw him briefly in town a few weeks ago,' Robert said.

'I had to see the solicitors because of father's death,' Henry briefly interjected.

'We spent some time talking and Standish mentioned that he wished that he could find his sister, as she was the only immediate family he had left. Then yesterday, when Richard mentioned your background, I sent an express, hoping to provide you both with a Christmas present.'

Standish suddenly gave a speculative look to the Fitzwilliam brothers. 'Did you perchance just casually mention the dowry?'

Robert grinned. 'No, I did not. Richard was most determined to marry the love of his life and does not give tuppence for wealth.'

Margaret turned to her brother. 'Henry, you know perfectly well that father denied me my dowry when I went against his wishes and married David.'

'He denied it to you then, but it has been sitting in the four percents, waiting for you to claim it, now that Taylor cannot get his greedy hands on it.'

The colour drained from Margaret's face. 'You mean that...' she could not complete the sentence.

Standish grinned. 'Indeed.'

~A~

Lord and Lady Matlock sat near the siblings and quietly listened as Margaret and Henry related the happenings of the last decade.

After dinner the previous evening, Lord Matlock had informed his wife that while their new daughter was poor, her antecedents were impeccable, a fact which had greatly relieved the lady. She did not have to worry that Margaret would embarrass the family by her behaviour.

She commiserated with Margaret over the loss of her parents but when Standish mentioned the dowry, even she was stunned. Could it be that Richard and Margaret would be financially not only secure but comfortable? Even a few thousand would make a big difference to the level of comfort they could enjoy and the future they would be able to provide to any potential children.

She barely restrained herself from asking, *how much.*

Her patience was soon rewarded, although the answer caused her to laugh hysterically, especially when she saw the pole-axed look on Richard's face.

Lady Matlock had pushed one heiress after another at her son, only to have him reject every one of those ladies. Yet when she stopped pushing and accepted his choice, the result exceeded even her wildest dreams and hopes.

It turned out that Margaret's dowry of five and twenty thousand pounds had been sitting in the four percents for over a decade, accumulating interest of another ten thousand pounds.

~A~

By the time everyone was ready to sit down and enjoy the Christmas feast, Lord Henry Standish, Baron Standish was fast becoming a favourite of Lady Matlock.

Considering that Margaret was now in possession of a fortune, Lady Matlock initially suggested delicately that her new daughter should immediately leave her employment, a suggestion to which everyone objected... not least of all Margaret Taylor herself.

'I cannot simply walk out on my friends. While I am technically an employee, I have always felt more like family in this house.'

'I meant no offense. I simply thought you might wish for time to arrange your trousseau.'

Margaret smiled sweetly as she explained, 'Neither Richard nor I care for the London season. In addition, he will still need several months to fully recover, and even though I only discovered my father's death today, I shall spend some months in mourning for him.'

She looked at Richard who smiled and nodded almost imperceptibly. 'I believe that all those situations will resolve themselves at about the time the season is over, at which point I would be happy to marry.'

When his mother looked ready to object, Richard pointed out, 'I have no wish spending the first months of my marriage as an invalid.'

Lady Matlock graciously conceded and simply enjoyed the festivities.

~A~

After the meal, the children went back to playing with their new toys, while the adults enjoyed tea and coffee in the drawing room.

The ladies took turns playing Christmas carols on the pianoforte and encouraged everyone to sing along.

As everyone was relaxing, Lord Matlock addressed Elizabeth, 'I am minded of my earlier promise. Would you care to engage in a game of chess?'

Elizabeth was so inclined and shortly taught Lord Matlock a valuable lesson.

Richard had watched the match with an enigmatic smile until the end when Elizabeth thoroughly trounced the Earl.

'Father, did I mention that Mrs Brooks and Darcy are evenly matched when it comes to chess?' he asked.

Lord Matlock gave Richard a mock disgusted look. 'No, son. You forgot to mention that little detail.'

Turning back to Elizabeth he bowed as best as he could while still seated. 'Thank you for this most informative lesson. I believe that I will never underestimate an opponent again, even if the opponent wears a dress… or perhaps I should say, particularly if my opponent wears a dress.'

Elizabeth smiled at him and said, 'You are welcome. Merry Christmas.'

~A~

Chapter 28

After Christmas, a flurry of letters crossed the country.

Since Darcy had mentioned to Georgiana how interested Richard had been in Mrs Taylor, who although she was forced to work for a living was everything genteel, they were not particularly surprised to hear that Richard was to marry the lady, although news of her background and newfound wealth pleased the siblings enormously.

Darcy immediately offered to look for a suitable estate for the couple. He advised that Richard and Margaret should consider settling further in the north, perhaps in a county like Derbyshire, as properties were cheaper than in the vicinity of London.

After discussing the advice, Richard and Margaret agreed to let Darcy make enquiries on their behalf, as he was more knowledgeable in this field.

~A~

Bingley also sent a letter to Darcy, in which he yet again extolled the virtues of Miss Bennet.

In a previous missive, immediately after his failed proposal he had explained the lady's reluctance for an immediate engagement, preferring an extended courtship. Now he wrote that he was grateful for the opportunity to become better acquainted with Jane, as he was learning about her character and became ever more convinced that she was the right woman for him.

He was hopeful that by summer he could achieve his dream of claiming her for his wife.

~A~

Anne de Bourgh received a flood of letters from her Fitzwilliam and Darcy relatives.

Darcy wrote to confirm the date he planned to arrive at Rosings for his annual visit. During these visits he went over the estate and the books with Anne to provide advice for which his greater experience made him eminently qualified. Now that Lady Catherine was not in a position to insist on a wedding between the two of them, the cousins were pleased to spend time together. This year, Darcy even requested permission to bring Georgiana.

Georgiana's letter to Anne focused on her brother's interest in Mrs Elizabeth Brooks and her hopes that Darcy would at last find the happiness he deserved. Knowing that Anne and Elizabeth corresponded, she obliquely requested her cousin's help in furthering the match.

Most of the Fitzwilliams wrote letters to Anne de Bourgh telling her of the latest developments in Hertfordshire.

Lady Matlock waxed lyrical about her future daughter who had convinced Richard to retire from the army, and who was wealthy enough for her son to become a landed gentleman.

Richard rhapsodised about the many admirable qualities of his fiancée. While the primary ones were her kindness and intelligence, he also appreciated her sense of humour and almost as an afterthought he mentioned that he thought her exceptionally beautiful. He also revealed that they planned to marry as soon as he was completely recovered from his injuries.

Even Robert wrote about the delightful people he had met in Hertfordshire. He described the various charming ladies he had met, and Anne noticed that he was particularly effusive about Miss Charlotte Lucas, whom she knew to be a particularly good friend to Elizabeth. Of course, when he discussed his brother's fiancée, he also had to warmly mention her brother, Baron Standish. As a matter of fact, he described the charming gentleman in great detail.

As a result of all those letters, Anne de Bourgh wrote letters of her own.

To Darcy she responded with an invitation for Georgiana.

To Georgiana she wrote that she would do her best for her cousin's happiness.

To Robert she sent an invitation to visit Rosings and casually mentioned that she was planning to invite Elizabeth and her friend Charlotte. Anne also indicated that she was curious about Baron Standish and offered him the hospitality of Rosings, if Robert wished to include the gentleman in the houseparty.

The final letter she sent to Elizabeth in which she urged her to come for a visit and if she did not feel comfortable travelling on her own, she could perhaps ask Charlotte Lucas to accompany her. It was of course purely an accidental oversight that Anne forgot to mention that Robert Fitzwilliam might also be present at Rosings to coincide with Darcy's visit.

~A~

Elizabeth was sitting in her study, holding a letter and staring into space when there was a knock on the door. When Elizabeth automatically called, 'Enter,' Margaret Taylor came into the room.

Margaret tilted her head as she observed Elizabeth and asked, 'Is something wrong? You appear... pensive.'

Elizabeth waved the letter and sighed as Margaret took a seat. 'I received an invitation from Anne de Bourgh to visit Rosings... at Easter of all times.'

'I see,' said Margaret, understanding Elizabeth's reservations.

Before her marriage, Elizabeth and Jane had been the closest of sisters, but during her year at Hunsford, Jane and Mary had formed a closer bond. When Elizabeth returned and became widowed, she did not wish to burden her sisters with her experiences. Margaret, as a widow herself, had gradually become a confidant to Elizabeth, especially after that incident, when she had explained to her sisters about the pitfalls of marriage.

These days, while Elizabeth enjoyed the company of all her sisters, particularly Jane and Mary, their lack of experience prevented her from having the close connection she used to share with Jane. That void had been filled by Margaret since she was the closest in experience to Lizzy.

Margaret waited and it did not take long for Elizabeth to explain. 'I suppose that you think me a coward, but the idea of going back to Hunsford fills me with dread, as I spent the worst year of my life there.'

'But you have been invited to visit the manor, not the parsonage.'

'But at the manor, Lady Catherine encouraged my husband in his behaviour towards me.'

What Elizabeth did not say was that she felt sick to her stomach at the very idea of setting foot into not only the parsonage, but also the area. She well remembered how the slightest criticism by Lady Catherine had caused her husband to punish her for improper behaviour. She had felt so utterly helpless, like a fly caught in a spider's web. The more she struggled the more she suffered. There was nothing which she could do to prevent Collins from doing what he considered his duty. Elizabeth was terrified that she would break down as soon as she arrived.

'But did you not tell me that Lady Catherine has been bedridden since you returned to Longbourn?'

'Yes, what of it?'

'You can visit Rosings without having to encounter the lady. And if you feel so inclined, you can gloat over the fact that you now have a good life. You have complete freedom to do as you please, while she is dependent on everyone for even the littlest things.'

'You cannot truly think that I would be so vindictive!' Elizabeth cried in horror.

'No, but you are human. It would be perfectly understandable if in the deepest recesses of your mind, you felt just the slightest amount of satisfaction that the tables have been turned and Lady Catherine has received her comeuppance.'

Elizabeth blushed furiously but did not contradict her friend any longer. After a moment she sighed and said, 'I confess that I have enjoyed my correspondence with Anne. She understands not only the challenges of suddenly being thrust into the position of being the master of an estate, but also of having been effectively a prisoner in her own home. While Lady Catherine did not beat her, she subjected Anne to the torture of doctors who, instead of helping her, only made her feel worse.'

'Yet, despite the decade or more of enduring that torture, she did not run away when she was no longer constrained.' Margaret tilted her head as she recommended, 'Perhaps it is time for you to return and exorcise your ghosts.'

Elizabeth took in a sharp breath as she was taken aback by the suggestion. As she considered the words, she started to nod and relaxed her shoulders. 'You certainly have a way with words. Yes, I believe you have the right of it. I will accept the invitation.'

'Excellent. If you would care for my opinion, I would recommend that you take someone with you.'

'Indeed. I cannot take Jane or Mary since they are courting. While Kitty and Lydia have come a long way in the last three years, I do not think they would be best suited to accompany me. Since they are staying at Longbourn, by necessity you need to remain as well, even if you were not busy with your own fiancée.'

'Richard is not such an invalid anymore that he cannot do without me for a few weeks and as you said, your sisters are not the wild girls anymore and do not need constant supervision. I could go with you,' Margaret offered, albeit reluctantly.

'There is no need for you to come, unless you particularly would like to accompany me. Anne is aware of the situation at Longbourn, and she suggested that I bring Charlotte.'

'What an excellent choice. I am pleased that you have an alternative,' Margaret enthused ensuring that Elizabeth was not concerned that she might feel slighted.

~A~

Charlotte declared herself delighted when Elizabeth applied to her for her company. 'I confess that since all those visitors left our neighbourhood, it has become rather quieter,' she said.

'Are you perchance missing the excellent company of one particular visitor?' Elizabeth teased. 'A certain Viscount even?'

'It was rather pleasant that a man paid attention to me instead of drooling over Jane,' Charlotte admitted. It had been more than just pleasant as her hopes had been raised that there might be the slightest possibility that she would not always remain a burden on her family.

It had been difficult for Charlotte to watch when even Mrs Taylor, who was not only a widow, but three years older than herself, becoming engaged despite being just as poor. Admittedly, Margaret was more accomplished, but she had been willing to share her knowledge with Charlotte.

After the arrival of Baron Standish, it had not taken long for the news that Margaret was wealthy to spread, but the Colonel had not known that when he proposed. So, if the Colonel did not care for wealth, perhaps his brother would be equally as open minded, especially as he did not need an heiress.

But it had come to nothing. He had left and Charlotte was still on the shelf. Therefore, the invitation to accompany Elizabeth to Rosings was most welcome. Perhaps there were other single men who were in want of a wife.

~A~

Once the decision had been made, Elizabeth bent all her efforts to ensuring that Longbourn would run smoothly during her absence.

Elizabeth prepared lists and schedules to ensure that her sisters had all the information they might need and recommended that Lydia should ensure that all purchases were charged correctly, a responsibility the girl was proud to be given. She also timed her departure and return so that she would be available at the beginning of March and again in April to pay all the merchant's accounts. Elizabeth also wanted to be back at Longbourn before the first of April, as she wanted to celebrate her coming of age in her home.

Knowing that there was only one carriage available at Longbourn, but there were several spares at Rosings, Anne had offered to send a coach plus a maid and a footman, to collect Elizabeth and Charlotte to arrive at Longbourn on the second of March.

On that day, after paying all the bills, Elizabeth had one final visit to make to her Uncle Phillips. She explained to him, 'While I am leaving Jane and Mrs Taylor in charge at Longbourn, I am afraid that I have to ask you to keep an eye on my sisters while I am away.'

Mr Phillips gave her a smile full of confidence when he said, 'You have everything and everyone at Longbourn so well organised that I cannot imagine that there will be any need for my assistance. But you may rest easy that if such a need should arise, I will be there to provide it.'

'Thank you, uncle, I knew that I could count on you,' she said as she smiled in relief before she frowned as she had to make another request. 'I also need you to make certain that your sister does not get the idea that she could take over my position in my absence.'

Phillips groaned, 'Good Lord, I had not even considered that possibility.' He dropped his head in his hands for a moment. 'I hate having to ask this, but would you station footmen at every entrance to Longbourn with instructions not to let her enter?'

Elizabeth sighed as she answered, 'Yes, I can do that. But if she makes the attempt, I need you to come quickest.'

'I will do that. In the meantime, I shall also speak to Sir William in his capacity as magistrate in case my sister gets it into her head to try to involve the law.' He saw the dismay on Elizabeth's features as she was about to change her mind about leaving. 'Do not worry. According to your father's will, I am still the legal guardian of your sisters and there is nothing Mrs Bennet can do.'

Elizabeth allowed herself to be reassured and took her leave to return to Longbourn for the final preparations.

~A~

Chapter 29

Early the next morning, Elizabeth, accompanied by Mrs Brown, the middle-aged maid from Rosings, collected Charlotte and her trunks from Lucas Lodge.

Anne had sent the large barouche box to convey Elizabeth and Charlotte to Rosings, giving them plenty of space to be very comfortable indeed. Yet despite the physical comfort, Elizabeth was exceedingly uncomfortable. Only the fact that she did not wish to disappoint her friends, stopped her from cancelling the visit.

All along the way Elizabeth fidgeted, being unable to focus on anything except her nervousness. After they had stopped for the first time to change horses, Charlotte teased her friend. 'I am sorry to point out that you are so flustered that if you were to flutter a handkerchief you might almost make me believe that I was travelling with Mrs Bennet.'

Elizabeth gave her a disgusted look as she snapped, 'I am nothing like that woman. I simply cannot help being reminded that the last time I travelled this way, was the beginning of my... slavery. It makes me feel... discomfited.'

'I am sorry, Eliza,' Charlotte said with sincere remorse. 'I had not meant to distress you with my rather bad joke. You can usually laugh at silly things, and you must admit, you fluttering a handkerchief is a ridiculous image.'

This statement did at last lighten the mood a little as it raised a wan smile. 'You are correct, I would never wave a handkerchief about, but perhaps I did inherit a nervous disposition from Mrs Bennet.'

Charlotte briefly embraced her friend and said, 'You are nothing like Mrs Bennet. You at least have a good reason for being distressed. I cannot imagine what it would have been like to be in your position.'

'You very likely would have had an easier time of it since I cannot imagine that your mother would have encouraged your husband to use a firm hand to guide you. And I expect you would have been much more diplomatic with Lady Catherine.'

'I suppose the difference between us is that I want a husband to provide a home of my own for me, whereas now you have a home.'

That comment set off a discussion of the relative merits of getting to know one's husband before or after the wedding. In this way Charlotte managed to distract Elizabeth for much of the journey.

~A~

Since they changed horses as frequently as the driver had changed them the day before, it was not too long before they reached Bromley, where they retrieved the horses from Rosings for the final leg of the journey.

Knowing they were nearly at their destination, Elizabeth again fretted until Charlotte took hold of her shoulders and gave her a good shake. 'Eliza, remember, that man has been rotting in the cemetery at Meryton for three years.' She lowered her voice as she was not certain the maid would not take offense at her next words, which she whispered into Elizabeth's ear. 'Also, Lady Catherine has been an invalid for the same period of time. Neither of them can hurt you again. You are alive and healthy. Cherish that thought.'

Either Charlotte had not been quiet enough, or the maid had exceptionally acute hearing. She smiled with great satisfaction as she said, 'The lady certainly had her comeuppance for treating the young Miss so badly. Now she is learning that being treated by incompetent doctors is no bed of roses. I may be speaking out of turn, but I hope the old harridan has a long and miserable life.'

That surprising sentiment did much to help Elizabeth relax and at least stopped her from jumping out of the carriage and running all the way back to Longbourn.

~A~

As soon as they stepped out of the coach, the door to the manor opened and Anne de Bourgh came down the steps to greet them.

'Welcome to Rosings,' Anne said with a huge smile when she saw Elizabeth's expression.

Elizabeth gaped at their hostess in amazement and in complete disregard of propriety she exclaimed, 'You look wonderful, I would hardly have recognised you from that frail little creature you were when I was here.'

The moment the words left her mouth she blushed and stammered, 'I am sorry, I should not have said that...'

'Nonsense. Never stop yourself again from speaking the truth. But the difference is not so surprising when you consider how much your strength can improve if you are not being bled at least once a fortnight.' Anne grinned as she replied, but there was a hint of bitterness beneath her words. 'But allow me to return the compliment. You too are looking the picture of health. Now, please, introduce me to your companion.'

Once Elizabeth performed the introductions, Anne led them into the house, chattering happily. The difference to how Elizabeth remembered Anne was so marked that it took her some moments to notice the difference in the house.

Elizabeth stopped in the middle of the foyer and looked around in wonder. Gone was the excessively opulent décor of the manor. Now it appeared simple and airy. The clean lines bespoke of elegance and taste rather than the oppressive and vulgar display of wealth.

Seeing the changes, Elizabeth felt something shift in her. Suddenly she felt lighter and at last she relaxed. Yes, unpleasant things had happened to her, but that was in the past. Anne seemed to have swept away all the reminders and now she looked forward to a pleasant visit.

~A~

Elizabeth was astonished and flattered that she and Charlotte were being housed in the family wing.

'It makes more sense to have you nearby, rather than at the other end of the house,' Anne prevaricated, not mentioning that she expected three bachelors to visit who would be accommodated in the guest wing, thereby ensuring that propriety was observed.

Once they were settled and had cleaned up after their journey, Anne was only too pleased to give them a quick tour of the house before adjourning to the parlour for tea.

Unlike Lady Catherine, Anne was much happier using the more modest sitting room rather than the large drawing room, even though her mother's throne had been removed.

'The difference is simply amazing,' exclaimed Elizabeth, or variations thereof, again and again.

Anne relished the compliments as she had spent considerable time and effort in making the changes which turned the house from an ostentatious mausoleum into a comfortable, albeit large, home.

They entertained a suitably horrified Charlotte with descriptions of how the previous mistress had chosen to decorate the house.

Amidst many gasps of horror and peals of laughter, by the end of the evening, the three ladies were becoming the best of friends.

~A~

As the weather had become capricious, it was several days before the ladies could explore the estate, although on the second morning, Elizabeth judged the rain would hold off for an hour, allowing her a brief walk, escorted by a footman.

Even though her health had improved considerably, Anne had not felt comfortable learning to ride. She therefore still preferred to use her phaeton, although the ponies had been retired and she was now employing horses to pull her conveyance.

Charlotte was happy to accompany Anne in the phaeton since she too did not ride, but Elizabeth preferred not to trust anyone else's skill and chose to ride.

Anne was about to chastise the groom for leading out a horse wearing an ordinary saddle rather than the mare with the side saddle which Lady Catherine had been in the habit of riding when Elizabeth explained that this was her preference. Anne was still dubious about the propriety until Elizabeth promised, 'I will explain later, when we have some privacy.'

The majority of Anne's reservations were laid to rest when she discovered that Elizabeth's riding habit sported a split skirt, which allowed her to ride astride while still fully covered.

Once they were underway towards the first tenant Anne was planning to visit, with a groom and two footmen following at a respectful distance, allowing them to speak without being overheard, Anne said, 'You were going to explain about the propriety or lack thereof of ladies riding astride.'

Elizabeth sported a mocking smile as she explained, 'It is considered improper because if a maiden rides astride, it can damage her maidenhead, which can raise questions after her wedding as to her purity. Since we live in this ridiculous age where men are expected to be experienced in matters of the flesh, but women are not educated in any way about such things, men wish to be assured that the seed planted in a new bride is their own. Hence, they want visible proof that no man has been there before them.'

Even though Anne blushed at the topic of discussion, her embarrassment did not last long, and she laughed gaily. 'I was given the impressions that there was something essentially sinful about riding astride, rather than such a simple and practical reason. If I had known about this, I would have learnt to ride years ago, but I did not feel confident riding side-saddle.'

Now it was Elizabeth's turn to blush as she confided to her friends, 'I suspect there is another reason why men do not like women to ride astride. It can create some rather pleasing sensation in one's nether regions and I believe that men may feel that it is unladylike for genteel ladies to experience such sensations.'

'You mean they want to keep all the pleasure for themselves,' huffed Anne. 'Well, I for one do not care what they think anymore.' She tilted her head and examined Elizabeth. 'I believe that I shall need to commission some riding habits.' She surreptitiously eyed Charlotte, who looked with longing at Elizabeth and thought that an extra riding habit would be needed.

~A~

The following week Charlotte was disconcerted when Anne insisted on her being measured for a riding habit by the seamstress which Anne had employed for her own new wardrobe.

Anne distracted her by saying, 'You should have seen the outfits which my mother used to commission for me. Stiff, scratchy brocades in the most unflattering colours.' Anne chuckled and shook her head. 'I looked quite ghastly and yet she expected that I could lure my cousin Darcy into marriage. She seemed to forget that he needs an heir, and I am unwilling to produce one.'

'You do not wish for children?' Charlotte asked in shock. 'I was given to understand that all women wish for the joys of motherhood.'

'I am selfish enough to prefer being childless and alive rather than a dead mother.'

The distraction worked and soon the seamstress was promising to have the outfits ready in a few days.

During those days, the young women spent their time exploring more of Rosings, while in the evenings they talked on a large variety of subjects, often until late at night. They soon cemented a lifelong friendship.

~A~

While Elizabeth was enjoying her outing with her friends, word had spread through Meryton that she had gone away on a holiday.

Mrs Bennet had weighed up her options for several days and decided that this was an opportunity too good to miss. While the interest on her jointure was indeed quite enough to live in modest comfort in a cottage rather than starve in the hedgerows, Mrs Bennet mourned the days when she was treated with the respect due to the mistress of Longbourn. Now that she was living in reduced circumstances in a cottage that respect had disappeared.

It never occurred to the lady to question whether she might have retained that respect if she were not such a greedy and grasping woman without any significant accomplishments. After all, other widows lived in Meryton, and they were accorded respect and some of them had never been the mistress of an estate, merely the wives of humble tradesmen.

Be that as it may, she decided that she could not allow her daughters to live without the benefit of their mother to guide them towards the enviable state of matrimony. She knew that Jane was being courted by Mr Bingley, but obviously Jane needed to learn how to encourage the gentleman to come up to scratch. After all it was time that Jane used that beauty of hers for something useful.

It had also seemed quite ridiculous when Mrs Bennet heard that John Lucas was calling on Mary. Her neighbours surely were confused, and he must be calling on Lydia under the guise of visiting her middle daughter. No man in his right mind would be interested in such a plain girl as Mary. It was such a shame that Elizabeth had not allowed Lydia to come out yet, as she could have done very well for herself when all those visitors were at Netherfield at Christmas.

Mrs Bennet was convinced that once she was back in residence at Longbourn, she would have her two favourite daughters married in no time, so that by the time Elizabeth returned from gallivanting about the country, she would have to acknowledge that mothers knew best.

She therefore donned her most impressive gown and marched off to Longbourn to carry the day.

~A~

Mrs Bennet was most displeased when she arrived at Longbourn, and the front door was not immediately thrown open for her. When she tried to enter by lowering herself to open the door with her own hands, she discovered the door locked.

Instead of gaining immediate admittance she was forced to knock and wait until Mr Hill opened the door. She was foiled again as he did not stand aside to let her enter, but quite deliberately blocked the door.

'Stand aside,' Mrs Bennet demanded imperiously. 'I have come to ensure my daughters receive the loving care only a mother can provide.'

Alerted by the commotion, Mary was coming down the stairs to investigate what was happening. She was amused when Mrs Bennet's lips pinched in displeasure before she exclaimed, 'Elizabeth, what are you doing here? I was told that you have gone away and left your sisters without proper guidance.'

In Mrs Bennet's defence it must be said that the stairs were not particularly well lit and seemed especially dim compared to the bright sunshine outside and vanity prevented her from considering that perhaps her eyesight could use the assistance of spectacles. Also, the lady had not seen much of her daughters in recent times. As she judged her daughter by general shape, colouring and mode of dress, she therefore concluded that her least favourite daughter had returned to frustrate her yet again.

'It does not matter where I am, there is no need for you in this house. Goodbye, Mrs Bennet,' said Mary and Mr Hill closed the door in the lady's face.

Mary was conflicted whether to be angry that her mother could not even recognise her daughters or amused to have so easily fooled the woman. Once she had given orders for Mr Phillips to be informed of the event, she decided amusement, while irreverent towards a parent, was infinitely more worthwhile.

~A~

Chapter 30

On Sundays, Elizabeth refused to attend services in the church at Hunsford.

Anne told her about the new rector to whom she had awarded the living after the death of Mr Collins. Mr Hayes was different from his predecessor in every respect. He was an intelligent, pleasant and active man of about thirty years of age, and he was more concerned about the wellbeing of his parishioners than the opinion of his patroness.

While Mr Hayes was always perfectly courteous to Anne, he never once fawned on her or asked her advice on scripture. The closest he came to discuss his sermons with her was after the service when Anne congratulated him on a particularly poignant one.

Since Anne had discovered that Mr Hayes often spent a considerable part of the tithes which he received from the parish on helping the poorest of his flock, she had agreed to fund half his charitable works.

Still, attending services in that church was a step too far for Elizabeth. She had no intention of ever setting foot in the Hunsford church again.

When Anne misunderstood her reticence and tried to encourage her by saying, 'Surely, you do not still miss your husband. I had not thought you to be particularly close,' Elizabeth broke down and related the true state of her marriage to the abject horror of Anne.

'You mean to say that my mother encouraged that... man?' cried Anne. When Elizabeth could only nod, Anne's eyes narrowed as she exclaimed, 'At the moment I am fiercely tempted to take a stick to my mother for her transgressions.'

She hesitated as another thought occurred to her. 'Perhaps her devoted attention to my welfare by engaging all those useless doctors were not as kindly meant. Or her insistence that I should marry William. My cousin Robert would have been a much better catch, but it occurs to me that his estate is only fifteen miles from here, an easy couple of hours. Whereas it takes at least three days to travel from here to Pemberley.'

Elizabeth pulled herself together and gave a small shrug. 'What does it matter anymore. My husband is dead, and your mother is an invalid. We have both survived to take control of our destinies. I am perfectly content to leave it at that.' She added with a small but mulish smile, 'But I still refuse to set foot in that church.'

Now that she knew the full story Anne readily agreed but determined to warn her cousin to exercise patience. No matter what Georgiana hoped, Anne did not think Elizabeth was ready to trust another man... even one as kind and gentle as she knew William to be.

~A~

On the second Monday afternoon, after Elizabeth's and Charlotte's arrival, a convoy of coaches descended on Rosings, carrying the expected visitors.

The leading coach carried Darcy, Georgiana and Mrs Annesley, Georgiana's companion. Robert Fitzwilliam and Henry Standish shared the second coach, while the third carried all the valets and Georgiana's maid.

As Darcy handed out Georgiana and Mrs Annesley, Anne came out to greet her guests, and Robert performed the introduction. As she welcomed her new acquaintance, Anne was pleased to see that the young Baron was just as Robert had described him. Before they even spoke, they each felt a sense of recognition.

When Anne addressed Standish formally, Robert suggested to her, 'Since all of us are family or good friends, do you suppose that you could forgo formality with our friend? Otherwise, he is very much the odd one out.'

Anne glanced at the Baron who gave her a hopeful smile and a slight nod, she said, 'Very well, you may address me as Anne and if you are agreeable, I shall call you Henry,' to which Standish heartily acquiesced.

As she led the party inside, Anne informed them, 'Gentlemen, I hope you do not mind but I have put you into the guest wing since I have single ladies visiting as well, who are all in the family wing. Georgiana, you have a choice whether you wish to stay near your brother, or you and Mrs Annesley can join us ladies in the family wing.'

Since Georgiana felt a little intimidated by the Viscount despite the fact that he was her cousin, she opted to stay with the ladies.

'Very well,' Anne agreed. 'I recommend that you refresh yourselves and I will have tea ready in the small parlour in an hour.

~A~

Once the new arrivals had washed off the dust of the road and made themselves presentable, they joined Anne and her other guests in Anne's preferred sitting room.

Robert and Henry were aware which ladies Anne had planned to invite and were therefore prepared to greet them pleasantly. Yet no one had informed the Darcys of the identity of the visitors, leaving Darcy stunned while Anne introduced Georgiana to Elizabeth and Charlotte.

Georgiana almost squealed during the introduction. 'Mrs Brooks, I am so very pleased to meet you at last. I have heard a great deal about you from... ah... all of my family.'

'I too have heard a great many things about you and was looking forward to meeting you,' Elizabeth replied with a smile at the enthusiasm of the young girl who reminded her a little of Kitty. 'But since I am on a first name basis with your cousin, will you call me Elizabeth?'

The offer was gladly accepted and reciprocated, while Darcy watched with an approving smile, pleased that the two women he loved most were immediately drawn to each other. When Darcy greeted Elizabeth with a brilliant smile, she caught her breath, thinking again that that smile coupled with his piercing look should be classified as a lethal weapon.

They shook themselves out of their reverie as Anne declared, 'As Robert suggested earlier, and since he is the most senior person present in age and rank, I quite agree that as we are all family or good friends, we dispense with formality and use only given names during your stay.'

Even though Robert laughingly protested that he was hardly decrepit despite his advanced age of two and thirty, all agreed to the suggestion.

Only Darcy requested a small alteration, 'Please call me William, otherwise Robert might answer when you address me as Fitzwilliam.'

~A~

The party enjoyed their tea, which included a variety of pastries and sandwiches, during which Darcy complimented Anne on the changes she had made to the house. 'I could hardly believe this is the same house over which Aunt Catherine presided with an iron fist.'

Anne smiled at the compliment as she said, 'I confess that I have tried to wipe away all reminders of her presence and attempted to make it as light and airy and welcoming as I could.'

'I know that it is impolite to raise such a subject in company, but I am concerned how you could afford to do so. After all, your mother nearly destroyed the estate with her extravagance.'

'As it happens, I made a profit from her extravagance as I sold all that tasteless junk with which she furnished the house. The new pieces I bought were significantly cheaper and much more tasteful.' Anne smiled and nodded towards Elizabeth. 'I have Elizabeth to thank for the suggestion and for putting me in touch with Mr Gardiner who helped with the sale.'

Robert chimed in, 'I have come to the realisation that every family needs some relations in trade, to ensure that they have someone who is practical. It also keeps noble families from thinking that they are above perfectly decent people, simply because they do not have a title.'

After the meal, Anne suggested, 'Would you like a tour of the house? There are some changes even Robert and William have not yet seen.'

Everyone agreed, and Darcy added, 'After several hours in a carriage, I could use some exercise.' He rose to his feet and offered his arm to Elizabeth. She raised a brow but accepted without demur.

Robert suggested to Anne, 'Since Henry has never seen the place before, you should show him around,' as he offered his own arm to Charlotte.

Henry smiled cheekily at Anne and offered his arm, 'Please my lady, lead me wherever you wish.'

Robert rolled his eyes and murmured, 'Up the garden path even.'

The three couples set off, with Georgiana and Mrs Annesley bringing up the rear. Just to ensure that no one went astray...

~A~

The following morning Darcy was awake at his usual time, just as it was getting light. Unable to sleep any longer, he remembered that he had promised Anne that he would speak with her at the first opportunity this morning, but he judged it much too early for such a conference. Instead, he rose and dressed, deciding to go out for a walk.

He was just putting on his coat, when there was a soft knock. Answering the door Darcy discovered a footman bearing a tray with coffee. 'Your valet said that you always rise at dawn and appreciate a cup of coffee,' the man explained as he put down the tray.

Darcy thanked the man and considered all the gradual changes to Rosings over the years since his cousin took over the management. Everything ran more smoothly, and guests were treated with more consideration. In Lady Catherine's time, he would have had to wait until breakfast for his coffee.

Sustained by his favourite brew, he set off on his walk.

~A~

As he strode along the lanes in the park, Darcy admitted to himself that he hoped to encounter Elizabeth as he had been unable to have a private moment with her since his arrival.

Ever since Christmas since he had that conversation with Georgiana about her potential future, he had felt a great anticipation. He wanted to journey to Meryton immediately to ask for Elizabeth's hand, but between his duties and the state of the roads due to the weather, his sensible side prevailed and he decided to wait until after this visit to Rosings to approach Elizabeth.

The more he missed her, the more he realised how much she had come to mean to him. Not only how much he loved her but how much he needed her in his life. Elizabeth had become his best friend, the person with whom he could discuss everything, even if propriety frowned upon some of the topics they had canvassed in their debates.

When he arrived, she was the last person in the world he expected to see here. But not only was she here, thanks to Anne and Robert, he was allowed to address her at last in the manner in which he thought of her... as Elizabeth. Or not precisely as he thought of her, since in his mind she was *my Elizabeth*.

But his hopes were frustrated yet again as Elizabeth did not appear.

~A~

Elizabeth woke in a pensive mood. Since her arrival at Rosings, she felt that her emotions were on a seesaw.

As she had feared, there were many reminders of her time in the area. Fortunately, the house had been completely redecorated, easing her apprehension, but then someone would say or do something, and she was again reminded of Collins.

The discussion she had with Anne a few days earlier had simultaneously made her feel better and worse. Better, because she felt like she was letting some of her anger at Collins and Lady Catherine go, but worse because it opened old wounds.

As a consequence, she decided to forgo her walk and instead find a book in the library with which to distract her mind.

~A~

When Darcy returned from his walk, he almost walked past the open door of the library until he spied the object of his desire within.

Elizabeth was curled up on the window-seat with a book in her lap, apparently completely engrossed in whatever she was reading. She made such a lovely picture and Darcy wished to see her like this at Pemberley.

He could resist no longer and entered the library, making certain to leave the door partially open.

As he approached, Elizabeth heard a slight noise and looked up. Seeing her good friend, she smiled in welcome.

That was enough encouragement for Darcy, and he said, '*In vain have I struggled. It will not do. My feelings will not be repressed. You must allow me to tell you how ardently I admire and love you.*'

Darcy forgot the speech he had worked on to convey his great feelings and instead spoke from the heart. 'For weeks I have searched my feelings and I have come to the conclusion that I cannot imagine a life without you in it. You are the most wonderful woman I have ever known. I love your kindness to everyone, and your compassion even towards people who have no claim on you. I love your intelligence and wit, and your ability to manage your estate. I could not help but imagine how much everyone at Pemberley would benefit from your attention. Even in the short time she has known you, Georgiana already loves you like a sister. And like I do for Georgiana, I wish to take care of you and shelter you and do everything in my power to ensure your happiness. I hope you will do me the honour of accepting my hand in marriage.'

As he finished speaking, Darcy's eyes glowed with the passion of his words and the certainty that he had conveyed his sentiments most eloquently.

Elizabeth was shocked by the speech and rose to her feet to respond in the only way she could. She sought to gain some distance by reverting to formality. 'Mr Darcy, I am honoured by your proposal, but I am afraid that I am unable to accept.'

Darcy was pleased when Elizabeth stood to face him to give her response and impatiently waited for her to say *yes*, so that he could seal their engagement with a kiss. He was staring at her luscious lips and was starting to lean forward when she stopped speaking, until suddenly the meaning of her words registered.

He flinched back as if he had been slapped. 'Did you say no?' he gasped, unable to believe Elizabeth had just rejected his proposal of marriage.

'While I did not actually use that word, that was the meaning I hoped to convey.'

'But I thought you like me, even perhaps love me.'

'I think you are an honourable man and I like you a great deal indeed,' Elizabeth said carefully.

'But why would you say no? I thought that you were expecting, nay... hoping for my addresses.'

Elizabeth suppressed a moue of distaste at the arrogance and said as calmly as she could, 'Mr Darcy, I have no wish to marry again.'

'Whyever not?'

'If we were to marry, would you be prepared to sign over all your worldly possessions to me?'

'Good heavens no, why should I?'

Before he had a chance to say that although he would be most generous in his marriage settlement, he had no intentions of becoming a pauper, Elizabeth asked, 'Or... would you be prepared to become a non-person with no rights of your own, for me to do with as I please?'

'Of course not. Whyever, would I want to do any such thing?'

'Exactly. You have your answer.' Elizabeth fought back tears as she curtsied and said, 'Now if you will excuse me...' and rushed out the door.

Darcy stared after her in complete and utter disbelief.

What had just happened?

~A~

Chapter 31

Darcy was still trying to work out why Elizabeth had rejected his proposal and what she had meant by the ridiculous questions she had asked, when Anne came storming into the room.

'Fitzwilliam Darcy, explain yourself. What did you do to Elizabeth to make her so distraught that she would not even speak to me?' she demanded furiously.

Darcy was shocked to hear that Elizabeth was distraught as she had seemed perfectly composed when she shattered his hopes before leaving the library. But not wanting to admit to what had just happened, he prevaricated. 'What makes you think that I did anything wrong?'

'Because she came from this direction, and you are a master at saying the wrong thing.'

'How can offering marriage to a woman be the wrong thing?' Darcy snapped, without thinking, at his cousin's insult.

Anne rolled her eyes and sighed as she asked seemingly apropos of nothing, 'Do you remember what I asked you to do this morning?'

'You wanted to speak to me about something... I assume it was about some matter with the estate,' Darcy was grateful to change the subject.

'Tell me exactly what I asked you to do,' Anne said carefully, but with an edge in her voice.

'You asked me to come and see you first thing this morning,' Darcy replied patiently as if speaking to a child.

'Try again, and this time try to get it right. And preferably without the attitude,' Anne snapped with considerable attitude of her own.

Darcy gave her an irritated look as he furrowed his brows and said, 'You said, and I quote, *come and see me first thing in the morning before you do anything else*. Happy now?' he growled.

'No, I am angry with you for ignoring my request. But I suppose that you suffer more for your stupidity and inability to follow simple instructions than I will.'

Seeing confusion added to Darcy's irritation she added, 'I wanted to see you to advise you to exercise extreme patience where Elizabeth is concerned. Visiting here has brought back many bad memories with which she has to come to terms. At the moment the last thing she needs is a besotted fool bumbling about and upsetting her.'

'WHAT?'

'I discovered that that young woman went through hell while she was at Hunsford, thanks to her husband and my mother and right now she has not the slightest interest in marriage.'

'I knew that her marriage to Collins was unhappy. After all, how could any woman as intelligent as Elizabeth be happy with an idiot like Collins, who enjoyed nothing better than to grovel at your mother's feet. But surely, he could not have been that bad since she chose to marry him.'

Darcy ran his hand through his hair in frustration that his cousin could possibly compare him to that idiot parson. 'But you know that I am nothing like that fool. I appreciate Elizabeth's intelligence. It was one of the things which first attracted me to her. With all that intelligence, surely, she can see that I would make her a much better husband.'

'Honestly, William, why would you expect an intelligent woman agree to become your slave unless she had no other choice.'

'A slave? What do you mean? And why are you changing the subject? We were speaking about Elizabeth's refusal of my honourable proposal of marriage.'

'But we are speaking of the same thing. You proposed to Elizabeth to become your slave.'

'I asked her to be my WIFE!'

'Please explain to me the difference between a wife and a slave under English law.'

Darcy was still too shocked by Elizabeth's refusal to think clearly. 'A wife has rights,' he stated distractedly.

Anne gave him a pitying look as she countered, 'The only right she has is that you are not allowed to kill her.'

When Darcy opened his mouth as if to argue the point, Anne went on relentlessly, 'In England, when a woman marries, all her property becomes her husband's, even the clothes on her back. She has no right to anything, not even her own body. She too becomes the property of her husband. She has no standing as a person in her own right. The husband has the right to make any demand of his wife and do whatever he wishes to her, short of killing her and she has no right to object in any way.' Anne glowered at her cousin. 'So, tell me, how is that different from being a slave?'

Darcy closed his mouth with a snap as the tirade brought him back to the present and reminded him of all the facts which he knew, since he had used them to frighten Caroline Bingley away from insisting on marriage.

But he never had thought about those laws actually being applied to himself and his wife, since he would never ask his wife to do anything to which she did not agree.

But since Anne listed the points of law, it made him think of the questions Elizabeth had asked and which had so confused him at the time.

She had asked him to agree to exactly what marriage to him would entail for her under English law and his reaction was abhorrence of the very idea. Yet, if losing everything including himself made him feel such disgust, how could he expect a woman like Elizabeth to subject herself to such an ordeal.

Darcy attempted to convey this feeling on the subject to Anne. 'But I would never ask anything of her that she was not willing to give, and I was planning on settling a significant sum on her to ensure that she will always be taken care of.'

'Were you planning to settle more on her than the value of what she already owns?'

'What she already owns?' Darcy repeated the words in confusion.

'Elizabeth owns an estate, just like I own Rosings. Has that featured at all in your considerations?'

Darcy had the grace to blush as he admitted, 'I had considered the estate to be a most suitable dowry as we could set it aside for our second son.'

'A dowry of which you would take possession and then decide where to bestow it at a time of your choosing, completely ignoring Elizabeth's wishes?'

'Ah...'

'Just as I thought,' Anne stated but said no more as she stood with her arms crossed over her chest while looking at her cousin in disgust.

'I was not planning on ignoring Elizabeth's wishes,' Darcy defended the one point which he could argue.

'So, you would be willing to pass Longbourn on to one of her sisters?'

'Certainly not. It should go to one of our sons.'

'But if you have no sons. Remember, Elizabeth is one of five sisters,' Anne reminded Darcy.

'She already had one son. There is no reason why she should not have more.' It was Darcy's turn to hold up his hand to stop Anne from interrupting as he added quite reasonably, 'But if we should only be blessed with daughters, I can leave Pemberley to one of them. And I suppose it is only fair that I should let her decide what to do with her own property,' he finished with a sigh.

Anne was somewhat mollified as she asked, 'So, you would not turn her into a broodmare and force her to endure the trauma of childbirth for as many times as it took for her to deliver an heir to you?'

'I would certainly not force her to do such a thing. But children are a natural outcome of... ah... marriage,' Darcy tried to phrase things as delicately as he could since he expected his cousin to be unaware of the technicalities because she was still a maiden.

Anne allowed herself to calm down, seeing that her cousin had simply not considered the implications of the law upon his own life. But as the subject was one about which she felt most passionate and perhaps just a tad obstreperous, she declared, 'For many women, marriage is a form of institutionalised prostitution as well as slavery.' She had the pleasure of seeing the colour drain from Darcy's face as she presented the worst interpretation of conjugal interactions.

'How do you come up with all those outlandish ideas?' he gasped when he found his voice again.

'I had many years when all I was allowed to do was to sit quietly and suffer.

'But do you not remember the felicity between my parents? Or that Georgiana was the result of my mother's ardent wish for more children?'

'Yes, and it killed her.' Seeing the pain on her cousin's countenance, brought Anne up short. 'I am dreadfully sorry, William. I had not meant to hurt you. I let my own irritation and frustration get the better of me.'

She sighed and blinked away tears. 'Unlike you, I remember my mother being anything but loving to my father. I realised quite early that she only married him for his wealth and when he kept tight hold on the purse-strings she became quite... vocal and distant.' She huffed. 'I suspect that was why, after his death, mother spent money like it was growing on trees and she was living in an orchard.'

Darcy sighed and let his shoulders relax as he gave a small chuckle. 'Just listen to us, we argue like a married couple.'

'Let us rather say, like family.' Anne gave Darcy a mirthless smile as she shook her head. 'I am afraid that I let my experience with my parents colour my attitude towards marriage. It can work for some people. But my initial point was that Elizabeth did not choose to marry Collins. Her parents forced her into that marriage, and she was badly hurt by it. As a result, she is not ready to trust any man. Especially one who blunders about without considering her feelings.'

'But I do care about her feelings,' protested Darcy.

'You may care about them, but do you have the least idea what they are? Have you ever asked her about those feelings?'

'It is most improper to raise such subjects with a lady who is unrelated to me.'

'So, propriety strikes again. How are potential couples ever going to know anything of significance about each other if propriety prevents them from being honest?'

'Since you are so full of wisdom and good advice just like your mother, what do you suggest I should do,' Darcy asked sarcastically.

'I would recommend telling propriety to go to hell.' She held up her hand to stop whatever Darcy planned to say. 'But in the meantime, I strongly recommend giving Elizabeth time to deal with her past.'

As much as it pained Darcy, he was forced to agree with Anne's evaluation.

~A~

Anne found Elizabeth in her dressing room pulling her dresses off the shelves and taking an armful into the bedroom to pack them, very badly, into the trunk which she had dragged out.

Looking at Elizabeth's tear-streaked face Anne took the dress out of her hands and set it aside in preparation for enfolding her friend in an embrace.

'I am sorry that you are planning to leave us,' she said quietly.

'Oh, Anne, I am sorry too, but I simply cannot remain,' Elizabeth sobbed as she clung to Anne.

'You should know that while William is a fool, he meant well.'

Elizabeth pulled away from Anne to ask, 'Did he tell you...'

'That he made a fool of himself? Yes, he did.'

Elizabeth slumped down onto the bed and sighed. 'He is such a good man, but I simply cannot...'

'I quite understand since I now know something of your history. But you never told my cousin about this, did you?'

'No, I did not. It is not exactly the sort of thing you can talk about casually. After all, can you imagine a dinner party where one lady turns to another across the table and asks, *and how often did your husband beat you this week*? And she answers, *only once, but he did beat me half to death.'*

Anne chuckled at the weak attempt at humour but was reassured that Elizabeth was not about to suffer a nervous collapse.

'I am afraid that he caught me by surprise with his proposal and when he had the arrogance to say that he expected me to be hoping for his addresses, I reacted more strongly than perhaps I should have done.'

'Did he actually say that he expected you to be hoping for his proposal?'

When Elizabeth simply nodded, Anne exploded, 'That piece of arrogance seems to have slipped my cousin's mind.'

'I suppose it is only to be expected. From all that I have heard, he is a most eligible gentleman and has been pursued as a matrimonial prospect for nearly a decade. Most women would have jumped at the chance at such a great prize.'

Anne sat next to Elizabeth and captured her hands. 'All joking aside, will you tell me how you feel about William? If you did not have to contend with your past?'

Elizabeth dropped her eyes from the intense searching look and coloured. 'Do you have any idea how much I have cursed my late husband in recent times, because I cannot blithely consent to marriage as I simply do not trust any man.'

'I can assure you that William is nothing like that man.'

Elizabeth's eyes blazed as she raised them and cried, 'My head knows that but the rest of me will not believe. That is why I now hate Mr Collins and my parents. They have robbed me of my innocence and trust in human nature. While I was never as naïve as Jane, I used to believe that most people are mostly good. Not perfect, but mostly good. Now I feel that I cannot trust anyone. Especially not someone whom the law gives complete control.'

'I get the feeling that you would like to trust...'

'Oh, yes. I would like nothing better than to be in a position where I could trust someone wholeheartedly.' Her face crumpled again, and she sobbed, 'I think I have hurt him abominably.'

'No. Do not trouble yourself on that account. While he is a good man, he never before really considered what marriage means to a woman in our country. He also needed to learn that he cannot have everything his own way. But I know that he can be patient.'

Elizabeth looked up again in shock. 'But I cannot guarantee that I will ever be able to change. I could not ask him to wait... potentially forever.'

'Perhaps you and he could talk, without paying propriety the least regard, and find out how each of you feel.'

'I am sorry, Anne, but at the moment I cannot bring myself to do so. Everything is simply too raw,' Elizabeth pleaded.

Anne took pity on her friend. 'I had hoped that you would stay longer, but I can see that this time it will not be. I will send Lucy and Molly to you to help you get changed and packed. The carriage will be ready to take you home in half an hour. Although I hope that you will not mind travelling without Charlotte?'

'Oh, Lord, I had completely forgotten about her.'

'Do not trouble yourself, I will ensure that she will get home safely when she is ready to leave.'

Elizabeth threw her arms around Anne. 'Thank you. You are too good to me.'

'It is my pleasure to help in any way I can. I hope that you will find the strength to be happy.'

Within the half hour specified, Elizabeth was ready to quit Rosings Park. It felt like she was running away, but she knew that having faced her fears, she needed time to recover.

~A~

Chapter 32

As Elizabeth and Anne approached the front door, Darcy stepped out of the library.

He bowed to Elizabeth from three feet away to ensure she would not feel pressured in any way and said quietly, 'Elizabeth, I am sorry that in my precipitousness I have caused you pain. It was never my intent. My only hope was to add to your happiness as well as my own.'

'Mr Darcy... William, you could not have known about the extent of my demons. Which is why I must take my leave to return to my home, but... I hope to see you and Georgiana in Meryton after Easter, as you had planned.'

Darcy's face lit up at the hesitant suggestion. 'Perhaps at that time we will have a chance to talk?'

'I think I should like that,' Elizabeth agreed quietly.

'In that case, I will look forward to seeing you then.'

~A~

As soon as the horses leaned into the traces and the barouche box started to move, Elizabeth relaxed into the squabs with a sigh.

Mrs Brown, who again accompanied Elizabeth on the journey, and who Lizzy had discovered was the head parlourmaid at Rosings, gave her a nod and a pleasant smile as she pulled her knitting out of her valise.

Relieved that her companion was content to travel in silence, Elizabeth let her mind wander over the last several months since she had met Mr Darcy again.

Ever since she had known the gentleman, he had been consistently courteous and respectful. He had always treated her as an equal and had seemingly enjoyed their debates when she had disagreed with him.

Not once had he given the slightest hint that he had anything other than his sex in common with her husband. Then why was it so difficult for her to trust the man?

He was intelligent, well read, kind and considerate towards his staff and tenants. By all reports he was a most loving and supportive brother as well as cousin to Anne. He was always there for everyone and never shirked a duty.

Elizabeth's eyes had been half shut while she pondered the situation. But as the last thought occurred to her, her eyes flew open as she sat up straight and gasped. A cold shiver ran down her spine as she thought again... he never shirked a duty.

Collins had considered it a duty to teach her how to act according to his understanding of how women should behave. Elizabeth knew that he had found no pleasure in his actions, but his mind had been too rigid to consider other teaching methods. Collins also had had an exceedingly rigid idea of women's mental abilities (none) and place (decidedly below any man). None of those ideas were conducive to accepting Elizabeth's differences.

But the crucial point was that Collins, misguided though he was, had always done his duty.

Darcy was always doing his duty.

Was that what held her back from trusting him? While his ideas appeared liberal, that was the face he showed in public. She could never know his true private face until it was potentially too late.

She started cursing silently. Knowing what was holding her back did not bring her any closer to a solution on how to overcome that issue.

Elizabeth had been able to hide behind the idea that they were just good friends where such things did not matter as they were two independent individuals. But Darcy's declaration of love and his proposal was forcing her to confront her own true feelings.

At last, she had no option but to admit to herself that she was hopelessly in love with the man but could see no way in which they could be together as she was terrified that she would be hurt again. But, contrary to what most people might think, it was not the physical pain but the mental anguish of not being able to speak her mind and being treated like a child, which had hurt the most.

All the brooding had exhausted her and because of her restless sleep the night before, the swaying of the coach lulled Elizabeth to sleep. She roused at times when the coach stopped to change horses, but she was grateful that nothing was required of her during the journey but to rest.

~A~

Elizabeth was even more grateful for the rest she had as she arrived at Longbourn to find quite a commotion going on outside the front door.

'What do you mean that you do not want me? I am your mother!'

The shrill voice of Mrs Bennet could be heard as the de Bourgh coach drew to a halt a short distance beyond the entrance, as the area immediately outside the door was taken up by a group of people.

As Elizabeth stepped out onto the top step which had been placed by the footman, she could see over the heads of the crowd consisting of Longbourn staff, the Netherfield party, Sir William Lucas and Mr Phillips, towards the combatants in the centre of the disturbance. Mrs Bennet faced Lydia, who was flanked by her sisters and Mrs Taylor. It appeared that Mrs Bennet was making demands of her favourite daughters, who had been rejecting every overture.

Elizabeth was just in time to hear Lydia respond. 'You stopped being my mother the day you abandoned me to move into your own house. At least my sisters stood by me, no matter what happened. Lizzy housed me, clothed me, fed me. She looked after my education, and she was there every time I needed her. She even nursed me when I was sick, which is something you never did, even when you were living here.'

'She also recognises family. What kind of mother cannot even distinguish her own daughters. Last time you were here you thought that I was Lizzy,' huffed Mary and took Lydia's hand.

'That harridan has poisoned your mind against me,' complained Mrs Bennet, seemingly more out of habit than conviction.

This time it was Jane who answered, cutting across whatever Kitty tried to say. 'No, Mrs Bennet. You stopped being a mother when you traded your daughter's wellbeing for your comfort and status. No real mother would purchase her luxuries with the pain of her children. Go away, you are not wanted here.'

Mrs Bennet looked from one daughter to the next and could not see the slightest softening in any of them. 'But...'

Sir William Lucas had stood by and observed but concluded that he needed to speak up to stop the scene. 'Mrs Bennet, leave off. You know that Eliza will reach her majority in just another fortnight. All the Misses Bennet are in excellent health. They are well cared for and accomplished in all the areas expected in young gentlewomen. And much as it pains me to say so publicly, you could not have done half as well by them if you had remained in charge of their education.'

'I thought that you were on my side,' Mrs Bennet rounded on her accuser.

'I am on the side of right and that is Eliza's.'

After several attempts, Kitty at last managed to make herself heard. 'Why did you come here today? I do not for one second believe it is out of concern for any of us. You never truly cared about anyone but yourself. You had five daughters, but you ignored all but the prettiest whom you could show off to your neighbours and gloat. I for one am glad that Lizzy is in charge now. Because she at least notices and loves all of us,' she made her own point while she glared at her mother.

As even her meekest daughter spoke out against her and accurately discerned her less than noble motives, Mrs Bennet at last conceded defeat. Without another word, but with unshed tears stinging her eyes, she turned away from the sisters and stalked up the drive not noticing the new arrival.

For the longest time she had told herself that she was only concerned about her daughters' welfare, even when she forced Elizabeth into that marriage, but Kitty's blunt words at last forced her to examine her true motives. As much as she did not wish to acknowledge them, because they did not paint a pretty picture of her character, they had a ring of truth to them.

~A~

Jane turned away from the retreating back of Mrs Bennet and spotted the bone of contention watching the drama. Her face lit up as she called out, 'Lizzy!'

Elizabeth stepped down and approached her sisters as everyone made way for her. 'Can I not even go away for two weeks without having problems occurring,' she said as she enfolded Jane in a brief embrace. As she stepped back, she smiled and praised her sisters, 'Although you seem to have the situation well under control.'

'We did have a lot of support,' Jane pointed out and indicated the assembled friends.

'Mrs Bennet must have been excessively determined to face such overwhelming odds.' Elizabeth smiled and nodded at everyone. 'You all have my thanks for defending my sisters.'

This was greeted by a variety of denials such as 'It was the merest bagatelle,' or 'Think nothing of it.' But seeing that Elizabeth had just arrived, her friends and neighbours took their leave to allow her some peace.

Elizabeth barely had time to inform Sir William that Charlotte was having a delightful time at Rosings and would return with the Darcys and Mrs Annesley, before her sisters claimed her attention.

~A~

Over the next few days, Elizabeth had plenty of stories about the happenings at Rosings with which to regale her sisters and friends.

She described many of the events in detail, with one notable exception. She did not mention the rather impetuous proposal by the Derbyshire gentleman.

Instead, she found an attentive audience in Margaret Taylor, when she related how her brother and Anne had immediately taken to each other. 'I suppose that they might make a true love match,' mused Margaret with a pleased smile. 'Henry is a gentle soul and has no need for further riches, which would appeal to Miss de Bourgh as he would not wish to control her life.'

Sir William proved to be ecstatic when Elizabeth mentioned that Viscount Fanshaw was visiting his cousin and had appeared to be pleased, but unsurprised to discover Charlotte at Rosings.

When she spoke to the gentlemen at Netherfield to inform them of the imminent arrival of Darcy and his sister, Elizabeth discovered that the Colonel had news of his own to impart. As of the end of the month, he would revert back to being the Honourable Mister Fitzwilliam.

Jane happily reported that her courtship was progressing well. She and Bingley spent many hours in conversation about how they hoped to live their lives in the future. She was also pleased that he was doing well at Netherfield and the tenants grapevine testified to his commitment to their welfare.

The youngest girls were thrilled because Mrs Taylor had given them a new project. They were to plan her wedding. Mary was in charge of the wedding breakfast, Kitty was to arrange the decorations as well as submit her ideas for a wedding gown to the bride, while Lydia was to coordinate the supplies and monitor the finances.

All three of them swore that Margaret's would be the best wedding Meryton had ever seen.

Elizabeth maintained a pleased expression for her family and friends while she silently grieved that such happiness was not to be hers.

But instead of moping, she threw herself into her duties and did not notice that she was often being watched while she went about her tasks.

~A~

The two weeks till Easter went by very quickly and there seemed to be a suppressed excitement in the air.

The three youngest sisters and Mrs Taylor spent much of their time at Netherfield. Elizabeth was given to understand that they, together with Mr Fitzwilliam and Louisa Hurst were planning the wedding.

Since this project was a good part of their lessons, Elizabeth had no issue with the location of the lessons. She did have a minor complaint with all the giggling and whispering in which the girls indulged when they were at Longbourn. But since the girls were happy and enthusiastic about their curriculum, Elizabeth ignored the side-effects.

Instead, she made the most of the warming weather and focused on visiting the tenants and inspecting the estate for any minor damage which might have been overlooked but found everything in good order.

The routine of her duties helped settle Elizabeth's raw emotions. She had survived seeing Rosings again. Not only that, but the friendship which she had begun via correspondence with Anne had become much stronger during the visit. It had been reassuring to see that Anne had survived her mother's tyranny for a decade or more and yet she had come out of it stronger than she would have been otherwise.

Elizabeth resolved that she would take Anne as an example and inspiration for her own healing.

~A~

As Elizabeth had returned early from her visit, she invited Bingley, Fitzwilliam and the Hursts to join her and her sisters for dinner at Longbourn on Easter Sunday, an invitation which they gladly accepted. Even though everyone had a wonderful time, Elizabeth mused that it would have been even better if the Gardiners, and especially their children, had been able to attend.

As the birthday of her majority was approaching, Elizabeth was a little surprised that no one seemed to pay much attention to the date, until Jane enquired if she wanted any special dishes prepared to celebrate the day.

'I am certain that Mrs Hill is already planning to have cook prepare all my favourites,' Elizabeth advised, a little relieved that at least her closest sister had remembered the occasion in all the other excitement.

'I believe that you are correct.' Jane replied and hesitated before she asked. 'I just remembered that I promised Louisa that we would have tea with her on Wednesday. Would you be amenable to attend?'

Seeing no reason why she would not want to visit Netherfield, Elizabeth agreed.

~A~

Chapter 33

April Fool's Day dawned bright and clear and promised to be a perfect day. As was so often the case when the weather was good, and occasionally when it was not, Elizabeth hurried through her morning ablutions at first light and headed out to Oakham Mount.

While she watched the sun rise from her favourite perch, she reflected that at last no one could dispute her right to own and administer Longbourn. Even though her uncles had been supportive, for three years there had been a niggling worry in the back of her mind that someone would try to take the estate from her.

Now at last she did not have to worry any longer. She was at last legally an adult and no one could wrest control of the estate or her life from her.

As she thought that, the image of an exceedingly handsome face rose unbidden in her mind. While no one could take control away from her, would she ever be able to willingly give up control? The temptation was getting stronger every day.

~A~

When Elizabeth returned to the house, she found all the inhabitants ready to pamper her.

Jane was waiting with a cup of hot chocolate to go with cook's best pastries, as well as a breakfast spread fit for a queen.

Once she was replete to the point of, *if I eat another mouthful, I shall burst*, Elizabeth was informed that Sally had her bath ready.

She indulged in that sybaritic pleasure as Sally kept adding hot water to allow her to soak for as long as she liked.

Despite thoroughly enjoying her leisurely bath, Elizabeth weakly protested, 'There truly is no need to go to all that trouble.'

'You are an undemanding mistress. It is a pleasure to give you a treat occasionally,' Sally protested in return.

Eventually, Elizabeth was ready to dry off again, after Sally had washed her hair and given her a final rinse. Wrapped in a warm robe, she lounged in front of the fire while Sally brushed her hair until it was dry. As she sipped the last of the hot chocolate, Elizabeth was vaguely aware of suppressed giggles in the house. She absently wondered what her sisters were up to, causing such merriment.

She was not left long to wonder. As soon as Sally left her, the room was invaded by her sisters carrying a number of items.

'Although we are not Greeks, we come bearing gifts,' declared Lydia as she held up a day dress which Elizabeth had never before seen.

'You must be properly attired when we call on our neighbours this afternoon,' declared Jane, who also held some garments.

Elizabeth soon discovered that her sisters had brought a complete new outfit, from the skin out, for her to wear.

'Happy birthday,' they cried in concert with big smiles at the astonishment displayed by Lizzy, before assisting their sister into her new finery.

~A~

Elizabeth was getting worried, as the closer they got to Netherfield the more Lydia and to some extent the rest of her sisters, including even Jane, became ever more restless.

Lydia was trying not to bounce in her seat but was unsuccessful enough to garner a reprimand from Mrs Taylor. 'Lydia, ladies behave with more decorum.'

The performance caused Elizabeth to ask,' What is going on?'

Replies of 'Nothing,' and 'What could possibly be going on?' delivered with innocent expressions did nothing to quell her anxiety.

Fortunately, the journey was short enough and soon they arrived at Netherfield where Messrs Bingley, Hurst and Fitzwilliam were waiting to hand the ladies out of the carriage.

'Welcome, ladies. I am most pleased that you were able to join us today,' Bingley greeted them and offered his arms to Jane and Elizabeth to escort them into the house. He was followed by Fitzwilliam with Margaret and Mary, while Hurst brought up the rear with the youngest girls.

As they approached the doors to the drawing room, these were thrown open from inside and a shout of 'Happy birthday' startled Elizabeth. Instead of only seeing Louisa Hurst presiding over the tea service, the room seemed to be filled with people.

~A~

Elizabeth was still trying to recognise all the occupants of the room when Mrs Gardiner enfolded her niece in a brief but heartfelt embrace. 'Happy birthday, Lizzy. I wish you all the very best on your majority.'

Madeline Gardiner was immediately replaced by her children who were all clamouring to wish their cousin a happy birthday.

The children were soon followed by Mr Gardiner, Mr and Mrs Phillips, Charlotte Lucas, as well as all the other company from Netherfield and Rosings.

The last one to approach her was Darcy, who bowed over her hand as he said, 'I too wish you a happy birthday and congratulate you on reaching your majority... and with it gaining your completely unfettered independence.'

The look which accompanied the words conveyed understanding and respect as well as something which Elizabeth struggled to define.

~A~

Once everyone had had a chance to express their congratulations, Elizabeth was at last allowed to take a seat and accept a cup of tea, which she sorely needed to settle after all the excitement.

She gave her sisters a mock severe look and chided, 'I believe that you were less than truthful with me since my return. Planning a wedding indeed...' She turned to Margaret. 'And you are no better. You were supposed to ensure that my sisters behaved properly.'

'As it happens, we were planning the wedding. It was simply not the only thing we planned,' protested Lydia with a wide grin, pleased with the success of the surprise. 'But I have a bone to pick with you. You caused us a great deal of inconvenience by not remaining at Rosings for another two weeks.'

Jane added with twinkling eyes, 'You had better brace yourself. This is but the start of your celebration.'

'Mrs Taylor allowed us to plan your ball as well as her wedding,' crowed Kitty.

'A ball?'

'Indeed. We felt it appropriate to mark the occasion by celebrating with all your family and friends. It is not often that we have the incumbent master of an estate reach their majority. And you always did love dancing,' Mrs Phillips explained.

When Elizabeth looked at her new dress with a somewhat dubious expression, Mrs Gardiner reassured her, 'Do not worry, an appropriate gown is waiting for you upstairs.'

'And we took the liberty of preparing a dance card for you,' Louisa Hurst said with a smile as she handed the article to Elizabeth. 'We have had many requests, but you may feel free to make any changes you please.'

Elizabeth read the entries and discovered that her first set was split between both her uncles, who would open the ball with her with one dance each. Every other gentleman in the room had claimed one set, except for Darcy, whose name was pencilled in against the supper and last sets.

When she saw the notation, her eyes flew up to meet his gently questioning gaze. A swarm of butterflies took flight in her stomach, and she struggled to tear her eyes away.

Elizabeth was only successful when Louisa asked, 'Does this meet with your approval? When we delivered the invitations, many of your neighbours requested dances with you.'

'When Louisa showed us the list of potential dance partners, we picked the best dancers for you, but you can make whatever changes you like. After all, it is your ball and you should maximise your enjoyment,' Mary added her own explanation.

'I thank you for your consideration. Your choices are perfect,' Elizabeth replied with a smile and a sideways glance at Darcy.

~A~

Having her immediate future settled, Elizabeth recalled herself to the present as well as the presence of the other guests.

'Georgiana, I must apologise to you for my abrupt departure from Rosings. I had hoped to get to know you for more than just one evening.'

'I understand that you were needed at home,' Georgiana replied diplomatically. Since Elizabeth had shared the information provided in Mary's letter about Mrs Bennet's attempt at gaining control of Longbourn, Anne had used this information to explain her sudden departure.

'As it turned out, it was not truly necessary for me to return as my sisters were well able to take care of the situation at Longbourn. But now that you are here, I hope you will find the company congenial.'

'I already met three of your sisters yesterday and they welcomed me most warmly,' Georgiana gushed. 'They also suggested that since Miss Lydia will be allowed to attend the ball, even though she is not yet out, because it is in honour of your birthday, I should also be allowed to participate. And my brother has agreed, and my cousin Anne has gifted me with a gown.'

Because Anne had been aware of Darcy's reasons for bringing Georgiana to Netherfield and the fact that Elizabeth's sisters planned this surprise for her, she had ensured that Georgiana had a gown appropriate for her age and the occasion.

Elizabeth gave Anne a stern look. 'So, you too were party to this conspiracy. Is there anyone in all of England who was not aware of this ball?'

Anne grinned, 'Since he was not invited, I suspect the only one who does not know is the Prince Regent.'

~A~

The receiving line for Elizabeth's ball was blessedly short. It consisted only of Bingley and Louisa Hurst as the hosts, Elizabeth as guest of honour and Robert Fitzwilliam as the ranking gentleman supported Elizabeth.

The greetings by the guests were almost uniformly warm, except for a couple of young ladies who had difficulty suppressing their jealousy at seeing the fineness of Elizabeth's new ballgown. Madeline Gardiner had outdone herself in the choice of colours, fabrics and style.

Fortunately, the London custom of being fashionably late had not made its way to the country and it did not take too long for the last of the guests to arrive.

Phillips and Gardiner led Elizabeth to the small platform where the musicians were located and had them play a small flourish to attract the attention of the assembly.

Once the room had quieted, Phillips addressed them. 'Dear friends, as you know, my dear niece Elizabeth has reached her majority today and we are here to celebrate the occasion. While it has been my privilege to be technically her guardian, over the last three years, she has proved to us all that she is perfectly capable of looking not only after herself, but also her sisters and her estate. While in the early days, some have doubted her abilities, I know that today we are all unanimous in our opinion that Lizzy is an excellent master of Longbourn, and we welcome her into the ranks of adults.'

As he paused a moment, there were numerous calls of 'Hear, hear,' until Phillips finished with, 'Happy birthday, Elizabeth,' which set off a cheer by all the guests.

Once the cheer died down, Phillips bowed to Elizabeth and led her to the floor, as the musicians struck up the first tune.

~A~

Darcy had been pleased when Elizabeth declared herself satisfied with the dance partners which Louisa and Mary had allocated to her.

When he and his party had arrived from Rosings the previous afternoon, he had wanted to go and speak with Elizabeth immediately upon his arrival. He had only been dissuaded from this course of action because he did not want to spoil the surprise everyone had worked so long and hard to make perfect.

Since he discovered that both her uncles would open the ball with Elizabeth, he had used all the charm of which he was capable to convince Louisa Hurst to reserve the supper and last sets for him. This arrangement worked out perfectly as it allowed him to dance the first set with Georgiana while their cousins and friends filled up Georgiana's dance card for the first half of the ball.

Georgiana felt nervousness and excitement in equal measure. She had been taking lessons with a dancing master, but this was the first time that she was dancing in public. When she and Darcy lined up for the first dance, he gently squeezed her hand and whispered, 'Relax and enjoy yourself. You will do very well.'

Those words were echoed a moment later by a widely smiling Lydia, who was being partnered by Mr Gardiner, as they were next in line.

Elizabeth's other sisters were also dancing – Jane and Bingley, Mary and John Lucas, Kitty and Robert Goulding. Nearby were also Anne and Henry Standish as well as Charlotte and Robert Fitzwilliam. Even Margaret and Richard took to the floor as he was recovered enough for a few dances.

~A~

Elizabeth was having a wonderful time. Mary and Louisa had arranged her dance partners so that they alternated between one of the gentlemen residing at Netherfield, with one of her neighbours.

Even Richard Fitzwilliam partnered her for a set, although in his case they danced the first and slower dance of the set, but sat out the second one, as he was not yet up to dancing for half an hour. But this gave Elizabeth a chance to rest her own feet for fifteen minutes, halfway through the first half of the evening.

Eventually it was time for the supper set and Darcy came to claim her. They danced in silence for a few minutes, neither quite certain how to start the conversation. Finally, Elizabeth teased, 'Come, Mr Darcy, we must have some conversation. It would look very strange indeed if we remained completely silent for a full half hour.'

Darcy smiled and replied, 'I have been wondering how to tell you the reason for my request for a second set tonight.'

'I confess that I am all astonishment. How did you convince Mrs Hurst to allow you a second set when no one else was allowed such a privilege?'

The dance separated them for a moment, giving Darcy a chance to reflect that it was indeed a privilege for him to be allowed to dance a second set with Elizabeth, unlike in town where ladies considered it a privilege if he condescended to dance with them at all.

'I explained to her that at the last ball at Netherfield, I was supposed to have two sets with you, but in the end, due to Miss Catherine needing a dance partner and then Bingley changing the music for the supper set, I only had a single dance with you. Therefore, I was owed another dance,' Darcy said in his most reasonable tone of voice and nervously waited for Elizabeth's reaction.

He was relieved when she laughed. 'That was indeed a most astute reasoning. I am pleased that Mrs Hurst was amenable to honouring her brother's debt.'

'I can only hope that Bingley does not get it in his head to be helpful again.'

'Do not trouble yourself, Mr Darcy. My sisters assured me that the musicians have been threatened with the most dire consequences if they deviate from the set program by a single note,' Elizabeth assured Darcy and was quite astonished that she felt reassured herself.

~A~

Chapter 34

The day after the ball, the majority of inhabitants of the estates around Meryton were having a late start and opted for a relaxing day to recover from all the dancing or at least the late night.

One of the few people who were up and about early was Darcy. He rose at his usual time and after a quick cup of coffee rode to Oakham Mount in the hope of encountering Elizabeth.

After sitting for nearly half an hour, Darcy started pacing as he remembered the last few months, especially the time before Christmas and his discussion with Georgiana.

He had left this area as he realised that he was becoming enamoured with the lovely, witty and exceedingly competent Mrs Brooks. At the time he had wondered whether society would consider her good enough to be his wife because she had no important connections.

In his hubris it had never occurred to him that she might not consider him good enough to be her husband.

He had been so proud of himself to have overcome his ridiculous pride to offer for the lady. But in retrospect he recognised that he still harboured the same pride as he had always had, since he expected her to be overjoyed by his condescension and eagerly accept his proposal.

But Elizabeth had no need for marriage. She was financially secure and did not need a bumbling nodcock with delusions of grandeur to give her consequence or even security. He had seen proof of her significance in this area last night when everyone had been eager to help her celebrate her independence.

Ever since his conversation with Anne after his failed proposal, when she had reminded him of the legal aspects of marriage for women, Darcy started to consider how he could ensure Elizabeth's security if she were to give him a chance. But would she give him a chance?

Elizabeth had promised to have a conversation with him after his return to Netherfield. But it seemed that this morning was not to be the occasion for their discussion. After waiting for two hours, Darcy gave up and returned to the Netherfield.

~A~

Later that morning, now that the party was over and Elizabeth knew of all the visitors, Charlotte Lucas went back to her family and most of the Gardiners relocated to Longbourn. Mr Gardiner had to return to London because of business, but he was planning to return on Saturday to collect his family.

In the evening after everyone else had gone to bed, Mrs Gardiner had a private conversation with her favourite niece.

'So, tell me, Elizabeth, what has been happening? I hear that you returned early from Rosings, but no one seemed to know the reason. Was it so very difficult to face your past?' the lady asked gently.

'Rosings was not so bad because Anne made a great many changes since she took over as mistress...' she trailed off with an embarrassed smile.

'What happened?'

Elizabeth let out a deep breath that was partly a sigh. 'Mr Darcy proposed to me.'

'Since no one mentioned an engagement, I presume that you rejected him.'

'He gave me the impression that he expected me to be thrilled by his addresses and that he never considered what I would have to give up if I were to marry him.' Elizabeth shrugged helplessly as tears trickled unnoticed down her cheeks. 'I could never agree to be less than myself again.'

'Oh, Elizabeth. It pains me to see you so hurt,' cried Mrs Gardiner and gathered her niece in her arms.

The sympathy was too much for Elizabeth. She allowed her grief free rein as she sobbed on her aunt's shoulder, partly in despair and partly in frustration. Would it ever be thus? Would she always be reduced to tears whenever marriage to an honourable man was mentioned?

Eventually Elizabeth calmed down. But despite discussing the problem for hours, she was still no closer to finding a solution.

She could at last admit that she had fallen in love with Darcy, but the thought of not being in control of her life made her want to run screaming for the hills.

~A~

The next morning, she walked quietly to her favourite hill, where she was unsurprised to encounter Darcy.

He rose from his seat and bowed. 'Good morning, Mrs Brooks. I wanted to apologise for upsetting you at Rosings. If you will allow, I would like to offer an insight into my thinking at the time as an explanation, not an excuse.'

'Good morning, Mr Darcy. I would be pleased to hear your explanation before I give you mine. But perhaps we could sit. This conversation could take a while,' Elizabeth suggested with a small smile.

Darcy waited until Elizabeth had taken a seat and sat within an easy speaking distance, but not too close to make her uncomfortable, before he continued. 'Until recently, I laboured under a misapprehension. I assumed that yours was simply a marriage of convenience as is quite common in our society. It was not until after I made a pest of myself that I found out from Anne that you did not choose to wed Collins but were forced into that marriage. I thought that since we are already friends and I believe that I am a better man than your husband was, you would welcome a proposal from me.'

He shrugged and with a small grimace turned both hands palm up. 'What can I say? All my adult life I was given to understand that I am a most eligible man and it never occurred to me that a lady existed who was not amenable to my wealth or position in society. I should have realised that such attributes would be immaterial to you.'

He stopped briefly with a rueful smile. 'I confess that I approached you with a great deal of arrogance. In my hubris it did not occur to me to consider the rules which apply to women under English law, which was why I did not understand your explanation.'

'I thank you for explaining, Mr Darcy. I accept your apology, especially as I had come to the same conclusions already. But Anne felt that you deserve an explanation why I could not accept your proposal.'

'I would appreciate knowing why you felt that you cannot accept.'

'My marriage to Mr Collins was more than just unhappy. For me it was the worst kind of prison,' Elizabeth said before she told Darcy about the kind of life which she had led at Hunsford. The more she spoke the angrier Darcy became, but he forced himself to remain quiet until she stopped.

'Collins is lucky to be dead. If he were still alive, I would cheerfully rend him limb from limb,' Darcy growled in disgust. His agitation could not be contained, and he rose and paced around the top of the mount for several minutes to work off his anger at the dead man. 'I cannot understand how any man can raise a hand against a woman,' he exclaimed at last, throwing his hands in the air.

'Mr Darcy, you still do not understand. The physical pain was nothing to the fact that I was not allowed to have opinions. Or worse, if they should disagree with my husband or Lady Catherine.'

Elizabeth grimaced. 'If I could have held my tongue, I could have saved myself several beatings. But I could not help myself, if my husband, or worse, Lady Catherine, was wrong, I corrected them.'

'You mean to say that he beat you for being right?'

'As far as he was concerned, whether I was right or wrong was irrelevant.' Elizabeth gave a mirthless huff and said, 'Your aunt was most insistent that I should learn how to act towards my betters. Maintain the distinction of rank, I believe she phrased it. If I had the temerity to disagree with him or his revered patroness, I was to be punished.'

'Was that man a complete moron?' exploded Darcy.

'Yes.'

That simple, quiet statement broke the tension and a slightly hysterical chuckle escaped Darcy.

As he stared at her, Elizabeth smiled and repeated, 'Yes, he was a complete moron. He had been taught how to behave towards a wife by his father, and Lady Catherine reinforced his education. But my experience with him taught me to distrust men. Or at least husbands, since they have all the rights under the law.'

Darcy at last understood the full extent of Elizabeth's reluctance towards marriage.

'I promise you that I would never raise my hand against you, especially not for disagreeing with me. A large part of what attracted me to you was that you have your own opinions and are willing to stand by them... unless I can change your mind by presenting a better argument.'

'Mr Darcy, I would like to believe you, but I simply cannot bring myself to do so.'

'We are at an impasse.'

'I am afraid so,' Elizabeth agreed helplessly.

They sat in silence for a few minutes while Darcy considered the situation. 'I understand that you have no wish to be trapped in a bad marriage again, but will you give me leave to court you and perhaps over time win your trust?'

'Mr Darcy, that could take years and there is still a chance I will never be able to trust again.' Elizabeth was horrified. She could not allow this wonderful man to waste his life.

Darcy shrugged and gave her a gentle smile. 'Elizabeth, I love you. I will never love another woman like I love you. I do not want to love another woman. There will only ever be you.'

Elizabeth was almost in tears as she managed to put her feelings into words. 'I do not want you to throw away your life on something that might never be.'

'But it might be, unless I do not try. I will take my chances. At worst, I hope to have your friendship,' he paused and was relieved when Elizabeth slowly nodded. 'But given time, you might learn to trust that I have only your best interests at heart. And I can be very persuasive.' He said the last with a smile.

Darcy held out his hand to her. 'Will you let me court you, Elizabeth?'

Elizabeth saw the steadfast love in Darcy's eyes and capitulated. She took his hand as she replied, 'I suppose that I have nothing to lose.' In the deep recesses of her mind she added, *except my fear and loneliness.*

~A~

~A~

Chapter 35

Darcy, with Hermes trailing after him, escorted Elizabeth back to Longbourn and they chatted about inconsequential topics along the way.

Both felt much lighter after their fraught conversation and having achieved some clarity about the other's thoughts and feelings. For the moment they were content to relax and let the future take care of itself. Nothing could be gained by trying to force an outcome.

Darcy had just made a comment about how well Mrs Annesley had helped his sister improve, when Elizabeth exclaimed, 'Drat. You just reminded me that I have to find a replacement for Margaret. While my sisters have come a long way in their education, we really should have a companion living in the house. Although perhaps it would be better if I chose an older widow this time.'

When Darcy's brows furrowed in a confused look, she added, 'We should not be as likely to lose an older woman due to marriage before we can dispense with her services.'

Darcy laughed. 'My cousin has often been in situations where his careless actions caused difficulties, although this is the first time where a family needed to seek a new companion.'

'Yes, well, you can tell him from me that his lack of care is not appreciated,' Elizabeth returned the tease.

~A~

When Darcy made his farewell at the front door of Longbourn, the couple were observed by most of the occupants, who descended onto Elizabeth as soon as she entered the dining room.

'You seemed to be in great accord with Mr Darcy,' Lydia, as forward as ever, commented with a sly grin. While she had meant to simply tease her sister, she was unprepared for the answer.

'Why should I not be in accord with Mr Darcy. I thought that state was customary for a courting couple. Is that not the case, Jane?' Elizabeth said, pretending casual disinterest. The words had the desired effect. Elizabeth's family and Mrs Taylor variously exclaimed.

'Courting?'

'You and Mr Darcy are courting?'

'A couple?'

'Indeed. But I am famished. What has cook prepared for us for breakfast?' Elizabeth casually strolled to the sideboard to fix herself a plate, ignoring the indignant looks from all the ladies in the room.

That nonchalance temporarily silenced the sisters, but as soon as Elizabeth seated herself, her Aunt Gardiner gave her a stern look. 'Enough of these games. Last night you were still determined never to consider marriage. What has changed?'

Elizabeth sighed as she looked her aunt in the eye. 'I encountered Mr Darcy on my walk today and we talked. I told him about my... history. He was suitably horrified, but he was also sympathetic to my attitudes.' She grimaced a little. 'I was unable to change his mind about finding another lady to marry.'

Elizabeth shrugged helplessly as she added, 'Mr Darcy is a most determined man. He refused to take no for an answer, even when I told him that I might never be able to change that reply. He claims that he will have none other than me. In the end, I agreed to let him try to prove to me that he only cares for my happiness.'

Kitty sighed and murmured, 'Oh, how romantic.'

Mrs Gardiner ignored the comment and asked Elizabeth, 'You do care for him, do you not?'

'Yes, I do... a great deal.'

'Oh, well. They say that Rome was not built in a day. Since he does not seem to be in a hurry...'

'And at worst, we will always be friends.'

Margaret nearly groaned as she thought, *do not let him hear that you used that f-word.*

~A~

Darcy was whistling a merry tune when he arrived at Netherfield and entered the dining room.

'You sound remarkably chipper,' commented Richard, who was sitting at the table with a plate filled with ham, sausages and eggs.

The other residents and guests looked up at the comment and confirmed that Darcy did indeed look to be in excellent spirits. Several of them put two and two together and came to the right and wrong conclusion.

'Elizabeth said yes,' exclaimed Anne with a huge grin. 'I knew you could not be so handsome for nothing,' she teased, having heard from Jane that a similar phrase had often been applied to her, and thought it appropriate. 'How soon are we to hear wedding bells for you?'

'You are rather precipitate. While Elizabeth has said yes, it is only for a courtship.'

'What a shame,' cried Bingley. 'I had hoped to share my wedding day with you.'

'But you are not engaged. Unless something happened of which I am unaware, you are still courting Miss Bennet.'

'True but the stipulated six months are nearly up and Ja... I mean Miss Bennet has not given me the slightest hint that she is unhappy with me. I am therefore hopeful that I will be able to propose to her in another month. And while I have no wish to be presumptuous, I am hopeful that she will accept.'

'I hope for your sake that you are correct. Miss Bennet is a charming lady and I think you two are well suited.'

'But what about you? I think Mrs Brooks would be ideal for you. You have so much in common. And at least you can be assured that she would be an ideal mistress of Pemberley.'

'Bingley, slow down. You do not have to tell me about Mrs Brooks' many sterling qualities. I am fully aware of them. Probably more so than you, since I have spent more time speaking with her.'

'Sorry, what can I say. You are my best friend and I want you to be happy.'

'Thank you, Bingley. But for the moment I am pleased that Mrs Brooks has agreed to consider me as a potential husband. But I do not wish for any of you to try to pressure her to rush into anything. To do so would be counterproductive. If she feels that you are trying to force the issue, she will most likely tell you and me to go to the devil.'

He let his gaze move slowly over all his companions until they all nodded in agreement. Then to change the topic, he told Richard about the trouble he had caused in the Longbourn household.

'While I am sorry to have caused the ladies an inconvenience, I cannot say that I regret the outcome,' Richard replied, unrepentant.

Mrs Annesley had listened to the conversation with amusement and delight. Being a companion meant that she was often overlooked and forgotten, allowing her to hear much. She was pleased that Mr Darcy at last had clarity about the situation and his intentions, and Mrs Brooks was at least giving him a chance.

When Darcy mentioned the need for a new companion, she spoke up. 'Mr Darcy, forgive me for interrupting, but I have a cousin who is looking for a position as a companion. She is a most accomplished and respectable lady. Mrs Brooks might find her suitable.'

'Ha,' exclaimed Richard with a mischievous grin. 'It seems that my marriage to my lovely fiancée will benefit not only me, but Mrs Annesley's cousin as well. Instead of berating me, you should thank me.' He sat up straighter and gave Darcy a haughty look.

Mrs Annesley suppressed her amusement at the banter as she said, 'Mr Fitzwilliam, please allow me to thank you on my cousin's behalf for giving her a chance at respectable employment.'

Darcy promised to mention Mrs Partridge to Elizabeth and set himself to enjoy his breakfast, speaking quietly to Georgiana, who had many questions as well as advice on how to impress a young lady. While Darcy was amused by many of the things his sister thought important, he listened carefully as some of the things she said struck a chord, particularly when she mentioned respect.

~A~

That afternoon, Darcy called on Elizabeth who received him in her library. As promised, he informed her about Mrs Partridge.

He was pleased when she seemed relieved to have found an option so quickly, causing him to offer to send for the lady.

Once the business was out of the way, he asked, 'Are you busy?'

'Not particularly. Since I returned early from Rosings, I have caught up on all my chores.'

'In that case, would you care for a game of chess? It has been a while since I had a challenging opponent.' Darcy gave her an open smile as he asked, as if it was the most natural thing in the world for a gentleman to challenge a lady to a game of chess. 'I promise I will do my best to trounce you.'

Elizabeth laughed at the reminder. 'It will be my pleasure to see who will win today.'

They had a hard-fought battle which ended in a draw, making both of them happy.

~A~

Over the next few days, Darcy wracked his brain for all the ways in which the law and unscrupulous husbands held women to ransom.

The law was relatively straight forward. When it came to unscrupulous husbands, he tried to remember the various stories which were bandied about in places like White's where gossip flowed like wine. Some of the men he had heard, bragged about how they had used their wives' better natures to control them and gain the advantage.

He made a list of all the ways he remembered in which women could be disadvantaged or controlled. The obvious were of course, finances, friends, and family, which included children.

Then he made another list of ways in which those issues could be mitigated.

When he had reached the point when he could not think of any other factors, he made an appointment to see Mr Phillips.

~A~

After the customary pleasantries, Phillips asked, 'You wanted to see me in my professional capacity. What can I do for you, Mr Darcy.'

'I would like you to draw up marriage articles for myself and your niece, Mrs Brooks.'

'While I would be happy to do so, I find it difficult to believe that Elizabeth has agreed to marry you.' When Darcy's mien darkened, he added hastily, 'I mean no offence; I just know my niece's attitude to marriage.'

'While she has not agreed to marry me, she has consented to a courtship. I would like the document prepared as an act of good faith, to ensure she knows what she can expect from our union, should she agree to it.'

'While that is commendable, are you not afraid that I might be biased and include clauses which would favour my niece to your detriment.'

'I most certainly hope you would do exactly that. I have prepared a list of clauses, which I would like you to reword into incontestable legal language. If I have missed anything which would ensure Elizabeth's safety, I most definitely want you to include those clauses.'

Darcy handed his list to Phillips. The solicitor's eyes got ever bigger as he read the document and he scratched his head. When he finished, he looked up and asked in disbelief, 'You truly want to include all these things in your marriage articles?'

'Do you have any issues with any of my ideas?'

'From Elizabeth's point of view, I have not the slightest reservations, but for you...'

Darcy smiled. 'As it happens, I trust the lady implicitly. I wish to ensure that she has the means to feel safe and protected. But as I said before, if I have missed anything, please feel free to include it.'

'I hope you will allow me a week or two to research the marriage act to ensure that there are no loopholes.'

'Take as long as you need for the finished article, but perhaps you could let me have a draft a little sooner. I would like to show it to Elizabeth for her consideration.'

'You are hoping to use the document to overcome her reservations,' Phillips stated rather than asked but was rewarded with a nod and an almost shy smile. Phillips thought, *you must love her very much to leave yourself as wide open as this*, but only said, 'I will have a draft ready for you by Saturday if that suits you.'

Darcy gave him a brilliant smile, 'That will suit me admirably. Thank you, Mr Phillips.'

~A~

For the rest of the week, Darcy saw Elizabeth every day, either due to a *chance* meeting on Oakham Mount or when he called on her.

Elizabeth, while she was still vehemently opposed to marriage, found herself looking forward to those meetings and their conversations. They rarely spoke of earthshattering topics, other than once when they mentioned the destruction of Pompeii. They talked of books they were reading, their families and their estates. They even discussed President Madison's embargo on trade between England and the United States of America. Naturally, they both abhorred this action.

Darcy was careful to arrange his visits for times when Elizabeth was at leisure and never to outstay his welcome, which made his visits doubly appreciated.

~A~

On Saturday, Darcy called on Mr Phillips and was pleased that the solicitor had the first draft of the document ready for him as promised.

He spent the afternoon carefully reading the contract and found that Mr Phillips had added a couple of clauses he had not considered. Once he was satisfied that everything was in order, Darcy spent a couple of hours carefully copying the document, substituting the names with the generic terms of husband and wife.

Once the ink had dried, he folded the new version and put it aside, ready to take to Elizabeth.

~A~

Chapter 36

As he had arranged to visit on Sunday afternoon to enjoy another game of chess with Elizabeth, he brought along his document to discuss it with Elizabeth if the opportunity presented itself.

A tray with coffee was brought to the library as they settled themselves at the chessboard and Elizabeth served them before they started their game.

Because Darcy was distracted by the contract in his pocket, Elizabeth easily defeated him at chess. Even though he was annoyed with himself for losing, he was pleased to have the perfect opening, when Elizabeth asked, 'Is something the matter? You seem distracted.'

'I have a document and wondered if I could ask you to read it and give me your opinion on it.'

'You should know by now that I am always happy to render whatever assistance I can. You have but to ask,' Elizabeth replied, wondering what could be so important about that document to keep Darcy from giving his full attention to their game. Even if she had been unwilling to help, curiosity alone would have brought about her agreement to read the document.

Now that Elizabeth was waiting expectantly for him to give her the contract, Darcy was having second thoughts about the wisdom of broaching the subject at this point in time as he was afraid that she might think that he was trying to push her into acceptance of his suit.

But, as he might never get a better opportunity, he reached into his pocket, drew out the papers and handed them to her.

Elizabeth settled back in her chair and started to read. She had barely begun when her eyebrows rose in surprise and her eyes widened. She had read perhaps half a page when she raised her head and looked at Darcy. 'Is this some kind of a hoax?' she asked in irritation as the document could be nothing but an elaborate joke.

'Not at all, although this is still a draft and can be changed, if necessary,' stated Darcy rather nervously.

'I see,' replied Elizabeth although she was still dubious. Shaking her head, she lowered her eyes again and continued reading. This time she paid close attention to the meaning of the words. When she finished, she read through the whole document a second time to ensure that she had not misunderstood what she thought she had read. But the words were still unambiguously the same and were not open to interpretation.

Eventually she dropped her hands which were still holding the paper into her lap. She gazed at Darcy in shocked disbelief. 'This is the most astonishing thing I have ever read,' she said with a look of bewilderment. To gain some time, she checked the coffeepot and finding it was still lukewarm, she poured herself a cup, adding more sugar than she normally used, and took a rather shaky sip.

When she put the cup back down onto its saucer she said, 'If I understand it correctly, stripped of the legal verbiage, the man referred to in this document is essentially offering to make his wife an honorary man, considering how many concessions he is making.'

Darcy was astonished at her wording but said carefully, 'As I understand it, he is offering his wife complete equality.'

'No, it is more than that,' Elizabeth disagreed. 'I have heard of marriage settlements where the husband agreed to leave the wife's property in her control, but that is usually because he has no choice as she is an heiress, and he is a fortune hunter who is trying to acquire a life of ease.'

She picked up the papers again and waved them about. 'This is several orders of magnitude beyond that. While I can understand that a wealthy man would make provisions for potential children, I think fifty thousand pounds is rather excessive. But that still pales in comparison to the other conditions. What man would voluntarily agree to...'

She glanced at the paper and ticked points off her fingers.

'One –let his wife keep complete control of all her properties... although that is the least surprising aspect of this document.'

She raised a second finger. 'Two – agree to consult her about the management of his own properties... I suppose that if she is knowledgeable about estate management that could be sensible. Surprising, but sensible.' She shook her head.

'Three – insist that she always speak her mind without repercussions of any kind –'

'Other than potential agreement by the husband after a heated debate,' Darcy interjected with a small smile. He was getting pleasure out of Elizabeth's careful analysis of the document and her reaction of bewilderment and disbelief as well as her comments which gave him an even greater insight into her personality.

She ignored the interruption and continued. 'Four – he gives her leave to come and go as she pleases and to reside in his homes or her own... with or without him. Again, it is not unheard of for husbands and wives to live separate lives, although the tone of this document does not suggest such an arrangement.' She shrugged and sighed.

'Five – if she is unhappy with her situation as his wife for any reason, she is free to return to her own home... permanently if she chooses, without let or hindrance by her husband. Now that is quite unusual. Most husbands want to dictate the movements of their wives as they are unwilling to give up control of their property.'

She looked at Darcy who simply said, 'One cannot cage a free spirit.'

'Six – and this is the most incredible point. If she chooses to return to her own home permanently, she is free to take her children with her and raise them as she sees fit. The only proviso that I can see, is that she is required to teach the heir how to be a good manager for her husband's estate.'

Elizabeth put down the papers and took up her cup for another mouthful of coffee to fortify herself. 'There are other minor points addressed in this document, but I believe that I have enumerated the major ones.'

'Do you think that this would appeal to an independent woman who values her independence and wishes to retain it?'

'I suppose it might, if she could bring herself to believe that the man was actually serious, and this is not some elaborate joke.'

'Supposing this is not a joke as you fear, are there any clauses which should be added to make the wife feel completely secure?'

Elizabeth gave Darcy a long searching look but could not detect any levity or deception. Trying to shake off a feeling of inevitability, she attempted levity of her own. 'There is only one real issue which I can see with this document. Any halfway decent solicitor would declare that the husband cannot be held to any part of this contract as he is mentally unstable and fit only for bedlam.'

'Ah. I had not considered that aspect. Do you have any suggestions on how to overcome that issue?'

'I cannot see how. What woman would consider marrying a man who should be in bedlam?'

Darcy gave her a mischievous smile as he said, 'I should not disclose the best kept secret of the male sex, but as you may have already discovered for yourself, men in love are rarely rational. They will go to any lengths to win the woman of their dreams.'

'Indeed?'

'Quite. Just look at Bingley. For the first time in his life, he has stayed in one place courting one lady for half a year. And my cousin, who enjoys his comforts, was quite prepared to live in a modest cottage to be with the lady of his choice.' He nodded at the paper in Elizabeth's hand. 'One could argue that such things are perfectly normal.'

'In that case, might I keep this document to study the aberrations of the male mind?'

'I should be delighted for you to consider the workings of the mind who conceived this manuscript.'

They chatted for another half an hour until Darcy reluctantly took his leave.

~A~

That night Darcy was thinking about their conversation.

He had been nervous that he was pushing too hard or too fast by giving Elizabeth the marriage contract. He knew perfectly well that she would not be fooled by his pretence that it was a hypothetical scenario.

But his gamble appeared to have paid off. Elizabeth had seemed very much in favour of the conditions in the contract despite her comments about bedlam. At her request he had left the document behind so that she could study it when she was not dealing with the surprise of first reading.

He was pleased that she wanted an opportunity to consider his offer and while he hoped she would come to a favourable decision soon, he was prepared to wait as long as he needed to.

At least she had not rejected the offer out of hand.

~A~

Elizabeth struggled to sleep as she too considered the contract which she had placed on her nightstand.

Despite the fact that there were no names in the document, she was in no doubt that Darcy had prepared the marriage articles for her to consider. Yes, he was presumptuous to do this when she had only just agreed to a courtship, but she could not fault him for the sentiments expressed in that contract.

The thought and care he had put into every single clause spoke volumes about his feelings. She could not help but think that he was the best of men. Especially as he appeared to understand that she needed time to let go of her past and he was prepared not only to wait until she was ready but to arrange matters so that she would always be in control of her own destiny.

It made her wonder what she had done to deserve such devotion.

~A~

During the night, Elizabeth had come to the conclusion that she needed more information. She therefore set out to visit her uncle first thing on Monday morning.

Since, despite her early arrival he already had a client with him, Mrs Phillips invited her to come into the parlour and have some tea with her. Elizabeth gratefully accepted as it was a cool morning, and she could do with a hot cup.

She had just settled back into the comfortable wingchair and taken a sip of the hot beverage, when the door burst open and a familiar and unwelcome voice exclaimed, 'You will never believe the ridiculous story I just heard. Can you imagine it, Lady Lucas just informed me that Lizzy is being courted by Mr Darcy? I suppose that if Charlotte can be courted by a Viscount, and Lizzy's governess is engaged to his brother, it should not be surprising that their cousin could be interested in one of my girls. But Lizzy? I could understand if he was interested in Jane, but that little fool only has eyes for that tradesman when I am convinced that she could have snared that Viscount. I really must get access to Longbourn to ensure that Mr Darcy picks a worthy bride, like Lydia. After all, what could he possibly see in Lizzy?'

'A woman who is his equal in every respect and who deserves respect,' said Mr Phillips who had just come into the parlour to collect his niece.

'But she is soiled goods.'

'And whose fault is that?' spat Phillips. 'But any soiling is due to emotional trauma caused by the husband you forced upon her. As a person she is a respectable widow who is entitled to admiration and happiness.'

Mrs Bennet sounded petulant as she said, 'But just look at her. She has no beauty. How was I to know that she would ever attract a husband? I thought that I was doing her a favour...'

Elizabeth had listened unobserved to the tirade. While she had initially been angry that her mother would continue to spout such vile nonsense, that last statement suddenly caused an epiphany. She rose and turned to confront the lady.

'You did indeed do me a favour,' she told Mrs Bennet with a sardonic smile reminiscent of her father at the shocked expression of the lady she addressed, 'as you put me into a position to ensure my beloved sisters are well cared for. I suspect that had you remained at Longbourn, you would have pushed them all out into society at the earliest opportunity and encouraged them to behave in the most unseemly fashion, ruining their chances at any marriage, let alone a good marriage.'

Elizabeth took a deep, cleansing breath. 'How could you have been so deluded that you thought that your actions would cause me to be well disposed towards you and allow you any consequence? By forcing me into that marriage you created your own downfall and removed yourself from that position of consequence you craved. Now my sisters are safe from your machinations and have the option to make independent choices for their futures. I thank you for that.'

As she spoke, Elizabeth realised that with one year of misery, she had indeed purchased the safety of her sisters and the potential for their lifelong happiness. One year out of a lifetime was not such a great price.

And she had achieved independence not just for her sisters. If she could just overcome that last hurdle of distrust, there was an excellent chance that she could have the same happiness.

If she had not gone through that period, she might have met Mr Darcy under very different circumstances which could have prevented them from becoming friends, and developing their mutual respect and affection. Knowing the fastidiousness of Darcy, it was entirely possible that he would have been put off by Mrs Bennet's manners.

That could not happen now. At last, she was free to make her own future. 'Now if you will excuse me, I need to consult my uncle on a legal matter.'

~A~

Elizabeth's conversation with Mr Phillips was quite short.

When she explained her concern that a good solicitor could make a point of calling the sanity of Mr Darcy into question due to his outrageous concessions, her uncle quickly reassured her.

'Simply by including an accompanying statement explaining that those clauses were necessary to make you feel secure due to your history, should negate any questions about the sanity of the gentleman.'

He smirked. 'If that is not enough, and someone wants to declare the contract null and void, and you to be subject to the law which makes slaves of women, due to the insanity of the gentleman as proven by him signing such a contract, you have a simple solution. Insanity is one of the very few grounds for the annulment of a marriage. You will never be controlled by any man again... unless you choose to be.'

Phillips patted her hand. 'Apart from that, no one will be likely to ever see that contract as he would have no intention of ever putting you into a position where you had to use it.'

Elizabeth gave him a relieved smile. 'I had not considered the full implication of the offer. He is the most incredibly generous man I could ever hope to meet.'

~A~

Chapter 37

Even while Elizabeth considered her potential future, life continued at Longbourn, Netherfield and the rest of the neighbourhood.

As Darcy had hoped, Georgiana immediately fell in love with Elizabeth, who in her turn came to love the young girl but in a more big-sisterly, not to say maternal, way. When she and Darcy discussed this, they agreed that it was probably because she had spent the last three years raising her sisters who were of a similar age to Georgiana.

Elizabeth laughed, 'Heavens, those girls sometimes make me feel quite ancient, as they seem to see me more as a mother than a sister. Sometimes even Jane looks to me for guidance, and she is two years older than I am.'

'I know how you feel, as I am more of a father than brother to Georgiana,' Darcy agreed.

Given those attitudes, it was not surprising that Georgiana became the best of friends with the youngest Bennet sisters, as they dragged her out of her shell.

~A~

Mrs Annesley had written to her cousin about coming to work at Longbourn, and as soon as Mrs Partridge agreed to meet the ladies, Darcy sent a carriage to collect her.

As expected from Mrs Annesley's description, Mrs Partridge was a motherly widow of nearly fifty years of age whose children were grown up.

'My daughters all have boys,' she explained during her interview with Elizabeth. 'While I am perfectly competent to teach girls all they need to know based on society's expectations, I do not have the classical training required to teach boys.'

As none of the younger Bennet sisters had any particular interest in the classics, that lack was not an issue, especially since the lady was an exceptional artist with paints, who would be able to further Kitty's talents.

The youngest girls all immediately took to the motherly woman.

The new addition to the Longbourn household relieved Margaret's mind as she was getting ready to marry Richard.

~A~

Netherfield and Longbourn were full to bursting. Richard's parents, brother and cousins were being hosted at Netherfield, while Margaret's brother as well as the Gardiners were staying at Longbourn.

Lord and Lady Matlock had initially suggested a society wedding in London but had been overruled by the principal participants who only wanted their family and friends to attend.

The ladies at Longbourn were excited to help their friend and former mentor get ready for her wedding. Despite Margaret having enough funds to provide her own trousseau, the sisters had insisted on providing her wedding dress as a thank you for the lady's dedication to their welfare. All the materials had of course been gifted by the Gardiners. Kitty had designed the dress and all the sisters helped with the sewing and embroidery.

On the morning of the wedding Mr Gardiner and Henry Standish were banished to the library while the sisters, as well as Mrs Gardiner and Mrs Partridge helped Margaret to get ready.

Lydia, irrepressible as always, quipped, 'I always heard that marriage ages women. But you look younger and prettier than ever.'

Mrs Taylor was torn between laughter and exasperation. Laughter won. 'You are an incorrigible scamp,' she complained. 'But I thank you for your sentiments.'

After that incident, everyone except Margaret, Henry and Elizabeth made their way to the church, alerting the others that the bride would arrive shortly. Henry was standing in for their father and Margaret had asked Elizabeth to be her matron of honour.

When they arrived at the church, Elizabeth gave her friend a fierce hug. 'I thank you for all that you have done for us. I hope that you will be very happy in your new life.'

~A~

Judging by the expressions of the groom and the guests, Lydia had spoken nothing but the truth. The bride was indeed stunningly beautiful, although some of the beauty must be attributed to the groom as Margaret seemed to glow when their eyes locked.

They barely noticed anything or anyone else and Elizabeth and Robert, who was standing up with his brother, each had to nudge their charges once or twice to get them to respond appropriately.

When at the end of the ceremony the vicar said, 'You may now kiss the bride,' Richard did not need a second invitation, although his brother had to nudge him twice to recall the happy couple to the present and their audience.

Lady Matlock watched with a delighted smile and could not suppress the satisfaction when she quietly commented to her husband, 'That bodes well for grandchildren.'

~A~

Mr and Mrs Richard Fitzwilliam were to spend their wedding night at Darcy House in London, Darcy having sent instructions to his staff to welcome the newlyweds. The transport was provided by the Matlocks, who presented the couple with a new coach.

After spending a few days in London, the couple were to spend their honeymoon at Pemberley, using the manor as their base while they looked around for a potential estate of their own.

Just before they set off after their lavish wedding breakfast, Jane informed them that she was engaged to Bingley, as he had proposed exactly six months after she had requested that timeframe for their courtship.

'But why did you not say anything before?' exclaimed Margaret.

'Because I did not wish to detract from your day. But I hope that you will be able to attend my wedding which will be in three months.'

Richard and Margaret promised to be there and, after a final farewell, set out on their own new adventure.

~A~

Now that both their siblings were married, Robert and Henry returned to their own homes. Since both of their estates were in relatively close proximity to Rosings, they offered to escort Anne as she returned home.

No one was particularly surprised when Anne invited Charlotte to accompany her as all four of them had become quite close during their stay at Rosings over Easter. The friendship had deepened while they were all in company at Netherfield.

Lady Lucas delighted in raising the envy of her neighbours when she related that Charlotte mentioned in her letters that during her stay at Rosings, the two noblemen often visited.

~A~

At the beginning of July, Darcy received a letter from his steward at Pemberley requesting his presence to deal with a tenant issue.

The letter also included a note from Richard, informing Darcy that he and Margaret had found an estate which showed great potential, but he was hoping for a second opinion while Darcy was at home. Darcy reluctantly agreed to journey to Derbyshire, but he promised Bingley to be back in time for his wedding.

While he was away, he requested that Georgiana could stay at Longbourn with Mrs Annesley. The request was gladly granted by Elizabeth, who commented, 'I believe Mrs Annesley and Mrs Partridge will treasure being able to spend some more time in each other's company as well.'

As Darcy took his leave from Elizabeth, she felt a wrench at the separation, but all she said was, 'I shall miss our Sunday chess games,' in as teasing a voice as she could manage. 'I hope that you have a good journey.'

Darcy felt a thrill, selfish though it was, at the sadness he saw in Elizabeth's eyes at his departure. 'I shall return as quickly as I can,' he promised.

Lifting both her hands, he placed a lingering kiss on each and was rewarded with a slight gasp and a blush.

When he had gone, Elizabeth chided herself, *stop being so foolish. You are no innocent maiden to blush just because an exceptionally handsome gentleman kisses your hands*. The admonishment did not seem to help, either then or when she remembered the sensation later that night.

~A~

Saturday afternoon, less than three weeks later, a dusty coach pulled up at Longbourn and a tired but happy Darcy stepped out.

He was in luck as Elizabeth was just returning from visiting the old Chalmers farm, where a new tenant was busy improving the land.

'Mr Darcy, welcome back. We did not expect you at least until next week,' cried Elizabeth with a beaming smile on seeing him standing outside her home.

'Forgive me for arriving like this,' Darcy indicated his own dusty appearance. 'But I could not wait to see you again.'

'Please, come inside and refresh yourself. Georgiana will be thrilled to see you again,' invited Elizabeth.

'Only Georgiana?' asked Darcy tilting his head. The intense look he gave her was again rewarded by colour creeping into her cheeks.

'Not at all. We are all pleased to see that you have safely returned,' Elizabeth prevaricated, turning towards the door to hide her embarrassment about how exceedingly pleased she was to see the gentleman. She thought that he looked particularly handsome in his less than immaculate state.

'I would not wish to get dust all over your house,' Darcy protested feebly, as he very much wished to spend time with Elizabeth.

'Nonsense. This is the country, not some delicate drawing room in town. Dust is a way of life here... as you should know.' She looked over her shoulder and gave him a teasing smile. 'Unless of course Pemberley is the rare place which never sees a speck of dust.'

While they were speaking, Mr Hill had come outside carrying a brush. 'Never you mind,' he admonished. 'I will have you fit for my lady's parlour in a jiffy.'

Darcy laughed as he bowed to the butler. 'Brush away. I am at your disposal.'

~A~

As soon as Darcy stepped into the parlour where Mr Hill had directed him, he was nearly knocked off his feet by Georgiana who rushed to embrace him.

'William, it is so good to see you. I had not expected to see you this early. But now that you are here, I have so much to tell you,' Georgiana gushed.

'Hold on. Who are you and what have you done with my sister? You look like her, but Georgiana is a timid little thing who would not say boo to a goose, and she would certainly never act in such an exuberant manner in someone else's house.'

Georgiana pouted as she said, 'Nonsense. I am amongst friends, and they do not hold with hiding their joy in being with family.'

'While we do not hide our pleasure in seeing a beloved relative, we do allow them to sit down and enjoy a cup of coffee after spending days travelling,' Elizabeth chided gently but smiled to take the sting out of her words.

Darcy reassured Georgiana that no harm was done, before he addressed Elizabeth, 'While I would enjoy a cup of coffee, I have spent those days sitting in the carriage and would enjoy the opportunity to stand if you would not mind.'

'Please yourself, as long as you are comfortable,' Elizabeth replied as she handed him a cup, fixed just how he liked it.

'So, tell us, how are Richard and Margaret? I presume you have seen them while you were at home. Was the estate suitable?' Georgiana peppered her brother with questions.

Darcy was delighted that his sister had become lively due to her association with Elizabeth and her family. As he glanced at the other occupants of the room, he could see that they were equally as eager to hear about their friend but were too polite to immediately demand answers.

He smiled as he replied, 'They are very well indeed. Marriage certainly agrees with Richard, and I believe Margaret is happy as well.' He took a sip of his coffee. 'The estate they have found is rather rundown but has potential as a stud farm. It will require work, but they seem to relish the challenge. And the advantage of the current state of disrepair is that the price is very reasonable.'

'Where is it?'

'You will be pleased to know that their new home will be only thirty miles or so from Pemberley. It will be quite easy to see them regularly.'

'Will they be here for Jane's wedding?' This time it was Elizabeth who asked. While she did need to know the numbers of guests for the wedding breakfast, it was an excellent excuse to interact with Darcy.

'They will make every effort to be here,' he confirmed.

They exchanged some more news, but the exertion of the journey soon caught up with Darcy. After confirming with Elizabeth that she would be available for their chess game the following afternoon, he made his way to Netherfield.

He was pleased that the long daylight hours of summer had allowed him to travel from Pemberley to Longbourn in only two days. The previous day he had left Pemberley at the crack of dawn, only stopping to change horses until dark. And, by leaving the inn, where he had spent the night, again as soon as the horses were able to see, he had managed to arrive in time to see Elizabeth today.

~A~

Darcy was not the only one who was pleased by his speedy return.

Elizabeth had tried to keep herself too busy to miss his company by throwing herself into her work with the estate and the preparations for Jane's wedding. She had been partly successful, except for those occasions when she wanted to share a thought with Darcy, only to remember that he was not there.

Her nights had been plagued by very different thoughts. She kept remembering her response to when he kissed her hands during their farewell. As confusing as that surge of desire was, since she had never experienced such during her marriage, Elizabeth could not help but wonder...

~A~

Chapter 38

Until the wedding of Bingley and Jane, Darcy divided his time between Elizabeth and Bingley unless he had to deal with correspondence to manage his own business affairs.

On occasion, Darcy even managed to spend a little time with Georgiana, who had begged to remain with her friends at Longbourn. The lack of interaction was because Georgiana was helping Kitty and Lydia, with the assistance of their companions, to finalise the preparation for Jane's wedding.

Spending time with Bingley and advising him on the finer points of estate administration stopped his friend fretting about his upcoming wedding. But Darcy was pleased that there was very little with which Bingley still needed help.

Bingley had come a long way in understanding the responsibilities of a landowner and had discovered that he enjoyed the lifestyle. Since Jane hoped to remain in the neighbourhood where she had grown up, Bingley convinced Mr Morris to sell him all of Netherfield Park, rather than sell it off one field or farm at a time. As Morris had long ago lost interest in the estate, Bingley was able to make the purchase at a good price.

When Darcy was not busy with Bingley, Elizabeth was pleased to have his company. At times, when Darcy called on Elizabeth, he would accompany her as she went about Longbourn, overseeing necessary maintenance. At other times they would converse on a variety of subjects while walking or sitting in the parlour at Longbourn if the weather was inclement. Sunday afternoons were always set aside for their chess games.

On one of those afternoons, Elizabeth commented that she had been unable to accept an invitation by the Gardiners to go on a holiday with them because she did not wish to leave the estate without someone to oversee its management.

Darcy asked, 'I remember you saying that you once tried to hire a steward, but you were unsuccessful...'

'I did try about three years ago when I first took over Longbourn, but I could not find anyone suitable.'

Darcy's brows creased as he said, 'I believe you said something about not finding anyone honest.'

Elizabeth nodded and explained more fully, 'They either did not wish to take orders from a woman, or they were not prepared to try new things, or they seemed to think that they could cheat me.' She shrugged. 'Perhaps I did them an injustice doubting their honesty, and they were just being patronising. In any case, I could not feel comfortable with any of them.'

Darcy nodded in understanding, as he could easily see that Elizabeth would have disliked any of those attitudes. 'If you still would like to engage a steward to take some of the burden off your shoulders, I may now have a solution for you. At Pemberley we are in the habit of training staff to take on greater responsibilities. At present, I have in my employ an under-steward who is ready for a senior position of his own. I could send for him, if you would like to meet him and give him a trial.'

Elizabeth considered the offer. 'Do you think he would take orders from a woman?'

Darcy laughed. 'He should not have the slightest problem with that, as he has been taking orders from Mrs Reynolds all his life. He is her nephew.'

Having heard many stories about the formidable housekeeper, Elizabeth chose to accept. It would be good to have a second opinion available, especially one trained by the man who managed an estate as large as Pemberley... if its master was unavailable.

A few days before the wedding, Richard and Margaret arrived to help celebrate with their friends.

They were accompanied by Mr Peter Stevenson, the new steward for Longbourn, a young man of five and twenty, who very quickly fitted into Elizabeth's staff.

~A~

Rising from the Ashes

The eagerly anticipated day of Jane's wedding arrived at last.

Mrs Gardiner teasingly complained that she and her family were spending more time at Longbourn than at Gracechurch Street lately.

It was fortunate that Jane was occupying the mistress's suite as all her sisters, aunt and friends wanted to help her get ready. Her wedding dress had of course been designed by Kitty, who was becoming the family's favourite designer, and made by the combined efforts of the sisters.

Once she was dressed, despite all the help, Jane chased, no sent, all the ladies but Elizabeth to the church.

When they were alone, Elizabeth asked, 'Are you happy to marry Charles today?'

'Ecstatic,' Jane replied with a beaming smile. 'But I want to thank you for your advice about an extended courtship. I have learnt enough about Charles that I am confident we will mostly be happy.'

'Mostly?'

'If we were to be happy all of the time, I am sure we would soon become bored and not appreciate our happiness. According to Aunt Gardiner, every marriage needs some seasoning, otherwise it is too bland. So, I shall be delighted to be mostly happy.'

'In that case, I shall be very happy for you.'

~A~

Mr Gardiner walked Jane down the aisle and Elizabeth once again had the role of matron of honour.

When they arrived at the altar, Bingley, supported by Darcy, were waiting for them. Several people noticed that Jane and Charles were not the only couple who only had eyes for each other.

Darcy kept glancing at Elizabeth throughout the ceremony and wished that the roles would be reversed. Since their discussion about her experiences, he had been very careful never to push her, hoping that his restraint and steadfastness would sway the lady to trust him. Admittedly, it was quite a strain on him as he fell ever more deeply in love with Elizabeth and wanted nothing more than her to allow him to protect her from the vicissitudes of life.

Even though she did not show it, Elizabeth was not unaffected by the gentleman and the situation. In her case the strain of her fear warring with her desires took as much of a toll as his restraint.

Her emotions were having a tug of war. Part of her wanted to throw caution to the wind and lose herself in his embrace, but then memories of her marriage intruded, and she pulled back again.

Standing next to her most beloved sister who was joining her life to that of the man she loved, strengthened the desire to have such happiness herself. The couple speaking their vows fairly glowed with happiness, and they had no doubt or hesitation.

As Jane promised to love and honour Charles, Elizabeth glanced Darcy and saw his gaze resting on herself with such love and longing, it took her breath away.

She tore her eyes away to stop herself from crying.

~A~

The happy couple only stayed long enough to fulfil their obligations towards courtesy, but at the earliest opportunity said their goodbyes to leave for London for their first stop on their wedding trip.

The Hursts planned to move to Hurst's estate as soon as the Bingleys returned but in the meantime remained at Netherfield to act as hosts for Darcy and his sister, as well as Mrs Annesley. Richard and Margaret were planning to leave the following day.

As much as the Darcys would have liked to be hosted at Longbourn, Darcy knew it would have been inappropriate... tempting, but for that very reason most inappropriate.

~A~

Longbourn felt strangely empty without Jane. Mary had taken over the mistress' duties, ensuring that the house was as well run as always, but it was still not the same.

Elizabeth wondered what would happen if Mary married and moved away. And in a few years Kitty and Lydia would also be old enough to start lives of their own, leaving her alone at Longbourn.

That thought gave her an idea and she asked Mary to have tea with her in the library.

After chatting for a few minutes about trivial household issues, Elizabeth broached the subject. 'Mary, I have noticed that John Lucas has been paying you a great deal of attention. Do I need to speak to him about his intentions?'

Mary blushed but she looked Elizabeth firmly in the eye. 'There is no need for you to do so. His intentions are honourable, but we are constrained by finances since neither of us wants to live at Lucas Lodge while Lady Lucas is still in charge.' Mary saw that Elizabeth was about to protest. 'I do remember that I have a dowry, the interest of which would allow us to rent a cottage, but John would prefer us to be in a situation where he can provide a home for us.'

'You told him that you have a dowry?'

'I did, but without giving any details. He is under the impression that the amount is only enough that the interest could pay for a cottage.'

'It seems a little strange, but I have been thinking along similar lines, although for different reasons. I wondered, now that Jane has gone and you are running the house, that in the fullness of time, you might wish to live at Longbourn until John comes into his inheritance. After all, Longbourn is considerably larger than Lucas Lodge.'

'Are you suggesting that you would consider having John live here?'

'Why not? John would be close enough to Lucas Lodge to help his father and you could take over the mistress's suite.'

'That is a very generous offer. I will consider it, but I am not in a great hurry to marry just yet. Perhaps in another year or so.' Mary suddenly gave an impish smile. 'If it were someone else making this suggestion, I would suspect that I was being pushed into marriage, but knowing you as I do, I am well aware that you have only my best interests in mind.'

Mary paused for a moment, turning more serious. 'I believe that I am in love with John, and he claims to be in love with me. But since I am only nineteen, I do not yet feel ready for a lifetime commitment. I certainly do not feel ready to be a mother.'

'There is another point to consider. If John is prepared to wait until you are ready for marriage, it proves that he truly cares for you.'

'Those are my thoughts as well,' Mary replied with a smile.

~A~

In repayment for the hospitality, Darcy oversaw the running of Netherfield in Bingley's absence. It gave him something to do when he could not spend time with Elizabeth.

Georgiana still visited Longbourn frequently and often shared lessons with the youngest sisters.

Elizabeth still enjoyed Darcy's company, but since Jane's wedding something had changed for her.

Instead of dreading that he might renew his addresses, she had begun to think that perhaps it would be rather pleasant if he did. But the gentleman seemed to have endless patience.

While he was always attentive to her and there was not the slightest doubt about his continued interest, he never made any move or said anything which could be construed as anything other than the most polite conversation. Of course, they still debated and disagreed, and each tried to win those debates, but nothing else was ever said.

It seemed they were at yet another impasse.

Elizabeth wanted to scream in frustration.

~A~

Elizabeth once again visited her Uncle Phillips in his professional capacity to draw up yet another contract.

She brought along several sheets of paper, some of them in the distinct masculine hand of Darcy, with notes of the various clauses she wanted to be included.

Mr Phillips raised both brows when he read through the notes. 'Are you quite certain that you wish me to draw up this document?' he asked.

When Elizabeth replied in the affirmative, he said, 'I have some suggestions you might wish to consider.'

They spent the best part of an hour discussing the exact content of the contract. In the end both declared themselves satisfied, and Mr Phillips promised to have the final document ready for her in a couple of days.

~A~

When Darcy came for his Sunday chess game, he thought that Elizabeth was rather distracted and not giving her full attention to the game. Being a gentleman, instead of taking advantage of the situation he called a halt to the game.

'You are distracted today. That is most unlike you. Is there a problem which you would like to share?' he asked with concern.

The question made Elizabeth even more nervous, but she gathered her courage and said, 'There is a document I have received, and I wondered if you could have a look at it and give me your opinion.'

'Certainly, I would be happy to do so,' Darcy replied. He was rather puzzled as he would have expected Elizabeth to ask advice about documents of Mr Phillips, but perhaps it was something more personal which she did not wish to discuss with a relative.

After a moment's hesitation, Elizabeth reached across to her desk and retrieved a folder which she handed to him, all the while thinking, *oh lord, I hope I am doing the right thing.*

Darcy noticed the abject terror in Elizabeth's expression as he opened the folder. For a moment he wondered what could cause Elizabeth to feel this way when she had asked him to read the document, and not wanting to be the cause for any further distress he was about to close the folder when the heading and two names caught his eye. After that, a whole herd of wild horses could not have pulled him away from reading the entire document.

He had to force himself to remember to breathe as he realised the cause for Elizabeth's nervousness.

He raised his eyes to meet Elizabeth's anxious gaze. 'What would you like me to do with this?' he asked carefully.

'Sign it... if you feel so inclined,' she whispered.

Darcy rose and put the open folder on the desk then turned and held out his hand to Elizabeth with an incredulous smile. She took it and he pulled her to her feet. Perhaps he pulled a little harder than absolutely necessary as Elizabeth ended up nestled in his arms.

'You had better ring to arrange for witnesses. I would not wish for there to be any possible doubt... if you are quite certain.'

'I am certain,' she said with an answering smile and reached out to pull the bell cord.

When Mr Hill answered the bell, he found Elizabeth and Darcy in a passionate embrace, the *Marriage Articles between Mr Fitzwilliam Darcy and Mrs Elizabeth Brooks, nee Bennet* forgotten on the desk.

'It is about time,' the butler muttered.

~A~

Chapter 39

As soon as Jane and Bingley returned to Netherfield, Elizabeth and Darcy were married by common licence. Having been patient for so long, neither was prepared to wait any longer. As it happened, their wedding day was exactly one year since Darcy's first visit to Longbourn.

They spent their wedding night at Longbourn, where Elizabeth discovered that in a love match, conjugal duties became a pleasure.

The following day they travelled to London so that Darcy could introduce Elizabeth to his staff as their new mistress. They took the opportunity to take in a performance at the theatre before continuing on their wedding trip to the seaside.

While they were at Ramsgate, they received an invitation to attend the double wedding of Anne de Bourgh to Henry Standish and Robert Fitzwilliam to Charlotte Lucas.

As Rosings was on their way back to Longbourn, Elizabeth and Darcy stopped at Rosings for a few days to attend the wedding as well as to lay the last of Elizabeth's ghosts to rest.

The day before the ceremony, Elizabeth visited Lady Catherine's chambers. 'Remember me?' she asked.

'Mrs Collins,' gasped Lady Catherine.

'Not anymore. Despite your best or should I say worst efforts, I have found happiness with a gentleman who treasures and respects my opinions.'

'Who would marry an impertinent hoyden like you? You, who drove her husband into an early grave.'

'I am not sorry to contradict you yet again, but he dug his own grave. And as to the man who would marry me... I am pleased to inform you that I am now Mrs Darcy,' said Elizabeth, and with a malicious smile she watched the blood drain from her former tormentor's face.

'You are lying. You are just saying that to vex me,' screamed the old woman as she attempted to lever herself out of bed to attack Elizabeth.

'She is speaking nothing but the truth, Lady Catherine. Will you not congratulate me on my most felicitous marriage to a wonderfully strong, intelligent and opinionated woman?' Darcy said as he walked into the room and stopped next to his wife.

'You, you, you...' screamed Lady Catherine with spittle flying from her lips as she collapsed back into her pillows.

'I just came by to wish you a long life during which I hope you will experience the same kindness and compassion you have shown to everyone in your previous life.' Elizabeth smiled and curtsied politely. 'Goodbye, Lady Catherine.'

A week later, Elizabeth and Darcy returned to Longbourn, where they collected their unmarried sisters and their companions and departed for Pemberley for the winter.

~A~

The following year, Mary and John Lucas married and for the lifetime of Sir William occupied the mistress's suite at Longbourn, while the master's suite was always kept ready for Elizabeth and Darcy. Once John and Mary moved to Lucas Lodge, Elizabeth's oldest daughter, together with her companion, took over Longbourn.

The year after Mary's wedding, Georgiana, Kitty and Lydia agreed to be presented and spend a season in London. They all decided that high society was not to their liking.

Georgiana and Lydia returned to Pemberley, where it took several years before they found suitable partners.

Having learnt their lesson, Elizabeth and Darcy insisted on rather draconian marriage settlements, ensuring that all their sisters could not be mistreated. Fortunately, since they all made love-matches, none of the husbands objected.

Kitty meanwhile remained in London with the Gardiners. With their assistance and her dowry, she opened Catherine's Couture. Within a few years, any lady who had any pretensions to taste insisted on wearing her creations.

Rising from the Ashes

~A~

As they had married in the same ceremony, it was no surprise to anyone that that the Standish and Fitzwilliam couples spent a significant amount of time together.

Lady Matlock was disappointed that her firstborn and his wife were childless, but since Richard and Margaret were blessed with two sons, she was reassured that the family and the title would continue.

As no one had expected Anne to have any children, it went almost unnoticed that she too did not produce an heir. To ensure that his title did not become extinct, Henry petitioned to allow Margaret and Richard's second son to inherit the Barony, since their first son was destined to becoming the next Earl of Matlock. This request was granted.

Despite being childless neither couple bemoaned that fact as they were perfectly happy with their chosen partners.

When eventually both Robert and Henry died within months of each other, Charlotte, on Anne's invitation, moved into Rosings where they spent the rest of their lives, while the Fitzwilliam and Standish heirs took up residence at their respective properties.

Once both Anne and Charlotte passed away, Rosings became the property of the third and youngest of the Darcys' children, a daughter.

~A~

Another couple which remained childless were the Wickhams, a situation about which Caroline had mixed feelings. The vain part of her rejoiced that she never lost her figure, but the rest felt a distinct lack.

Their estate and title eventually passed to the second son of Jane and Charles Bingley, who had lived mostly happily at Netherfield.

~A~

The only ones who were truly unhappy with their lives were Lady Catherine and Mrs Bennet.

After her marriage, Anne moved Lady Catherine to the dower house where, apart from the staff who looked after her with indifferent efficiency, she remained alone for the rest of her days.

Mrs Bennet became a bitter old woman, who could never understand what she had done wrong.

~A~

Elizabeth did spend time at Longbourn over the years, but always in company of her adoring, adorable, and adored husband.

The main reason for the regular visits was to familiarise their older of two daughters with the estate she would inherit while her younger brother was to take over the reins of Pemberley when the time came.

Knowing that she had options and the ability to make her own choices, allowed Elizabeth to find the courage to deal with situations which caused her some discomfort. While at times she would have preferred to run away when her demons plagued her, Darcy's patience and willingness to discuss their issues always won out.

Even though they had their share of problems, most of the time they had a happy marriage and there were many occasions in their long lifetime when each of them thanked the fates which brought them together and gave Elizabeth a second chance at a happy life.

~A~

Books by Sydney Salier

Unconventional

An Unconventional Education (Book 1)

Unconventional Ladies (Book 2)

The Denton Connection

Mrs Bennet's Surprising Connections

Don't flatter yourself

It's a Duke's Life

Lady Alexandra's Hunt

Don't flatter yourself – Revisited

Other P&P Variations

A P&P Christmas Carol

Compromising Mr Darcy – The Accidental Rake

Consequence & Consequences – or Ooops

Mr Bennet leaves his study

No, Mr Darcy

Reversed Fortune

Surprise & Serendipity

The Colonel & The Lady

This is not a laughing matter

Turnabout

You asked for it

Short Stories

Remember, you wanted this OR Be careful what you ask for

Original Work

Lady Alexandra's Hunt

Made in the USA
Middletown, DE
19 September 2023

38789950R00177